Happy Bir

FROM The Gardening Club

and Ben,

John Bowman.

ii

The Gardening Club

by

John Boman

Grosvenor House
Publishing Limited

This book is published by
Grosvenor House Publishing Ltd
28–30 High Street, Guildford, Surrey, GU1 3HY
www.grosvenorhousepublishing.co.uk

A CIP record for this book
is available from the British Library

ISBN 978-1-907211-68-3

Acknowledgements

The seed of the idea for *The Gardening Club* began to germinate. The plant that emerged fought for a life of its own, but it needed the love and care of an expert to battle the weeds that grew amongst it. A lucky break occurred when the best editor in the UK's botanical garden began nurturing the rough chapters. It might have withered and died without Linden Stafford's patience, professionalism and above all expertise. Her skill helped to make it bloom.

For my wife Carol, who encouraged me to write,
and for Sophie and Honey Louise,
my beautiful daughters.

Our England is a garden, and such gardens are not made
By singing:- 'Oh, how beautiful', and sitting in the shade.

(from Rudyard Kipling, 'The Glory
of the Garden', 1911)

Chapter 1

The thin trail of smoke from the little blackened chimney tried to find its way through the low early-morning mist that covered the allotments. Everything was mono-chrome. The cobwebs on the eaves of the shed were hung with bright droplets of dew. Frozen over each of the dirty windows on the sides of the shed were more cobwebs heavy with dew. The melting frost on the roof and the ground steamed in the watery January sun that was trying its best to find a way through clouds and mist and smoke.

The heat of the cast-iron stove and the warmth of the men's bodies inside the shed had begun to spoil the zigzag patterns that the ice had formed overnight on the grimy glass.

Pete Wilson could just hear the crackle of wood burn-ing in the stove and the murmurs of familiar voices as he pulled his overcoat tighter round his chest. He leaned his bike against the side of the allotment shed. He stamped his feet and shuddered. Reaching for the cotton hand-kerchief in his overcoat pocket, he wiped a droplet from his cold, red nose, then stamped his feet again as he opened the shed door.

'Bloody hell, what are you lot trying to do – kipper yourselves or smoke a ham?'

Pete peered through the fug inside as he took off his brown leather gloves and warmed his hands over the black iron stove. He let out an involuntary shiver as the heat and the smoke leaking from the stove engulfed him. He gazed round the shed's interior and greeted the other occupants. The three men each returned his greeting.

Richard Owen-Davies was the first to speak. 'Morning, Peter.'

Brian Young managed to choke out an almost incoherent 'Good morning' before a fit of coughing brought on by age and Old Holborn roll-ups overcame him. His bloodshot eyes streamed and his face turned various shades of red and purple. As he attempted to calm his spluttering, he winked at Pete. The others watched him rub his freckled fist in one eye-socket then the other. He winked at each man in turn and muttered a barely audible curse.

'You should give that filthy tobacco up!' snapped Richard. 'You'll be in the next funeral we'll all be going to, if not.'

Brian winked at Pete again and nodded his head in the direction of Richard. Taking a deep, defiant, drag on his roll-up, he tipped his head back and blew smoke at the shed ceiling, secretly aiming it at a knot of very dry onions hanging from an old rusty hook there.

Ernie Evans had waited for Brian's coughing to subside before he in turn greeted Pete, and handed him a mug of tea.

Pete cupped his hands gratefully around the steaming mug. 'Brrr, I should have come in the car this morning. I looked out of the window when I got up and it looked quite bright ... Got to stay fit, got to ride the bike as much as I can. Stay fit.' He trailed off as he thought of his wife. 'Liz needs me to stay fit.' Pete sipped the hot tea as he sat down. He reached in his jacket under his overcoat for his cigarettes, then lit one with satisfaction, smoke pouring from his nostrils. 'First today,' he said, looking at his wristwatch. 'Not bad. Ten-thirty before my first smoke.'

'You should give up smoking as well.' Richard peered over his mug, staring directly at Pete, his bushy white eyebrows twitching up and down, as they did when he spoke.

The four men fell silent for a while, each sipping his tea and each gazing at the glowing stove.

Brian broke the reveries of his fellow allotment holders. 'Where's Bill this morning? He's late.'

All three stared at him as if he had said something stupid. He unfastened his battered old tobacco pouch and began rolling another cigarette, looking from one to the other as he licked the gummed edge moist and fingered the paper and tobacco lovingly, rolling it to a better shape between two thumbs and forefingers.

'Anybody seen him?' Brian glanced from one face to the next. 'He's normally here waiting. He's normally the first here – rain, sun, whatever the weather, he's first, sitting here or out working on his patch. I came here back in the summer at six-thirty one morning and he was already making tea. He'd been here before it was light, he said.'

'I wonder why he never got married – Bill, I mean,' Pete added as if they might not know who he was talking about.

Ernie stood up and went over to the bench, filled the blackened kettle with water from the big plastic drum they kept their clean water in and lit the little gas ring.

'Who wants another cup?'

The other three all grunted their agreement.

'In my opinion Bill is a very nice man – lonely, I guess, but a decent man.' Ernie poured the boiling water into the large brown teapot, stirring the teabags inside as he did so. 'Perhaps that's why he isn't here. Have you thought about that?' Ernie straightened up, putting down the tea-stained spoon and replacing the teapot lid with a rattle of enamelled tin. 'I mean, here we all are – our so-called gardening club on a Monday morning – and Bill has had all weekend to think about what we were talking about on Friday in this very hut. He's a decent sort of bloke and it might be worrying him, what we were all saying last Friday.'

'No, I don't think so,' interrupted Pete.

Brian laughed and coughed again. 'He had a lot to say Friday – he had plenty of ideas on how we could go about things.'

'Yes,' said Pete, 'he was agreeing with the whole idea. He was as keen as any of us, don't you think so, Richard?'

'Yes, I do. He started off the whole conversation, if I remember rightly.'

Brian gave a wheezy chuckle of agreement.

'Well,' said Ernie, returning to his theory about Bill's absence. 'I must admit, I've spent the whole weekend thinking about what we were saying, and maybe Bill has and he thinks better of it.'

The group of retired men fell into silence, each going over Friday's conversation. How could they, the gardening club, get rid of pests? That was Friday's subject here in their shared hut at the allotment.

Pests in their town, not in their allotments or their gardens.

Willbury is an unremarkable town sitting in the modern multi-cultural United Kingdom. It has its leafy avenues for successful entrepreneurs and solid long-established family houses for lawyers and professional families to live in, families that have given their names to the town for street names, local parks and Victorian buildings of red-brick splendour. They share their avenues now with garden centre owners, people 'in computers' and even in the media. Now these avenues house a few minor celebrities, even a BBC Radio 2 presenter. Range Rovers and Mercedes adorn their in-and-out driveways. A scattering of Willbury University professors occupy bungalows and smaller houses built in the 1930s in and around these more pleasant parts of town. A large family of former Ugandan Asians of several generations were quickly absorbed into these quiet streets, their ambitions fulfilled from long, hard hours in corner shops and careful accumulation of cheap hotels and bedsits in other parts of town. They now live next door to Willbury Rovers FC's once illustrious manager, although cricket is a sport they know better. Still they pass the time of day across their adjoining hedges with perfect politeness.

The town was built on its two converging rivers, once the motorways of commerce. Silk has a long since faded association with the town but is now lost somewhere in an archive. Agriculture in the surrounding countryside used to contribute much to Willbury's development.

American computer companies and insurance conglomerates have added plenty of growth since the swinging sixties – although the myth of 'swinging' all but swung very wide of Willbury. The biscuit factory of Harris & Cohen, H & C's to townsfolk, once employed nearly four thousand dogged souls of Willbury and housed them in rows of terraced houses on the east side of town. Gone now, the same way as the Wills cigarette factory and many other large employers; gone to Scotland or in many cases to China. Willbury makes very little these days. Workshops, factories and warehouses have been turned to rubble, and office blocks now occupy their sites, buildings in concrete and glass containing multiple floors with rows and rows of computer screens where many of their occupants seem to vanish into the ether upon reaching forty years of age.

Like most towns in the early twenty-first century, Willbury does not seem to be aware it shares its space with an even larger population that swung to the Beatles, the Stones or even Eddie Cochran and Cliff. They must be there somewhere – perhaps out on the 1960s and 1970s council estates, or in the new developments of the 1980s and 1990s. The rows of workers' terraced houses are now cottages inhabited either by social workers or by original *Windrush* Jamaicans or Bajans who brought the sunshine of their islands to their grey and rain-soaked colonial homeland. Lord Tanamo, Prince Buster and Desmond Dekker once enjoyed these draughty little houses on vinyl disc at parties that throbbed to their ska in these older districts.

Willbury's football team once reached the FA Cup semi-final and even entertained Arsenal and Newcastle United but now it fights for survival in League 2. The ground that once regularly squeezed around 30,000 supporters on to its terraces begs in the local newspaper to add to the faithful four of the 4,000 or so locals who obstinately cling to the belief that the glory days will return, perhaps next season. The faithful four console themselves that they haven't gone the way of Lowestoft, Gateshead or more peculiarly Wimbledon's league football clubs.

Brian Young had been brought up in Garibaldi Street, a typical road among the terraced houses of Willbury. He had shared it with his mother, his father, his older brother and his sister. His father had been on the maintenance team at H & C's. He had taught Brian to mix muck, his mortar, and how to lay bricks. Brian had been earning nearly four times the last wage his dad had received before his redundancy back in the late 1960s. Not for Brian the cruel subsistence wages of H & C's. 'I know it's regular, your job with H & C's,' he had told his dad many times, 'but I can earn more on piece work in a day than you can in a week.' And he could.

Brian had helped build half of Willbury, he'd tell anyone who would listen in the King's Head, his local pub. His eyes sparkled with fun, which his retirement had not extinguished. This pub, the only Victorian building still standing near to where Brian now lived in his sand-faced, fletton-brick, semi-detached house built in the late seventies. The original wooden window-frames had long been converted to UPVC, as were most of his neighbours' houses. Pete Wilson, his best mate, wouldn't have to paint his windows any longer.

Pete Wilson had been to the same school as Brian, and had been brought up near Garibaldi Street, but they hadn't become friends until they both starting drinking in the King's Head in the 1960s. While Brian had become a bricklayer, Pete was a painter and decorator, and they had often worked on the same building sites. For all that time, they had shared the same pub.

As young men in their twenties, they had drunk their pints of light and bitter together, they had wavered around the Olympia ballroom together. They still talked about the times back then when Screaming Lord Sutch had brought his band, the Savages, to the Olympia's stage – not to mention the Hollies, the Undertakers and other groups they saw during those happy days of piece work, beer and occasionally girls. They still puzzled that neither had been present when Chuck Berry had played the Olympia. Pete still gloated that he had seen Bo Diddley and his magic home-made guitar, and the honking saxophones of Bo's rocking band. Brian had missed it through working too late that summer night.

Now, over forty years later, the Olympia was no more. Its replacement, Loose Juice, played no jazz or rock and roll ; house and hip-hop were now its multicultural fare. When young Pete and Brian had staggered out at 11.30 p.m. to weave their way home, they could not have imagined in their wildest dreams that the place would carry on until four in the morning, when it now hustled out its last customers. Crowds of menacing young men and shrill, semi-clad girls spilled out into the chill morning air, looking still for something they knew but Brian and Pete could not have contemplated. But they had both now seen endless documentaries on their television screens showing fighting girls being separated by police in bright yellow fluorescent jackets. They had watched the running battles, the vomiting and shouting, youths urinating in the street and standing upright with difficulty. Pete and Brian were nearly as familiar with these scenes from their television screens as the resigned desk sergeant at Willbury Central police station. In apparently every town across the United Kingdom the local police force plied their trade around the local pubs, bars and nightclubs. When the familiar landmarks of Willbury appeared on his TV screen, Brian was genuinely shocked. After he picked Pete Wilson up on their way to the allotment, he couldn't wait to ask if he had seen the same. Pete hadn't, but it came as no surprise.

'Why should Willbury be any different to any other town, Bri?' he asked his friend. 'There's no respect anywhere these days. We had a laugh when we were young but we didn't get into fights for nothing, and we didn't just smash things up for the sake of it. No one I knew did, and you and I knew a few rascals back then.'

As they drove towards the allotment where they spent so much time since retiring, Pete pointed out graffiti and the strewn broken glass of a bus shelter that had obviously been smashed overnight.

'Just look at that, mate. Can you tell me why somebody has to do that?'

'Bloody sure I can't, Pete.' Brian dropped a gear and turned into The Elms, one of Willbury Council's allotments. Their allotment.

Pete had talked Brian into this new hobby. He had told him at the King's Head one Sunday lunchtime some years ago how much he enjoyed growing a few vegetables, or a patch of rhubarb. Pete had said how much better they tasted when you grow them yourself. Brian had laughed and taken the mickey out of his friend for some weeks but had relented one Monday morning during a boring but dry October day. He had been retired for two years then, although he still did a few small jobs and his wife Debbie had even suggested he try to get some part-time teaching of his bricklaying skills. 'Not for me, Deb, sorry,' he had said. Brian was often bored, and it was difficult to fill the day after an active life outdoors. He wandered down the local betting shop a few afternoons most weeks but this soon palled. He visited a few different pubs at lunchtimes to kill time but it just made him doze off when he got back home. Debbie was not amused to find him asleep on the sofa when she got in from work. Besides, Brian thought, both the betting shops and the pubs in the daytime were full of either bored or boring old men like himself, moaning about everything from the Prime Minister to foreigners, or else, if they were young, Brian could not contain his irritation.

'Doesn't anybody go to work any more?' he would ask Debbie or Pete. 'Seem to have plenty of money to drink all day.'

Pete and Brian had still not quite come to terms with the changed licensing laws allowing their pubs to stay open all day. They would often agree, 'You knew where you were if a pub opened at twelve o'clock on Sunday and closed at two o'clock.' 'Home for a nice roast dinner then,' the other one would add.

Brian parked his ancient Escort van by the allotment shed.

'Here we are, Pete boy. Second home.'

Pete lit a cigarette. 'You're glad I talked you into this now, eh?'

Brian grinned and wheezed as he drew on his self-rolled cigarette. 'Yeah, mate, it certainly passes the time.'

'And you get some nice vegetables.' Pete climbed out of Brian's van and leaned across the top as Brian got out. 'And you don't have to lock your van when we're here.'

'That's true. I caught a little bastard trying the back doors of my van in the car park last week at the supermarket with Debs. Saw me coming and ran off. I suppose he thought I'd have tools in there he could nick,' he growled.

Pete Wilson shuffled a bunch of keys, looking for the right one to unlock the large brass padlock on their allotment shed door. They shared the shed with two others – Bill Choules, a retired clerk, and Ernie Evans, a retired shop worker – but neither was here yet on this sunny autumn morning.

'No Bill or Ernie then, mate,' observed Brian as Pete unlocked the door. 'Just us.'

'I expect they'll be here later,' Pete said as he stepped inside.

Chapter 2

Pete had started on nodding terms with both Ernie and Bill long before Brian joined him after taking a rented plot of ground from the council. All the men shared ideas and produce with others on the allotment. But it was Brian who had secured them the invitation to share the rickety old shed used by Bill and Ernie when he volunteered to help renovate it. 'On condition,' Brian had joked, 'that me and my mate can share it.' His joke had gained them regular use of the shed a couple of years ago.

Brian and Pete had added new mineral felt to the roof and fixed some broken window-panes, and Pete had given it two coats of chestnut-coloured wood preservative he had found in a corner at the back of his garage at home. They had thoroughly enjoyed doing it up, and it looked very smart when they had finished. Bill had given them huge bunches of chrysanthemums in thanks. Since then, they had both taken home plenty of Ernie's produce too.

Bill had initially felt slightly uneasy at sharing with these two newcomers. He'd even said to Ernie, 'Bit rough, these building workers, Ernest.' Ernie hadn't replied; he'd enjoyed the extra company, especially when his wife Grace died just afterwards. Brian and Pete were more sociable than Bill, and they had helped him get through his grief over the loss of his wife of more than fifty years. Ernie had quickly come to like both men, and they had fun together. He already knew Pete, having had many brief conversations with him for some years. Pete had appreciated Ernie's help and guidance when he first taken on a plot. When Pete was a boy, his father had an allotment. Pete always remembered how much he'd enjoyed going there with his dad all those years ago and had promised himself to get one some day.

The four men would sit and chat for hours if rain kept them inside. Ernie sometimes secretly hoped for rain, since living alone did not agree with him. Bill, on the other hand, was used to his own company, having never married. He had reached and passed into retirement long after the death of his parents, with whom he had always lived. He would join in occasionally but seemed to the others content just to be there with his own thoughts.

Brian had fixed the wood-burning stove in the early days as well. It was now a regular companion. Everyone made a habit of bringing bits of wood from time to time, even Bill. Pete had donated a gas ring which he'd had for years. It was his duty to change the gas bottle when necessary. In the past he'd used the ring to boil a kettle on building sites with no electric power. 'Can't beat a fresh cup of tea,' he used to tell young painters. 'Not the same if it's stewed in a flask.' Pete had been the target of many jokes about this habit on various sites, mostly from the younger ones who brought cans of Coke instead. Of course, everything anybody did on site was fair game for taking the piss. It was one advantage of working on a site rather than in a private house tip-toeing about carefully on their fitted carpets. In more recent years Pete was glad of the warmth and having somebody else – perhaps the lady of the house – to make cups of tea or coffee for him, but he had preferred the carefree feeling of building sites in the old days. Sites he'd shared with Brian. 'You start 'em – I finish 'em!' he would say to Brian. He'd enjoyed the camaraderie of carpenters, plumbers, plasterers – 'spreads', as Pete always called plasterers – and the fun of Irish drain-laying and ground-work gangs back in his past. He would sit in the shed with Brian these days and recall different characters, when Ernie or Bill were out on their plots.

'Real characters then,' Brian would agree about a mutual acquaintance they recalled. 'Like Billy Kelly, the little digger driver. He knew more jokes than anybody I ever met before or since.'

'Not like Brody, the ganger on the same site?' Pete added.

'No, he was spooky, he sort of frightened me.' Brian reflected for a moment, then added, 'Vanished one day never to be seen again, ol' Brody. Bet he was IRA.'

Pete agreed. 'Yes, everyone thought he was before he left, and there were bombs in London not long after as well. Wouldn't mind betting he was involved in those.'

'Yeah,' Brian grunted. 'Me too. Good job those days are gone though, mate.'

Pete put the kettle on the gas ring. 'Let's have a cuppa.'

'I'll get the milk from my van.' Brian got up from the old painted wooden chair that he'd rescued from a skip on his way to the allotment one day some months before. This was Brian's duty: milk. Ernie tea, Pete gas, Bill water. Somehow this had quickly become established without any of the four men verbally agreeing it. It had just grown into a habit and an accepted order.

'Have you seen the shed over by the south fence, you two?' Ernie asked Brian and Pete after he and Bill had arrived that sunny autumn morning.

'No, I haven't.' Brian glanced round as he drank his tea.

'Nor me.' Pete shook his head.

'Some vandals have burnt it to the ground. I'm surprised you didn't notice,' Ernie continued. 'They've done all sorts of damage over the other side of the allotment. Bloody kids. A gang of kids, I suppose. No respect for nothing.' Ernie's cheeks coloured even more than usual. His small beady eyes darted from one to the other. 'Trampled plants, pulled things up. Set fire to the shed. I'd lock 'em up.' He sighed.

'I blame the parents,' Brian said as he sipped his tea. 'No control. No respect. This town is not a nice place to live any more.'

He then proceeded to tell Ernie of how he had seen Willbury town centre on the television, in last night's documentary about the police dealing with drunks and yobs coming out of clubs and pubs.

Ernie had seen similar programmes on television but he hadn't seen Willbury, his own town. 'Sunderland and Brighton, I've seen those on the telly, but not Willbury. Though I've seen enough yobs in the town centre.'

'That's why there's no copper about when you need one,' Brian threw into this conversation. 'All in bed from night work.'

Pete laughed.

'What's so funny?' Brian snapped. 'You try finding a bloody policeman if you get burgled then. You might see one about two weeks later if they can spare the time.'

'Don't be so silly, Brian. They're not that bad.' Pete grinned and shook his head.

'They fucking are.' Brian sounded genuinely angry now. He busied himself rolling a cigarette and glared at Pete.

Pete noticed Bill quietly 'tut' at Brian's expletive.

Ernie agreed with Brian. 'So much crime these days. The *Willbury Reporter* is full of it every night. Muggings, stabbings ... If they *are* about, they don't seem to catch many. They seem to think it's enough to put in the paper, "If anybody has any information ..." Why don't they go looking for the culprits?'

Brian calmed down. 'Sorry, mate,' he said to Pete. 'Didn't mean to get ratty with you.'

'And mind your language, Brian.' Bill surprised everyone when he spoke.

'Never mind my language, Bill. These bloody yobs get away with too much these days,' Brian said.

Bill did not reply. He stirred his tea methodically and silently.

Pete tried to defuse the tension that seemed to be developing but he couldn't resist teasing Brian now he could see the other man had calmed down. 'You really will have to watch your language soon, Brian.'

'Yeah, and why is that, Mr Peter the Painter? Are you gonna start going to church? Have you become a born-again Christian?' Brian smiled a toothy grin at his own question.

'No, but I invited a posh customer of mine to come and join our little allotment group. He's thinking of taking over old Hatch's plot. You know – near Ernie's.'

'I know old Hatch died months ago. Who is this new man then?' Brian was curious now.

'Who is he then?' echoed Ernie.

'He's a retired civil servant. Lives over on Linden Avenue.'

'Woooo! Posh road, that.' Brian stuck his little finger out from his tea mug. 'Perhaps he could bring biscuits to go with our tea.' He chuckled. 'Chocolate ones maybe sometimes.' Brian's laughter caused the usual fit of coughing. He spluttered and went red in the face until his eyes ran. Then he mopped them with his sleeve.

'He's a very nice gentleman,' Pete continued, ignoring Brian's sniggering. 'Loves gardening. He's got a big garden and even a part-time gardener, but he's just like us, bored. Not enough to do since he retired. I suggested he join us. He said he'd think about it but I reckon he will. Then, as I said, you'll have to watch your swearing, Brian.'

Brian growled an incoherent noise and continued chortling to himself.

Bill sat forward but eyed Brian from the corner of his eye as he spoke. 'A gentleman, you say, Peter?'

'Yes,' agreed Pete. 'Just like us.'

Brian and Ernie cheered sarcastically and both laughed.

Bill sat back and said nothing.

'When's he coming then, Pete?' asked Ernie.

'I don't really know,' Pete answered honestly. 'I don't really know at all.'

It was a week later, as the men sat in their allotment shed discussing the merits of compost heaps, that they were interrupted by a light tap on the closed door. They looked at each other.

'Come in if you're rich and good-looking!' Brian called out towards the door.

'Good morning, gentlemen. Good morning, Pete.' A tall man, neatly dressed in a tweed jacket, stood expressionless in the doorway.

'Come in, Richard,' said Pete, and dragged a wooden chair forward. 'Take a seat.' As the other man sat down, Pete announced, 'This is Richard Owen-Davies,' and went round making the introductions.

Ernie handed the newcomer a mug of tea. 'Do you take sugar?' he said, in the tone of voice he used in his former occupation when serving customers.

Brian nudged Pete and indicated Ernie with an eye movement. Pete grinned back his acknowledgement of Ernie's affectation.

In spite of the initial nervousness, Richard soon became another regular visitor, and one day during his second week when he brought in a pack of digestive biscuits even Bill found himself chuckling along with the others. Brian felt obliged to explain the joke but was unsure whether the new member understood the explanation.

'Oh, the biscuits with tea for civil servants,' Richard had said with a cautious smile of comprehension. He would soon learn to ignore Brian's teasing.

'Get any trouble with yobs in your ...' Brian hesitated. '... avenue, do you, Richard?'

The ensuing conversation confirmed that Richard shared their disappointment in Willbury in particular and the world in general.

Over the coming weeks they spent more time outside on their individual plots. Ernie insisted that Richard should have a compost heap, and explained how to start one with grasses and weeds. As Richard gradually transformed old Mr Hatch's neglected plot into what he wished it to be, the men shared ideas about seeds and cuttings as well as produce and conversations. Richard found he had never in his whole life slept so well. The fresh air and the damned hard work, he supposed. He still got blisters on his hands, and he even laughed at himself now when Brian or Pete or even Ernie teased him.

The men's conversations over tea, before or after work, as ever revolved around their perceived disintegration of British society. Each annoyance, disturbance or reported crime was discussed at length. The weeks came and the weeks went, with the frosts of November and the rain of December.

Willbury Rovers were out of the FA Cup too early. Fireworks exploded where they shouldn't; screaming rockets broke through the glass roof of Bill's greenhouse at his home. The men exchanged their discontent with each other. Occasionally there was a mention of a mutual acquaintance in the death column in the *Willbury Reporter*. Another gone. Ernie always seemed to creep into himself a little more if he recognised a name. It made him miss Grace a bit more intensely. This effect would subside until the next one.

'I dread getting old,' Pete said one December morning.

'You *are* bloody old.' Brian laughed. Rain was pouring hard down on their plots, and inside the shed the air was full of cigarette and wood smoke.

Pete smiled but continued, 'No, I mean *really* old. When you can't help yourself. When dignity goes. Lying in your own urine or worse. You know what I mean. Hospital or an old folks' home.'

'Your daughters would look after you, wouldn't they, Pete?' Ernie asked.

'I wouldn't want them to, mate. They've got their own lives. I wouldn't want to be any sort of burden on them.' He had said as much to both his daughters.

Ernie considered Pete's answer. He would like his only daughter to look after him – although he knew there was no chance of it happening.

Pete thought about his wife and her dependency on him. How would he cope in the future?

'What you gonna do for Christmas, Bill, or you, Ern? What you gonna do? It's soon, you know.'

Ernie and Bill exchanged a look.

'I'll be on my own as usual apart from the Church,' said Bill matter-of-factly. 'Christmas doesn't worry me. Just another day.'

'I'm having my Christmas dinner with old Ada in the flat next door,' said Ernie. 'Not as good a cook as my Grace, but it'll be nice to have it cooked for me. I expect my daughter Anne will run in and run out in five minutes on Christmas morning, just to see if I've bought her anything or to scrounge some money.' He released a sigh. Their shared hut remained quiet for some minutes until Brian broke the silence.

'Come on, you miserable old buggers. Cheer up. You're not dead yet.'

Pete nodded and smiled at his mate. *Good old Brian*, he thought.

'What about you, Richard? Your family coming round to you?' Brian asked.

Richard hesitated. He was just beginning to feel part of this group but he still found personal questions or information about his background slightly embarrassing to talk about.

'No, we will be going to my son's house for a few days.'

To Richard's relief, this seemed enough to satisfy Brian.

'Big family Christmas, lovely,' Brian concluded.

At the end of December the rain was back again. Four of the men sat drinking tea and chatting in their haven, but Ernie was missing.

'Where's Ernie today?' asked Richard. 'He hasn't ever failed to turn up since I joined your gardening club. In fact he's usually one of the first to arrive.'

'Yes, it's not like him to be late,' said Brian.

Suddenly Ernie appeared in the doorway, small and grey, but this morning his ruddy cheeks looked more hollow. He had a graze on one cheek and a black eye.

Pete jumped up. 'Christ, man, what's happened? Come in. Sit down. Get him a mug of tea somebody.'

Pete led Ernie to a wooden chair, the one with arms. He had a hand under Ernie's elbow.

'Sit down, mate, and tell us what's happened to you.'

Ernie told his rapt audience, 'It was yesterday afternoon. About four o'clock. It had only just got dark. I'd just reached the gateway to our block of flats when three boys ... yobs ... came up behind me. They snatched the two carrier bags I was carrying. One tripped me to the floor and punched me in the face.' He paused, and stroked his bruised eye socket. 'This spotty one kicked me in the ribs. Then he took my wallet from the inside pocket of my jacket. When I started to pick myself up, they all ran off.' He stared at the others. 'They could have killed me.'

Each man sat back. Pete reached for his cigarettes. Brian rolled himself one. Richard hadn't stopped clicking his tongue. He had tut-tutted throughout Ernie's report.

'Little fucking bastards,' said Brian.

'Yeah,' agreed Pete.

Bill stood up abruptly, his tall frame towering over the seated men. 'That's it! That's enough! We can't just keep talking about yobs and crime and muggings.' He looked intently at each of the other men to make sure he had their attention. 'Enough talk. Now we have to so something.'

He sat down slowly and watched the others' reactions.

CHAPTER 3

Bill Choules was a large ungainly man. Large limbs, large face, large eyes, large feet – size 13s in fact. It was always difficult to buy shoes, let alone size 13 wellington boots for his allotment jobs, and his thick woollen socks always seemed to have holes in the toes. He hated darning them but it was better than trying to find new ones big enough. Although both his parents were long since dead, he still lived in the house where he was born seventy-one years ago. He still thought of it as their house, Mum and Dad's house, even though it had belonged to him since his mother followed his father out of this world nearly twenty years ago.

Dad had been a strict man, no nonsense, and played the organ adequately in St John's up the road. Mum had been a good wife, submissive and quiet as a good wife should be, Mr Choules had once told Bill. It was during their one and only man-to-man chat fifty years ago, Bill recalled. His twenty-first birthday, £21 in an envelope with a card from Mum and Dad 'with love', it had said. Bill sometimes asked himself where that love had been before and after that day. On that day long ago his dad had said, with a solemn face, 'I want to talk to you, William.' His father had never called him Bill, though his mother did when her husband was not around.

'Now listen, son, that's a lot of money in that envelope and I don't want you to waste it. Save it for your future.'

Bill had saved it.

Mr Choules had worked for the same company all his life. He was in his early sixties by the time Bill was twenty-one and had found Bill his job in the office at the biscuit factory where he worked. At Harris & Cohen his dad had progressed to foreman on the cream line. His fellow workers were afraid of their foreman, so strict and unsmiling. You dared not be late for work. If Mr Choules caught you, then you were in the office at tea break explaining how many minutes you were late and asking – yes, asking – for that time to be deducted from this week's pay. That was Mr Choules on the cream line. No nonsense.

'When you get married, William, you must find a good woman like your mother, a quiet one who doesn't answer back, one who keeps a clean house and cooks well. Good wholesome food, ready on the table when you come in from work.'

Bill had blushed at his father's talk. He had been worried what else his father was going to say when he had started talking about marriage. Even today he could still remember that talk, and had recalled it many times over the years. His dad had never really talked to him ever again during the rest of his life, never mentioned marriage, never questioned Bill why he hadn't got married. That talk was the most his father had ever said to him at one time. 'Yes, Dad' was all Bill had said at the end of it, waiting to be sure his dad had finished speaking. His father had simply got up at the end of his speech and gone out into the garden. 'Off to do a bit of hoeing,' he had muttered. 'Must keep the weeds down.' No wait for a reply, no smile – he had just stood up and walked out of the house without looking back.

Bill was fifty-one when his father died, and all he ever really got from his dad was to take over his allotment. Of course he had spent much of his childhood and a large part of his adulthood with his dad at the allotment. They had sown potatoes, onions, planted out runner beans together as the seasons came and went. But Bill made one change to their allotment after Dad had gone: he was able to grow chrysanthemums there. When years earlier he had suggested growing some flowers for Mum, his father, who so rarely laughed, had laughed.

'Flowers, lad, flowers? You can't eat them.' No discussion. End of subject.

Bill hadn't argued, he knew better than that, nor did he ever suggest it again, but three years after his father died he covered his mum's grave with the chrysanthemums he had grown that year on his plot. Tracey Wallers, Decorative Keystones, early Yellow Symbols, Mavis Shoesmiths, Davines, Koreans, Pom Poms, sprays and singles. His mum had received many varieties over the years since, though she wasn't aware of it. Bill knew his chrysanthemums now. He had had his battles with aphids, and also eelworms in his plant leaves. One year had been particularly wet, and the eelworms had nearly deprived his mum of her sprays of chrysanths. He remembered the first signs of yellow-green blotches on the leaves, and some purple discolouration. Eventually he had found the answer in Percy Thrower's book, which his mother had given him for Christmas one year, and he won the battle at the end of the season. 'Immerse in hot water for five minutes or so,' Percy had advised, and it had worked. His mum would have been pleased with the next year's blooms, if she had known. Then the leaf-miner had found his plants one year. These days he knew to look for the eggs, but they had also been a real pest. He could feel the anger now as he thought about the pests.

Disease he could cope with, spotted wilt he'd conquered, as he had done with aspermy. His natural gentleness came into effect to treat his chrysanthemums for these problems, but the pests made him furious. He sometimes had sleepless nights when the pests invaded his plants. He would sit in his kitchen, 'Mum's kitchen', make tea and feel his anger rising.

Bill tried dahlias for a few years but he had never stopped growing chrysanthemums ever since his mother died. She would have been proud of the many prizes he had won over the years. Bill would be out in the early morning, nobody else on the allotments, enjoying the quiet stillness. He would be peacefully selecting and cutting blooms or just de-budding, choosing the tall stems, removing the bottom leaves, crushing the stems before putting them in a bucket of clean water under the stairs, in the dark, before the show. The flowers would be ready to tease gently with a child's paintbrush on the morning of the show.

His heart swelled at the memory of the first time he'd returned to the marquee to see 'First Prize' on the table in front of his vase, Mum's vase. It was not the first time he'd put chrysanthemums on his mother's grave, but when he put his first prize blooms on her grave that night he cried – whether it was tears of joy or sadness he didn't know – but he hadn't cried since. In later years she had had sprays that had won national competitions, but he hadn't cried. On more than one occasion he had noticed that bunches had disappeared the next time he had visited her grave with yet more chrysanths. He got angry, not sad – angry at the pests taking them. Did they watch and wait till he had gone? While they were fresh, did they watch him, and wait for him to go home and then take them? Once when he had laid them there quite late at night, he found they were gone the following morning when he returned with some special Mavis Shoesmiths with their beautiful incurved heads. The pests had got them. It had to be adult pests, not child pests.

On this cold, frosty January morning he was slow to get going, slow to make his tea, slow to fry his egg and the fried bread that he liked on Mondays. *The others will wonder where I am*, he thought, as he busied himself. *They'll think I feel ill or something*, he supposed. He was excited this Monday morning. He had spent the whole weekend indoors – well, nearly all of it, apart from having done a bit of shopping on Saturday morning, thinking, thinking, all the time. He had thought up some good ideas for getting rid of pests and congratulated himself. All weekend he'd thought of nothing else but getting rid of pests. He was confident his pals down at the allotment shed, the 'gardening club', would be pleased with him.

When Bill was twenty-seven he had met a girl. A shy, quiet girl had come to work in the office next to his at H & C's, in the buyers' office, with Mr Holmes as her boss. Occasionally he had lunch with Mr Holmes in the canteen, and he would daydream sometimes that Mr Holmes would introduce him. For months he had imagined having lunch with Mr Holmes and that he would talk to Bill about the new girl. Sometimes he tried to get this conversation going. 'How is the new girl getting on, Mr Holmes? She's quiet, isn't she, the new girl in your office, Mr Holmes?'

He felt so nervous that sometimes he blushed when he asked. Mr Holmes would simply eat his lunch or talk about the factory football team or biscuits, but never the new girl. Bill knew he would have to pluck up courage and be more direct one day.

With his new resolve, on the next occasion he began: 'Mr Holmes, what's the name of the new girl in your office?' He had blurted it out as the older man was eyeing his shepherd's pie with anticipation.

'Oh, the new girl – Brenda,' replied Mr Holmes, chewing his first mouthful, not questioning Bill, not looking up from his meal. 'Brenda, she's a quiet one.'

For a moment Bill was lost for words, but he told himself he must continue. 'Where does she live then? Where does she come from?' His voice had sounded to him higher-pitched than normal. 'Brenda, eh?' he ploughed on. 'Nice name, Brenda. Where does she live then, Mr Holmes – near the factory, does she, Brenda?'

The office manager had briefly stopped eating and had fixed Bill with a grin. 'Bill, I do believe you fancy her. You keep asking questions about her. You've been asking questions about her for weeks.'

Bill's face had grown very hot when Mr Holmes said this. 'No, no, just wondered,' he had stammered out.

Mr Holmes had glanced up at that point and looked Bill square in the face. 'Young Bill,' he began. He had known the younger man since he had started work in the next office when he was sixteen – young Bill, Mr Choules the cream line foreman's boy. 'Yes, you do fancy her, it's obvious. I'll tell her if you want me to, see her reaction, if you're too shy to ask her out yourself.'

'No,' Bill had heard himself say, while of course he was thinking, *Yes please, yes please.*

The older man laid his knife and fork tidily across the centre of his empty dinner plate. 'How old are you now Bill – twenty-six, twenty-seven? Do you know, I've never heard you talk about girls and I've never seen you with one. So it's about time.' He rearranged the cutlery on the plate as he spoke. 'She's very quiet but she seems a nice enough girl to me. For God's sake, ask her out, man.'

'OK, Mr Holmes. Don't rub it in.' Bill had finished the cold dregs of his cup of tea and said nothing more.

Bill stood in his kitchen remembering how he had eventually plucked up courage to wait outside the factory for Brenda. How he had planned to leave quickly that afternoon to make sure he was outside the gates before she came out, to wait for her and to talk to her. He had waited, and she came out on her own. His heart seemed to want to jump from his chest, and he felt breathless as she approached. He smiled, she smiled back, he had said hello to Brenda in not much more than a whisper, but she had replied, 'Hello, Bill. Waiting for somebody?'

His heart was thumping, his mouth had gone dry, but he had managed to stammer out, 'Yes, yes, I am ... You. I was waiting for you to come out.' He had spoken before he had realised it. His words had just come out. 'How do you know my name is Bill?'

'Mr Holmes just said that Bill in the next office had been asking questions about me, so you must be Bill. What questions have you been asking?'

Bill recalled that he had never felt so peculiar in his life before. His mind had seemed to trip over itself – what to say, how to answer. He blurted it out before he had decided what to say.

'I like the look of you. I wanted to ask you out. You know, the pictures, or go for a walk or something.'

Her eyes had lit up at this outburst. 'Are you going to, then?' she teased him.

'Yes, yes.'

'Well, then …' she began, really tormenting him now.

'OK.' But no other words had come out.

'I will,' then Brenda replied. 'Yes, I will.'

'You will what?'

'Go out with you to the pictures or something.'

'OK,' said Bill again, his mind in turmoil. 'OK,' he repeated.

Brenda had smiled to herself at his diffidence. As he remembered now once more, rerunning the events in his mind as he poured himself another cup of tea here in his cold kitchen, all these years later. He recalled once more that first conversation with her, he could see that lovely peaceful look on her face, that smile he could remember now, those gentle brown eyes. That same smile she gave him as he held her hand for the last time only a year later when he saw her the day before she finally died. His eyes filled with tears once again. He still couldn't really acknowledge that people as young as twenty-one died of cancer. His heart swelled in his chest, the bile in his throat was so bitter, he shook his head as if to shake the memories from it and take the ache away.

'Wait till the others hear my ideas for getting rid of pests,' he said aloud. Then he finished his tea and left the stained cup on the sink's draining board.

CHAPTER 4

The knock on the shed door made them all jump. Bill walked straight in, clutching the doorframe.

'Everything all right, Bill?' enquired Ernie.

Bill looked around the familiar, smoky shed. 'Good morning, everyone.' He was more cheerful than usual. They all noticed almost at once. He didn't have the lugubrious look that was more usual, not quite; not quite normal in fact.

'He didn't seem himself, I thought, as soon as I saw him,' Brian remarked to Pete later on at the King's Head, or the King's, as they generally called their pub.

'Cup of tea, Bill?' Ernie asked, trying to stop staring at him as the others all seemed to be.

'Yes please, three sugars, Ern.'

'Three?' Ernie queried.

'Yes, three.'

All eyes were on Bill; they knew this wasn't Bill's regular amount of sugar.

Ernie sat down again after handing Bill his tea with the three spoonfuls of sugar in it. The four old men were seated on a variety of ancient wooden chairs and stools that the shed contained, among all the rest of the usual tools and odds and ends that adorned their shared hut. Bill remained standing, sipping his tea, his eyes shining, his face relaxed. His large eyes began to gaze slowly round at his friends, studying each one deliberately, from one to the next and back again. They in turn watched him closely, each sensing something, each unsure what to say or do but not knowing why. No one spoke. Each man was waiting for Bill to break the growing silence. Pete fished in his jacket pocket and rummaged for his cigarettes and lit one without taking his eyes from Bill. Brian rolled himself one but only looked away from Bill as he checked the gum on the paper and licked gently. At last Bill began, quietly, slowly at first, then gaining momentum as he spoke.

'I've had a few ideas to put to you all about getting rid of the pests, like we were talking about last Friday. I've been thinking about it all weekend, at home, getting rid of pests. We are gardeners, agreed?'

The others muttered puzzled agreement.

'We are the gardening club, agreed?'

Richard, Brian, Pete and Ernie nodded dutifully.

Bill continued, answering his own question: 'Yes, we are the gardening club. And we as the gardening club hate pests.' He looked around for reactions. 'We all hate pests, don't we?'

No one uttered a word, no one took their eyes from Bill, his broad forehead glistening bright pink in the dim January light of their shed.

'So we start getting rid of pests.'

Brian took a deep drag on his roll-up, blew smoke in Richard's direction with a slight cough, and glanced back at Bill. 'That's what we all do anyway, Bill.'

A flash of irritation crossed Bill's face as he looked directly at Brian. 'Not the garden plant pests, Brian – the pests of the nice town we once all lived in. Those pests, the pests we were talking about on Friday, the yobs, the bullies, the criminals, those sorts of pests.'

And he spat out the final 'pests' with a spray in Brian's direction which made Pete smile as he caught Brian's eye over the sleeve crossing his face. The other two members of the gardening club shifted in their respective seats. Pete lit another cigarette from his last one.

Richard tutted in Pete's direction and waved his open palm as he took up the baton. 'Yobs, junkies, dealers, burglars. Illegal pests that the police don't seem to do anything about.' Richard leaned forward and continued. 'My grandson had his bicycle stolen a couple of weeks ago. We phoned the police, but they didn't even send anyone around to my son's house. My grandson knew the boy, a yob, near where you live, Pete.' Pete looked sheepish. 'The police as far as we know did not go round there either. The yob just told him to get off his bike, and he did because he was frightened, he told my daughter-in-law. The other boy just rode away on it laughing. It cost £300 or so, that bicycle.'

'My wife has to put up with a gang of yobs by the shops shouting at her,' Brian chipped in. 'Fancy shagging an old man, they say to her. Sleep with your dad, do you? And worse sometimes. If I get hold of them ...' He looked around for support or comment. Neither came.

Ernie joined in with the same story he had told on the previous Friday. 'My grandson has changed so much lately, abusing his mother, my daughter. I swear he's on drugs. He used to be a good kid, but last time he came to my flat I noticed my video had gone after he'd left. I didn't want to believe he'd taken it. I didn't say anything to my daughter or to anyone – I don't use it ever anyway – but it's gone and I can only think he took it. My own grandson! I ask you. I haven't been broken into, although that's a surprise because everyone around our block of flats has at some time or other. I suppose they know I haven't got much.'

'This is it,' interrupted Bill, raising a huge pink hand as if to stop their anecdotes. 'Nobody does anything to stop these things.' He paused. 'But *we* can. We can take action to stop them. Who would believe five old men like us would do anything? They wouldn't suspect us. Here's one of my ideas. We name a pest – say, a slug – and then we call yobs slugs so that we know what we're talking about but others don't. Snails could mean junkies, that sort of thing, garden talk.'

'Aphids,' said Richard.

'Aphids,' Bill repeated.

Richard was anxious not to lose his train of thought. 'Aphids are a gang of yobs. Slugs are not just yobs, Bill, as you suggested. Slugs come out and do damage at night, eating up our plants the way drugs eat up young people. By that I mean drugs eat up the users' self-respect and decency so they end up stealing from decent people. Decent people plant plants, and slugs eat them.'

'And snails are as bad,' added Brian. 'Are they druggies?' Once more he looked around the shed for support or agreement.

Richard thought for a moment, running his hand back across his balding head. 'We would have to differentiate between pests and their analogies so that we five alone would know the difference. Good idea, Bill. It wouldn't make sense to anybody else but we must know. Why don't we draw up a list of garden pests and a list of the town pests and then put them together, rather than this haphazard way? I suggest that tonight we each write a list of each of the pests and that when we meet tomorrow, assuming you can all make it, we then compare notes.'

They all agreed that Richard's idea of lists was a good one and confirmed they would sort it out tomorrow with their individual lists.

'No Latin names, Richard,' said Brian. 'Me and the others won't know what your list is about.'

Richard tutted but smiled. 'No Latin, I promise. I don't know the Latin for yob anyway.'

Pete concluded the morning's business. 'Who's coming down the King's for one then?'

CHAPTER 5

Bill had the kettle on and the wood stove was roaring and crackling with its door wide open as Richard arrived the next morning. It was another frosty morning, but Bill hummed and whistled tunelessly to himself as he turned to see who arrived first.

Richard had noticed that Bill seemed to be standing straighter than usual. He was a big man anyway compared to the rest of the group, 'six foot four without shoes,' Bill always added when asked his height.

'Good morning, Bill. Early this morning, aren't you?'

'Yes, I felt like getting up early and getting on. I don't have anybody to slow me down like you other blokes, no one else in the house to get in the way.'

'You're right there, Bill. My wife is always up before me and seems to be everywhere I want to be in the mornings.'

'I don't have that problem.' Bill stirred the teapot, not really listening to Richard as the retired civil servant continued.

'Daphne always says every morning, "I'll be glad when you go to that allotment of yours, not that I can begin to imagine what you find to do around there for so long."' Richard did his best to mimic his wife's way of speaking. 'Every morning she says the same. She has all her charities to support, but *I* can't imagine what *she* finds to do all day every day since I retired.'

'How long since you retired, Richard?'

'Nine years. Retired at sixty, an advantage of being a civil servant, eh? A long boring life but a decent pension at the end of it. There were plenty of times Daphne tried to get me to leave. Why wasn't I more ambitious?' He mimicked her voice again.

'I spent my whole life working for the same company,' Bill added, more to himself than to Richard. 'From sixteen to sixty-five. The directors wouldn't have known me after forty-nine years ... Gave me a greenhouse at the end, a retirement present, "for our loyal member of staff", Mr David said at my farewell do, on my last day. I had to pay Brian to put the greenhouse up for me. It spent nine months just lying in the garden before I could use it.' He shook his head at the memory.

'You called all the directors by their Christian names then, did you?'

'Mr David, yes. Three brothers – David, Giles and the arrogant Jeremy, the youngest. Mr David was OK but the other two didn't know I existed.' Bill sighed.

Richard helped himself to a cup of tea just as Pete and Brian arrived together.

'No bike today, Pete?' Richard asked as they brought the cold air in with them.

'No, Brian picked me up. I got so cold yesterday, and Brian rang and asked me if I wanted a lift.'

'Poor old bugger. Painters are all soft, not like us brickies.' Brian let out a gruff, gravelly laugh.

Pete grinned. 'Get the bloody tea ready. Soft, eh?'

'That's right. I'll have a cup as well, please,' called Ernie as he walked into the shed, rubbing his hands and stamping his feet. 'Well, I don't know about you lot, but I must do some work today. I must finish digging over my patch if the frost isn't too deep.' Ernie looked around at the others for reactions.

'I've got some spare seed catalogues if any of you would like one. Or have you all done this year's order?' asked Richard.

'Good old Richard, always organised.' Brian clapped his hands in mock applause before he added, 'What about these lists then? Never mind catalogues, Richard.'

'I've done mine,' Ernie announced.

They each produced pieces of paper from various pockets.

'You're used to paperwork, Richard, and you, Bill, so I vote you two sort them out.' Brian handed his to Richard.

Richard studied Brian's list of pests of both kinds.

'Can you read my writing, Richard? My Debbie says she can't decipher my writing. She says I should have been a doctor.' Brian smiled, held out two large fleshy hands and studied the palms closely. 'All right for cutting bricks with my trowel but pity the poor bugger whose appendix I take out.'

Pete flicked ash from his cigarette into the open palms. 'I'd stick to laying bricks if I were you, mate,' he said with a friendly grin.

Brian shot a playful punch at Pete's shoulder, almost knocking him off balance.

Bill and Richard were already studying the lists and ignoring the others.

Richard's list was neatly laid out and printed on his personal computer. Brian teased him with over-exaggerated praise. Pete let out a whistle of genuine admiration. Ernie screwed up his small scrap of paper and shoved it back in his jacket pocket, murmuring something about not really needing his.

'Right,' said Bill, standing up to make his point. 'Let's get started ... Let's agree on these pests.' He sat down again and glanced at Richard. 'You explain.'

Richard shuffled Bill's list on his lap. The small neat handwriting so clear.

'I'm not ignoring your lists, Brian, or yours, Peter, but Bill's and mine are very similar and so I'll start with them, and please speak out if you agree or disagree with what we've done.'

Brian winked at Pete. Pete grinned back at Brian. Ernie sipped his tea.

Richard began, 'We've already identified most of the pests but now we can confirm each type for our code. Leatherjackets, the tough-skinned larvae of the crane-fly, live in the soil and mainly feed on the roots of plants.'

'The crane-fly – the daddy-long-legs – is harmless,' interrupted Bill, 'but the larvae are not.'

'Yes, yes.' Richard continued, 'Leatherjackets therefore are the type of pest or criminal who hides beneath something. Those who perhaps organise or remain beneath a surface of respectability but nevertheless do so much harm on the surface.' He glanced around the hut for approval. 'Does this make sense?'

Bill nodded enthusiastically, and Pete and Ernie agreed that they understood.

Brian lit a roll-up and felt the others looking at him. 'You mean like white-collar crime or con-men, people like that?'

'Sort of,' replied Richard. 'People' – he hesitated as he searched for his words – 'people less obvious, people beneath the surface, like the damage done to plants by eating the roots, as leatherjackets do. If healthy plants have their roots eaten, then they wither. In the same way, society is undermined by hidden forces beneath the surface – probably the more cunning types of criminal … those who carry on their work with disregard for the consequences to the rest of us law-abiding citizens.'

Brian stared at his roll-up. 'So how do we recognise a leatherjacket, Richard?'

'As the larva,' Richard explained very slowly, 'the leatherjacket feeds itself to become a crane-fly – a daddy-long-legs, as you say, Bill – it eats the root of the plant for its own purpose, and the plant rots and withers, to the detriment of us gardeners. Us gardeners are the normal law-abiding majority who merely wish to see healthy plants. Is that clear?'

'I get it,' said Brian through a cloud of exhaled smoke.

'Do you?' asked Pete.

'Sounds a bit complicated to me, but yeah, I get it. I'm not that thick, mate.'

'I didn't say you were thick, Brian.' Pete put a hand on Brian's forearm reassuringly.

'Yeah, well.' Brian shrugged.

'OK,' said Richard. 'Let's get on then.'

Bill cleared his throat and shifted in his chair. 'Percy Thrower said in *Everyday Gardening* that anyone who has tried to kill one of these larvae by stamping on it will know how well named it is – the greyish skin is extremely tough and resilient.'

'Thank you, Percy.' Brian winked again at Pete and Ernie. Bill momentarily glared at Brian.

'Aphids,' said Richard, 'I know we'll all agree, are a crowd or group that get together with the purpose of colonising areas and causing disruption. Sometimes they put fear into people just by hanging around in a gang, or in large numbers. Like football hooligans. Aphids, blackfly and greenfly – masses of them doing damage to plants by force of numbers, colonising leaves and fresh new shoots.'

'Taking over our streets. Aphids are gangs.' Bill kept nodding.

'So we understand leatherjackets and aphids? On to slugs and snails then. These are almost the same.' Richard was aware he might be confusing the situation. 'Slugs and snails mainly come out at night and do their damage.'

Ernie had grown anxious to be seen and heard to participate. 'Slugs and snails, the most regular criminals, the thieves, the burglars, the drug dealers?' He looked around at his fellow gardeners for approval.

'Yes!' agreed Bill and Richard.

'I think we should separate burglars and thieves from drug dealers.' Brian's expression was serious. He went to continue as he rolled another cigarette, but suddenly stopped himself, unsure.

Pete said, 'We can't have too many different pests. It will get confusing. Surely it's the drug culture that makes for so many burglaries and shoplifters, you know, to pay for their drugs. Surely these are mostly the same people, aren't they? The same sort of pests?'

The shed went quiet for a few minutes, Bill looking to Richard for a decision or conclusion.

'I think Peter is right.' Bill broke the silence.

Ernie agreed. 'What do you think, Richard? We don't want too many types of pests, do we?'

Richard rubbed the top of his head with a smooth palm, his involuntary habit when thinking. They all watched him, waiting for a lead.

'Let's just think about it for a moment. Let's make another cup of tea and just take a moment to think.'

Ernie filled the kettle and lined up the five mugs in readiness, while Pete stood up, stretched one leg after the other and lit a cigarette. Ernie poured the tea when it was made and passed each of the others a mugful.

'There are so many different sorts of pests in a garden and so many different sorts in life.' Ernie sighed as he handed Richard his mug. 'Every night in the *Willbury Reporter* I read of so much crime. Old ladies knocked to the ground for a few pounds, young blokes left in the gutter with broken jaws or worse. When I sit and read the paper it seems half full of crimes of all sorts. There was always crime in the old days but it was big news because it was so rare. It was sometimes hard not to feel sorry for people who shoplifted then. People who'd stolen food from the shop I worked in were always prosecuted. But they were stealing to survive then. To feed their family. In desperation for something to eat. Now with Social Security it's not necessary. It's just greed. People, however poor, can get money so easily for food and basics nowadays. I haven't got a problem with that.'

Bill interrupted Ernie. 'That's why I don't have a newspaper, Ernie.'

Richard had become aware of the difference between his life and the others'. He had rarely come across the same levels of poverty as the other four men. Conscious of his somewhat cosseted lifestyle, he knew he'd never really been short of money or comforts.

Brian confirmed his thoughts when he agreed with Ernie. 'When me and Pete couldn't work because of the weather, or when we had no work in the winter, we could've easily started nicking food.'

'You're right there, mate,' said Pete. 'I've had enough times with nothing in the cupboard and wondering how

Liz managed to come up with a meal. When you're self-employed you don't get any money from Social Services. I couldn't even get the basic sick pay when I had my hernia operation. They said I was three National Insurance stamps short during the previous three years. It was only about £56 a week but I didn't get anything. I don't see how people who've never paid anything in can get money from Social Services when I'd paid in for about forty years and wasn't even entitled to the basic. I'd never even tried to claim anything until then. I was supposed to rest for six weeks, but I had to go back to work after three weeks. No work, no money.' Pete realised he could go on and on but silently shook his head.

'This isn't getting our Pest List done,' announced Bill.

'Now where were we?' asked Richard. 'Ah yes, it was about the length of the list and the grey areas of different pests. I think we should keep it simple and short. There are so many in both categories of pest. Leatherjackets we agree on. Aphids we agree on.' He glanced around for confirmation. Nobody spoke.

'Slugs and snails we stopped at – thieves, burglars, druggies. I actually think these belong together for simplification, but maybe drug dealers should be classed as leatherjackets.'

The other men each agreed with this. Keep it reasonably simple.

'After all,' Pete pointed out, 'this is only for us to know. It doesn't really matter.'

Richard nodded and rubbed his head once more. 'Yes, the main thing is for us to have a simple code to use if we write anything down, or if we talk about our pest control in front of other people. If anyone overhears, they'll think we're just talking about gardening. So we must keep it simple, otherwise we'll get confused and we won't be able to use the code at all.'

Abruptly Bill stood up and began to speak, not really addressing anybody in particular. 'Cockchafers, the large white grubs of the cockchafer beetle, also live in the soil like other larvae, feeding on fibrous roots ... Frog-hoppers suck the sap of plants ... Leaf-miners – their larvae are also destructive ...' He hesitated between each item as if thinking aloud and enabling the others to inter-rupt if they remembered any other pests that should be added to their code. 'Yes, there are endless pests in the garden and in our town,' he added, to no one in particu-lar. 'Yes, Willbury could do with less pests.' He blew his nose noisily into a ragged handkerchief.

Bill was imagining all the pests that he had battled with in protecting his chrysanthemums. *Yes*, he thought. *Aphids, the gangs. The eelworms creeping into the leaves of my plants – extra troublesome in rainy seasons. The leaf-miner too. The fly laying its eggs on my prize plants, their grubs tunnelling inside the leaves, eating the tissues as they go. Weakening my plants.* Thinking about these pests made him feel so angry.

'Come on, gentlemen.' Richard tried again to galvanise their thoughts. 'Let's agree our list of pests. Leatherjackets. Aphids. Slugs and snails. These three groups pretty much cover all the human pests in Willbury.'

'No, I think weevils should also be included.' Bill spoke loudly.

The others stole looks at one another.

He continued, 'There are lots of different types of weevils that do so much harm to different sorts of plants, as so many pests do in our town.'

'Yes, but, Bill, what category of human pests are weevils?' Richard asked what all the others were thinking.

Bill gulped a large mouthful of his tea before he spoke. 'Weevils are the pests who are difficult to see until the damage is done.'

'Give us an example then, Bill,' said Brian.

'Well, I think drug dealers should come into this category.' The big man shifted his weight on his creaking chair and then stood. 'Weevils should be included separately – the human weevils who destroy so much without being seen until it's too late.'

The men could see Bill's determination to make his point. It seemed to them inappropriate to the discussion, unnecessarily forceful. Brian and Pete had been nudging and eyeing each other while Bill spoke, Brian alternately winking at Pete and adopting an exaggerated expression of serious concentration. Pete meanwhile struggled to keep a straight face at Brian's antics. He caught a disapproving glare from Richard. Ernie shifted uneasily on his chair while studying a knot in a floorboard. When Brian mischievously nodded to Pete to look at Ernie, Pete had to fake a cough so as not to laugh out loud. His eyes watered and he felt for his cigarettes to distract himself.

The gardening club hut then fell silent for some minutes. The silence seemed to grow and seep into each dusty corner. Occasionally the five men each glanced round at one another but no one spoke. Ernie had his hands between his knees and his chin on his narrow chest.

At last Richard broke the silence. 'Can we all agree that weevils should be a separate category of pest?' The others immediately murmured their agreement. 'That will make four categories,' Richard added. 'Leatherjack-ets, aphids, slugs and snails, and weevils.'

Bill sat down slowly, unaware of the uneasiness he had caused in the other men. 'Four categories of pests,' he said quietly. 'That's good.'

'Come on, Ernie. Let's go and do something useful and think about this,' said Pete, pulling his scarf more tightly round his neck, while Ernie buttoned up his coat. 'You've got ground to dig and I want to put something over my rhubarb to force it.'

Bill glanced from Richard to Brian, and cleared his throat as if he were going to make a speech.

'I know I've probably jumped the gun but I have to tell you I've already begun on the pests.'

Richard didn't appear to hear this but Brian stopped rolling his cigarette midway.

'What do you mean, Bill?'

'I mean I did something to a pest over the weekend.'

Richard looked up now and gazed from Bill to Brian and back again. 'You have?'

'Yes.'

'Well, you'd better tell us what, then.' Richard frowned and glanced at Brian.

'I'll tell you when Pete and Ernie come back in. They won't be out there long in this temperature,' Bill added cheerily.

Pete had placed an old plastic dustbin upside-down over his rhubarb, and when he had finished he wandered over to Ernie. Ernie, the oldest of the little group at seventy-three, was a small, wiry man with ruddy cheeks that made people who didn't know better suspect he was a drinker.

'That looks like hard work, Ern,' Pete remarked as he reached Ernie's patch of allotment.

'I'm getting too old for this,' agreed Ernie. 'I'd really hoped to finish turning this lot over, for the frost to break it up a bit.' He leaned on his fork with one hand and waved the other in the general direction of his plot.

Pete peered around the allotments furtively, checking that no one else was about. 'What do you think of this pest control idea then, Ern?'

Ernie straightened up, pushed his fork deeper into the ground, rubbed the middle of his back with both hands and let out a sigh. 'It worried me when I first understood what Bill was saying last Friday. I mean we're always putting the world to rights, aren't we? You know what's going wrong in Willbury. In the country. In the world. You know what we should do. All blokes do it, don't they? Everywhere people are always moaning about what's wrong. One thing or another. What the government should do. Or what the police should be doing.'

He drew his scarf tighter round his neck and gazed across the white-sprinkled allotments. He took in the low layer of mist over the ground towards the perimeter fence. Then, looking up at Pete directly, his small watery eyes fixed carefully on his fellow gardener, he said, 'I've worked all my life. I own nothing. I paid rent to the council all my life. My wife died three years ago now. My daughter hardly ever comes to see me. You blokes seem more like my family. This used to be a nice town to live in. Neighbours aren't friendly any more. The yobs do just what they like. So I'll be glad to play my part, I'll be glad to help get rid of pests.'

Pete could see his old friend meant what he said. He noted a sad despair in Ernie's eyes too. 'Yes, it might be

fun. Come on, let's go back to the shed and get warm ...
have a cup of tea.'

Ernie shivered, as he and Pete huddled round their
wood-burning stove. Pete pushed a couple more small
pieces of wood into the top, and it crackled and spat out
a few sparks. He lit a cigarette and viewed their shared
haven.

'Well,' he said, blowing a cloud of blue-grey smoke.
'Have we got our lists together?'

Brian eyed Pete and Ernie. 'Bill and Richard have
sorted the lists out into one list. Pests and pests. And Bill
has something to tell us, haven't you, Bill? Bill has
already done some pest control, haven't you, Bill? Tell us
what you've done.' Brian winked at Pete.

Four sets of eyes, watery old eyes, fixed on Bill. For a
few seconds Bill looked slightly embarrassed and
awkward. He cleared his throat, first with a growl, then
with an almost dainty little cough.

'When we were talking Friday, I got to thinking.
I couldn't sleep Friday night. I hadn't gone to bed,
I didn't feel sleepy. I sat in my sitting-room, which as you
know is at the front of my house. I didn't have my
records on. I was just sitting thinking about what we'd
all been talking about that morning.'

Bill looked from one to the other, cautious, it seemed,
wary of what his friends might think of him.

'Come on, Bill. Confess.' Brian was growing impatient.

'I'm getting to it. I could hear voices outside the
house, people coming from the pub, I thought. Well, not
talking, more like shouting, effing and blinding at the
top of their voices in fact. I ignored them at first,

thought they would carry on up the road. Then I looked out of the front window. They didn't see me, I didn't have the light on. There were about four or five yobs still outside, just past my place, larking around, swearing and making lots of noise. I watched. They began to move on. But then they go into my neighbour's front garden and appear to be messing about with his car parked there. They break off his wipers. Laughing and joking out loud as they do it. They lever off his hub caps, break his wing mirrors off. Then just as one of them starts peeing on the bonnet my neighbour's lights come on, the porch light comes on, and out he comes. He chases out, they all run away but he catches one of them. Only a kid, about seventeen, too young to be drinking in a pub in my opinion. I go out to help and as I get there the lad punches my neighbour in the face. He lets go and the lad runs off. So I help my neighbour back to his house. He is OK, really angry but OK. His car isn't but he is. He tells me he knows exactly who the boys are and I know them as well. They're part of the gang that makes a nuisance of themselves outside the shops down the road. I have a cup of tea with my neighbour. He tells me he can't be bothered to phone the police since they won't do anything anyway, and even if they do come they'll keep him up as well, and so he goes off to bed – he works Saturdays. I don't go back indoors. I follow the boys. I know where one or two of them live. I get to their houses and I damage two cars on the front. I throw mud over the front.'

'Is that all?' Brian seemed disappointed.

'Well, no.' Bill hesitated again. 'I slashed the tyres of both cars with my pruning knife. Well, stabbed the tyres more than slashed. The cars probably belong to their parents, but so what? The questions will still be asked, I guess.'

Silence fell once more in the hut. Pete blew smoke. Ernie's jaw looked slack, his eyes wide open. Richard was stern-faced, Brian grinning broadly. All eyes were still on Bill, who was looking from one to the other until he turned to fill the kettle.

'Who wants another cup of tea?' he simply concluded.

'Bloody good on you, Bill! I for one am proud of you.' Brian, still grinning, slung a thick arm round Bill's shoulder, almost on tiptoe to reach. 'Well done, mate. Give the pests some of their own medicine, that's what I say.' Brian was full of glee, smiling and rubbing his horny hands together. If it had been quieter in that shed you might have heard the hard corns on his hands scratching at each other. 'What sort of pests were they then, Richard?'

Richard ran his hand across his balding head in a circular movement as if to add to the shine. 'Aphids.'

Brian's eyes twinkled. 'What do you think of that then, Pete boy, eh? Ernie, what do you think? You, Richard, what's your opinion?'

Richard considered quietly before saying, 'Actions speak louder than words, my friends. Well done, Bill.'

Bill stirred five mugs of tea, the relief obvious on his face. At times like this, his face looked somewhat baby-like, belying his seventy-one years, with his wide eyes, pink cheeks and shining forehead. He was clearly pleased with himself. 'Help yourselves to sugar,' he said.

Pete and Ernie seemed to be scrutinising each other. 'What do you think, Pete?' Ernie whispered. 'What do you make of that?'

Brian had heard Ernie's question. 'Yes, what do you think? Is he a vandal or a hero?'

Pete sat down with his tea, watching it revolve within his mug. He looked up slowly to find all the rest of the gardening club studying him, waiting for his reaction. At last he spoke.

'Did you know the rest of the yobs' addresses?'

The hut filled with voices as they all seemed to talk at once.

'Do you mean that?'

'You agree with Bill, then?'

'Let's go get 'em.'

As the cacophony faded, it was Richard, calm and businesslike, who summed it up.

'Well, it seems, gentlemen, that the pest control has begun. It just remains for everyone to understand our code, but I think we will all remember "aphids" as a gang of pests.'

They spent the next hour or so discussing their new code and then all left together, each with his own thoughts, each with his own ideas on pest control.

CHAPTER 6

Brian dropped Pete off at his neat semi-detached house. They would be back at the allotment tomorrow for sure.

'Cheerio, mate. Beware of aphids.' He winked at Pete and clunked his van into first gear.

Pete shut the front door and hung his coat on one of the row of hooks at the bottom of the stairs.

'Hello, love, it's only me!' he called out to Liz as he hurried down the small hallway to the kitchen, filled the kettle and flicked the switch on.

He walked across the lounge and on through the door of the partition wall that separated off the room at the back of the house that was his wife's bedroom. Pete had built the partition wall himself so that Liz could have a bedroom downstairs, making the lounge smaller – two rooms now instead of one large one. Leaning over the back of the armchair she sat in, he kissed the top of her head.

'Hello, love. You all right?'

'Yes, I'm all right. Bored as usual but all right.'

'What do you fancy to eat?'

Liz replied that a sandwich would be OK. 'Cheese if we've got any in the fridge or cream cheese if not.'

As Pete looked around the small room, his shoulders sagged. A bed, an armchair, a sideboard of sorts covered in bottles, boxes of pads and bits and pieces that were needed to look after someone with MS. Multiple sclerosis is a disease that will take some to an early grave, but Liz was dubbed 'lucky' by her GP, because she had a less aggressive form. She couldn't walk, her speech was slurred, her hands were stiff and awkward, but she was 'lucky', the doctor had said.

'Usual nurse this morning, love?'

'Two this morning, Kathy and a new young one. They have to come in pairs now. They're not insured for one to move me on her own. New regulations, Kathy said. In case they hurt their backs, I'm told.'

'What was she like, the new one?'

'Pretty girl, only in her twenties, I'd guess.'

When over thirty years ago Liz had started walking badly, dragging one foot at first, Pete had thought it would get better. It was only temporary, he'd thought. Then one day when he came home from work their daughters, Sally and Vanessa – then aged six and eight – were both crying in the front garden as he pulled his van in.

'Mummy has fallen over,' they had told him, sobbing. 'She can't get up.'

What a day that was, he recalled. That was when he knew life was about to change. That was when he realised his wife's limping would not go away. Over the years they had coped the best they could, but Liz had needed a wheelchair permanently almost from that day. The council – it wasn't called social services back then – had arranged for a home help. Some home helps stayed for years, visiting every morning, cooking, cleaning and generally helping Liz. In those days she used to cry a lot – out of frustration, he supposed; not sorry for herself but frustrated.

For years Pete had carried her upstairs to bed, but he couldn't do it now. The nurse came and bathed her and helped her with the toilet. Menstruation time was difficult. Liz often said during the menopause that at least it was one blessing of getting old. The menopause, a blessing! Now the home help visited for an hour at the most in the morning. Social services seemed to keep cutting back with help.

'Your family will have to do more,' they always said, if he ever asked for more assistance. As Pete was getting older, it would get harder, he guessed. Still, he was retired now, although he occasionally did some small painting jobs for old customers; the cash was useful. His daughters laughed at him a few weeks ago while they were all discussing the lack of help. When Pete said he was middle-aged, they had laughed till they cried.

It was Sally who said it first. 'If you're middle-aged, Dad, that means you'll live to be 134!'

Pete smiled at his own silliness and the memory of their laughing so much. Well, he might be old but not that old, he told himself. Liz did feel a bit heavier when he helped her into the downstairs toilet, but he hoped he'd manage. His mate Bob had done him a good deal, he thought, converting the old larder into a downstairs toilet. It was a pity it was under the stairs, a pity the ceiling wasn't a little higher so he wouldn't hit his head so often.

'Here's your cheese sandwich, love.' Pete handed Liz her lunch. 'Kettle on, tea in a minute.'

Liz looked out of the patio doors that took up most of the outside wall of her bedroom. She'd moved down here some years ago, after Pete's hernia operation, to save him having to carry her upstairs. How he'd managed it as long as he had still surprised her when she thought about it. The garden, her view, was ugly at this time of the year. Cobwebs with dew, bare soil, only a few shrubs and bushes that formed the borders to the small lawn beyond the patio that Pete had laid all those years ago.

'I was thinking, Peter ... ' She generally called him Peter when she was being serious or upset but also when she was angry. '... Couldn't you put a roof over the patio so I can sit out in the summer?'

'Yes, I suppose I could,' he murmured without much enthusiasm.

'It would save you having to rush home when you're out if it rains and I'm out there. I know it was unusual last summer when it was raining here but not on that blessed allotment of yours. Only about a mile away, raining here but not there. I got saturated that day. There wasn't anything I could do. I shouted and shouted for the neighbours but no one heard me. I'd still be in the fresh air but dry if that happened again. You know, a clear plastic roof, that's all it would need.'

'You're right, my love. Good idea. I could get Brian to give me a hand.'

Pete was glad she couldn't turn round to see him. He couldn't help smiling wryly as he remembered that day he'd put her out on the patio in her wheelchair at lunchtime, then gone back to the allotment at 2 o'clock and stayed there till nearly 6. It had rained at home from about 2.30. Liz was soaked. She looked a sorry sight that day as he took off her wet clothes, poor girl.

'Looking at the garden now, I wonder what on earth you can do every morning on the allotment.'

'Well, there are jobs to do in the winter, but mainly I enjoy just seeing the lads round there. I did cover some more rhubarb this morning – that forces it on quicker. Ernie did a bit of digging.'

'How is Ernie? It's quite some while since his wife died, and his daughter doesn't live locally, does she?'

'He's OK.'

'He must be very lonely without Grace.'

'Yeah, I suppose.'

'What do you do in that hut of yours?'

Pete was by now in the kitchen making a pot of tea, having switched the kettle back on. He went back in.

'You didn't hear me,' Liz said. 'I asked you what do you do in that hut of yours.'

'We sit and drink tea, chat about gardening mostly. We've got our wood-burning stove, which we all take any old bits of wood for. Keeps us warm. We talk about football sometimes, though it's only me and Brian interested – none of the other three are. We discuss a bit of world politics, sort out world problems. That's Richard's favourite subject. Bill, well, Bill is just Bill. You ask about Ernie, is he lonely? Well, he said to me this morning he thinks of our little gang as his family. It was sad really to hear him say that. At least we've got each other and the girls, and the grandkids to come to see us sometimes. Even Sally's Garry pops in sometimes when he's not playing golf, I suppose.'

'It doesn't seem healthy to me, five old men sitting in a shed all morning, every morning.' Liz wasn't nagging. She never really complained about anything much.

Pete was thinking of the punctured tyres as he ate his cheese sandwich. He chuckled silently to himself. Liz, he reckoned, would not much approve of what they had agreed to do. He wasn't sure himself about what the gardening club had set out to do – to clean up Willbury.

Liz interrupted his thoughts. 'Why don't you invite them round here? I'm sure it's more comfortable than that old shed. Invite Ernie round at least. He always seemed a sad little man to me, I mean even before Grace died.'

'He's OK. He likes his own company as far as I know, and Bill, the other one who lives alone, has been on his own for years too.'

'What's Bill's house like?' Liz changed the subject, enjoying the chance just to talk.

'Bill's house is like a time warp.'

'What do you mean?'

'Well, he has all these charts, maps or whatever you like to call them, up on all the walls of the lounge – maps of his rose bushes with their position in his garden and their names. The rooms can't have been decorated for twenty years or more, and everything in the house is old and shabby. Not that I've ever been upstairs, but I guess it's the same or worse.' He chewed the last of his sandwich. 'The kitchen still has a stone sink with a wooden draining board. His pots and pans must have been good-quality originally, but they're very old. Everything he has is ancient. The curtains are dusty and frayed, the net curtains are grey and dirty. His garden is beautiful in the summer, though, masses of roses front and back, apple trees galore at the bottom. But the house is a museum – apart from his hi-fi music system. Bill loves classical music, opera and orchestras. That stereo system, I think, is the only modern thing in the house. He doesn't even have a TV or radio. He hasn't even got an electric kettle – just an old-fashioned kettle, big enough to cater for an army troop.'

'Poor old chap,' said Liz, anxious to keep the talk flowing.

Pete thought for a moment, and the image of Bill stabbing tyres flashed through his mind.

'I don't know about "poor old chap", he must have thousands in the bank, never a house to pay for, never seems to buy anything, no car to keep him poor, no wife or kids to keep him poor. I've even seen in his kitchen cupboards – never much in them. For a big bloke he doesn't seem to eat much.'

'Funny him never getting married.'

'Bloody sensible if you ask me.' Pete stood up and ruffled Liz's hair as he said it. 'Why make one miserable if you can make lots happy? That's what I say.'

Liz didn't answer this last tease, she had heard it so often before.

A few minutes later Pete peered round the side of the armchair and saw that Liz was fast asleep. Quietly he went into the lounge, to sit in his favourite armchair. He soon drifted off. A strange dream of policemen banging on the front door in full body armour, combat hats, guns, the house, his house, floodlit from the road. He awoke with what felt like a head full of cotton wool, and it seemed as though minutes, though it was perhaps only seconds, passed before he realised somebody really was knocking at the front door. Pete rubbed a fist into each eye as he stood up. Certain now that he wasn't dreaming, he opened the front door.

'Hello, Bill, what can I do for you?'

The big man stood on the doorstep, looking cold.

'I've got the addresses of the other boys – aphids, I mean. I thought you might like to come and help tonight.'

'Come in, Bill, come in.'

'No thanks, I won't interrupt you. Besides, I'm going to call on the others. Arrange to meet at my house tonight about eight-thirty if you can. Let's get started on some work. Can you make it?'

'Yes, I can. And I'll ring Richard to save you going round to him.'

As Bill left, Pete stood at his front door and watched him ride off on his bike, not entirely sure what he had just agreed to, or why. *Where is this going?* he thought, closing the door behind him and walking back to join his sleeping wife in her bedroom.

He sighed audibly as he studied Liz. A heavy feeling suddenly filled his whole being. 'What's it all about, love? he whispered. 'What's the point?' The inexplicable sense of foreboding engulfed him. He bent and kissed his wife gently on the cheek, careful not to wake her.

It was in quiet moments like this that Pete had lately begun to experience a deep despair about his and Liz's future. The thoughts slipped silently into his mind. He saw himself struggling to get Liz to the toilet. This process seemed to become more difficult by the day. What if the despair overwhelmed him? Sometimes as he lay in bed he'd imagine a pain in his groin, and wonder whether it was another hernia, on the other side. When he'd had his operation last time, his daughter Sally moved in for a while to help, but it wasn't pleasant for her children or her husband. That was when he had finally given up carrying Liz upstairs and rearranged the house to create Liz's new room downstairs. He still missed her beside him in the double bed. And he couldn't help gagging when he had to clean Liz up if she had an 'accident', as they euphemistically termed her incontinence. They both became distressed every time. He would reassure Liz, of course, but he would never get used to it – rolling her about to change the bedsheets.

Should he open the patio doors to clear the air? Squirt air-freshener around her? Her doleful gaze would follow his every movement.

Pete couldn't see it getting any easier. In fact he supposed it would get even harder. Right now their lives were on hold. The future looked bleak, and for the first time he wondered how long he would still be able to cope.

Chapter 7

Richard Owen-Davies sat in the study of his large, detached, 1930s house in Linden Avenue. When the children were small, the study had been the playroom, and Peter Wilson had redecorated it in a fine Regency stripe of white and maroon. Richard still thought it looked smart, with his big ruby-leather-topped desk, his bookcases, his old school photograph. The heavy brocade curtains that his wife, Daphne, had chosen for his study still hung well from the dark wooden pole.

He pushed his rimless glasses back up to the top of his fleshy nose, a bit nearer to the bushy white eyebrows. He leaned back in his buttoned-leather chair and looked out at the light grey sky beyond the curtains. That was how he had met Peter Wilson. They were both about the same age. Richard had just retired at the age of sixty-one, and Peter had told him he had passed retirement age. Richard preferred having this older tradesman in his house rather than some young painter with an earring. They got on; they both liked gardening. It was Peter who had suggested he might enjoy having an allotment, even though his garden was about one-third of an acre. It was beautifully laid out, and well maintained by himself, Daphne and old Mr Ritches, who came round for two hours every Tuesday and Wednesday afternoon.

Richard had considered the idea for a while. There seemed to be too many hours to fill, with no train to catch, no rush, no meetings; the days seemed endless. He had looked forward to retirement but he soon wondered why. Daphne's days seemed full of activity. He even suspected he was slightly jealous of Daphne. She didn't appear to need him. She certainly didn't want to go anywhere with him, not even to the garden centre. She said she had too much to do, so many meetings, so many friends to see. It had taken only a month before he decided to take a look at the allotments. Peter had written down directions for how to find The Elms, as the allotments were called.

All the men had all been there, and it was kind of them to find an extra mug of tea from within their shared shed. He had felt like an outsider for a while but something drew him back. It was agreed with the council that he would take over old Mr Hatch's patch the following week. Mr Hatch had died suddenly, his runner beans still to be picked. Richard was offered the fifth key to the shed that very first week. He was hooked. He found he enjoyed the open air, even some of the harder work. His hands had blistered that first year, though. Brian had laughed when he'd shown him them one morning over tea in the shed. He found this gruff but jovial man amusing. He could not recall ever having talked to a bricklayer in his life before.

Richard sat reflecting on his early days at the allotment, so different from his life before, his well-ordered, well-organised routine. It filled the void very quickly. Soon he had a new routine and some ... well, yes ... friends. Yes, he had enjoyed the relaxed personalities of Brian and Peter, their lack of inhibition, their straight-

forward, informal ways. Daphne would not have understand if he had ever told her the ease he felt in their
company. He wasn't sure he would have believed it
himself once upon a time. Bill was not an imaginative
man, nor was Ernie, but they were clean and decent.
They didn't swear as much as Brian. Sometimes Brian
had seemed coarse to him, but he ignored it now. Still
from time to time it puzzled him, their easy acceptance.
Their skill not mine, he had concluded. He still did not
feel at ease with them in the King's Head pub, but he
didn't have to go there often. He was still irritated sometimes at the over-familiar jokes and the mickey-taking
about his boarding school or civil servants drinking so
much tea. He didn't like to remember his boarding
school days, that was probably it. He shook his head as
if to shake out the memories now. *Get on with the job in
hand, Owen-Davies*, he scolded himself – the job in hand
made easier from his well-stocked bookcases: *Garden
Pests and Nature's Poisons* by G. P. Alexander.

Daphne's car crunched on the shingle drive. He was so
engrossed in his studies that it made him jump. Feeling
somewhat guilty, he quickly returned the book to its
place on the shelf. At that moment the phone rang and
Daphne picked up the receiver in the hallway before he
had begun to reach for his handset right there on the desk.

'It's for you, Richard!' she called out.

'Hello, yes ... Peter, yes.' He hesitated. 'Yes, I suppose
I could come ... Yes, fine ... Eight-thirty tonight, yes ...
Bye for now.'

'Who was that, Richard?' Daphne leaned round the
study door from the hall.

At sixty, Daphne was still an attractive woman, still a
size 12, slim ankles. Her hairdresser, Kurt, had told her

many times, 'There really isn't any need to colour your hair, Mrs OD,' as it amused him to call her. She, of course, knew there was, but she still hadn't tired of hearing him say it. 'Pale blue eyes need blonde hair,' he always told her. *Such a waste*, she thought to herself, *that he prefers men to women – he's so charming*. Richard could be dull and predictable. But he provided well for them, and Bobby and Oliver had been so successful that it compensated. Their daughter Roberta – Bobby, as she preferred to be known – now ran a successful dance school. Oliver was a partner in an estate agency with three branches, Owen-Davies and Blagrave. Daphne was proud of both their children.

'Just a friend from the allotments,' Richard replied, and shrank a little as he said the word.

'Nobody interesting then,' she said, gliding away from the door jamb.

Richard sighed, and slid slightly lower into his chair, annoyed with himself for allowing his wife to make him so easily feel diminished. He reached into a desk drawer and found a note he had made of the address of the boy who had stolen his grandson's bicycle. *I'm sure we'll have time for that as well*, he considered – a visit to a leatherjacket.

The *Willbury Reporter*, delivered each afternoon, dropped through the letterbox. Richard went out and picked it up, reading the front page as he returned to his desk. As if he needed a reminder, the front headline informed: PENSIONER AGED 80 HAS HER HAND-BAG SNATCHED. *For full report, see page 4*. He turned to page 4 and skimmed through the article. In broad daylight, at three in the afternoon, a pensioner had been knocked to the ground and was now in a critical condition ... Her handbag had contained her pension book and six pounds in her purse ... The police would like to talk to witnesses of this brutal attack ... The suspect was wearing a black puffa-type jacket, white trainers, and a black woollen hat with an emblem on the front ... This was the third snatch this month ... As Richard read the report, he shook his head slowly. Then he rang the police station, thinking while he waited so long that he was glad he wasn't reporting a crime.

'Desk,' a flat voice said.

'Yes, I've just read in the *Willbury Reporter* about the elderly lady who had her handbag snatched and wondered if I could help.'

'Help, sir? Did you see it happen?'

'No, but ...' He didn't know what to say next.

'Well, then, how do you think you could help, sir?' the tired voice at the police station asked.

'I don't know. Sorry. Goodbye.' Richard put the handset down, wishing he had thought it through beforehand. *Fancy reacting like an idiot*, he scolded himself.

The desk officer shook his head in bewilderment and returned to his crossword.

Daphne and Richard ate their dinner in silence, sitting at each end of the polished mahogany dining table. Richard rested his cutlery gently on the plate as he finished, then cleared his throat, trying to sound casual.

'I've just got to pop out shortly, Daphne. I have to meet someone at eight-thirty. I won't be gone long.'

Daphne did not disguise her surprise at this announcement. 'Out? You never go out in the evening, Richard. Where are you going? Who are you meeting?'

'Just some of my gardening friends.'

'Gardening friends, allotment friends? You haven't been yourself since you started going to that dreadful place with those awful men. Coming back here with your clothes smelling of smoke and tobacco.' She feigned a shudder of disgust.'Surely not in that filthy shed that you seem so fond of? Not at night as well!'

'No, dear – just meeting them. We have something to discuss.'

'Discuss? Won't it wait until tomorrow morning? I'm sure you'll all be back there tomorrow morning.'

'No, this can't wait.' He tried his best for this to sound conclusive.

To his relief, Daphne merely shrugged. 'Oh well, I'll clear the plates, and you get off to your important meeting.' She stood up and started collecting dishes.

Richard found himself thinking of his childhood and his life almost used up. It was a long way from Aberystwyth, the town of his birth. He put his coat on, picked up his car keys from the hall table and shut the door behind him, still annoyed at the feelings Daphne always managed to stir in him.

Once in the car, he pulled out of the drive and headed for Bill's house. He checked his pocket for the address of the boy who had stolen his grandson's bicycle. *I'll show you, Daphne*, he thought to himself.

CHAPTER 8

The five gardening club members were all present at Bill's house. Brian had given Pete a lift there, but Richard and Ernie had arrived separately. They all lived fairly close to each other, but Bill's semi-detached house was almost central. Bill had quickly found a leadership quality he didn't know he had until now. It was he who had organised this meeting. Besides, as he lived on his own, there was no one else to question the pensioners assembled in Bill's sparse lounge. Later they would each agree that they had never seen him so animated.

'He was not his normal docile self,' Richard observed afterwards to Ernie and Pete. 'He was more alive, more confident.'

Bill had told them all earlier, 'Give some thought to where we might start. Think of some targets. We'll all go out tonight and make a start. No time like the present.'

Sitting in Bill's house now, they discussed where each would go and how each would tackle his targeted pest. So far, their discussion had been haphazard and more than a little vague.

Bill tried to stiffen their resolve. 'Have you all got a knife of some description?' he asked. 'I have the other addresses to visit. Slugs and snails can do a lot of damage overnight, I'm told.' He let out a deep chesty laugh at his own rare joke.

The others were like-minded but still found themselves shifting uneasily in their chairs. Richard, to his own annoyance, found himself recalling schooldays once more. He remembered the times when at his boarding school during the summer term they were allowed to take their bicycles to school. They had Sunday afternoon rides instead of the Sunday afternoon walks during the other two terms. During the summer term some of the boys would sneak out of the dormitory and ride their bikes at night. He had never been caught by his housemaster or prefects. He had only agreed to go twice. In those days he had been fearful of the consequences, just as now he felt apprehension. He remembered two boys being expelled for having broken into a local sweetshop on a night trip. It was not a prefect or the housemaster but the shopkeeper who had returned them to the school. Among the boarders back then, it had seemed a major incident, with lectures about obeying rules, warnings of punishment and expulsion. Richard had steadfastly refused ever to go on any night trips after that, though others still went.

Pete had Liz in his thoughts.

Ernie found he was enjoying himself. *This is better than sitting in front of the television again*, he thought. *I've never done anything wrong in my life*, he told himself, *and look what it got me*. Ernie had come from a big family, and had three brothers and two sisters. His family was not so big these days; his three older brothers had all been killed in the war. But Ernie still had the framed black-and-white photo of all six siblings with their mum and dad on his bedroom wall. Poor little Sam, next up from Ernie, was only seventeen when he was blown to bits. He could remember his mother crying when she opened the third telegram. He had cried himself. His sisters had hugged him, but he pushed them off and went to sit in that cold outside toilet for hours till his mum coaxed him out. 'Come on, Ernie, your dad wants to use it.' He couldn't remember his dad crying. It was his dad who got him the job at fourteen at the local Co-op and it was now his meagre Co-op pension that kept him above the poverty line.

Brian rolled a cigarette. Bill watched the spilled strands of tobacco fall on his threadbare carpet as if it had been laid last week, but he didn't say anything. Not even when Brian lit the end result with a cough.

'All ready, then?' Bill asked as he buttoned his huge overcoat.

'Just a minute before we go,' Richard butted in. 'I have one more address to find.' He explained that he had kept the address of the boy who had snatched his grandson's expensive bicycle, and grumbled once more about how the police didn't seem interested.

'This is what it's about.' Bill waved his hand towards Richard. 'If they can't be bothered, we can.'

It had been agreed that they would be too noticeable if all five travelled together as a group. Now that they had four rather than three addresses to visit, they decided that Richard and Pete would go together because Pete knew the road where the 'leatherjacket' lived. The other three men were given one address each. According to their plan, they would all go straight home after the pest control and each would report tomorrow at the allotment shed.

The members of the gardening club left Bill's front door and walked towards their respective vehicles. Ernie unlocked his VW Golf and was soon away, Brian not far behind in his Escort van. Bill climbed on to his bike, his scarf pulled round his face, his eyes glistening in the light from the lamppost outside his house. Pete closed the passenger door of Richard's Renault, fitting into his seat and finding the seat belt.

'Nice car, Richard.'

Richard shifted in his seat, settled himself comfortably as he started the engine, and clicked the headlights on. 'Yes. Except it's French. I always had Rovers in the old days. It makes me angry to think we have no motor industry of our own. My wife has a Mazda, Japanese – silly little sports car, at her age.'

'Yes, I know. I've seen her in it. I thought it was neat, I must admit. Not like an MG, though.'

Pete gave Richard directions and away they went. The heater was blowing noisily, directed to clear the windscreen.

'I assume, Richard, that you have some idea of what we're going to do when we get there.'

Richard glanced momentarily across to his passenger.

'It would have been better if we had all had some sort of plan, don't you think? We're all charging off in different directions, none of us knowing what we're doing really. Don't you think we should have planned this better?' As he watched the road ahead, Pete repeated, 'I really hope you have some idea of what we're going to do. All I know is that you want to follow up where your grandson's bike ended up.' He thought of Liz and wondered what on earth he was doing in this car.

Richard gazed straight ahead. 'I do have a plan, but it depends on what we find when we get there. You tell me this boy – the leatherjacket – lives on the estate near the shops. It depends on whether we can actually find the bicycle at the house.'

'He's probably sold it already.' Pete stared hard at his driver.

Richard shot a brief look back at him. 'You know, you're probably right. I hadn't thought of that, the little bastard! Yes, you're probably right. Why hadn't I considered that?' He hesitated before continuing. 'To be honest, I thought we would steal it back and that would be that.'

'Left at this roundabout, Richard, then second left into Wycliff Road.'

Richard changed down a gear and followed Pete's directions into a road of similar houses, grey concrete, new windows. Dim orange street lights glowed against a clear black sky.

'Odd numbers this side,' observed Pete. 'Number 37 must be coming up. I've just seen 21. You can find somewhere to park any time now.'

Richard slowed and stopped and reversed the car into the kerbside.

'This will do,' said Pete. 'I can see 31 and 33.'

Richard switched the headlights off and stopped the engine. The sky was clear, the stars bright, over the rows of similar terraced houses. Some were in blocks of four, some in blocks of six. The curtains were drawn in most of the houses, with a glow of light showing through. A few were in complete darkness. A dog barked somewhere nearby and another answered. A battered Transit van crawled slowly by – slow enough to be looking for an address? Two silhouettes were visible in the front of the van. The windscreen was misty and the side windows running with condensation. It was a cold night. Frost sparkled on the roofs of parked cars. White frost formed on the pavement beside the parked Renault. The

Renault's occupants saw the rear lights of the Transit van glow brighter, and they glanced at each other. They watched and waited.

'Do you mind if I smoke in your car, Richard?'

'I would normally ask you not to, Peter. Daphne would moan if she could smell it. Carry on, though, but perhaps you might open the window.'

Pete lit a cigarette and opened the car window a few inches. As the cold air flowed in, the car's warmth vanished quickly. The Transit van up in front of them had stopped, but the driver had made no attempt to pull into the kerb. It had parked in the middle of the road. No car could get by now, but none came while the two gardeners sat watching in silence. Pete nipped the end of his cigarette out of the window and dropped the tip on to the kerb beside their parked car. He wound up the window, then rubbed the back of his hand across the now misting windscreen. Richard produced a cloth and did the same on his side.

Suddenly two men emerged from either side of the van. One opened the back doors and both men set off towards a house on the left. Pete nudged Richard, and touched his arm as he whispered that they must have reached number 37. Richard shifted his body up in his seat, leaned forward and wiped the windscreen again with the cloth. Pete could clearly see two men, with a figure that looked like a teenage boy. Each was pushing a bicycle out of the front gate and across the pavement, making black lines on the frosty path. One man held two bikes as they reached the open van. A shadowy figure vanished into the cavern of the van's body. The third passed a cycle up on to the van, then took a second from the man holding the bikes.

'Well, well, well,' Richard breathed out loud. 'This is interesting.'

'Bloody hell,' Pete added. 'More leatherjackets than aphids.'

'Yes,' Richard whispered back.

As the third bike was loaded on to the van, two of the figures returned through the gate in the privet hedge in front of number 37 Wycliff Road. Pete and Richard didn't have to wait too long to see them returning with two more bikes. The third man jumped down from the back of the van, the other man and the teenager loaded the two bikes into the van, and the rear doors were shut with a metallic clunk. One of the men handed something to the boy, whose breath was visible in the dim street light as he spoke to the two men before turning and disappearing from view through the gateway in the hedge.

The van's rear lights came on and a cloud of smoke belched from the exhaust. Richard waited until the van had begun to move away before he started up his engine, put the car in gear, switched the headlights on and pulled away from the kerb. The heater quickly blew the windscreen clear from the bottom upwards.

'Let's see where they go, eh, Pete? We'll come back to number 37 later perhaps.'

Pete agreed, leaning forward in his seat and wiping the windscreen to assist the blowing heater. They followed the white Transit van out of the estate, back to the roundabout and straight on. In the brighter street lighting, Pete glanced at his watch as they drove round the roundabout.

Richard noticed. 'Are you worried about the time?'

'A bit,' agreed Pete. 'Liz will wonder where I am if I'm too long. Don't worry, though. We have to follow these rascals.'

'Rascals?' repeated Richard. 'These are obviously professionals, Peter. These are weevils or leatherjackets, aren't they?'

Pete did answer. Weevils? Leatherjackets? He was confused now after all their talk that morning in the shed.

After several miles, right across the other side of town, they found themselves watching the white van turn off beside a short parade of small shops. Richard stopped the car across the road from the shops. The van had disappeared out of sight. The shops, however, were clearly visible – Gregg's the chemist, Hairflair, Dryden the newsagent's, and the fourth shop fascia bearing the sign 'On Yer Bike'. Posters in the window proclaimed 'New and second-hand bikes at unbeatable prices'.

Richard broke the silence as the two men stared across the road. 'The bastards! The leatherjackets steal them, the weevils buy them to resell them. No wonder the prices are unbeatable.' He shook his head in disbelief. 'I had no idea of this sort of thing went on.'

Pete looked at his friend. It did not surprise him nearly so much. 'What now, Richard?'

'I've come to the conclusion we should rid the garden of some pests.'

A glow of light appeared in the window of 'On Yer Bike' and went out a few minutes later. The two men in the Renault kept watch. Soon, headlights appeared from the side of the shop parade and the van turned back the way it had come.

'The shop or the van? Quickly, Pete, a decision!'

'The shop,' replied Pete. 'We'll recognise the van again, and we know where its owners have their business and which house it visits.'

'I agree.' Richard turned the sidelights and the engine off.

'If they haven't got business premises they can't do business. That will slow the bastards down.'

'What have you got in mind, then?' Richard asked.

'We set fire to the shop,' said Pete, 'phone the fire brigade fairly soon after, so it can't take hold of the other shops, and our friends will have a problem.'

'Do you have a lighter? Yes? Let's go.'

Richard got out of his car, walked round to the boot and took out a plastic petrol can. Pete followed and caught Richard's eye.

'An old habit of mine, to carry some emergency petrol,' Richard said by way of explanation to Pete's enquiring look.

It was not yet ten o'clock, and there was still some traffic going by as the two men crossed the road. The rear of the shops was in darkness. Together they searched around for something with which they could start a fire. Richard soon found some bundles of old magazines and newspapers behind the newsagent's next door to the bicycle shop on the end. He loosened the bundles and quickly built up a pile against the back door to the cycle shop. Then he poured petrol down the door and over the pile of paper.

'Light it up, Pete, and let's go.'

Pete hesitated, then lit a roll of newspaper and placed it carefully against the pile Richard had made. It flared rapidly as they stood watching until they were sure the flames were setting fire to the door. Then they turned and hurried back to the car, checking both ways. There was nobody around. Richard started the engine but didn't put the car lights on as they fastened their seat belts. Both stared anxiously across the road at the parade, wondering if the blaze would catch the bicycle shop? Pete looked at his watch. A quarter past ten, it told him. They had been sitting there, engine running, for five minutes or so. Pete just wanted to be at home now. This had begun to seem crazy.

'You anxious to get home, Peter?'

'Yes, but I'm more anxious to see what happens ...'

He didn't finish. They could both see smoke coming over the roofline of the shop on the end and a glow was flickering inside the shop. Richard switched the headlights on, put the car in gear, U-turned in the road and accelerated away from their night's work.

'Look!' Pete pointed. 'There's a phone box just ahead. Let's call the fire station.'

Richard stopped the car and got out, but the call-box had been vandalised. It stank of urine, and somebody had obviously tried to lever the box from its fixings. Richard returned to the car and climbed back in.

'Typical,' he grumbled. 'The phone's been vandalised. But we've got to find another call-box quickly, Peter, before the fire gets out of control. We mustn't endanger the other shops, so we need to phone the fire brigade quickly.'

'We should have thought this through before,' Pete muttered.

Richard did not reply but drove off fast.

'Over there!' Pete pointed to another call-box across the road.

Richard stopped again, jumped out and almost ran across the road. Pete watched anxiously from the car. He could see Richard pick up the handset. *Please work*, he thought.

Back in the car, Richard blew air from his mouth noisily. 'That's done,' he said. 'I've phoned the fire brigade. They're on their way. Let's get home. I'll drop you off.'

Tilting his head back into the car's headrest, Pete closed his eyes and silently exhaled, lips pursed. Nothing more was said between the two men for the rest of the journey to Pete's house, where they merely exchanged their goodnights. Pete got out of the car, closed the door as quietly as he could and watched the rear lights of Richard's Renault until they disappeared out of sight.

Pete sighed as he shut his front door and took his coat off. He checked in on Liz, who was sound asleep, before slipping upstairs. As he climbed into bed he wondered how the others had spent their evenings 'gardening'. He switched the light off but he couldn't sleep.

In a detached house not far away, Richard sat in his study.

Daphne was not surprised to see Richard sipping a glass of brandy as she opened the door to wish him goodnight – he often did. She might have been curious if she had seen the size of the drink when he had first poured it.

Perversely, Richard wondered if his grandson's bike was in the fire. This was his last thought before he fell asleep in his study chair, his head on his hands on the desk. He didn't hear the siren in the distance.

Chapter 9

Smoke trailed from the chimney of the shed on the allotments as Brian got out of his van. He chuckled to himself as he recalled the night before. He had had a quick pint at the King's, and Debs thought he had been there all evening, although he didn't normally stay till closing time these days. He saw Bill's bike leaning on the shed but no sign of Richard's smart Renault or Ernie's little Golf. Pete was here, though. Brian had parked next to his Ford Fiesta.

'No bike today then, Pete boy? Too cold for you old painters?' Brian chuckled again. This was a good laugh, this gardening club, he thought to himself as he lit the cigarette he'd rolled before leaving his warm van. He wished he could tell some of the others down the King's what a laugh having an allotment could be. The young 'uns wouldn't take the piss as much if they knew what a laugh being a gardener is sometimes. He wouldn't tell Domino, though.

'Morning, Pete. Morning, Bill.' Brian sat down. 'Where's the tea then, Pete the painter?'

'I'm a *retired* painter,' replied Pete, 'and a retired tea-maker.' But he handed Brian a mug of tea.

'Have fun, you two, last night?'

Pete searched his pockets for his cigarettes.

Bill turned from stoking the fire. 'I did,' he said, his large face pinker than usual. 'And I know Peter and Richard did.' He glanced conspiratorially at Pete.

'What have you been up to then, Pete? What does Bill mean?'

It was Bill who answered. 'They set fire to a shop on the other side of the town, that's what they got up to!'

Brian laughed.

'Not a joke, Brian.' Pete was straight-faced and serious. He related the story to Brian and Bill, obviously enjoying the tale all over again. Brian listened to every word carefully, his weather-beaten face occasionally changing from a frown to a grin and back again as he followed the story.

'Bloody hell!' was all he managed to say when Pete had finished. 'Fuckin' 'ell, mate,' he repeated several times.

After the three men had returned to their own thoughts for a few minutes, Brian spoke up. 'Right, I'll tell you my story now.'

'Go on, Brian,' said Pete, and he and Bill turned to listen. Brian had agreed the previous evening to try to annoy some of the boys who had taunted him in the past.

'Well,' he began, 'when I got to the address I'd been given, luckily I found some dog shit outside, so I pushed it through the letterbox. Remember I told you last night that manure might make them grow up? I hadn't been sure what I'd do when I got to the house. But there's always too much dog mess around. It's my pet hate, as I've often said. So I felt I'd made a sort of point. You know … aphids and garden manure. Bloody silly really.' Last night he had justified it to himself with a chuckle as he threw away the polythene carrier bag he had used as a glove to push the excrement through the letterbox. Then he'd got back into his van and gone to the King's Head for a pint. 'Not so exciting as you, Pete. I just thought manure for aphids.'

'Phew, fuckin' 'ell. Messy job!' Pete laughed uncomfortably but looked straight at Brian. 'Can't wait to see tonight's paper – see if any shop fires are reported. My co-conspirator is late. And Ernie … I don't suppose you know how Ernie got on. I hope he didn't have to run away from anything.'

They laughed at the thought of old Ernie trying to run. Many years ago, long before they knew him, he had been a useful sprinter. Not now, though.

'What about you, Bill?' asked Brian. 'What's your story, you old rascal?'

'I'm proud of Richard and Peter. They excelled. Weevils as well as a leatherjacket! I think they make my attempt look feeble, like a schoolboy prank by comparison.' Bill hesitated before he spoke again. 'My target was aphids. I put Superglue in the front door locks and around the front windows of my target's house. There weren't any lights on in the house, so I thought maybe it would be a good idea if they were out and couldn't get back in. I'd also got a small bottle of water in my coat pocket, so I poured water on the path to the front door. It was a concrete path and already frosty when I got there. I nearly slipped myself – that's why I thought of the water. I just chucked it on the path as I left. Then I went home. That's all really. I can only hope the yob was out and couldn't get in the front door.'

'Got to start somewhere,' said Pete.

Brian agreed. 'Yeah, Bill, yours is better than mine, especially if he couldn't get back in his bloody front door, eh?'

Bill looked pleased with this encouragement, this endorsement of his retribution on the aphids.

'Not far from Ernie's flat, those aphids,' Pete observed.

The men amused themselves by speculating on the consequences of Bill's efforts. Bill joined in, but his suggestions became quite macabre, with youths frozen to the front door and the pathway, and the milkman finding them blue-faced and stiff. The other two exchanged glances behind Bill's back – Brian moving his eyebrows down with a frown to express his concern, while Pete gave a careful a nod.

Brian changed the subject. 'Anyone got any proper jobs to do today? Pete, you? Bill, you? Got any real jobs to do?'

'Yes,' replied Bill. 'I have. I'm going to put some more straw in my cold-frames. My chrysanthemum cuttings won't like these freezing cold days and I'm not sure I've put enough in them. I'm going to take a few more cuttings that I should have done the other side of Christmas. I've got some chrysanths to go to shows early, I hope, that I should have sorted out weeks ago.'

Buttoning up his coat, Bill opened the shed door and stepped out. As soon as he had left, Pete made a face at Brian.

Brian was so familiar with Pete's expression, he could read it. 'Come on, what's up with you?' he asked.

Pete hesitated a while.

Brian waited.

'This is all a bit crazy, isn't it, mate?'

Brian said nothing.

'It's all right talking about it ... you know ... pests ... but how on earth ... ?' Pete shook his head. 'I don't know. Five old blokes. We shouldn't be doing this, mate. None of us knows what we are doing ... No plans ... But I'm not so sure we should be doing anything at all. What if that fire had caught the other shops, with people in the flats above?'

Brian shrugged but remained silent.

Pete continued. 'A lot of silly chatter at Bill's house last night, and off we all go willy-nilly. Nobody really thought through our actions, the implications, with all this nonsense about aphids and leatherjackets, slugs and snails.'

'I'm not sure what you are saying, Pete,' Brian interrupted.

'I'm not sure myself, mate. I think I'm saying we should not have started this pest control thing. Aphids ... leatherjackets ... It's all very well talking about what should be done ...' He sighed, fished in his jacket for his cigarettes and lit one. 'I mean ... five silly old men out at night thinking we are vigilantes or something. It's not right, surely, Brian. I'm worried about the future. You know, looking after Liz as we get older. I worry these days how I'll cope with that.'

'I think I know what you mean, Pete. It seemed fun talking about it but ...' Brian stopped. He rested a freckled hand on his friend's arm, sensing his confusion and apprehension. Brian had never heard Pete sound so depressed before. 'Cheer up, mate ... It'll be all right.' Brian tried to reassure Pete with his platitude, though he was aware the other man felt no comfort.

Almost an hour went by before Ernie arrived. He looked smaller than ever today.

'Like he's shrivelled up a bit overnight,' Pete remarked to Brian while they were outside the hut smoking. They agreed that Ernie didn't look too good this morning. That was why, though they were anxious to know, they hadn't asked how he had got on with his 'assignment'.

The two former building trade workers went back into the warm shed, where Bill was now sitting close to the crackling stove, thawing out his large hands.

'No Richard?' asked Ernie of nobody in particular.

Nobody answered, and Bill related the story of how Pete and Richard had followed the white Transit van. Ernie listened quietly until Bill seemed to have finished.

'I let you all down,' he finally confessed. 'I got to the house I was supposed to go to, I got out of my car, then I got back in and went home.' He hung his head, addressing the last words to the floor. 'I didn't do anything. I couldn't, somehow I couldn't. I'm sorry.' He trailed off without taking his eyes from the floor.

Brian went over and put a meaty hand on Ernie's shoulder. 'Don't worry, mate, it doesn't matter.' Bill and Pete murmured comforting words.

Ernie looked up, a weak smile on his face. 'Sorry, fellas.'

'No matter,' Pete consoled him.

Ernie straightened up soon after this exchange. There was a little more light in his eyes. 'Don't worry, though. I've got some ideas of my own. I won't let you down in the future, you'll see.'

Bill briefly returned to his gardening jobs. Pete, Brian and Ernie chatted for a while. Richard hadn't arrived by the time they all left the shed. As Pete snapped the large brass padlock shut, they said their goodbyes. Each returned home, each reflecting on what they had embarked on, each separately concluding that they liked one another, they were good mates, with things in common.

The weak sun tried to warm the allotments, but it had succeeded only in creating steam from the frosty ground. The hazy mist clung to the deserted shed and the frozen water butts. Cobwebs on abandoned runner bean poles glistened with dew. A few crows were hopping over the broken soil on Ernie's patch, waddling, pecking, seeking something to eat. A blackbird chattered noisily in the hawthorn hedge. Was it a complaint about the weather? One of the crows had apparently had some success on Ernie's patch, for several more arrived all at once to fight over whatever they had found. They hopped and fluttered and croaked out loud. When the crows flew off together, the allotment was absolutely still, with no movement except wisps of mist creeping over the cold ground.

On the other side of town, the wisps had been smoke. At 'On Yer Bike' the front windows were black. Mr Dryden, the newsagent, had got up even earlier than usual. He had been woken around 11 o'clock the previous night by the sirens and the flashing blue lights in front of his shop. He'd been asleep since half past nine, his usual time. He hadn't smelt smoke, not even the rubber tyres burning next door. As he had told one of the firefighters, 'If you did the hours I have to work, you wouldn't wake up either.' The fireman hadn't been interested. Dryden knew nobody ever was when he told them. 'I do on average two weeks' hours of a normal job every week.' He did, it is true, but no one seemed to care when he told them, not even when they complained about their papers being delivered late. 'Kids today aren't reliable like they used to be. It's hard enough to get paper boys at all these days, never mind reliable ones.' He always defended his business with this explanation. They didn't seem to listen, though.

'Arson, we think,' said the chief fire officer. Mr Dryden hadn't slept properly when he went back to bed, but he sold more papers than usual that morning. The word had spread quickly. Everybody wanted to know what had happened next door. By 10 a.m. he was fed up with telling people. He had had enough trouble settling the paper boys down, sorting out the papers for their rounds. The boys were excited about the fire next door, more interested in that than getting the papers out on time. 'Little whatsits.' Mr Dryden had heard enough about the fire long before the police came to interview him. What could he tell them? He had been asleep and was lucky to be alive because the fire brigade arrived before it reached his shop. But his shop now smelled of smoke and burning rubber, and he wondered if his insurance policy would cover smell. Perhaps he could make a few bob, he wondered, if it did. Perhaps he could afford to get a relief manager in for a week's holiday. That couple last summer did quite a good job. He'd enjoyed his coach trip to Scotland last summer, despite the rain; despite being on his own since his wife had run off with the greetings cards rep. At least he could look at his own top-shelf magazines in peace now she had gone, he'd reflected the week after her disappearance. The Saturday girl was nice to brush against. He smiled at this thought. Pretty little thing, Lisa, and only £10 per day.

Mr Dryden did not notice the Renault car across the road, even when he went out the front to clear away a crowd of boys and girls on their lunch break hanging around outside, bikes everywhere, effing and blinding at him, laughing at him. 'Little whatsits,' he repeated to himself, but satisfied he had got rid of them. 'Two at a time only in my shop,' he had yelled at them, 'and if you don't want to buy anything clear off.' At least the fire was more interesting to them today than trying to steal his KitKats and magazines.

The Renault driver had seen some of this action but it wasn't what he had been looking at. He was checking on his handiwork and wondering *What next?*

Chapter 10

Richard had waited across the road from the parade of shops until he saw the van pull up with the early edition of the *Willbury Reporter*. Then he left his car and crossed the road to the newsagent's. Richard watched Mr Dryden cut the straps from the bundle of newspapers, while guilty feelings seeped into him. *Ridiculous*, he thought. *Nobody is going to connect me to the fire*. He had to clear his throat, however, to ask for a paper as the newsagent flopped the pile of fresh newspapers on his counter with a thud.

'Lucky it didn't spread to your premises,' he observed to the newsagent before he realised what he had said. He pointed to the front-page headline: 'Arson suspected at bicycle shop'.

'Somebody phoned 999 fairly quickly, from what I gathered off one of the firemen last night.' Mr Dryden eyed his customer.

Haven't seen you before, he thought to himself. He knew most people who came to his shop, if only by sight. From early-morning builders for their *Sun* or *Star* and their fags, to the retired old ladies mid-morning who he always had a job to stop talking. To the bloody schoolkids at lunchtime and afternoon, the pretty young mothers buying sweets for the little ones in the afternoon after infants' school, right down to the smarmy office types popping in for an evening paper, never bought anything else, well perhaps a top-shelf magazine sometimes. He knew most faces even if he didn't know their names. Richard studied the front page unaware of Mr Dryden's watching eyes, certainly unaware of Mr Dryden's thoughts. He folded his paper and went to leave the shop.

'Good job they did,' Mr Dryden agreed, but his customer had left.

Back in his study Richard read the full story in the *Willbury Reporter*. The owners of the bicycle shop, a pair of local businessmen, brothers David and Graham Bastin, related how they got a call from the police at 3 o'clock in the morning. David had taken the call and phoned his brother Graham straight away.

'By the time we got there the fire was out. The whole inside of the shop was black.' The firefighters' lights revealed the extent of the damage.

'If it was arson, then we'll find who did it,' Graham was quoted as saying. 'What are people like these days? Nobody is safe.'

'We're just two people trying to make an honest living,' David was reported to have remarked.

Richard sneered as he read this. He sat back in his chair and reflected on a job well done, and it crossed his mind again to wonder if his grandson's bike was still in the shop, as he was now sure it had been at some time recently. Was it one of the cycles they had seen the men loading on to the Transit van? Richard ambled into the kitchen to make himself some tea, taking the paper with him. He stirred the pot and reached down from the cupboard a fine bone-china cup and saucer, part of the silver wedding tea-set Roberta had bought for Daphne and himself. Idly he flicked the newspaper pages over on the worktop beside the teapot. Something caught his eye a few pages inside, just a small article. 'MAN DIES OF EXPOSURE. An elderly man, Mr Reg Scrase, was found in the early hours of this morning frozen to death on his own doorstep. His grandson found him with his front door key in his hand.' The address given in the report seemed familiar to Richard, though he couldn't think why. He reread the report of the fire on the front page, *continued on page 3*. Then he placed the teapot, the cup and saucer and a small jug of milk from the fridge on to a tray, which he carried back to his study. He sat down and absent-mindedly read some letters to the editor, finding that he agreed with most of the written sentiments and complaints. Then it came to him why the elderly man's address was familiar. He picked up the phone.

'Peter, Richard here. How are you?'

'I'm fine. How about you? ... Where were you this morning?'

'I slept badly last night.'

'Me too,' Pete told him, assuming it was for the same reasons.

The retired civil servant did not explain how easily he fallen asleep while leaning on his desk after several large brandies. Richard had woken shivering with cold at 5 a.m., his whole body stiff and aching. The central heating was not timed to come on until 7 o'clock.

'I've got a copy of the *Willbury Reporter*,' he said. 'I'm afraid we're front-page news ... Hello, Peter ... Hello, Peter, are you still there?'

'Yes,' Pete replied after a pause. 'I haven't seen the *Reporter* yet. I have mine delivered but it hasn't arrived yet.' He looked at his watch – 4.30. The paper was usually delivered about now, but sometimes not until around 5 o'clock. 'What does it say?'

'Arson suspected.'

'We could confirm that then.'

'There's something else in the paper that puzzles me.'

'Go on,' said Pete.

Richard told him about the elderly man who had frozen to death before he asked, 'Have we got somebody called Reg Scrase at the allotments?'

'I don't know.' Pete's heart was thumping in his chest. His mind was racing, tormented with a scenario that seemed to fit this report. He was reaching in his pocket for his cigarettes before he realised he was lighting one.

Liz called out, 'Pete, are you smoking indoors? You are! Who is on the phone? Why are you smoking indoors?'

'Peter, are you there?' Richard asked again.

'Excuse me, Richard – Liz is calling me.' Pete walked to the back door and threw the lighted cigarette out on to the neat slab-paving pathway. Then he returned to the phone and picked up the handset again. 'Richard, does it give an address in the paper, an address for this bloke Scrase?'

'Yes, it does. That's what caught my eye really – the address seemed to ring a bell. That's why I called you. That's why I was curious.' He read out the address to Pete.

'Richard, this morning at the shed Bill told us he'd Superglued the front door lock of a house last night. The yob he'd gone to punish lived there. It was the pest control. The others had one address each. That was Bill's target address.'

Without a word, Richard put the phone down.

Pete clicked the telephone rest, repeating into the mouthpiece, 'Richard, Richard, Richard, are you there?'

Liz called again. 'Peter, who is it?'

Pete put down the handset and hurried through to his wife's room.

'What made you light up a cigarette, love? You've always taken care not to smoke indoors – you know I don't like it. You've always respected that. I realise you enjoy a cigarette. I never nag you, but you always go outside to smoke. What's different today? Is there something wrong? I don't mind you smoking – you've got to have some little pleasures, looking after me all the time. A cigarette, a pint. I don't want to deny you your pleasures.' Liz went quiet.

'All these questions,' Pete said softly. He looked into her eyes, which had filled with tears. 'What's up, love?' He took his wife's hand, its fingers stiff and distorted. 'Come on, love, no tears. What's this about a cigarette?'

'Not cigarettes.' Liz had started to sob. 'I may not deny you the little pleasures of a cigarette or a pint of beer down the King's Head, but for years we've been denied another pleasure.'

'I'm too old for that, love, don't worry.' He forced a smile.

'You may be, but a kiss on the top of my head is not …' Her voice trailed off to a whisper. 'Has it ever occurred to you that I miss it?' She dabbed her eyes with the tissue Pete had handed her.

He added, 'We don't ask for much, do we, either of us?'

'We could try sometimes, you know. You could squeeze into my bed for a while, you know, before you go upstairs.'

'Yes, we could try, love, but ...'

'Has it ever occurred to you that I miss the intimacy – the warm glow, the feel of you beside me? What is my life? I rarely see anybody. I can't go anywhere, do anything. What's the point of it all? It's only going to get more difficult for us. What's the point? I sometimes think I might as well be –'

Pete interrupted. 'Hey, hey, old girl ... That's enough of that sort of talk.' But he knew what she meant, and was beginning to think she really would be better off dead. Sometimes he thought his own life was not worth living now either. And he dreaded the future. But all he said to Liz was 'Oh, come on, love. Don't upset yourself.'

Liz's sobbing subsided, slightly. 'We don't get as much help these days as we used to, and you are not getting any younger. You could do with more help, not less.' Liz smiled up at him tearfully as he handed her another tissue.

'I'll make us a nice cup of tea, love – cheer you up.' Pete had heard the newspaper come through the front door letterbox. He moved away to get it.

Liz sighed to herself, her thoughts still on the same subject. She recalled with a dull ache in her heart the last time they had tried. Her eyes began to glisten again.

Out in the kitchen, Pete filled the electric kettle, put it on its stand, automatically flicking the switch on. As he stared at the headline, 'ARSON SUSPECTED AT BICYCLE SHOP', he was surprised to discover that he felt no guilt. Rather, he felt positively elated. He was amazed at his reaction to the rerun of his own evening out reported on the front page. He allowed himself a wry smile. Not 'suspected' arson, mate; it really was. He mouthed the words silently at the front page on the neat Formica worktop. His reservations caught up with him soon enough, however, as he remembered what he had confided to Brian that morning. They shouldn't be doing these things. It was ridiculous. Pete kneaded his fingers into his forehead as he watched the kettle. *No, it's crazy. Why am I so pleased to be reading this? It's completely wrong.*

He looked around his kitchen as if seeing it for the first time. Pete had refitted it himself, with the help of a couple of mates who had done the plumbing and the electrics. He still liked the antique pine doors, the black worktop, plain white tiles and sunny yellow walls. He had pretty much refurbished the whole house in the last few years before he packed in full-time work four years ago. The bathroom had been quite expensive, even though Dave, his plumber friend, had done most of the work. Pete had spent eight days decorating Dave's hall, stairs and landing as payment for the bathroom – eight days not actually earning money. Still, the old avocado bathroom suite that had looked so modern back in the 1970s when Liz chose it had really looked dated by then. Liz hadn't seen the sparkling new white suite or the electric shower he had added. He hadn't really no-ticed which particular day it was when it had become more difficult to get in and out of the bath. Both his daughters were impressed when he installed the shower. He recalled taking a photo each morning and each evening as the work progressed, to show Liz. She had shed a few tears when she saw the final photo. 'It's beautiful,' she'd sighed. She'd loved the white, and the bright grass green he had painted the sections of wall that hadn't been tiled. 'I would never have picked that colour but it looks good.' He had copied that idea from a house he had worked on. The young wife had what Pete regarded as some way-out notions of colour, but he had admired the effect in one of the bathrooms on that job, and he had used the leftover paint on his own. It was the same job that gave him the idea for the black worktops in the kitchen, except the young couple had real granite worktops.

Pete flicked the pages of the paper as he stirred the teabags in the two mugs of tea, looking for the other report. The smaller one was a couple of column inches on page 8: 'MAN DIES OF EXPOSURE'.

'Jesus Christ, Bill, what have you done? What have we all done?' He felt for a cigarette but stopped himself.

Liz broke his thoughts. 'Have you been to China for that tea?' It made him jump.

'Coming, love.' He placed her mug of tea on the little table beside her. 'What would you like to eat?'

When she replied it made him shudder from head to foot. His scalp prickled. 'Cold meat with something, please, Pete.'

CHAPTER 11

The frost had vanished overnight, and now it was raining. Dark grey clouds chased each other across the sky. There was no watery sun today, just a fine mist of rain. Bill turned up the collar on his greatcoat. The damp overcoat smelt musty, a bit like cold cabbage. He mounted his cycle, sniffing the coat sleeve before he set off from the kerbside outside his house. He shrugged his lack of interest but he had noticed it. *They don't make coats like this any more.* He had been demobbed with it from his National Service and it had served him every winter since.

His journey to the allotments took him past the house where he had glued the locks. Tape rippled around the front garden, and he wondered why. There was a police car outside.

Bill was unaware that the yob lived with his grandfather or that they shared the same pub. Grandson and grandfather had spent the whole evening in the Wicket Keeper down the road by the shops. Granddad had gone home, and Darren had gone back to Kirsty's house until her dad had come thumping down the stairs and told him to leave.

'Fucking cheeky old git,' Darren told Kirsty. 'Your fucking old man has got a cheek!'

Kirsty had agreed with him but told him he had better go, anyway, that it was nearly three o'clock. They had kissed goodbye at the front door.

Kirsty's dad had called down the stairs again, 'Come on, Kirsty. Get to bed! I have to go to work in the morning, even if he doesn't.'

Darren had waved a one-fingered sign towards the staircase and squeezed Kirsty's left breast with his other hand at the same time. They'd giggled together but Darren had set off back home to his granddad's house.

He had spent the rest of that night getting cold, and visiting the local police station, as he recounted in the pub at lunchtime.

'"Hello, Darren, how's your granddad?" the fucking copper said on the fucking counter when I fucking got there,' Darren told his mates in the Wicket Keeper. 'He was a fucking cheeky shit, that one. I wiped the fucking smile off his face when I fucking told him, "You'd better get one of your fucking blokes to come and fucking look at my granddad. He's fucking dead." There he was, fucking dead on the fucking front doorstep when I fucking got there.'

'Fucking hell,' his mates gasped.

'Then what?' One of them asked what had happened, and what the coppers had done when they got there.

Darren related the rest of the night's events to his enthralled audience. He told how the copper then made him a cup of tea and gave him a fag. How it had been almost an hour before two of them took him back to his home in a cop car. How his granddad had still been lying there in the same position with the front door key in his hand. Blue in the face and his eyes open. And his mouth blue.

One of his mates interrupted the story. 'Poor old bugger.'

Darren continued, explaining how this young copper had gone back to the car and phoned for a funeral place to come and get him. 'A doctor came first. Then an old black Transit arrived with two blokes, who picked Granddad up, put him in a body bag and took him off to the mortuary.'

Darren laughed out loud as he told the next part. 'The other copper said, "A cup of tea would be nice, if you've got a key and know how to make one." "Course I got a fucking key," I told him. Then it got interesting because I couldn't get the key in the lock. The coppers were looking at each other. They both tried the key and they couldn't open the door either. Then we all went back to the police station. I was fucking freezing by now, the first time ever I've been fucking glad to be in the nick.'

His mates all laughed at this.

'First time I ever agreed with the Old Bill as well. They reckoned somebody had been fucking about with the lock. Fucking Superglue or summat.'

Darren's mates were genuinely shocked. 'Who would do that to an old man?' one asked.

'The fucking coppers had better find who did it,' another demanded.

'Your granddad got any money?' yet another asked.

Darren hadn't thought of that, but he did now. Then again, he didn't consider how he could continue living in his granddad's house. His granddad was a council tenant. Darren would have to find somewhere else to live, somewhere else to deal from.

Bill Choules fished in his coat pocket for his keys to open the lock on the shed. He hummed an aria he particularly liked from *Der Rosenkavalier*– not Elizabeth Schwarzkopf quality, but in tune. He was unaware of Darren's granddad's return from the pub and the subsequent events. As he raked cold ash from the wood-burning stove, he winced at a wave of pain in his stomach. He took a couple of sips from a water bottle he produced from his pocket, then filled the kettle, lit the little gas ring and put the kettle on. He undid his coat, sniffing again at the sleeve while recalling emptying the bottle of water on to the pathway last night. The large man hummed to himself as he watched the kettle intently. *The others will like my next idea*, he told himself as he hummed a louder version of the aria.

Ernie made him start as he entered their shared haven, which was not a haven yet, since the stove was still unlit.

'Morning, Bill. You sound happy.'

'You made me jump, Ernest. You're early.'

'So are you, big man.'

Ernie stoked the fire with fresh wood, an old split wooden gate he had dismantled and piled into his car boot yesterday. He lit the newspaper he had stuffed in the bottom.

'Where was Richard yesterday?'

'Don't know,' replied Bill, wincing again at the same pain in his stomach.

'What's up, Bill?'

'Oh, a bit of indigestion, I think ... been getting a few pains lately. Nothing to worry about.' But he was sure that something was seriously wrong. These pains had been getting more frequent.

'More chrysanthemums this year then, Bill? Are you doing the county show again this year?' Ernie enquired, wondering what the funny smell was.

'I planned to, yes,' replied Bill. 'I'm trying a new variety of *Chrysanthemum carinatum* for this year's shows. You know, tricolours.'

Ernie nodded but he didn't really know what Bill meant. Ernie much preferred growing vegetables. Grace had been a good cook and encouraged him to grow all sorts of different things, such as artichokes, which it would never have occurred to him to grow. He didn't really like them himself when he'd agreed to grow them. His own carrots were his favourites, and his peas, nothing so sweet, with a little mint. Grace used to enjoy scooping the peas from their pods. 'Relaxing,' she would say, sitting on the back doorstep on a Sunday morning when Ernie brought some back from the allotment. 'I find it relaxing shelling peas.'

'Don't have to put sugar in my peas,' Ernie would tell Grace at this point. Anne, their only daughter, once enjoyed helping with this task, but Ernie believed she used to eat more than she put in the colander. Ernie would say, 'Save some for my dinner, Anne.' A long time ago now; he had to give most things away now, Ernie reflected as he watched Bill pour boiling water into the teapot.

'I let you all down the other night,' Ernie told Bill, 'but I have an idea for our pest control. I was listening to one of those phone-ins on the radio, the local radio ... at home. People were ringing in about the drugs problem, you know ... Mainly they were saying things like how it costs so much and how they do burglaries and shoplifting to sell things to pay for their drugs. Their 'habits', as they kept calling it. Hundreds a week it costs, you know, Bill. A druggie himself rang in at one point. He was talking about it costing him about two hundred pounds a day. Two hundred pounds a day, Bill. I was not getting much more than that in a week, before I retired. A *day* Bill,' he repeated, with incredulity in his soft voice.

'Anyway,' Ernie continued, 'this druggie was somehow excusing himself for being a burglar, as if it was his right to steal. Some of my neighbours have been broken into so many times I've lost count. Every time they get new stuff from the insurance money, back the burglars come and nick it all again. It made me think, Bill, if we could somehow contaminate their stuff – you know, their drugs – it would teach them a lesson.'

Bill pondered for a moment.

Ernie was impatient for a response. 'What d'you think, Bill? I bet Richard would know what the drugs look like and what we could add to them to make them ill or something like that.'

Bill sipped noisily at his tea before he spoke. 'I've been thinking on the same lines as you. If there was a way to get rid of those sort of people the town would be a better place without them.'

Pete and Brian arrived at the same time again. Brian had picked Pete up.

'What are two old reprobates talking about then?' asked Brian.

Bill and Ernie glanced round.

'An idea I have had.' Ernie looked pleased with himself, his forehead less furrowed, his eyes with more life in them than usual.

'Has either of you two heard from Richard?' Pete was keen to talk about the subject he had on his mind – the news he had just told Brian on the way here this morning, about the elderly man in the paper. Both Bill and Ernie knew nothing of this.

'You wait till you hear this, boys,' said Brian. 'Tell them, Pete.'

Pete told the other men about the newspaper report of his expedition with Richard – the fire in the bicycle shop. When he described the other article in the *Willbury Reporter* Bill's face went white. Ernie's face turned grey. Brian handed Pete a mug of tea, and for several minutes nobody spoke. The silence stretched until Bill finally broke it.

'Better than I hoped for!'

The others looked at Bill with surprise. Was this the man who put so much effort into his chrysanthemums? Who took so many flowers to his mother's grave? Who wouldn't say boo to a goose? Was this their gentle giant?

'You surprise me, Bill,' Brian exclaimed. 'You're pleased another old man has died a miserable death on his doorstep?'

'Yes, I think I am,' said Bill. 'The other day, we all talked about the different outcomes that might happen. We were just speculating at the time. I'm glad, because if he was that yob's grandfather, the same family, then he was probably no good anyway. He was only a no-good as well.'

'You don't know that, Bill,' Pete pointed out.

Brian coughed. 'I do,' he said. 'Bill's assumption is right. I go into the Wicket Keeper pub sometimes, and it's common knowledge in there that that old bloke is a fence of some sort. Never done a day's work for years, and yet he's always got a fat wedge of money on him. Yeah … he's known to deal in stolen goods – or was,' he added.

Brian sat back and sipped his tea, eyeing the others over his mug.

The talk continued in the shed for some while, Bill and Ernie asking questions, Brian making jokes about the whole thing. Pete was more serious, perhaps less confident than the others of what they had embarked on, the gardening club's new preoccupation. He might be part of this but he wasn't sure it was right – though he would certainly like to have his town back, the town he thought he could remember anyway in the good old days. He realised he was part of this activity, but now someone had died as a result, and it was no longer just a diversion.

'Want to hear my idea?' asked Ernie, looking round as if no fire had taken place, as if no old man had frozen to his doorstep.

'*Our* idea,' Bill snapped.

They all agreed it was a good idea to try to tamper with some drugs, but it was Brian who volunteered to visit the Wicket Keeper to get some practical ideas of who to target and how to do so.

'That's where all the dealers hang out,' Brian told them. 'You can buy anything crooked in the Keeper's – I thought you'd all know that! I've never understood how the landlord and his wife allow it all to go on.'

Brian didn't mention, though, that he had once bought a video recorder from the said establishment, or even that that was where he occasionally went to buy his Old Holborn tobacco at less than half-price. Some of the boys on the building site used to refer to it as 'The Smugglers' Rest', not the Wicket Keeper.

'Where's Richard? We'll need him to advise us on drugs and how we can tamper with them.'

Nobody knew where Richard was. He still hadn't visited their shed. Was he having second thoughts? Remorse?

Chapter 12

Richard had not joined his fellows but he had not been idle. That morning he had returned to the address that he and Pete had visited in Wycliff Road. He had knocked on the door of number 37. When a teenage boy answered, he had described his grandson's bike and said he wanted to buy one like that. He had told the teenager he understood that he sold bicycles. The boy had been evasive. At first he had vehemently denied he sold bikes, and, when Richard persisted, the teenager had begun to close the door in his face. Then Richard had produced the £20 notes, crisp and flat and clean from the cash machine, fanned out for the boy to see.

'Why is a posh bloke like you,' the young man had challenged, 'knocking on my door asking for a bike?'

'I had a word with David and Graham Bastin, told them what I wanted, and they gave me your address,' Richard had explained.

At this the boy had softened. 'Come back in a few days, see what I can do for you, Pops,' he said as he shut the door, picking up the milk bottles from the doorstep and taking them in with him.

Richard had returned to his car and driven off. He would not be back for a bicycle. But it was clear he had found the culprit. He imagined the boy putting the milk bottles in the fridge for his mother without noticing the minute needle holes in each foil lid. Richard wondered what would happen next. He had read up on his subject before making a solution to fill the hypodermic syringe he had taken with him. His other research had pleased him the day before when to his relief he had seen the milkman delivering to the house he was watching. One benefit of early rising, he thought. Not many people had doorstep delivery of milk these days. He did himself, but his own milkman had told him that more people buy from supermarkets than have a daily delivery. 'More's the pity,' he had grumbled to Richard, 'but we won't turn the clock back now, will we?' Richard had agreed: more's the pity.

'*Atropa belladonna*, deadly nightshade,' his large botanical encyclopedia had informed him. 'Also known as devil's cherries among other names in other parts of the world. Parts used: root, leaves and tops. Habitat: central and southern Europe, South-West Asia and Algeria. Cultivated in England, France and North America.' Richard had read on: 'Chiefly a native of the southern counties of England, being mostly confined to lime-rich soils. It grows under the shade of trees, on wooded hills on chalk or limestone, forming bushy plants several feet high.' Richard's home-grown specimens were not several feet high, and they grew in the furthest corner of his garden, around the old laurel bushes and trees at the edge.

'Sometimes used as an antidote to opium.' This fact had seemed ironic to Richard as he read, thinking of the drug addicts. Many beneficial extracts were taken from this plan, but he was not a chemist looking for a cure. What had intrigued him more was a paragraph quoting from George Buchanan's sixteenth-century *History of*

Scotland. According to this account, when Duncan I was King of Scotland, Macbeth's soldiers had poisoned a whole army of invading Danes with an infusion of 'Dwale' supplied to them during a truce. Suspecting nothing, the invaders drank their fill, slept deeply and were easily overpowered and murdered in their sleep by the Scots. Richard's encyclopaedia mentioned that 'Dwale' was an ancient name for deadly nightshade. Belladonna was also supposed to have been used to poison Marcus Antonius' troops during the Parthian wars, and Plutarch had supplied a graphic account of its effects. In the sixteenth century it had also been used as a sedative during surgery. Richard had discovered more and more interesting facts. It seemed that the berries could kill children but the root was more poisonous. Still he could not fully assess the strength of the concoction he had crushed from the root and injected into the milk bottles. Richard was not sure what effect it would have, if indeed it would have any effect. He had read about the symptoms and hoped some would afflict the targets of his pest control.

Symptoms

Feelings of giddiness, yawning, staggering or falling on attempting to walk. Dryness of mouth and throat. A sense of suffocation, swallowing difficult, and voice husky, voice fading completely sometimes. Face at first pale, later suffused with scarlatina-like rash extending to the whole body. Pupils widely dilated. Pulse at first bounding and rapid, later becoming irregular and faint.

Would the occupants of number 37 report any of these symptoms to their GP? He couldn't wait to tell the gardening club about *Atropa belladonna*. He still had plenty of the poisonous liquid left and, besides, other deadly nightshade plants were still growing in his garden. Richard was pleased with his morning's work so far. He had been so nervous before he left home that Daphne had noticed. He didn't think she took any notice of him these days.

'Your hand is shaking, Richard,' she had commented. 'Does this portend some excitement at your allotment?' She was laughing as she left the room.

If only she had known why, he had thought as he finished the coffee she had handed him. Of course he had still not carried out his plan then, and as usual she had undermined him without a glance over her shoulder. But Daphne had actually made him more determined without even realising her own effect.

When Richard left the house to undertake his mission, her perfume still lingered in the hallway, the unmistakable Jardins de Bagatelle by Guerlain which she always wore in the daytime. He had bought her first bottle himself during one of his frequent visits to the new Russia. After *glasnost* and the opening of borders, he had been seconded by the government to assist the Russians with the setting up of their job centres. The new Russia would certainly need these for their entry into the free world. The irony had amused him immensely. Those visits had been a welcome distraction in his previously well-ordered life. On his first trip he had not foreseen the yet-to-come added bonus of Tatyana, his interpreter. He still found it hard to believe how easily he had succumbed. For he still imagined he had been seduced; he did not recall having consciously been the seducer. He had been a willing pupil, however. Daphne still sometimes mentioned how surprised, if not shocked, she had been when she demanded how he knew what perfume to buy. He wondered now if she had ever been suspicious, though he thought not. Her life was so busy. And he knew for certain that she did not know what pleasure he derived daily from the fragrance she wore. He had told her in his quiet, straightforward manner, 'My interpreter Tatyana recommended it.' He had even told Daphne that on his final visit to Moscow he had presented Tatyana with the same perfume and how she had wept with joy, how overcome she had seemed. He remembered Daphne's comment then: 'Not often you can be said to bring a woman joy, Richard. Well done.'

So patronising, so hurtful. But the memory of Tatyana's small flat had eased the poison dart. Daphne could never take that away from him. And as long as she wore the perfume he could recall Tatyana.

Richard drove past his own house, continuing on towards the allotment. He felt sure they would all still be there in the shed. At times like this, he told himself, he did not have to ask himself why he enjoyed seeing the rough simple men he met there. But, although he did sometimes think of them as 'the rough simple men', he had never known such friendship all his life. His spell in the army for his national service had not brought the comradeship so many talked of. The men he served with did not respect him, Major or not, and the regular officers looked down on him. He had been glad to return to his office in the ministry. Richard recalled expressing this to Daphne, thinking she would understand. When, after a month back in his office, he had told her how happy he was to be back, he expected her to be happy for him. She hadn't said anything at the time but he remembered the expression on her face and he knew he had lost her respect. He knew it so long ago, when they had not been married long. They had stayed together, of course, they had had a daughter and son, but on that day he realised that Daphne no longer felt the same about him, that his life was destined to be more barren. How he had dreamt about a bright future during his period of duty in the army. Had he changed or had she? Perhaps that was why Tatyana was part of him still, even though that blissful time with her in Russia was gone too. She knew he had a family in England, yet she remained unselfish throughout their love affair. For a moment he thought he caught a familiar scent right here in his car as he shut off the engine and pulled on the handbrake. *Oh, Tatyana*, he thought to himself, *what would you think of me now, old and befuddled? What would you think of what I've done this morning? What my friends and I have done and are yet planning to do?*

Richard opened the shed door, and four faces looked back at him through the wood and tobacco smoke. The smoke smelt so good this morning, more poignant than he could ever explain to anyone, least of all Daphne.

'Good morning, gentlemen. All present and correct,' he saluted the assembly. Happy to be here. Ready to report his latest manoeuvres.

Willbury General Hospital received a call around 9 p.m. from a local general practitioner. A whole family of six together with a middle-aged neighbour and a teenage boy who had not yet been identified needed to be admitted. Dr John Wilde GP reported to the registrar that he had never encountered such a phenomenon before. Some sort of food poisoning was his provisional diagnosis. He knew the family and his initial reaction was reluctance to call. They were in the habit of expecting him and his colleagues in the practice to make house calls far too often. There was even a Post-It note attached to the mother's record card alluding to this. Dr Wilde felt a little guilty when he realised that the main symptoms appeared to be atropine poisoning. Three ambulances took the patients to Accident and Emergency. Dr Helen Sillence, the consultant toxicologist, who had been summoned from her dinner party, was on her way. Her expertise would very probably be needed tonight. Eight patients at once would put pressure on a depleted staff.

Chapter 13

Brian stood at the bar in the Wicket Keeper public house. With one elbow on the bar, he gazed around at the weekday drinkers.

'Busy for a weekday evening,' he observed to Betty, the landlady.

Betty took glasses from the steaming washer, drying them carefully and putting them on the shelf. 'We're always busy, whatever the night,' she replied eventually.

He watched and listened, noticing groups of men of all ages and a few young women. Noise and cigarette smoke filled the air. He recognised a few of the customers. He had spoken to two fellow bricklayers. One of them was a man he had helped to train, Domino, who came from Barbados; Brian had never learned his proper name. Middle-aged now, Domino still wore only a T-shirt in the middle of winter. Maybe he wanted to show off his fresh tattoos, bulging muscles and flat stomach. Brian thought he himself was once like that, and for his age of sixty-eight – well, nearly sixty-nine – he was still quite power-ful. He still had a ruddy outdoor complexion, and the palms of his freckled hands, with the thick meaty fingers, were still hard. One hip was stiff now, perhaps the result of his fall from the scaffolding back in the seventies, he sometimes wondered. It was worse in the mornings when he got out of bed. These days he usually had to come down the stairs sideways, but once he got going he was OK. In the winter his fingertips would crack open; that was a bricklayer's curse from cold mornings on the trowel. Plumbers' knees went; painters' necks went; carpenters' backs and shoulders went; and who knows what for ageing plasterers. Brian was glad he hadn't been a plasterer. Recently he had bumped into one of his old hod carriers, a ragged, sad little man, once strong and quick, and now his head was permanently turned to the side, the nerves in his neck dead. This labourer hadn't worked in the building trade for the last twenty years, but had been scraping a living from cleaning toilets in factories, or picking up paper on garage forecourts. The jukebox played an old country and western hit: 'He stopped loving her today,' sang George Jones. Brian idly wondered who would put it on, as though he wanted to talk to whoever it was. Willie Nelson was his all-time favourite, but 'He stopped loving her today' was a single he loved.

Brian remembered when the first generation of Jamaicans had first arrived in Willbury. He'd loved having a drink with them. There was Big Hughie, who drank strong Bulldog pale ale mixed with Cherry B., and Style, who flashed gold rings and wore sharp baggy suits. He'd told Brian and his mates that he'd come over to Britain to please the ladies, to show the white boys how to do it. They were good fun, 'black Irish' Brian always described them, always ready for a drink and a laugh like the Irish. Not quite so ready for a fight as the Irish contingent in the pub, though. He remembered Billy Kelly, the digger driver. Lovely man, Billy, unless you upset him. He wondered where they were now. Birmingham, Ireland – he didn't know. Back in Ireland, Jamaica or Barbados perhaps, the Irish and the Afro-Caribbeans he remembered from back then.

The youngsters in the pub tonight all seemed to be posing with an aggressive attitude – like the teenager shaking the jukebox to make the record jump. 'All BMWs and never done a day's work.' That's how Brian described the grandsons of his old drinking pals from the Caribbean. Brian didn't ask himself whether this was his own prejudice; it was just a fact to him and to most people he knew, for that matter. He liked the old Irish and the old West Indians. He wasn't sure of his feelings about the younger Asian and Afro-Caribbean men, but he was sure it was all better in his day. Somebody had to be responsible for changing the town and he was certain it wasn't him. Even Brian knew the smell of the different sort of cigarette smoke he was aware of now – the sweeter, herbal whiff.

'Is something burning?' he asked Betty when she was near his end of the bar.

'Don't think so.' Betty knew his question was a joke. She looked up at Brian while drying another glass, straight-faced, a dull, tired look in her eyes. Her low-cut black dress from another era revealed the wrinkled creases on her breastbone travelling down to the top of her dress, looking for somewhere to hide. An array of gold chains failed to conceal those wrinkles.

Brian did not pursue his question. He was just trying to make conversation, but it wasn't working.

'Coming, love,' Betty called, and off she went again. 'Two pints of Stella and a Jack Daniels, darling,' she said, repeating the order.

She served the customer at the bar, a shaven-headed man wearing two thick gold earrings and a tight white T-shirt, with a Chinese tattoo visible just below his T-shirt sleeve.

Brian wondered if it was obvious that he was trying to listen to conversations as he studied the jukebox. He rested his pint glass on the top of the box, took out his tobacco pouch and loosened a knot of tobacco he'd pinched between finger and thumb. Pulling it apart delicately, he began to roll a cigarette, licked the paper and lit up.

'What you smoking, man?'

Brian looked to his left and saw a pair of dark eyes in a shiny black face staring unsmiling at him.

'What you smoking, old man?' Ace Card fixed his eyes on Brian.

'Old Holborn,' Brian finally replied. 'Not your stuff.'

Ace Card laughed. 'This old man, he smokin' the weed and he's tryin' to tell me it's Old Holborn.'

His mates made tut-tutting noises with their tongues. 'You'll be in fuckin' trouble for that,' one said.

Brian found himself unsure how to react to this teasing. He knew it was teasing but was apprehensive of where it might go.

'What you gonna put on the box for us?' another said. 'Play us some music, old man, and none of that Country and Western crap.'

Brian shifted his feet and picked up his pint glass from the top of the jukebox.

Ace Card smiled at Brian, a wide, white grin. 'What you like, man, them oldies, the Beatles and t'ing. "I Wanna Hold Your Hand" and t'ing.'

They all laughed as Ace Card took Brian's meaty hand and held it in his own. As he did so, the 'two pints of Stella and a Jack Daniels' shaven-headed man pushed their hands apart and put Dolly Parton's 'I Will Always Love You' from the Country and Western hits section on the jukebox. Brian spilled his beer. Ace Card's smile vanished.

'He's our friend, man. He was gonna put his favourite Sixties tune on. You pushed him. You spilled his beer.'

The white T-shirt swelled as its occupant continued to press buttons on the box.

'You didn't hear me, man. My friend gonna play some music.'

Ace Card kicked the jukebox, and Dolly Parton finished when she'd hardly begun. Suddenly fists started flying, chairs, bottles, glasses, beer and bodies were being hurled around, and a girl screamed. Brian tried to pick himself up from the floor but his hip was painful and his elbow hurt on the same side.

'Stop it! Stop it!' A shout came from the landlord.

Brian looked up from his prone position, his head slightly dazed. *How did I get down here?* he wondered. Two young Asian men were approaching and they helped him up. He recognised one of them as Mr Athwal's son from the newsagent's.

'You OK, Mr Young?'

Two uniformed police burst through the door. The pub's customers turned to the door. Brian sat down on a hard wooden chair. The fight seemed to stop as quickly as it started. Four or five young black men sneaked out through the door left open by a policeman.

Ace Card pointed a finger at a group of young white men. 'You fuckin' regret this!' He spat the words out, blood trickling through his eyebrow as he left the pub. Johnny Cash sang 'A Boy Named Sue' to the chaos around him. White T-shirt and his group leaned with their backs to the bar, grinning and making V-signs in the general direction of the door.

'Are you all right, Mr Young?' Mr Athwal's son stood over Brian. 'That's not the first time it's happened in here. My dad told me not to come in here.' His smooth brown face was calm. 'They are rival gangs. I tell my dad they don't pick on me when both lots are in here.'

'Pick on you?' Brian asked, trying to regain his senses, now aware of the young man talking to him.

'Yes, Mr Young. It's the white ones that call me "Paki" and silly names. They don't even understand we're Indian, not Pakistani. They're ignorant, so I ignore them.'

'You're Mr Athwal's son from PK News, aren't you?'

'Yes, I'm Raj, and this is my friend Jai.' He waved an arm in the direction of the other young Indian. 'We've been friends since school, and now we're both at uni. He's going to be an accountant and I'm training to be a pharmacist.'

'Can I get you a drink, Mr Young?' Jai said. 'You look like you need one.'

And he was right. Brian was shaken up, still wondering what had happened. One minute he'd been standing by the jukebox, the next minute he was looking up from the dirty floor. He brushed his sleeve and rubbed his bruised elbow.

'Yes, please … Jai, did you say?'

'Yes, I'm Jai.'

'A pint of bitter please. Jai, do you want some money?' Brian fished in his pocket.

'No, no, I'll get it for you.'

Jai brought the pint of beer from the bar, put it on the table next to Brian, and the two friends drew chairs up closer. Now that the policemen had gone and the pub had settled down, the buzz of voices and layer of smoke filled the air once more.

Brian rolled another cigarette, took a large gulp of beer, closed his eyes momentarily and blew smoke at the yellowed ceiling.

'A quiet drink on my own, eh?'

He raised bristled eyebrows as far up his wrinkled forehead as they would go. Jai and Raj laughed quietly.

'They're drug rivals,' Raj told him. 'This a white pub, but members of a black gang have recently started coming here.'

'They should know better,' said Jai. 'There's no way the white dealers will allow the black guys on their patch.'

Brian spent the last hour before closing time enthralled by the two Indian students' information about where the young people of Willbury bought their drugs. He bought them each a drink in return. This time Jai fetched them, while Brian paid. One of the places frequented by drug users and dealers was a place called Mr Kool's Bar, and Brian made a mental note of this, hoping he would be able to remember some of the other details they'd told him about the two rival gangs, black and white.

The two students insisted on walking home with Brian, and the three parted company at his gate. Brian was grateful for their presence and didn't put up much opposition when they suggested it. His hip still hurt and he had to take it slowly. At the gate, Brian thanked them again for helping him. 'You're good blokes, the pair of you,' he said.

'No problem, Mr Young,' said Raj. 'Anyway, my dad likes you. He says you always treat him with respect. Not many do, you see, Mr Young, and Dad notices which customers are respectful when they come in his shop. All that's why me and Jai have told our fathers we don't want to run shops like they do. Who wants to work those long hours, with kids stealing, and rude customers? Our parents had to when they first came here, but we don't. Anyway, my mum always wanted me to be a doctor, and that's partly why I chose pharmacy.'

After they had said their goodbyes, Brian put the key in his front door and went inside. He limped into his lounge, where Debbie was watching television, legs curled up under her in an armchair. He had married Debbie only fifteen years ago, after his first marriage broke up, when he was fifty-three and Debbie thirty-five.

'Hello, you look tired, Brian,' she said. 'Want a cup of tea? Sit down and I'll make you one. Enjoy your pint?'

Brian sat down heavily on the sofa. 'Yes please, Debs, and no, I didn't.'

She brought him a cup of tea, and placed it on the coffee table that she had pushed near to him. 'So why didn't you have a good time? Did I see you limping?'

He told her about his eventful evening, but he didn't mention the conversation with Raj and Jai about the rival gangs of drug dealers. That was information he couldn't wait to reveal to the other gardening club members.

'Come on, you silly old bugger. Let's go to bed,' Debbie said with affection. She switched the television off and laid a hand on his arm. 'Come on, Brian. You've had an exciting night. You must be exhausted.'

Brian had and he was. His ideas about the pest control would keep until tomorrow. He rubbed his hip as he went upstairs. *Perhaps Pete is right*, he thought to himself.

Brian didn't always buy a national newspaper but he did the next morning. Inside PK News, he told Mr Athwal what had happened the night before – or, at least, a shortened version. As Anil Athwal listened, his head moved from side to side. Part of him really wished that Raj would take on the shop, but he was proud of his son for looking after Brian, he told him. His wife Nina would be pleased to hear about it when she came downstairs at nine o'clock. He would tell her before he went to the cash-and-carry. He would see Jai's dad there, and he would be proud of his son too. Maybe this country was not so bad after all.

Brian was first to arrive at the allotment that morning. It was cold enough to light the stove, but at least it was not raining or frosty today. He lit the stove and then put the kettle on. He checked the football results from last night, inside the back pages of the paper. There'd been a big crowd at Liverpool's Anfield ground for the European game, which had ended in a result of 2–1, with Auxerre scoring an away goal. Willbury Rovers had been beaten 2–0 at Darlington. Bloody useless, Brian thought, and determined absent-mindedly not to go to the ground on a Saturday until his team won a few more games. He'd been a regular during the whole of the fifties and sixties, when he was still playing himself at the park on Sundays.

He turned the pages back to front, noticing Willbury's name again in a small article headlined 'FAMILY POISONED MYSTERY'. Brian read it without much interest, but saw it referred to Willbury General Hospital. *'Eight people have symptoms of poisoning, including three young children, who are the most seriously ill, and a teenage boy. Six are from the same family, one is the next-door neighbour, and the identity of the teenager has not yet been revealed. There are rumours that the poison is deadly nightshade.'* The reporter wondered how this could happen in the twenty-first century.

Brian was sure he didn't know, but he soon would. He showed the article to Bill, Pete and Ernie when they arrived. He showed Richard too when the others had stopped quizzing the last arrival about where he had been during the last two days.

Richard read the short article slowly. No one took any notice of him until he closed the paper and made his surprising announcement.

'I am responsible for the mystery illness.'

They all stopped whatever they had been doing and stared at Richard, who shrugged his shoulders.

'Did you recognise the local address, Peter?'

'I did, but I couldn't remember why when Brian showed me,' Pete replied. 'Of course,' he continued. 'It was the address of the boy who stole your grandson's bike, the bike thief and his family, I suppose.'

Richard told them how he had crushed the roots and berries of the deadly nightshade in his garden shed at home. He told them about the syringe, and the milk bottles. They were in awe.

Bill was the first to speak, his excitement plain to see. 'Well done, that man! We're on our way!'

'We'll see,' said Richard with a sigh. 'I've researched another potion too, in a book I have on poisons. You see, I also have autumn crocus in my garden, as well as *Atropa belladonna*.' He glanced at Brian. 'Deadly nightshade, I mean. Autumn crocus or *Colchicum autumnale*, sometimes known as "naked ladies", is another plant that can produce a pretty toxic result, perhaps more deadly than nightshade. Poisoning from autumn crocus resembles arsenic poisoning. The symptoms appear some hours after it's been swallowed. There's a burning in the mouth and throat, diarrhoea, stomach pain, vomiting and kidney failure.' He spoke dispassionately. 'And often death follows from respiratory failure. There's no antidote.'

'From the flower?' Bill asked.

'All parts of the plant are poisonous.' Richard stroked his head. 'It's not actually a crocus, though the flowers look like crocus flowers. It's actually a member of the lily family. Colchicine is the poison, and it's usually extracted from the corms – the bulbs – and the seeds.'

Ernie shifted in his seat. Bill stared at Richard intently. Brian and Pete stared at each other.

Richard continued, 'The extract, colchicine, has been used as an application to treat gout or other forms of rheumatism and arthritis. People have sometimes been known to eat the bulbs accidentally by mistaking them for wild garlic. I've read a case on the internet of accidental death from eating some.'

They discussed Richard's information on his latest potion, each with his own thoughts on the subject. The shed fell silent for some minutes.

Bill broke the silence. 'How did you get on, Brian, with your detective work at the pub?'

Brian rubbed his elbow. 'It wasn't a pub. It was the wild West.' He recounted his story, and this time he was able to tell his friends what Jai and Raj had said about where the drug dealers found their customers. 'The white gangs mainly hang out at the Wicket Keeper, but apparently the black dealers sell their stuff at Mr Kool's Bar.'

The five old men were having difficulty absorbing everything they were learning that morning in their shed. It was taking each of them several minutes to digest what they had managed to stir up in Willbury.

Ernie, who generally had less to say than his friends, broke his natural quietness. 'I for one have to admit, my friends, that I think we're heading in the right direction. Aphids, weevils, look out! Your days are numbered! The pest control brigade from The Elms allotments are coming for you!'

This was quite a speech for Ernie. It galvanised the others' minds.

Brian limped across to refill his mug. 'Well said, old friend, well said. We need a plan, Richard. We have a lot going on now that needs organising. Let's form a plan so that we all know what we need to do.'

Richard stood. 'I agree. We need a plan of action to pursue our enemies, Willbury's enemies. And while I am on the subject – leatherjackets, aphids, slugs and snails and weevils, Bill. Nobody seems to remember our code. Ernie is making an effort, but the rest of you need to try harder. What was the point of discussing these originally? Please use the codes.'

He sat down again and they continued listening to Brian's information on the drug dealers, the two gangs and their regular haunts.

'Peter and I have used our information on the brothers from the bicycle shop. These seem to be our current focus. I suggest that we make our next target the drug dealers. I know you agree with that, Ernie and Bill. Let's make a plan of action for how we might tamper with their stuff, their drugs, as the next campaign in our pest control.'

All the men murmured their agreement.

'What kind of pests are they?' Brian grinned at Pete.

'Lets just get on with it,' said Bill.

CHAPTER 14

Nina Athwal sat on her stool behind the counter at PK News. Her husband Anil had gone to the cash-and-carry. She glowed with pride as she reflected on what Anil had told her about their son Raj and his friend Jai, how they had helped Mr Young last night. Although she disapproved of public houses, that didn't stop her from giving her son some money from the till to go there. She didn't understand why he liked going to the pub, but she accepted that young people born here in this country had very different ways from how she had been brought up back home in India. Nina remembered her father telling her she was to marry his friend's son and go to England. All she knew about England was that it was cold and always rained, but here she was, all these years later. She was daydreaming about this as the bell on the door jangled its announcement of a customer, interrupting her thoughts.

The man who had entered rolled what looked like an ordinary woollen hat down across his face as he approached the counter. He saw that the woman behind it had not looked up. She hadn't seen his face.

'Open the till, lady.'

Nina was suddenly aware of someone in a black balaclava in front of the counter. Then a knife flashed in the glare of the strip-lights overhead as the man drew it from his pocket and brandished it at her.

'Give me the money.'

Nina did not appear to understand at once.

'Open the till and give me the fucking money. Now!' the man shouted, glancing over his shoulder. He banged his fist on the counter. 'Now, quick! Understand? Now!'

He leaned across the counter and tried unsuccessfully to push the button on the till to open it. Instinctively Nina put her hands on the till to protect it.

'The till is empty!' she shrieked. 'No money in till. My husband take it to cash-and-carry. All money gone.' She trembled with rage and fear.

The man slashed out at her hands with the knife. A sharp pain seared through her body. Blood spurted over the till, across the newspapers laid out neatly on the counter, each title in its own pile. A rack of chewing gum went flying as the man tried to lean across the counter. He pushed her hard, sideways, and she sprawled on the floor, the stool falling on top of her. The man kicked out at her.

She screamed again and cried, 'No money, till empty!'

The blood from her hands and wrists was forming a pool beside her head. Nina looked at it and fainted.

Suddenly the shop door opened, and the bell rang. An elderly grey-haired woman, wearing a big green overcoat and bedroom slippers, shuffled through the shop, fingering through her purse for the exact money for her *Daily Mirror*. The man with the black balaclava knocked into her as he ran out of the shop before she realised what was happening. She fell against a rack of crisps. A few bags popped open with a crackle as she pulled herself up stiffly, holding on to the side of a greetings card rack nearby. There was no one at the counter, and the door was wide open. The woman clutched her purse and walked slowly to the counter. Then she saw the newsagent's wife lying behind the counter, blood everywhere. The brown face had a bluish-grey tinge to it, the eyes flickering.

A young woman came in the shop, pushing a buggy awkwardly between the rows of shelves. The infant cried and sniffed, its eyes closed tight with frustration and cold.

'Quick!' cried the old woman to the young one. 'Phone an ambulance.'

'What's going on then?' the young mother asked.

'Look, look!'

The young woman saw the blood on the floor by the counter before she noticed the Indian shopkeeper lying there.

'Oh, what's happened?' She chewed her gum more quickly as she tugged her mobile phone from her pocket and keyed in the number. 'Yes,' she said to it. 'Ambulance and police ... Both, yes ... PK News, Gratten Street ... Yes, the newspaper shop ... Yes, yes, quickly please. The lady is bleeding badly.'

Inside the cash-and-carry, Anil Athwal and his friends heard the siren go by and one of them observed, 'Too many times we hear sirens ... this country is going bad.'

It was an hour before he returned home. He was just about to bring stock from his estate car into the shop when he saw a police vehicle parked outside. There was a line of police crime scene tape across the front door.

'Mr Athwal?' A uniformed policeman approached him.

'Yes, I am. What has happened? Where is my wife?'

Inside the shop he saw blood on the floor and the cash till open and empty. Before the policeman began to explain, Anil guessed what must have happened.

Ten minutes later he was climbing into his Nissan estate car to rush to Willbury General Hospital. After parking his car, he hurried through the automatic sliding doors of the Accident and Emergency department. He'd been here before once when some boys had beaten him up, so he knew the way.

'Where is my wife, please?' he asked at reception. 'Mrs Athwal.'

'You must be Mr Athwal.' Sister Sarah Smith, her name badge informed.

'Yes, yes. Where is my wife? She is here somewhere, I think.'

'Calm down, Mr Athwal. Your wife is fine. She is here, yes, and the doctor has seen her. The ambulance brought her in. Mrs Athwal was robbed at knife point. She has some nasty cuts to her hands and wrists but she is fine.'

'Not fine with cuts!'

He didn't mean to sound rude, it wasn't his way to be rude, but it sounded sharp to the sister, although she understood his anxiety. *We seem to see more and more stabbings*, she thought. *These things would not be happening in Barbados. Only two more years before I retire back home to the sunshine and peace.* She pictured the beautiful bay she and Wesley had in mind. *Two years more, that's all.* They said it to each other so often. Three years, two years, soon. No more politicians telling them how they were going to stop street crime. It had been good when they first came here, cold but friendly. They were young and optimistic then, looking forward to a new life with a decent jobs.

'This is a bad country,' Anil heard himself say. Sister Smith agreed, but she didn't say so aloud.

'Come on, Mr Athwal, I'll show you where she is.'

She led him through to a cubicle and pulled back the curtain; the young male nurse looked up as he finished the dressing to Nina Athwal's hands. 'All done,' he said, and left the cubicle.

Nina smiled weakly at her husband. Her face was bluish-grey under the brown, her large brown eyes watery and doleful.

'Oh, Anil, who is looking after the shop?'

'The police are there right now,' he reassured her. 'The shop is closed. It's a crime scene now.'

'Would you like a cup of tea, Mr Athwal?' asked Sister Smith.

'Yes, I would, thank you.'

He sat on the spare chair in the cubicle, while his wife related what she remembered of the events earlier that morning.

'This is a bad country,' Anil repeated, shaking his head slowly from side to side.

In another part of the hospital there had been a death. The police had been called back. Dr Helen Sillence, the consultant toxicologist, had reached the conclusion that it could not be an accident that eight people had swallowed atropine. A child of six had died that morning, two more children were in a critical condition, and a middle-aged couple she presumed were the parents and three young adults were still quite ill. Dr Sillence had given instructions to the medical team and signed the report.

The young Afro-Caribbean man in the next cubicle nursed his hand. That morning his doctor told him he thought he'd broken a bone and had sent him to A&E. Ace Card had waited most of the morning to be seen, and to get his hand X-rayed, and now he was waiting to have it set in plaster. He ground his teeth in anger. No, it wouldn't surprise him if he or one of his mates got the blame for the knife attack on the Indian woman who was in the next cubicle. The police always harassed him when there was a mugging in Willbury. But they should know he didn't need to knock over defenceless old women. *Got good business of me own.* Ace Card had a good idea who might have attacked the shopkeeper's wife, though. He knew the area where the shop was located and had gradually pieced together the story from the conversation he'd overheard from the next cubicle. Now he would tell the Indian couple, and keep the cops off his back.

Anil and Nina listened attentively to the young black man who had pulled aside the curtain to the cubicle. Nina clicked her tongue and Anil shook his head silently as they took in Ace Card's information. Nina glanced almost guiltily at her husband when told to mention the Wicket Keeper pub to the police. They would remember to report that the name Gary Beesley had been suggested to them.

Ace Card settled back to wait to be called to have his hand set in plaster. He smiled to himself as he cupped his injured hand in the other. His name could not be used when the couple were interviewed, because he hadn't given it.

CHAPTER 15

During the rest of January, the five old men had spent more time in normal gardening pursuits. The events of those few days recently had left them determined to carry on with their other plan, the pest control. It had also left them reflecting – some concerned or worried, some eager to keep up the momentum. They had concluded in the end, however, that they would do no more than make plans. For the next few weeks, the new agenda was to do nothing but think or talk about their ideas. They had agreed to do more research, to develop their schemes but take no action. Let things settle down a bit.

The gardeners had shared a load of manure that Richard had located at a local farm. They had jointly paid for it and had it delivered, a big steaming heap that they spread out over their respective plots. 'Organic and traditional,' Richard announced.

The weather remained cold and wet but there were some bright days too, chilly but sunny, just right for gardening work. They planted some early crops, shallots and broad beans under cloches. Pete had planted a couple of apple trees. Ernie was trying some sweet peas for the first time, though vegetables were still his preference. As for Bill, who had stuck to his chrysanthemum preparation, with not much to do other than taking some cuttings, he frequently remained in the shed on his own.

Richard often stayed away, preferring to work at home in his greenhouse, pricking out and seeding. He had visited both his son and daughter, as though he was on holiday from something.

Pete too spent more time at home with Liz.

'Aren't you going to the allotment again?' she would ask.

'Not much doing this time of year,' he would reply.

On the last day of January, all five met up at the shed.

'I'm bored with this,' announced Bill. 'I want to get on with our plans.'

'Trouble with you, Bill, is that apart from your cuttings you haven't got enough to do,' Brian said. 'You ought to try other things as well.'

'I want to try other things but not growing plants. I want to get on with tidying up our town, not our allotments and gardens.'

Bill's frustration had been growing for a while, and he was finding it difficult to contain it. The pain in his insides was not getting any better. He had steadfastly refused to visit his doctor, although he was concerned when the others kept pointing out that he was losing weight. 'Aren't you eating properly, Bill?' Ernie had asked this morning.

What was the point, he'd asked himself. What was his future? Recently he had decided that he'd had enough. It was not melancholic sentiment, nor self-pity, merely a practical conclusion. If the cause of the pain was serious – and it hurt enough to suggest it was – there was little time left for getting the job done. Bill had made one visit, though. He had booked an appointment to make a will. He wouldn't tell anyone, least of all those concerned. Peter, Ernie and Brian, he considered, would know soon enough. They could share the proceeds of his house and his bank and building society accounts.

Bill felt a grip of pain as he put the kettle on the gas ring. He rubbed his stomach gently and took a small sip from a bottle of water.

'I've had a gang of aphids hanging about my house lately, and my next-door neighbour's.' He added after a pause, 'They seem to think it's funny to shout and throw things at our houses. Stones and empty beer cans. They can't be old enough to drink beer. I think they're the same ones who damaged my neighbour's car. They come up my front garden and bang on the door. If I or my neighbours go out, we get filthy abuse from them. Girls as well as boys. My neighbour told me he's thinking of moving. He grabbed one in his garden and three or four more came back. The little ...' He hesitated, searching for his definition. '... The little sod punched him on the side of the face and he had to let him go. My neighbour ran in to call the police, but by the time they arrived the aphids had vanished. So then he was up late telling the police what's been happening. They said they'd keep an eye.' Bill grunted. 'They seemed more amused than concerned. We haven't seen a police car drive by as they promised. If anything the gang of aphids has got bigger.' He watched the kettle boil.

'Christ, Bill, why didn't you tell us?' Brian said.

Bill stared hard at Brian. 'This is why we must get on with the pest control. We haven't done much lately, against pests that is. We must get a move on.'

They agreed as each took a fresh mug of tea from Bill.

'Let's get to work with the plan,' Bill said as he handed Richard his tea.

The general plan, decided during recent discussions, was to use Richard's poison solutions on any villains whose addresses they knew. They had laughed when Richard Owen-Davies announced so coolly that he knew where lots of villains lived – pests of all sorts, housed in the same place. He had dismissed their laughter with a shrug. They had said, almost in unison, 'And how do you propose to get into a prison?'

When Richard had explained his theory Bill had encouraged him. Ernie had gone quite pale when Brian joked, 'We'll all be in there soon anyway.'

Richard and Bill had spent the next ten minutes discussing weevils and leatherjackets, and became quite angry at Brian's jokes at their expense. Bill had remarked abruptly to Pete, Ernie and Brian that he was very disappointed they'd not used the agreed terms of leatherjackets, weevils, slugs and snails when discussing community pest control.

Their current aim was to cause as many poisonings as possible. Since news of the family poisoning that Richard had carried out had even reached some national newspapers, they believed that more of the same would achieve even greater publicity for their cause.

'It may become obvious to the authorities which type of people become sick,' Richard had observed. 'In my opinion the media these days go into so much trivial detail just to fill the news that they may well ask questions, if it becomes apparent that certain types of people are being targeted.'

Pete and Brian had quietly agreed they were getting bored with Richard's continual talk of plans. They reckoned Ernie was probably thinking the same but hadn't said so, and Bill, they had privately noted, seemed to be becoming stranger by the day. They'd assured themselves that no more children would be harmed. When they'd heard that the second child had died in hospital, they had all lost some enthusiasm.

'Probably saved the town from a few problems in the future,' Bill had remarked when Richard produced a newspaper cutting of the report.

Richard had agreed with Bill's remark but had thought better of saying it. He wasn't unhappy with the result.

They had now agreed to administer as much as possible over a few days to create an epidemic. More publicity, they concluded jointly.

'Perhaps it'll get on the TV news,' Brian had added with a grin.

The campaign would restart from today. They would continue, of course, to come down to the allotments regularly, not to arouse any suspicions by breaking habits and routines.

Ernie was determined not to have cold feet this time. He would do his bit, he had muttered apologetically without much conviction. 'I haven't done anything yet, except let you down when I did have something to do. Your deadly nightshade solution, Richard, can I have some tomorrow? In fact can we all have some tomorrow? Our plan to copy your success with the milk bottles is a good one. We each know where to go, we each know who to target. I, for one, am ready to make that big surge we've talked about. I know exactly where I'm going to start with mine.'

'Good man,' said Bill.

'By the way,' Ernie added, 'I've put quite a few syringes in that cupboard in the corner. As some of you

know, Grace was diabetic, and she had to inject insulin.'
He sniffed. 'There were plenty of syringes left over when
she died.'

Willbury was meandering on through the winter as January moved into February. The town was gloomy and grey to match the skies. Collars turned up and faces down for its unsuspecting townsfolk. Willbury Town FC had been removed from the FA Cup by non-League Halifax Town. Only florists were optimistic, getting ready for the Valentine's Day sales bonanza.

Brian put his phial in the glove-box of his van, dropped Pete off with his, and winked as he said goodbye.

'See you, mate. See you tomorrow.'

He had a list in his glove-box, mostly compiled from Raj and Jai's information but including some rogues he knew himself. His writing wasn't too good; he didn't suppose anybody else could read it, but he could. School had been an inconvenience to Brian years ago, and it wasn't much use when he was laying bricks. He had decided to go out that evening, to see what he could find for carrying out his bit of mischief.

Brian hadn't been into Willbury town centre for years, at least not at night. He hoped his old parking spot was still there by the old market place. It was, but it was a paved area now, with a sign: NO ENTRY. He swung his van round with a three-point turn. *I know*, he thought. *There's a place round by the library.*

'Right, second time, Brian,' he said aloud to the steering wheel as he parked his van. He rolled a cigarette, lit it, and reached for his list and his phial. He was surprised how easy it was to fill the syringe. Quite a few people were out in the town, mostly young, and none his age. Brian walked up the road purposefully, towards tonight's target, Mr Kool's Bar. Raj and Jai had told him that some of the young people obtained their drugs from dealers there.

It hadn't occurred to him how much he would stick out in Mr Kool's. A few people of his age might inadvertently stroll in at lunchtime but they would be a rare sight at night, judging from the odd looks he received. Undaunted, he pushed through the crush of customers and forced his way to the bar, where he ordered half a lager. He didn't really like lager, not proper beer to him, but he thought this would help make him less conspicuous. Mr Kool's didn't sell his brand of best bitter anyway.

As he cautiously glanced around, he saw that nobody was taking much notice of him any more. They all seemed to have returned to their own conversations, engrossed with one another, mostly standing in small groups. He wandered about the dimly lit bar, his half-pint glass in one hand and his phial in the other. A drop here, a drop there. He thought at one point a young woman had seen what he was doing. His heart raced, and he looked for the door, ready to leave hastily. He even overheard her say to her friends, 'What's that old bloke doing?' Some of the girl's group looked round at him .

'Fucking old junkie. Yuk, disgusting!' one muttered.

A drop here, another drop there. He was beginning to enjoy himself. Draining the last dregs of lager from his glass, wincing slightly at the taste, he left the way he had entered.

As he started up his van again, ready to head home, Brian chuckled to himself. He had done his job. His heart thumped as he pulled away. He was almost home before it crossed his mind how indiscriminate he had been, for somehow he had emptied the whole syringe. Then he shrugged. They were drug addicts after all, he reassured himself. It would just teach them a lesson.

Ernie was up at five the next morning. He whistled to himself as he made a pot of tea while shaving in the kitchen, his old habit.

He had decided to walk, and keep going until there were no more milk bottles at the addresses, or until he had run out of the liquid, or until he was too cold or tired. He would see what happened.

Next door but one, Ernie knew the man who lived in the ground-floor flat had a reputation for being a child molester, or a paedophile as they called it now. He had done time for it some years ago, but the man's history wasn't common knowledge; not many had lived here very long, so they didn't know. Ernie had seen children go in there. The flats were mostly occupied by either single mothers or elderly people now. The older ones might have heard about the man, but they weren't the ones in danger. Ernie knew for sure there would be milk by this man's door; there always was. *An early start*, he thought, as he injected a little of the fluid through the foil bottle top, careful to make the smallest hole he could.

He hurried on up his own road. It was cold, but Ernie didn't feel it today. At the next building, the resident had an expensive car but never seemed to work. Ernie was sure the man must be up to no good to afford that car. No milk on the step, though, so he would escape punishment. As Ernie Evans continued up the road, he felt tempted to inject the foul liquid into any milk bottles he saw, even when he did not know who lived behind the doors. He crossed over to the home of a known target, a boy who had cheeked Grace some years ago. Although he couldn't recall the details, he knew the boy had said something that made Grace furious that day. He walked up the path and carried out his retribution for the unremembered crime. A light in the hallway came on through the obscured glass panels at the top of the door. Retreating back up the short pathway as the front door opened, Ernie ducked beneath the fence. He heard the chink of the two bottles being picked up and straightened uneasily as the front door slammed shut again.

Ernie walked briskly away, his brow glistening with sweat. He looked at the syringe, still half full. *More jobs yet, Ernie, my boy*, he told himself. He continued on along the pavement, noticing that a few lights were on upstairs, fewer downstairs. A big 4x4 was half parked on the pavement in front of him. *If you live round here, sonny, you can't afford that thing. You didn't get it honestly.* The house was not on his mental list of targets but, unfortunately for the vehicle's owner, three milk bottles stood on the adjacent doorstep. Ernie quickly applied his fledgling skill. *This bloody area I live in*, he pondered, *is full of 'em.* Enough left for one more. He knew where he would dispense the last drops. Arriving at the parade of shops, he muttered 'Yes', inaudibly but with satisfaction, when he saw the milk bottles outside the women's hairdressing salon, Cut & Curl. He was certain they belonged to the flat above. So few people seemed to have a doorstep delivery these days, and he was pleased at having found a few in the right places.

The moneylender who lived above Cut & Curl, whose name was Alfred Sutton, had made his daughter's life a misery. Anne had borrowed money to clear overdue debts – hers or his grandson's Ernie never knew. Anne refused to discuss it with him after he told her he couldn't afford to lend her any more money. Why couldn't she make do, as he and Grace had always done? Credit was just too easy these days. He'd had many conversations with Pete and Brian over this aspect of so-called modern life. Credit cards, loans, so many people caught in a trap of self-generated debt, 'firefighting' with more loans they couldn't afford to re-pay. But the extortionate demands this moneylender had made when collecting from Anne still filled Ernie with a mixture of incomprehension and anger. ALFRED SUTTON: the name was printed next to a doorbell by the upstairs entrance.

This was a task he would greatly enjoy. Gently he pricked the bottle tops and released the remaining fluid from the syringe. He waited a while nearby, bought a paper from PK News and set off home. The pest control brigade from The Elms allotments would be pleased with him this time.

In another part of town, Bill Choules left his semide-tached house and set off on his bicycle. In the early-morning gloom the front light of his bike was a mere yellow dot. The hazy orange streetlights looked down with a misty indifference. His old legs pumped hard at the pedals, and his eyes watered in the cold, damp air. The big man hummed a familiar aria to himself. A few cars passed him, and one of the first double-decker buses of the day growled to a halt at an empty bus stop, fully lit for the two passengers it had already found. Bill caught it up and waited behind for it to pull away with its lightweight load. He coughed at the acrid diesel smoke that filled his lungs momentarily. It made him angry, and the tune in his head abruptly ceased.

Quietly he leant his cycle at the front of the Wicket Keeper public house, looking both ways up and down the road. A delivery van went by, BILLY BOY SAUSAGES AND MEATS TO THE TRADE. He crept round to the rear of the building. He had rarely in his life been inside bars or pubs; he didn't enjoy their atmosphere, and he didn't like alcohol for that matter. His mother had bought a bottle of Harvey's Bristol Cream sherry each Christmas, despite his father's vehement preaching against the demon drink. It was when Brian had described his visit to the Wicket Keeper last month that Bill decided it would be his target. On previous reconnaissance trips he had watched the delivery man leave six pints of milk at a side door, where the morning cleaner would soon let herself in. She would carry the milk into the pub and put the bottles in the fridge in the downstairs kitchen.

Removing his gloves, Bill fumbled with the syringe in his cold fingers. He hummed nervously to himself as he pricked each silver top with the needle, his thumb releasing a tiny amount of Richard's concoction into each bottle. His hands were shaking so much that he nearly knocked one bottle over, and he looked over his shoulder anxiously. With relief he remounted his bicycle at the front of the pub and cycled away as fast as he could push the pedals without casting a single glance over his shoulder. Plumes of condensation were forced from his lungs through his mouth. His eyes streamed with tears, tears from the cold, not emotion. He contained a chuckle of excitement and fear. He cycled towards the shed on the allotments, heading for his first cup of tea. On the way he stopped at a convenience store, open early, and bought a carton of fresh milk for his tea.

As Willbury woke, it could not know that a small gardening club were so busy this cold, grey February morning. Babies would be born today, lives would expire today, business would be done today, letters typed, goods made and sold. Life for most of Willbury would be its normal round of duties and obligations, its usual routine of work, school or college. Yet some doctors and nurses would be busier than normal today.

As Pete Wilson made the early-morning coffee for Liz, he thought of the vile liquid in the small glass bottle in his coat pocket: Richard's second potion made from the autumn crocus. He wondered what the others were doing right now. Pete plumped up the pillows behind his wife's head, hooked his arm under her armpit and heaved her to sit upright. His mind was elsewhere, not on his usual routine. He helped Liz use the bedpan as he did each morning, then emptied and rinsed the bedpan. He would then sit with her to help with the coffee.

'Like a piece of toast?' he asked, as he did each morning.

He returned to the kitchen to make some toast and marmalade, one for her, one for him. Liz's two carers would arrive in an hour or so, to wash and dress her, then get her seated in her armchair for yet another day. They came each morning to get her up and they came each evening to put her to bed. Christmas Day was the only day of the year the carers didn't visit, and his daughters helped then, or he did it himself. Liz would usually cry each Christmas morning. 'I wish you didn't have to do this,' she would say each year, part of the Christmas ritual.

Pete would not be putting Richard's toxic concoction into milk bottles. Richard had thought it might be deadly, and in any case all the milk bottles would be gone from doorsteps and it would be light by the time Pete could go out. He tried to picture the others performing their tasks. *Is this right, what we're doing?* he found himself thinking. He strove to dismiss the thought but the doubt kept returning.

Liz smiled at him as he handed her the toast. 'You are quiet this morning. You haven't even put the radio on in the kitchen. Do you feel all right? What's the problem?' She paused and shook her head. 'I know you, when something's bothering you you're different. You're always quiet when you've got something on your mind. What is it?'

'Nothing,' said Pete absentmindedly, without conviction. He looked at his wife's tired face, her damaged body. He propped her up with pillows as best he could and sipped the tea that he had made at the same time as Liz's instant coffee.

Sitting down in her armchair in the corner of her room, he studied her as he drank his tea. He loved her, he knew, he always had, but it was now the idea came back into his mind. He closed his eyes briefly. His thoughts raced, they tripped over each other, he argued with himself, wishing this particular thought had never crossed his mind. *It would be kind.* The inner turmoil overwhelmed him. *But it's outrageous, horrible.* He couldn't dream of it. Then again he reflected that today many people would be ill from mysterious symptoms, and another poisoning would not be conspicuous. In the small glass phial was Richard's new potion made from the autumn crocus, a potion as yet untested.

'Would you like another cup of coffee, love?' Pete's voice was almost a whisper.

In a smarter road nearby, Richard Owen-Davies started his car. He was about to play his part. Richard marvelled at his own coolness, puzzled at the inner confidence this adventure seemed to have given him. Perhaps this was his destiny, he wondered. In a perverse way he wished Daphne knew why he had got up so early.

For her part, Daphne had certainly been curious as she lay in the warmth of her own bedroom listening to her husband moving around. When she had heard him in the bathroom, she had propped herself up on one elbow to see the clock beside her bed. She had laid back down, eyes open, listening and wondering. It was much earlier than usual, for sure. Richard had been acting oddly of late. His whole manner was different these days. She couldn't quite put her finger on what exactly had changed in him, but she was sure he was up to something.

Their lives had gradually become virtually separate. They had, for many years, been travelling on parallel tracks, and to the outside world they were going in the same direction. It was important to Daphne how others perceived them; respectability was vital to her. There was no reason for her many friends and acquaintances to question her private life.

It's something to do with that damned allotment, she concluded as she lay in bed. She could not imagine how it was connected to that filthy old shed and those coarse old men, as she thought of them, but it must be.

Daphne had never hidden her disapproval of this hobby that had so engrossed her husband since his retirement. She could not, however, begin to work out why, on this winter morning, he should get up so early. Gardening was not one of her interests but she knew enough to realise that not much happens in February. Occasionally he had risen early in the summer to drive to the allotment, but never at this time of year.

As she heard the car start up underneath her window, she turned over, pulled the duvet up under her chin and drifted back to sleep.

The gardening club members had agreed during their renewed resolution that it was often difficult to locate the pests. That was when Richard had made the suggestion that he was now to follow up.

'Our local prison is full of pests, contained and captive!'

'And living at taxpayers' expense,' Ernie had added.

Brian and Pete had laughed when he had proposed his plan, but Richard had resolved to ignore them. He'd show them! The time had come for action. Bill had been in favour, Ernie had even asked if he could come along, but Richard was adamant that it would be easier on his own and Ernie reluctantly backed down. What the others didn't know was that he intended using the new colchicine potion that had not yet been tested on any pests.

Richard drew a few slow, deep breaths as his car pulled out of the drive. He glanced up at the bedroom window and pictured his wife there in bed, then consciously wiped the image from his mind and changed up a gear.

The retired civil servant nosed the car slowly out of his drive, headlights on. He turned the car radio on to his regular companion, Radio 4. The familiar voices discussed the American economy in the light of Japan's apparent economic downturn. The White House spokesman assured the world that the USA would remain robust. '*Wall Street is confident that if anything the Japanese economic crisis will be to the advantage of the States. I see no signs of recession here.*' Another car bomb had exploded in a food market in Baghdad, with thirty killed and many more injured. The presenter introduced the next report in a tone of despondency.

Suddenly Richard caught sight of the bakery truck he had been searching for in his headlights. He knew it delivered to Willbury General Hospital before it drove to the prison gates. He would have only moments while the driver was inside the hospital's catering department. Richard switched the car lights off and parked in the road beside the hospital. He made his way between the buildings to where he knew the truck would be parked up. No one would take any notice of him, he felt certain. Hospitals are busy twenty-four hours a day, and one old man would surely not arouse the slightest interest. Peering round the corner of a red-brick single-storey building – the Outpatients' Eye Clinic – he could see the truck backed up to a door, the lights from the building forming a pool of yellow brightness in the early-morning gloom. Richard watched and waited, then crept nearer to check whether the delivery man was inside, leaving his truck unattended. Sure enough, the bread-delivery driver was passing down plastic trays of wrapped bread and rolls to the hospital kitchen porter. Richard muttered to himself at his good luck when he heard the porter ask the driver if he had time for a cuppa this morning. The driver said he did.

As quickly as he could, Richard hurried round to the open back of the truck. He had not considered until now how high the truck's bed was from the ground. Grunting with the exertion, he pulled himself up on to the platform bed of the truck. He didn't know how to use the hydraulic platform, which in any case would have been too noisy. Richard entered the truck's cavernous body, only half full now, its bowels stacked with trays of wrapped loaves as well as rolls, cakes, buns and assorted confectionery. With the syringe needle he easily pricked through the plastic loaf wrappers at the side of the trays, as many as he could, up and down the racks as rapidly as he could manage. He did not suppose the tiny pinholes in the bread wrappers would be noticed. Quickly refilling the syringe from another glass phial, he continued to inject the colchicine solution from his autumn crocus manufacture. He breathed hard and fast as he clambered unsteadily over the back edge of the truck.

When he slid down, his feet were planted too flat, and his knees and hips jarred as he landed. His right leg gave way. Richard winced with pain, steadying himself with one hand on the truck's rear. Suddenly he heard a voice call out.

'Cheerio, mate! See you tomorrow. Thanks for the tea.' The driver was returning.

For a few seconds, Richard could not move. He leaned on the back of the truck and eased his weight on to his left leg. It was then he felt a hand on his shoulder. His heart seemed to stop. He turned to see the driver frowning at him. His mouth went dry, his knee hurt, and the soles of his feet throbbed.

'You all right, mate? Do you need a hand?'

Relief rushed through Richard with the realisation that the driver suspected nothing and had seen nothing unusual. The man reached up for the rope and pulled the shutter down at the back of the truck.

'One more delivery to make, to the prison, and then back to the yard to load up some smaller drops for the corner shops. That's my day,' he informed Richard. 'You sure you're OK, mate?'

Richard thought quickly. 'Do you know where the casualty department is?'

'Yes, mate. I'll give you a hand.' The driver snapped a padlock through the rings at the base of the shutters to the rear of the truck. 'Come on, mate, I'll give you a hand over there, if you like.'

Richard thanked him and leaned heavily on the driver, his arm round the man's shoulder. 'This is very nice of you. I'm a silly old fool getting lost.'

'What have you done to your leg?'

'I tripped over the kerb right outside the hospital as I got out of my car – I was going to visit a friend in here.'

'Bit early for visiting, isn't it?'

Richard gave no answer. The man didn't pursue his question.

As they reached the Accident and Emergency department, the double doors shushed open automatically.

'You can leave me here. I'll be all right on my own. I don't want to make you late. And thank you very much for your concern.' Richard stood his weight on his left leg.

'If you're sure you're all right, at least you managed to hurt yourself in the best place. Good luck. Hope you haven't broken anything. Bye.' The driver left him leaning by the open doors.

Richard limped over to a vending machine in the reception area. He would have a cup of coffee, have a sit down, get warm and gather himself up together. Nobody else was in the large waiting area. He fished in his trouser pockets for change and selected his drink. Then he sat down heavily in a plastic chair and sighed, cupping his hands around the hot Styrofoam cup.

A quiet sense of achievement flooded over him as he recalled how and why he found himself here. *A job well done*, he told himself. He jumped from his thoughts as a voice said, 'Need any help?' He looked up at the young man in a white cotton coat standing over him.

'No, I'm fine, thank you.' Richard smiled at the young doctor, who shrugged and left without another word.

Richard took his time over the coffee, dropped his empty cup into a bin and then began to limp slowly back to his car.

Shall I go home or straight to the allotment? he asked himself as he started the engine. He glanced back at Willbury General Hospital as he pulled away. *You will be busy later on.*

CHAPTER 16

Richard was surprised to see a car, a van and a bicycle silhouetted over by the shed as he turned into The Elms allotments. Smoke was already drifting from the little chimney, a white trail against the dark sky. The glow of streetlights met the sky across the black outlines of the houses forming the horizon beyond the allotments perimeter.

He could hear muffled voices from within as he approached. His bladder ached, and he could not refrain from relieving himself at the back of the shed, steam rising from the pool as it seeped into the soil. He stepped awkwardly into the shed, the only light on the three faces there the blaze of the wood-burning stove and the flame of the gas ring they used for boiling their kettle. The faces looked older in the mottled light. It was a surreal picture: white hair and eyes shining; the glow from the end of Brian's roll-up; the men animated. All eyes on him.

'You hurt yourself, Richard?' Brian enquired. 'You're limping, aren't you?'

Richard sat down uneasily on a stool. Ernie handed him a mug of tea. Three members of the gardening club studied Richard's face. They looked through the gloom at each other questioningly. Nobody spoke for a while, the previous chatter interrupted by the fourth member's arrival.

Richard began to relate his adventure to his friends. They listened intently; nobody interrupted. He told them the whole story, right up to his coffee in reception. They each absorbed the account without a word. Then Brian coughed and broke the silence.

'You didn't actually get seen by anyone for your knee then?'

Richard assured him that he had not, but mentioned the young doctor who had checked on him.

'It was lucky there were so few people about,' he continued. 'It would not have done to have left my name and address at reception, would it?'

They smiled and nodded agreement. Bill and Ernie congratulated him on his bravery, and Brian's face could not hide his admiration. Then they told their own stories again for Richard's benefit.

Outside the dark sky was lightening to different shades of grey over the shed. The men continued to quiz each other about their individual exploits, speculating on the outcome of their deeds. A cold, fine drizzle began to fall over Willbury and the allotments.

Over at a neat and tidy semi nearby, Pete Wilson forced back tears as he watched Liz drain her second cup of coffee and said his goodbye to her, wondering what the carers would think of her condition this morning. He kissed her gently on the cheek and left.

As he started his car, Pete Wilson could not hold back any longer. His eyes streamed and his nose ran as he set off for the allotments, his whole body trembling. His throat constricted uncomfortably, and he tried to cough to clear it. He could not contemplate what he had done. He had known it was today or never. When he emptied the small glass phial into the cup after he had spooned in the coffee granules, his stomach knotted and his throat ached. He watched the liquid gradually absorb the sugar and coffee granules. As he poured in the water and milk, Pete could not acknowledge what he was doing, what he was about to do to the woman he loved. He had watched her frustration in the early insidious days of the disease, the mother of his two daughters, married themselves now and mothers of his grandchildren. Liz was his lifelong friend as well as his wife. He had seen her health deteriorate, her distress when the disease made her incontinent, her beautiful hands stiffening. She was no longer able to do the things that gave her pleasure, no longer able to walk. She would be happy soon now, he thought. *Please do not make it too painful – no more suffering for her, no agony.* Tears burned his eyes, blurring his vision.

He couldn't remember driving to the allotments. It wasn't far, but Pete had no recollection of changing gear, feet on pedals, no memory of stopping or turning the engine off. He almost fell into the shed. The gardening club members were so consumed already with their own adventures, they weren't prepared for the shock to come as Pete incoherently gasped out what he had just done. There was a stunned silence as it slowly dawned on the group of men what Pete was telling them.

Richard and Bill looked stern-faced in the flickering light. Brian put his arm round his old friend's heaving shoulders, shaking his head from side to side in total disbelief.

'Oh, mate, what have you done? Oh, Christ, mate, what have you done? … Your Liz, your lovely Liz. Oh, Jesus Christ!' Brian's eyes swam as he struggled to express his feelings.

The shrill cry of a siren rushed past somewhere nearby, and they all jumped, eyes wide. The day was dawning reluctantly over Willbury.

Pete lit a cigarette with trembling hands. He sucked hard on it. His eyes closed tight to squeeze the hurt from his head. There was a nauseous hollow feeling in his stomach. Thoughts raced around in a whirlpool in his mind – his wife, his daughters; an empty house.

Brian stood in front of Pete, a hand on each shoulder. 'Tell me again, Pete. What have you done?'

Pete looked up at his friend's anxious face. 'She'd had enough, Brian,' his voice croaked out. 'Our lives are a waste of time now. Hers, mine. She told me recently.'

'Told you what?' Brian snapped. 'Not that she wanted to die? Oh, Christ, man, what the bloody hell have you done?'

'Yes, she did. Yes. With all that you lot have been doing this morning, it will add to it ...' He tailed off and gasped out a huge sigh from deep in his throat.

'You mean you'd had enough of caring for Liz? You wanted rid of her?' Brian's voice was harsh.

'Don't say that! I loved Liz. It was the best for both of us.'

'Did she ask you to poison her? Didn't you realise it would be a painful way for her to die?' Brian turned to glare at Richard, the veins in his neck bulging, his fists clenched tightly at his sides. 'Fuck you, Richard, and your fucking poison!'

Richard opened his mouth as if to speak but nothing came out.

Pete could not reply. He started to sob. Terrible feelings of remorse overwhelmed him, aching in his skull.

After all, Liz had never asked him to end her life, had she? What if he was wrong? Was he a murderer?

The men stayed in their hut. No one spoke a word now. Occasionally they would sip quietly at another cup of tea that one of them would make to lighten the atmosphere. This dilapidated shed contained some dark secrets now. None of the gardeners could bring himself to be the one to break the silence, the crackling of wood burning in the stove the only sound. Time passed slowly. Occasionally they glanced at each other. Pete just sat there either staring ahead, unseeing, or with his head in his hands. Sometimes a sob would disturb the stillness. The rattle of a teaspoon stirring a mug of tea jarred as if the volume had been turned up. Brian would cough sometimes over another intake of tobacco smoke into his lungs. Pete would sniff and shake his head. Bill's breathing sounded heavy and noisy. Ernie was quietly contained. No one knew what to say or least of all what to do. Richard rubbed his knee once or twice, but the silence rolled on inside the shed. More sirens wailed in the distance. On each occasion they would all glance round at each other and still nobody spoke. Finally, as each wondered how long they could stay like this, it was Pete who broke the spell.

Before any of the others realised what was happening, Pete sprang up and swiftly crossed the shed to the cupboard where Richard's foul liquid was stored in an a coffee jar. The colchicine. He snatched the lid off and as if in slow motion he gulped the pale yellow liquid down. A dribble ran down on either side of his mouth. His eyes were wide, staring straight ahead.

'I can't take what I've done! I don't want to live with what I've done!' Tears rolled down his cheeks. 'My poor

Liz.' Pete dropped to his knees, his face in his hands, and he howled a long guttural sound.

'Brian, get your van to the door quickly!' Richard commanded.

Brian raced for the door. Bill stood up.

'Bill, Ernie, help me!' Richard took charge. 'Get him into Brian's van and take him down to the hospital.'

Pete shook them off. 'I don't want the hospital.'

He wrestled his arm from Bill's grip, pushed Ernie away and dropped to the floor on his knees once more.

'Leave me alone! I don't want to go to hospital. I want to die. I want to die!'

Brian rushed back in. 'What the fuck is going on?'

Pete moaned again, 'I'm not going anywhere, Brian. Leave me alone please, all of you.'

'Do something, Richard! ' Brian shouted. 'You made the stuff, you should know what to do.'

'It doesn't kill.' Richard rounded on the other man.

'What about those kids in the hospital the other day?'

'Not adults.'

Brian squared up face to face with Richard. 'This is the other stuff you made, the autumn crocus stuff. That's what he's drunk. Not the deadly nightshade.'

'Make him sick! Put something down his throat!' yelled Richard.

Pete struggled furiously as Bill and Ernie again tried to hold him down. His pupils were beginning to dilate and his face had grown very pale, his breath rasping. Brian tried to get his fingers into Pete's mouth. Pete writhed and fought, and bit Brian's finger. Suddenly he vomited. Ernie recoiled. Pete coughed and gurgled, his breathing laboured, his face now becoming red.

'He won't be able to resist now he's gone under the influence of it. He won't fight us off now. Let's get him into your van, Brian,' Richard insisted. 'Bill, Ernie, come on, try again. Quickly.'

The four men grabbed a limb each and struggled with him out of the shed door and into the passenger seat of Brian's van, the men panting from the exertion.

'Go, Brian, go fast!' Ernie shouted as he slammed the van door shut, against Pete's body.

Pete's head rolled back and his body slumped across the seat. He fell across Brian's arm as his friend tried to change gear while driving out on to the road. The old bricklayer steered as best he could with one hand pushing Pete back across the van. Pete slumped against the passenger door with a thump. His head rolled back again and he slid from his seat into the footwell, half on the seat and half off. Brian let out a squeak of fear and anxiety. It made him cough convulsively, and his eyes began to stream. He finally turned into the hospital when he saw the Accident and Emergency signs.

Brian braked outside the double doors, then ran as best as his stiff old legs would allow up to the reception desk. The place was busy now – almost every chair taken. He banged one thick palm down on the counter.

'Quick! I need help!' he gasped.

A nurse looked up from her computer screen. 'Won't be a moment.'

'Now!' he shouted. 'Now! I need help now, for my friend!'

He pointed to his van outside. A man in a navy-blue uniform was coming in through the doors.

'Is that your van there, sir? I'm sorry but you can't stay there.' *Hospital Security*, his badge announced.

'I have someone in the van who's ill, seriously ill. I need help to get him in here. Please help me.' He took the security man's arm and tried to drag him out through the doors.

'It's not my job to get involved with patients,' the man protested. 'Ask at reception for a porter.'

Brian rushed back to the desk. 'Please help me. I need a porter,' he pleaded.

The nurse had seen what had happened and she had sent for two hospital porters and a trolley. By now the porters were already lifting Pete out of the van and on to the trolley. They wheeled the patient through the automatic doors and into a cubicle. Brian meanwhile was giving details to the nurse at reception, who filled in a form.

'What can you tell me?' the nurse asked. 'What seems to be the problem?'

'It's poison ... he's taken poison,' gasped Brian. 'That's all I know.'

The security man, seeing the van now empty, returned through the doors. 'Will you please move your van now, sir,' he demanded.

Apologising to the nurse, Brian left the building and climbed into his van. When he returned from the visitors' car park, an ambulance had filled the space he had vacated. The same porters were at the rear of the ambulance with another wheeled trolley as a paramedic appeared at the trolley's side.

'It's another poisoning – similar symptoms,' Brian heard the paramedic say inside the hospital to a doctor.

'Jesus Christ!' the A&E doctor exclaimed, staring at the trolley.

It most certainly would not be the last they would have to deal with that day.

Brian paced up and down outside the double doors leading to A&E, stopping only to roll another cigarette. He drew hard as he lit the latest one. 'Pete, Pete, Pete mate … Oh, Christ,' he muttered to himself. A young woman glanced nervously in Brian's direction as she got out of her car. She hurried two small boys along with her.

Brian returned to reception once again. 'Any news of Pete Wilson?'

'I'm sorry, Mr Young. I've told you already he is being looked at. We're doing all we can for him … Ah, here is one of the doctors coming now. Perhaps he can tell you more.'

It was past six o'clock in the evening now and Brian felt his stomach knot. He had been at the hospital all afternoon. He was tired and hungry. He had phoned Debbie to tell her Pete had been taken ill and that he would be at the hospital. His mouth was sour from too many roll-ups, and his head throbbed with a dull ache.

The young Asian doctor smiled. 'You are Mr Young, Mr Wilson's friend, I understand.'

Brian nodded. 'How is he, doctor?'

'I need to know what may have caused Mr Wilson's problem. We've had many people admitted with what is obviously some form of poisoning. Mr Wilson is not reacting in quite the same way. Nor is his wife, who I'm also attending to. Have they eaten the same thing, can you tell me? They are both seriously ill.'

Brian felt frantic. What could he tell them? That Pete had fed his wife some poison, a concoction made from autumn crocus bulbs, and then drunk some himself?

'It really would help me.' The doctor glanced at the nurse behind the desk – anxiously, Brian reckoned.

'I think they may have eaten some bulbs by mistake in a salad. They must have thought they were shallots or spring onions or something ...' Brian's voice cracked at his lie.

'What bulbs? Please calm down, Mr Young. What bulbs? Not onions, surely.'

'Flower bulbs,' said Brian.

'What flower?' The doctor raised his eyebrows to the nurse, who shrugged.

'Autumn crocus bulbs,' Brian gasped out. 'Autumn crocus.'

'But it is not autumn, Mr Young.'

'I know it's not autumn,' Brian said with a sigh, 'but they've eaten autumn crocus bulbs. Autumn crocus are different from the usual crocus you get in spring. Autumn crocus aren't even really crocus, they're something different – lilies, I think.'

'OK, Mr Young. Please calm down. Our toxicology team are run off their feet at the moment, there are so many patients being admitted with symptoms of poisoning. I have sent for the consultant toxicologist, but in the meantime I will see what I can find out myself.'

Brian stood by the desk and watched the white-coated doctor disappear through the door to an A&E ward.

Dr Singh sat down at his desk and stared at the computer screen. With not much hope of finding anything useful, he entered 'autumn crocus' in the search engine, and found a link to 'Colchicum autumnale'. 'Colchicum autumnale is most commonly known as autumn crocus. It is native to Europe, a perennial herb in the lily family. The bulb can unfortunately be mistaken for a wild onion.'

This was unfamiliar to Dr Singh, and he quickly scanned over the rest of the text until he spotted a reference to 'colchicine poisoning'. The doctor knew of colchicine as a treatment of gout, but against his expectations he seemed to have found something useful. He clicked on the link to this information and read on.

'Colchicine poisoning is rare but serious. It can be potentially fatal, and there is currently no available antidote.' He read a case report, his eyes racing over this information. 'Liver injury ... rapid organ failure ... Gastro-enteritis ... Unpredictable outcome from patients suspected of colchicine intoxication.'

Dr Singh sighed, and telephoned to reception. 'Dr Singh here, nurse. Would you please tell Mr Young to go home, if he is still here ... He is? ... Tell him there is nothing he can do by waiting. We will do all we can, but it will be some time before we will know the outcome ... Thank you, nurse.'

The nurse relayed the message to Brian, who reluctantly agreed to go home. Thanking the nurse, he walked out into the dark frosty evening, to locate his van in the car park.

Dr Singh called the nurses' station on his ward. 'About Mr and Mrs Wilson, the patients with symptoms of a different poisoning ... Yes ... I shall have to refer these patients urgently to Dr Sillence or one of her team. This is a new poison, not the substance seen in the other cases. We'll need some expertise if we are to save them.'

Chapter 17

Ernie had never expected Willbury to feature so much on the radio and television news, even though he remembered Brian and Richard speculating on the media coverage they hoped for. He returned to his kitchen to read more. The newspapers were full of articles about Willbury and its mystery illness. He had gone down to PK News to pick up a national paper to read its front-page story. 'An epidemic,' it said. 'Another victim has died.'

Yesterday's *Willbury Reporter* was positively revelling in it. 'How can this be happening?' the *Reporter* asked. 'The hospital is at full stretch.' Ernie read on. 'More operations have been cancelled. The NHS cannot cope. Are they using this epidemic as an excuse? Do consultants do too much private work? Nurses should be paid much more. The NHS is collapsing.' Ernie sneered and tutted as he read.

The MP for Willbury, Jane Hopkins, was making use of her frequent opportunities to appear on television. Ernie had seen her on a morning news programme, when she had assured her constituents that she would get answers for them quickly. She had added that she was confident the Tories could do no better in the unusual circumstances, and nor would the Liberal Democrats.

Ernie's thoughts drifted back to that terrible moment last week when Brian had come to tell him that Pete and

Liz Wilson had died within hours of each other during the night. Brian had sat in Ernie's cold lounge and sobbed out the dreadful news he had brought from the hospital. He had refused a cup of tea and only stayed a few minutes, just long enough to tell Ernie.

'You get yourself back home, Brian. And thanks for coming round.' Ernie could almost feel Brian's pain. 'I agree with you, mate. Enough is enough. There'll be no more pest control from now on.'

Distraught, Ernie had watched from the window of his flat as Brian climbed clumsily back into his van and drove away.

Yesterday morning Ernie had gone down to the allotments to chit his seed potatoes, laying out the tubers under the shed window to sprout. When the chits had formed, he would plant them out. It should have been done by now, he knew. He didn't really think a week or two late would hurt. He had sown his peas in a length of old guttering in his cold frame. They seemed to be growing well and he decided he might as well plant them out. He had picked up this tip from a gardening programme on the television. You merely had to dig a shallow trough similar in size to the guttering, slide the length of compost with its growing peas straight into the trough and press down the soil around the compost. A good tip, and he had followed it ever since. He had also potted up some of his fuchsia cuttings and a few pelargoniums. Grace had loved fuchsias. He had finished the few jobs he had promised himself to do before he went to the church this afternoon.

He took his only suit from the walnut-veneered wardrobe in his bedroom. Plain grey: the day he bought it, Grace had told him it would be smart in most circumstances. He found his black tie, a bit crumpled but he hoped no one would notice. Ernie stared at the tired old face in the mirror. Grey suit, white shirt, black tie. He couldn't remember ever attending a double funeral. He had worn this suit to Grace's funeral and he had wanted to follow her since. His only daughter was no comfort, his only grandson even less. *At least Pete and Liz are going together*, he thought as he straightened his tie. *I should have liked that.* He pulled his tie knot tighter, trying to disguise the fact that the shirt collar was loose on his neck now.

The new vicar had not known either Peter or Elizabeth. He expressed his condolences to their daughters, sons-in-law and families. 'We all have to die some time when God calls us but he doesn't generally call husband and wife together.' Sally and Vanessa, the vicar informed the congregation, had told him how much pleasure their dad had derived from his garden and allotment. At this, Brian squeezed Debbie's hand even harder. He could not explain to her how these deaths had happened. When she asked, he'd said only that he was as puzzled as she was, and Debbie had accepted this. Later that day she told him she didn't think she would ever see him cry at a funeral.

'I've known them both a long time,' Brian responded, briefly but truthfully. 'Most of my life,' he added quietly.

Richard Owen-Davies did not bring his wife, and only told her he would go along to pay his respects. As the two coffins stood side by side at the front of the church, he finally recognised his intense feeling of guilt and responsibility. This would weigh on him increasingly in the following days. He would avoid the allotment for over a week, unable to come to terms with its secrets, the secrets of what they had done – what he personally had caused. The deaths of Pete and Liz were his fault, he came to realise.

Nobody had heard Bill's baritone singing voice before, and he used it to good effect with the two hymns. Most people mumbled or mimed these days, but Bill sang out heartily. Sally and Vanessa both noticed. 'The big man, yes, one of dad's allotment friends,' they agreed later. Brian they already knew, and he introduced Richard, Bill and Ernie as their dad's allotment friends. Each man had squirmed inwardly with guilty complicity when expressing his condolences to Pete's daughters.

The police were already investigating a number of suspicious deaths as well as the non-fatal poisonings. A family of six had been poisoned, fatally in the case of two children. A husband and wife had also died, and members of two other families were seriously ill. Among other victims were several individuals from a public house including the cleaner; a moneylender who lived over a shop; customers of a bar in town; and many inmates as well as staff in the prison. The survivors could not explain their illnesses. Willbury General's consultant toxicologist, Dr Helen Sillence, announced that two separate poisons had been identified – *Atropa belladonna*, commonly known as deadly nightshade, and a more lethal substance, colchicine, from a plant named *Colchicum autumnale*. The fact that both were poisons with a botanical background was a mystery.

The prison had more than its share of victims, and its sickbay had overflowed. Three prisoners had died, although apparently healthy young men. Their autopsies revealed, along with the poison they had ingested, a mixture of other drugs already in their bloodstream. How they came to have used heroin and cocaine would provoke calls for yet another inquiry into how easy it seemed to be for inmates to get hold of drugs in prison, and the prison governor would insist upon stricter searches of visitors.

Detective Sergeant Dave Wallis could not help commenting to Detective Constable Barbara Booth, 'It seems somebody is trying to help us out a bit here.'

Dave Wallis was forty-two years old. He knew he would not achieve any higher rank; besides, he would not want it if he was offered it. Barbara Booth was part of a new breed, twenty-eight years old, with a university degree in psychology – and who knows how high she could go? Higher than he ever dreamed of, thought Dave, but he was not resentful. How could he be? He enjoyed working with her and she was pretty. He wouldn't have to do many more years anyway.

Dave could look forward to a decent enough pension and his dream of a bar in Spain, in Torrevieja or thereabouts, he had agreed with his wife. The boys, his two sons, would be in their twenties when he retired and old enough to make up their own minds whether they stayed here or went with their parents to Spain. He could see himself as mine host, a bit of karaoke in the bar in season, a few locals in the winter months. What more could a man want? Sunshine most of the time and no more villains to worry about, no more shift work. Every Christmas Day off.

'The connection I make here,' Dave had confided, 'is villains. One way or another, most of the victims and the addresses are known to us, except for the husband and wife who died. We'll have a nose around the pub first, since we've been given the honour of investigating this mess. The Chief thinks you and me are up to this one, Babs.'

When the two detectives had shared their early thoughts on the case with the Detective Chief Inspector, he was impressed by their observation that there was a connection between the cases, in that most victims were known to the Willbury force. DCI Bob Harris felt confident in having assigned this task to Wallis and Booth. In his office he studied the toxicology reports from the hospital. He would have a word with their own forensics people.

DS Dave Wallis grinned across the police station canteen at his fellow officer. 'What do you think? The pub? A good place to start?'

'Sounds good to me,' DC Booth agreed.

More interesting than most cases, they reckoned, as they pulled out of the garage heading for the Wicket Keeper, a pub they knew well. As Barbara drove, Dave returned to his musings about villains being victims. Was this some kind of vendetta?

DC Booth turned into the car park beside the Wicket Keeper and found a parking space. Dave's reverie was nudged away with the clunk of his partner's driver's door slamming.

She tapped on the side window. 'You coming in or not?'

CHAPTER 18

Richard swallowed hard as be drove past Pete's house and saw the estate agent's board. It had his own name on it: OWEN-DAVIES & BLAGRAVE.

It was the first day since Pete's death that he had felt like going to the allotment and the first time Daphne had ever suggested that he did. That puzzled him, but here he was anyway. Only Bill was there, fire crackling, kettle on.

'Morning, Bill. How are you?'

'A while since we have seen you, Richard. Haven't seen you since' – he hesitated – 'Pete's funeral.'

'No,' agreed Richard wryly. 'Not much to do this time of year, is there?'

'I've still been down here every day,' Bill informed his friend. 'So have Ernie and Brian some days.'

'How are they, Brian and Ernie?'

'Brian is very quiet for him, and Ernie is Ernie. Though somehow Ernie looks older.'

'Seventy-three? Seventy-four?' Richard queried.

'One or the other.'

'How do you feel about the mayhem we caused, Bill? How do you feel about the exercise we've started?' His bushy eyebrows moved in unison.

Bill pondered for a moment, rubbing his unshaven chin. 'I think precisely that we have started' – he emphasised the word 'started' – 'and that we should carry on.'

He continued to rub his chin and eyed Richard almost suspiciously. He had been eager for Richard to come back to the gardening club, and he had also been keen for their pest control not to stop. He was not even sure that Richard would return. 'After all, he's a different class to the rest of us,' Bill had observed to the others.

'Do Brian and Ernie feel the same?' asked Richard.

Bill poured Richard a cup of tea. 'Ernie definitely does. He told me it gave him a purpose in life. He was really positive. Brian's not so positive. Brian's been so quiet I'm not sure what he thinks. He misses Pete, I know … it shows.'

Richard considered the answer. He wanted to continue but he had become less sure about the modus operandi.

'What's your opinion then, Richard? I thought you might not come back, you know, when you didn't show up for a while.' Bill stood over Richard now, clutching a mug in his large hands.

'I'd like to continue, Bill, but I do believe that we can think of something a bit more subtle than poison, a bit less physical from my own part as well. My knee still gives me a twinge to remind me of that.' Richard rubbed at his knee. 'We may be able to come up with other ways of making our point. Other ways of controlling pests.'

Bill beamed, relieved to hear Richard was still keen to participate.

At that moment, they heard Brian's van pull up, and then his voice, addressing somebody outside the shed. Both men strained to hear who Brian was talking to.

'It's only Ernie as well as Brian.' Bill relaxed again, visibly.

The two men came in discussing some new strawberry plants they had ordered between them.

'Time to get them in, Brian,' Ernie was saying.

'Ah, Richard is back!' Brian turned to Ernie as they entered.

'Yes, I am, and how are you two?' Richard smiled cautiously as he watched Brian.

'I'm OK,' murmured Brian.

Ernie went on to reiterate some of Bill's thoughts, that he too had wondered if Richard would return at all. Richard turned both palms upwards at arm's length and shrugged.

'Richard and I were just saying that we want to continue our work, our pest control. Richard was suggesting we should go at it a bit differently in future. Not with poison, that is. Another way. More subtle, he said.' Bill sat down as spoke.

'I'm not sure I want to continue.' Ernie glanced at Brian.

'You, Brian?' asked Bill.

Brian licked a cigarette paper he was holding and looked away. Pete flashed through his thoughts. The funeral. Liz. The two coffins. 'No more …' He tailed off as if he were going to add something but he didn't.

'We should be more discriminating in future.' Richard stood up, his mug cupped in his hands as he surveyed the troops. 'Our targets must be more defined.'

Brian briefly worried about the slightly military terminology. His spell in the army years ago did not bring happy memories of his National Service spent in Cyprus.

'Any ideas then?' Richard asked Bill enthusiastically. 'What about you, Ernie? You told us you had some idea ages ago.'

Ernie's shoulders sagged a little.

'I propose,' said Richard, 'that we go back to where we started. First we should identify the pests. Then we should jointly devise their downfall, one by one.'

Bill got up from his chair. 'It says in a Percy Thrower book I was reading recently, an old but informative book, and I quote: "At first it may seem rather a burden to remember which foes attack particular plants at which season, but surprisingly quickly one finds that all this becomes almost second nature." He said this in his section headed "Pests and Diseases". More Percy Thrower for you: "Look ahead and take preventative measures whenever this is possible. When walking round the garden one should develop the habit of looking for early signs of attack on plants. Pay attention to garden hygiene. Many gardeners pile trouble on their heads because they do not bother to destroy immediately diseased plant material." There you are, Richard. I think we would do well to remember what Percy says. Diseased plants are our targets, and we should destroy them as soon as we see the trouble they cause. So let us put specific weevils, aphids, caterpillars ...' He hesitated at this point. 'This is what Percy Thrower was telling us about our own weevils, etcetera. Pests.'

Bill held a mug of nearly cold tea to his lips. His back to the others, he walked over to the bench, filled a kettle and returned it to the gas ring.

'The scum who stabbed the owner of my paper shop's wife, let's try to find him,' offered Ernie.

Brian looked up at Ernie. 'What did we say, Ernie?'

'Come on, Brian, we can't stop now for Pete's sake,' Ernie retorted.

'Hang on, hang on, fellas. I'm not so sure. It didn't seem so wrong when we first talked this way. Pests and slugs and snails. But it's more than just silly talk now. Worse. People have died. Ernie, you were not so keen when we talked this morning. I'd thought it would be a bit of fun or just talk, but it's gone too far for me. I know I'm as much to blame as the rest of you so far, but enough is enough. Well, it is for me. Bloody leatherjackets and weevils ... Fucking nonsense. And wrong.'

'Yeah, but ...' Ernie began. 'Willbury needs us.'

'Come on, Brian. We need you more now,' Richard interrupted. 'They haven't gone away, you know.'

'We are all the gardening club,' Bill pronounced.

'We understand how you feel about Peter, Brian.' Richard gently placed a hand on Brian's sleeve.

Brian looked from one to the other. He could feel his resolve evaporating again.

'For Pete's sake,' Ernie repeated.

'But we are just five ...' He corrected himself. '... Four silly old men who talked too much and somehow found themselves doing ridiculous things to people ... All this nonsense about slugs and weevils seemed more like ... well ... a joke.' Brian's voice tailed off.

'No joke, Brian, not at all.' Bill stood over Brian. 'We have a job unfinished.'

'What about Mr Athwal's wife ... you know, at the paper shop, Brian?' Ernie spoke quietly, ignoring Bill. 'Nobody has been arrested for that yet.'

Brian turned to Ernie. 'I'm not sure.'

'Leave him for now, Ernie,' Richard instructed. 'He'll make up his own mind.'

Brian rolled a cigarette and lit it, saying nothing.

'Bill, Ernie, any more suggestions?' Richard continued.

All eyes were on Brian. An uneasy silence fell, until Bill finally broke it.

'Percy Thrower could name many more pests if you cared to read him. Cockchafers, leaf-cutters, frog-hoppers, greenfly, blackfly, mice, ants ...' He hesitated. 'Lots more pests to destroy gardens, not forgetting our aphids, leatherjackets and weevils –'

'Stop talking nonsense, Bill!' Brian interrupted. 'Bloody Percy Thrower! What's he got to do with poisoning people?'

'Weevils are the pests who are difficult to see until the damage is done. That's what Percy Thrower said.' Bill looked sullen.

'The drug pushers – they probably escaped Bill's efforts at the pub, those weevils,' Ernie muttered.

'Don't you start, Ern.' Brian glared at Ernie and sighed.

'We agreed to call them weevils,' said Richard, 'because they attack the roots of society.' He spoke aloud as he wrote in his notebook: 'Weevils: chemicals applied.'

'What about the bicycle thieves?' asked Ernie. 'Have they been dealt with? The young 'un and his family have, but what about the brothers from the bike shop, David and Graham Bastin? I know their shop has been fumigated, but what about the brothers themselves? Might be difficult to find them now.'

'It's always difficult to be sure with any pest that one had been completely successful with one's treatment,' Bill said to no one in particular. He had a faraway look in his eyes. 'Cockchafers,' he added.

The others eyed him suspiciously.

'Fat white grubs, larvae of the cockchafer beetle. They live in the soil and feed off fibrous roots of plants. Did you know that, Brian?'

Brian wasn't sure whether he should answer or not, so he didn't.

'Aphids, the *Aphidae*,' Bill continued. 'That's Latin, isn't it, Richard – *Aphidae*?'

He didn't wait for an answer. The others glanced around, questioning each other with their looks.

Bill was not to be deterred. 'Small insects in vast groups sucking the juices of plants ... Greenfly, blackfly, whitefly ... their colour irrelevant but the damage the same.'

Brian nudged Ernie and winked, nodding in Bill's direction. Bill seemed undaunted and unheeding of the others, as though lost somewhere. Brian lit a cigarette.

'The *Tipulidae* family with their tough-skinned larvae, who turn into reasonable creatures on maturity. The young of the cranefly live under the soil, wreaking all sorts of destruction to roots, but when mature do no harm at all. Slugs and snails, on the other hand, cause enormous visible damage to plants, particularly young fresh ones, as any gardener knows. As we know, Brian, and you, Ernie, and you, Richard.' As he named them, Bill looked at each man in turn.

Richard cleared his throat and began to join in. 'Like caterpillars –'

'Yes, Richard, I know those too, and yet they can turn into such beautiful creatures when mature butterflies. But the young do harm.'

Richard looked irritated and tried again. 'What about the sawfly larvae, Bill? Those can turn a leaf into a mere skeleton.'

He sat back in his chair momentarily and then leaned forward again.

'What about your roses? You must get trouble from leaf-cutter bees, or leaf-hoppers and their larvae. Ant armies and even birds can do harm. Not to mention mice and rats. Nowhere is safe with all these troublemakers in the garden.'

Bill turned to Richard alone. 'Eelworms. Thrips. Wireworms.'

Richard was now eye to eye with Bill, although the fact he was sitting and Bill standing was giving him a stiff neck. 'Narcissus flies,' he said.

'Frog-hoppers,' Bill added.

'Leaf-miners,' Richard countered.

'Cuckoo spit,' retorted Bill.

'That's from frog-hoppers,' Richard pointed out.

'Red spider mites on fruit trees then.' Bill glared at Richard. 'Nowhere is safe with this amount of potential troublemakers wishing you ill in the garden. Remember all the other diseases that can affect healthy plants too.'

Brian, a twinkle in his eye, clapped his hands together loudly to stop the duel.

'Come on, you two ... Bill, Richard. Haven't we had enough of pests and disease?'

He looked to Ernie for support.

Ernie nodded almost imperceptibly. 'Yes, we know ... we know. Thank you for reminding us.'

Brian winked at Ernie. 'Did anybody see the match on telly last night? Fantastic game!'

Nobody answered. The shed fell silent, with all eyes on Bill. His forehead glowed, his eyes were wide, his wispy white hair was less disciplined than usual. He glared at his fellow gardeners, the surviving members of the gardening club.

'I think you're going soft, my friends.' Bill's voice was clear and loud, with a bitter tinge. 'You say you want to choose specific targets. Does that mean you want to reduce our war on pests? I do not agree. The whole idea was to take the battle all over Willbury to make our statement – wherever we could. To make them think about their own actions. To destroy those that harm or kill others. I for one won't stop now. My life till now was ineffectual. Nobody knew I existed. They walked over me, used me, exploited me. Now I've found a way of getting back. I may not live too much longer, and so I'll do everything I can to destroy pests. I have –'

Brian interrupted Bill's flow. 'Hang on, Bill. You're getting carried away.'

Richard agreed. 'Yes, steady on, my friend. We can't take action as indiscriminately as we have.'

Ernie in turn looked uneasy, unsure of Bill's growing zeal. He had known him for many years, a quiet man like himself, insignificant despite his size. This was a different Bill that he studied on this dank winter's morning in the gloom of their communal shed. A gentle giant, many had observed. All his fellow allotment holders had used the well-worn description at some time or other. That was how they thought of him. A gentle giant, a bit lonely, a grower of chrysanthemums.

Bill looked angry at the interruptions to his soliloquy. 'What's up with you? Don't you want to make a difference?' he snapped. He glared from one to the other. 'You, Brian, your best mate – don't you want revenge for him? You, Ernie, you've never in your life done anything useful. As for you, Richard, you have taken a well-paid living from this country. Do you want to see it go down the drain, taken over by yobs, hooligans, criminals, cheats, scum, druggies, foreigners, liars, bastards, people who want to give nothing and receive all? The police don't care. They whinge about their lack of resources and men. They hide in their offices and cars. Some are as bad as the ones they can't be bothered with. The namby-pamby social workers who are conned so easily by scum – they can't protect those they are paid to protect. Their salaries are money by deceit, so the bullies and the cheats can prevail.'

Bill Choules could not be stopped. His hands gesticulated wildly, and a trickle of saliva ran from the corner of his mouth.

'Look at the people who're supposed to protect us. The do-gooders, the soft liberals who've allowed this town to become the cesspit we live in. The well-heeled politicians, indifferent to the damage, more concerned with lining their own pockets. The company directors with their huge obscene pay packets. The pornographers fêted by politicians preaching one set of values, while living by another, feathering their own nest, several large homes each. Look at the judges, lenient towards the scum that come before them. Rapists and child molesters given psychiatric help and not punishment.' He was almost shouting now, the others fearful of interrupting him, allowing him to go on. 'They say, "Try to understand them, not punish them." No help for the decent people, no help for the weak. Asylum-seekers coming through so many other countries to get to ours. To cheat our system, get houses and money –'

'Whoa, Bill, you're getting yourself worked up.' Richard was the first to dare to interrupt. 'Calm down, man.'

'Calm down?' Bill growled back, his eyes bulging in Richard's direction. 'Well, if you people are not going to help, if you people can't be bothered, I will have to continue on my own.'

In silence he buttoned his coat, strode out and slammed the shed door behind him, leaving the three other men wide-eyed and dumbfounded.

'Well,' said Richard, breaking the ensuing hush. 'What have we set fire to in Bill? He frightens me. I didn't expect that tirade from Bill of all people.'

Brian blew a large cloud of cigarette smoke deliberately and noisily out of his pursed mouth. 'Bloody hell.'

Ernie studied the floor before raising his eyes to view the other two men. 'I can't say I disagree entirely with him.'

Brian and Richard shared a glance before looking back at Ernie.

'If we're not to arouse interest in ourselves, we'll have to be more measured than I fear Bill wants to be. It worries me that that amount of anger will make him careless about how he behaves and what he does. He seems to have gone ...' Richard Owen-Davies stopped himself from finishing the sentence.

Brian and Ernie thought they knew the word Richard was about to use. *Mad*, thought Brian.

'Do we make our own detailed plans now or what?' Ernie seemed unsure of himself.

'Well, I'm going home for now,' announced Richard.

'Me too,' said Brian. 'I've had enough of weevils and the like. It's become ridiculous. A shambles. A catastrophic shambles! Bloody pests, huh!'

Ernie turned the gas ring off and checked the stove for safety. They all left the shed silently, each lost in thought about Bill's ravings, each wondering where this might lead. Perhaps pest control needed control.

As Bill cycled away from the allotment, he hummed a stirring military march noisily to himself.

CHAPTER 19

DS Wallis stood at the empty bar of the Wicket Keeper pub. It was too early for opening. Unseen by Dave Wallis, the landlord shifted his feet, hidden by the bar between them. The temporary cleaner the landlord had hired after the poisoning busied herself at DS Wallis's side, cleaning tables and putting out ashtrays.

DC Booth sipped the coffee that Betty, the landlady, had produced.

DS Wallis repeated his earlier questions. 'So you've no idea who could have managed to bring poison into your premises, sir? No strangers? No oddballs? Nothing unusual? Nothing out of the ordinary? Are you sure neither of you can add anything, sir?'

The landlord shook his head again. 'Nothing at all.'

Dave turned to his partner. 'Well, we'll have to leave it for now. DC Booth, when you've finished your coffee ...'

The unmarked Ford Focus pulled up outside number 37 Wycliff Road. Both detectives had visited this house before for various reasons. The father, Steve Johnson, was a well-known villain, and his wife's son, Jason Kelly, had lately attracted their interest even more at this address.

DC Barbara Booth rang the bell beside the grubby door, DC Wallis standing close behind her.

A stocky, balding middle-aged man opened the door.

'Mr Johnson?' Dave Wallis enquired. 'I'm DS Wallis and this is DC Booth.'

'What do you filth want? Don't you think we've got enough trouble. Two children dead, all of us ill – and here you are at my door instead of catching the bastards who did it to us.'

Dave sighed aloud. 'We just want to ask you some questions.'

Barbara Booth showed her warrant card. 'Mr Johnson, I know who you are and what's happened, so there's no need for that kind of talk. We're here to see if you can help us find who did this to you and your family.' Barbara put as much sympathy into her voice as she could affect. 'Would you like us to come in and discuss it, sir? We're here to help, if we can.'

'Yeah, all right,' Steve Johnson agreed, his voice surly. 'Come in, both of you. Wipe your feet, though.' Reluctantly he stood back from the door to let them in.

Barbara stepped into the small hallway, thinking, *And I'll wipe them on the way out as well.* Dave made the same observation when they got back into their car a short while later.

'No help there, then. So evasive to every question we put to them.' He snapped the seat belt buckle into its socket. 'Waste of time, that lot.'

'Where to now then, Sarge?'

'We can perhaps find out more from the Indian shopkeeper. Gary Beesley's been arrested for stabbing his wife, so perhaps he'll be more helpful than Johnson and his family. Perhaps he might know something about his neighbour, Alfred Sutton, the old moneylender who lived over the hairdresser's next door to him. He was another victim of the poisonings. He died, you know.'

'Yeah, I know, Sarge.'

'It's Dave, not Sarge, when we're on our own, Babs.'

DC Booth put the car into gear and the Ford Focus headed towards the parade of shops across town. They parked opposite and went into PK News first.

'How is your wife, Mr Athwal?' DC Booth asked the newsagent.

'She is doing fine.' Anil's eyes misted slightly. 'It is difficult to get to the cash-and-carry without her help. I have to ask my son to help out. He doesn't like to be in the shop, but he helps. I do not like to interrupt his studies. We will be glad when my wife is strong again. It's just the shock, you know.'

Dave Wallis was direct. 'You knew Mr Sutton, the old man who lived above Cut & Curl? As you've doubtless read in the newspapers here, he was one of many people who were all poisoned at around the same time. He was not the only one to die, though most were only ill. Two children were also among the fatalities. We believe these cases are connected, and we're hoping someone … maybe you, sir … can give us some clue as to that connection.'

Barbara absentmindedly read the headlines on the papers in front of her on the counter.

'I heard about old Mr Sutton,' Anil Athwal replied, 'but I knew him only by sight. They said he was a money-lender, and I used to see people ringing his bell, and going up the stairs to his flat. But they always hurried inside, so I never got a good look at them. Anyway I would have nothing to do with a man like that. Before my wife and I came to this country –'

Dave cut in, 'So you saw no one hanging around? Nothing to account for how he came to be poisoned?'

Anil shook his head. 'No, we only saw the ambulance arrive that day. It was a shock. My son Raj and his friend Jai go into the public house where they also had this trouble. He was not ill, nor was Jai. But he was in there the night before it all began. I read in the *Willbury Reporter* about all these sick people at the hospital, so I know some people died as a result of the same illness.'

DC Booth looked up from the morning papers. 'You say your son was in the Wicket Keeper the night before, Mr Athwal?'

'Yes, I don't like him going in there. It is not a nice place. I don't like him drinking alcohol, but what can I do? The young are different. When I left India and came to this country with no money, all I had time for was work –'

'Yes, yes, I can understand,' DS Wallis interrupted the shopkeeper before he could relate his whole life history.

'Where is your son now?' DC Booth brought Anil Athwal back to the present day.

'He went to the university this morning. He could get away about eleven o'clock, he told me.' The newsagent glanced over his shoulder at the clock above the rack of cigarettes behind him. 'Yes, he will be here any minute, so that I can go to the cash-and-carry.'

'We'll wait then if we may, Mr Athwal. But can you tell us anything you may have noticed at about that time, anything unusual happening in the vicinity of these shops?' Barbara Booth waved her hand in a sweep towards the shop front.

Anil Athwal smiled to himself. 'When I go to bed I hear nothing. The hours I am in the shop, the long hours I work, I do not stir one bit until my alarm clock goes off at five o'clock. I hear the young people hanging around the front of the shops sometimes ... their swearing and shouting and their noisy radios. I hear them before I go to bed. I normally wait till they have gone before I go to bed, to make sure they do not try to get in the back of the shop. They try sometimes. They always gather near my shop after I have closed. Summer and winter the same, nothing else to do. Filthy mess they leave. Bottles and rubbish I have to tidy up every morning at the front of my shop. I even find condoms in the doorway sometimes. Filthy beasts.' He finally answered the question. 'No, I saw nothing unusual.'

At that moment, Raj came in through the front of the shop. Nice-looking, Barbara considered. Smart, clean-cut and tall. Lovely big brown eyes.

Mr Athwal was speaking to his son in a language the police officers could not understand. Barbara thought it might be Hindi.

'Yes, Dad,' Raj answered in English. He shook hands with both officers. 'We've been interviewed about the attack on my mother in this shop. We do hope you can convict the man you've arrested.'

His father had presumably explained who they were, but not the purpose of their visit.

'We're not working on your mother's case,' Dave Wallis informed him. 'We're here about the mass poisoning in this part of town. In particular the old bloke who died next door, a Mr Sutton, in the flat above Cut & Curl.' He explained to the son the circumstances he had described to his father.

Barbara looked into the brown eyes that she found so attractive. 'The night before the cases of poisoning began to occur, your father tells us you were in the Wicket Keeper pub with your friend.'

'Yes, with Jai,' Raj agreed.

Barbara continued, 'The people in the pub who were taken ill either worked there or were customers at lunchtime. We are trying to establish what connection, if any, there is between the various groups of people who were poisoned.'

'I'm training to be a pharmacist,' said Raj, 'so I understood the reports in the papers. Atropine was apparently the main poison that caused the illnesses, certainly for the people in the Wicket Keeper, and old Mr Sutton. Atropine is a substance that comes from what you would call the deadly nightshade plant, *Atropa belladonna*. It has several pharmaceutical uses. Most often it's used in eyedrops for dilating the pupils in examinations of the eye. But, in some of the cases where there were deaths, I read that blood tests found another poison, colchicine, which is also of botanical origin.'

Barbara was impressed. Dave Wallis joined in, even though he could see his partner was pursuing a line of thought.

'You seem to know something about poison, young man.'

'Of course I do,' agreed Raj. 'That's part of my studies, of course.'

After his father had left for the wholesalers, Raj told the police officers what had happened in the pub that night when the fight had broken out between the black and white drugs gangs.

'They knocked over an old guy, and he fell down and bruised his hip. He was badly shaken up, so Jai and I walked him home, to make sure he got back safely.'

'This old man, do you know him?' Barbara asked quickly.

'Yes, well, sort of. He's a regular customer in the shop. My dad knows him. He's a builder, I think ... or he was ... he's retired now, I believe. Brian Young is his name. My dad likes him, says he's a nice man. Mr Young always makes jokes when he comes in here.'

'Do you happen to know where he lives?'

'Yes, I do actually. I found out when we walked him home.' Raj scribbled the address on the back of a till receipt and handed it to Barbara.

'Thank you, Raj. You've been very helpful. Can you think of anything more that may assist us?'

Raj thought for a moment. 'No, I can't. But, if these were the poisons found, it strikes me as interesting that both are derived from plants, not chemicals or minerals. That's unusual. The plants have to grow somewhere. Deadly nightshade is not very common, I understand. Who would want something as poisonous as that in their garden? Perhaps if you can find where it's growing it will provide some clues.'

Even DS Wallis was impressed with this suggestion. It was definitely something worth considering. They both thanked Raj for his help, and Barbara expressed her hopes that his mother would be soon be fully re-covered. Then she felt Dave tug her sleeve and saw the impatient look in his eyes. She knew that look. *Enough*, it said. She hadn't worked alongside DS Wallis for long but she was already beginning to understand how he reacted.

They left the young man to his father's shop.

'Thank goodness the shop was quiet,' Barbara observed. 'Not one customer while we were in there. Does the business pay?' she wondered aloud, more to herself than to her partner.

'We'd better have a quick word with the hairdresser's next door before we go,' Dave said, staring up at the flat above Cut & Curl.

Half an hour later they were back in the Ford Focus, feeling at last that they had a few leads to follow up.

'I didn't think they would be much help in there,' Dave remarked. 'But it was interesting what they had to say about disgruntled customers calling on Alfred Sutton. It might pay us to look through his records and customer details. Certainly sounds like he collected a few enemies. Nasty piece of work from the hairdressers' description of him. You get the chief to get us access when we get back, Barbara.' Dave stroked his chin in thought.

'Will do, Sarge ... er, I mean Dave,' replied DC Booth.

'Next, I think, we go and have a word with this Mr Young. If he's a retired builder, he'll be old Mr Young.'

Dave laughed at his own joke. Barbara didn't. She was attempting to make sense of a particular set of thoughts that were beginning to form a connection.

Chapter 20

Bill Choules turned up the volume on his hi-fi. His normal preference was opera but this mid-morning he had found some of his father's old mono long-playing vinyl records, mostly famous marches – mainly recordings of military bands, the Coldstream Guards Band among others. Bill watched the needle arm rise and fall gently. He usually preferred more romantic melodies from opera – Rossini, Verdi or Puccini – but today this more strident music suited his mood. When he returned home he had felt a compulsion to put some music on. He skipped both of his mother's Nat King Cole LPs, presents he himself had bought for her many years ago. She would play them sometimes when his father was out at his allotment on Sunday mornings as she prepared his favourite dinner, roast beef, always beef. Bill ignored his own vast LP collection too.

No Beethoven's *Für Elise* today, he snarled to himself. He had let out a hideous, disgusted laugh at this thought. His head felt as though it was bursting. He shook it from side to side in disbelief and anger towards his fellow gardening club members and their weakness. As far as Bill was concerned, they had betrayed the cause. 'No, Herr Beethoven, you will not soothe me today. I refuse to act weak and watery as they are. Specific targets, huh!' He ground his dentures, his jaws aching, unaware or not caring about the saliva that trickled from his mouth. A whitish foam formed on his large lips. His bloodshot eyes bulged with inner rage.

Bill forked one pickled onion after another into his mouth. Ernie's annual gift of jars of picked onions had been still unopened in his sparse cupboard. This was all he could find to assuage his hunger. He chomped noisily on one after the other, the sharp vinegar stinging his tongue. He forked in the next onion before he'd swallowed the previous one. Vinegar was splashing from the jar over his already stained trousers. Bill Choules was oblivious to these details of decorum. He returned to his kitchen cupboard for another jar, its small handwritten label recording the date the shallots had been bottled. The band boomed its music from the speakers. 'William hungry,' he muttered as he twisted the lid off and threw it across the room. Then he returned to the kitchen larder, took out a dry hunk of yellow cheese, Canadian Cheddar, although the 'use by' date had expired seven days ago. He would not have cared even if he had noticed. The big man bit a corner from it and pushed another pickled onion in behind it. 'William hungry,' he muttered again, while particles of half-chewed cheese and onions fell on to his chin. 'I'll show them,' he told the military band as he turned the LP over and set the stylus on the edge with a large trembling hand. He marched up and down the small back room, his music room, his long arms swinging high, his long legs making small steps, up and down, up and down, stopping occasionally to stoke up with some more cheese or onion.

The two police officers, DC Booth and DS Wallis, were standing at a front door after having lunch in the Handy

Diner café. Barbara Booth, having refused the sausage, egg and chips preferred by her partner, had chosen instead a poached egg on wholemeal toast.

'Afternoon, sir.' Dave Wallis spoke cheerily to the man who had just opened the door. 'Are you Brian Young?' They both held out their ID cards for him to see.

'Yes, that's me,' Brian said cautiously.

'Do you mind if we come in a minute?'

'What for?' Brian's heart rate was speeding up, and he half feared the police officers could detect it.

'We would just like a few words about an incident that happened in the Wicket Keeper pub recently,' Wallis explained.

Barbara studied the old man's face. Was it her imagination or were there signs of relief in the weather-beaten features before her. Did his expression change? Did his facial muscles relax a little? She thought she had spotted the almost imperceptible signs she had been trained to observe.

'Yeah, yeah, but I don't want any fuss. I didn't even report anything. I was OK. No bother.' He stepped sideways and backwards from the front door to invite them in. 'I don't want to make a fuss about it ... it was nothing.'

The three sat down in the comfortable lounge. DC Booth couldn't help noticing how modern the décor looked, not quite what she had expected to see, judging from the man she had followed in.

Brian rolled a cigarette and eyed the detectives across his lounge. 'What can I tell you?' He peered over his hands as he licked the gummed Rizla edge.

Wallis would take this one first, he had decided, as they pulled up outside the house. It hadn't been very difficult to establish that this was the right Mr Young, the customer the young Asian had mentioned.

'Just tell us what happened, that's all.'

'I don't want to make any formal complaint. I just happened to get bowled over. It was more like an accident, when the white bloke went for the black one.' Brian explained about the jukebox – how the two black youths had been teasing him. 'Not nasty, just taking the piss really. I'm used to that sort of thing. They meant me no harm.' He described the fight when the white gang had arrived, and he told them how the young Asian student and his friend had helped him up and sat with him for a while.

'Do you know about the poisonings locally?' DC Booth interrupted, ignoring his story.

'What I've seen on the news and in the *Reporter* – of course I do. Big news for Willbury.' His heart fluttered uncomfortably.

Again Barbara thought there was an odd look on Brian's face, *fleeting*, she registered, *a mere twitch*. Was he telling all he knew? She wasn't sure he was.

Brian, though he felt slightly uneasy, reassured himself they couldn't possibly connect him with the poisonings. It was Mr Athwal's son who had pointed the police in his direction, because of the fight in the Wicket Keeper. Just pure coincidence, he reasoned to himself.

'You don't work these days then, Mr Young?' Barbara asked with a smile.

'No, I don't. My days of climbing scaffolding and freezing my nuts off are over. My fingers cracked every winter.' Brian gave a wry grin and turned both palms towards her. 'I do some small jobs in the summer – garden walls, that sort of thing.' 'What do you do with your spare time then?'

Brian laughed. 'All my time is spare now.' The laugh made him cough, and his face reddened.

'How do you spend your days?' she persisted. Was he being evasive? She had a nagging suspicion that he was, but she wasn't sure. This nice old bloke couldn't be a poisoner, could he?

'I've got an allotment near here. I go there sometimes and I do my garden here, and that's about all. Watch a bit of daytime TV if I'm really bored.'

'Why do you want the extra work of an allotment at your age?' DC Booth had become alert at the mention of an allotment. It reminded her of Raj's comments about the poisons, that they were from plants, including deadly nightshade. *The plants have to grow somewhere*, Raj had said. 'What do you grow there?' she asked Brian.

'Oh, I grow mainly vegetables there. My wife likes us to have grass and flowers here at home.' He nodded in the direction of the back garden. 'So I use the allotment for vegetables. I've had it for years. The allotment that is.' Brian looked puzzled.

'Bit cold this time of year, for gardening.'

'Oh, we don't get cold. I've got mates down there. We share a shed with a wood-burning stove and a little gas ring to boil the kettle. Our little home-from-home. We have a cup of tea, have a chat about this and that.'

Dave Wallis couldn't imagine how this line was getting them anywhere but Barbara persisted.

'What do gardeners do at this time of year, especially on an allotment?'

'There are a few jobs gardeners have to do in the winter – preparation, that sort of thing.' Brian leaned forward to stub out his cigarette.

Barbara was not familiar with 'that sort of thing.' She hadn't realised that allotments still existed. Her grand-dad had had one. She remembered him telling her about it when she was little, before he died when she was twelve or so.

'So where is this allotment?'

Dave Wallis let her continue. Something intrigued his young partner, and it was warm and comfortable here in this house. The Detective Sergeant was more concerned that his eyelids were becoming heavy, and it was so warm that he might just fall asleep.

Brian explained where The Elms allotments were before he asked casually, 'What has this got to do with anything?'

DC Booth caught something in the old man's eyes. Then she turned to her partner, saving him from his dread of drifting into sleep.

'Detective Sergeant Wallis, are you with us?' she asked him with a knowing grin.

'I was relieved you spoke to me then,' he told her afterwards as they returned to the car, glad of the cold air on his face. He inhaled hard and took a large gulp of air through his mouth to clear the fuzziness that had been forming in his brain. 'I might well have nodded off any minute.'

'I could see that,' his partner agreed.

Barbara Booth turned at the gate. The old bricklayer was still standing at his open front doorway watching the detectives.

'Bye then, Mr Young. Thanks for your help. Stay out of trouble.'

Brian chuckled weakly at her joke and half raised a hand in a wave.

Barbara hesitated. Was there a reaction?

Back in the unmarked Ford Focus, she explained her inner suspicions to Wallis.

'I can't fully explain. I just sensed that he might not be telling us something. Nothing in particular, but something made me think he was uneasy.'

Dave Wallis interrupted her thoughts as he settled in his seat and clicked his seat belt into its socket. 'Most old blokes react like that to us, especially his type, building trade workers. It's just part of them not wanting to have anything to do with the police.'

'I'm not so sure that explains what's going round in my brain.' She put the car into gear. 'It's more than that, Sarge. I keep remembering what Raj told us about the poisons having botanical origins. *The plants have to grow somewhere*, hc said. I think we should go and have a look at these allotments – see what Mr Young is growing there.'

'As you please,' Dave said, sliding lower into the passenger seat. 'Won't do any good, though.'

As soon as the car was out of sight, Brian phoned Richard and then Ernie.

CHAPTER 21

Daphne Owen-Davies prided herself on her looks. She was, indeed, always fashionably dressed, always well groomed. Her blond hair, she considered, took at least ten years from her age of sixty. People had told her this often.

She pulled up her shiny red Mazda MX5 behind her son's main office. She was very proud that Oliver had done so well for himself. His company had grown quickly during the last property boom. Oliver's estate agency was just the sort of business she had once hoped would interest Richard. Still, that was long ago. Her aspirations for Richard to make money had long since evaporated.

'Once a civil servant, always a civil servant,' he had always replied whenever she tried to get him to consider resigning. 'I'm not for changing.' Daphne had long ago given up trying, concentrating instead on her children and finding a life of her own, once Oliver and Roberta had left home to go their own ways.

It seemed fair to her that, after helping Bobbie financially to set up her dance school, she should give Oliver assistance too. Of course he knew brokers galore who would readily arrange finance, but she could at least help with money to buy houses for development. In this way, mother and son had set up in business together. He was ambitious and he made friends with people who were useful to his business. The solicitors he knew often put probate houses, ripe for modernisation, through his agency for sale. These had become a good resource for their joint venture. His own estate agency of course provided a steady source of properties he could under-value a little. His clients were pleased when a customer who came to view their property – it was usually a widow – made such a quick decision to buy. The same explanation had satisfied the house sellers so often.

'Why not take the offer?' Oliver would suggest to the vendor. 'Yes, I know it's very quick but it's for the full asking price. We pride ourselves on only sending quality purchasers. We work hard at identifying which proper-ties may suit our potential buyers. You're benefiting from our expertise.'

This was the pitch he had used so many times now. It nearly always seemed to work. Occasionally he had been forced to reduce his commission rate slightly, to appease the more aggressive sellers, but the profits from the refurbishments were significant enough to warrant sacri-ficing some commission. The vendors who complained about paying a fee for so little work when a property sold quickly could always be persuaded with a discount. There were always plenty of builder-developers willing to show their gratitude in a plain fat envelope. He could usually agree a condition to re-sell the refurbished prop-erty too, enabling the agency to profit a second time, while he and his mother prospered ever more.

Oliver's business partner, David Blagrave, had some-times complained that Oliver was far too generous in discounting their company's commissions. 'No need to retrospectively discount, just because we have sold so quickly,' David would argue at the monthly sales meetings. Oliver Owen-Davies's business partner did not complain too hard or long, though. Not when Oliver seemed to have this knack of getting so many fast sales compared to David's or those of any of their sales staff. It was company policy for a partner or member of staff to be responsible for seeing each individual sale through to conclusion. Each new property they took on their books was designated to one partner or salesperson.

When Daphne had first given Oliver the capital he had asked for initially, she had no idea how easy it would be to amass so much money. Of course, now she was fully aware how easy it was, and she smiled with satisfaction as she entered her son's office.

'A semi-detached in Glendevon Road, Mother,' Oliver announced from the peace of his private office to the rear of the showroom area where most of his staff had their desks.

All initial enquiries went through Oliver. Everyone understood this rule. It was he who designated who would handle each sale, and even David accepted this.

Oliver leaned back in his swivel chair, his hands clasped behind his head. His mother sat across the desk from him, her legs elegantly crossed.

'Two daughters selling their parents' house. Both parents died of poisoning within days of each other. The husband gave some to the wife and then himself, or so I understand. A gruesome business. Part of the poisonings that have plagued our lovely town of Willbury lately.' Oliver sat forward and rested his elbows on the desktop. 'I think this is just our sort of property, Mother, don't you?' He gazed at his mother's impassive features. 'One of the daughters instructed us only yesterday and I got the impression from her that they are rather anxious to be rid of it quickly.'

'I'm not surprised. Go on.' Daphne raised a well-plucked eyebrow.

'Quite, Mother. It did allow me to undervalue it in the circumstances. You won't have to visit it. They gave me the keys, and I understand they've already taken away whatever personal effects they wanted from the house. They're happy for me to arrange for a sale of the contents. It's a very tidy little semi. We'll have no problem selling it to a deserving widow, I think.'

He smiled and stroked a hand backwards across the top of his head – a mannerism his mother knew meant he was pleased with himself.

'What number Glendevon Road ? I'd better know that at least when I'm signing documents for its purchase.' Daphne uncrossed her legs as she spoke.

'Don't worry, Mother. I'll sort everything out as usual. I'll give it a week or so for credibility, before we accept your offer. I'll keep you informed.'

They chatted for a few more minutes. Daphne declined her son's offer of coffee and kissed him goodbye as he opened the office door for her.

'If you have nothing else for me to go and see, I'll get off to lunch.'

'No, Mother. Nothing else worth buying at present. See you next week.'

Oliver kissed his mother's soft cheek, her familiar floral fragrance lingering in his office as she went.

Daphne loved her little car, even though she could afford much more. The Mercedes Sports she had looked at was just what she would really like, but Richard would no doubt question her ability to pay for it. Ironic, really, that she had found it so easy to talk him into buying the MX5, just as it had been easy enough to explain the updated model a few months ago. The garage had made such a good offer on the old one from the same showroom, 'so little more to find, I can do it myself', she had told him.

She would have got a good offer anyway. Daphne had made the original purchase from his salesman but she had been sleeping with Terry Flynn, the dealership owner, for some years now. If 'sleeping' was the right word, since it was generally daylight when she saw him. A cosy relationship with no ties; a man's ego is so easy to flatter, she had long ago concluded. The villa she had bought just outside Marbella with Terry had been financed from her house purchase dealings with Oliver. She could close her eyes at any time and picture the beautiful view from the terrace there. Of course Richard knew nothing about it, and in any case he disliked the sun. Daphne hated his white legs most of all when she had the misfortune to glimpse them. She had clung to Richard's respectability for so long before the children had left home. Now, however, she sometimes wondered why she stayed with him, but always concluded that it still suited her at present. It was perhaps a habit that was hard to break. She would know when the time was right, if it ever was, to leave Richard.

Daphne had been in awe of Richard's background, his schooling, his parents' obviously comfortable life. It had not been a hard decision to marry him. She even supposed she had really loved him once upon a time.

Today she enjoyed her lunch with Rose, her oldest friend. They air-kissed each other on both cheeks in the restaurant car park and said their goodbyes – 'Same time next week.' She could not have foreseen such a pleasant way of life when she left school at fifteen to work in the local government office as a junior. Still, she had always had her looks. The assistance she had received from the London clinic had helped more recently. She laughed quietly to herself at the knowledge that she had obtained her various treatments at Richard's expense. How would he know she could afford much more herself than he could?

Richard was pulling his Renault out of the drive when she got home. *Strange*, she thought. *He never leaves the house in the afternoons as a rule.* She shrugged as she locked her car.

Roberta Owen-Davies, Bobbie to most of her family, acquaintances and pupils, switched the lights off at her dance school. Her mother had helped her to buy the converted chapel, which the church authorities had instructed her brother to sell. Bobbie was beautiful by any standards: tall and lithe, with a body honed to perfection. Fiona, her special friend and lover, appreciated her good looks. An accident had curtailed Bobbie's professional dancing career but teaching had mostly compensated since. Fiona would comfort her whenever Bobbie had expressed her disappointments. That was how the relationship had started, not long after Bobbie's own dance teacher had explained the physical restrictions that she would never overcome in order to become a professional dancer. Bobbie Owen-Davies had not had much experience with boys. Her whole world had revolved around dance and, with mother's encouragement, her ambitions for a show-business career.

Bobbie Owen-Davies had been beautiful from a very young age. Her uncle Terry had told her so that time he called round when her mother and father had gone out and left her, happy to be on her own, for a whole Saturday while they attended the wedding of a friend's son. 'You needn't come,' her mother had told her that morning. 'You're thirteen years old and quite capable of looking after yourself.' She remembered her excitement at this compliment, her relief at not having to go to the wedding with her parents. The young Roberta didn't understand then why she had never heard of an uncle Terry. Now Bobbie knew very well why she had never seen or heard from him again. He had seemed so nice at first, talking about her parents at the door before she had let him in.

'Your mother asked me to pop round to make sure you're all right.' Uncle Terry had said he sympathised with her not wanting to go to the wedding. 'So boring, weddings. Especially when you don't know anybody.' That was how he eventually brought up the subject of wedding nights. She had blushed with embarrassment at some of his descriptions. She had never mentioned to anybody except Fiona what had happened that day. Bobbie had certainly never told either of her parents.

Richard pulled into the allotments, the sky overhead a palette of mixed grey, white and black, the skyline over the houses beyond tinted a purple-pink, calling the day to an end. The weather had been kind for February as the night prepared to take over from day. Richard had not panicked when Brian rang but considered it prudent to pop down to the shed, however. He had reassured Brian that it was near impossible that anybody, particularly the police, could know of their activities. 'I'll just make sure there are no traces of the liquid concoctions in the shed. I really don't think there are, but I'll check, to be on the safe side.'

Richard was astonished to see a car by the shed and two people wandering round it. He guessed they might have seen him drive in, but he turned the Renault round and left. They might well be the two detectives. He could make out a man and a younger woman, as Brian had described them. *They won't break into the shed*, he assured himself.

DC Barbara Booth nodded in the direction of the Renault when it pulled in by the gate. 'Bit late for allotments … a bit late for gardening on a February afternoon, Dave?'

'You're getting paranoid, Babs.'

'Maybe,' she replied.

'Come on, let's go. There's nothing unusual here. A hut on an allotment used by old men. Come on, let's go. I'm getting cold.' DS Wallis headed back to their car.

DC Booth settled herself in the driving seat and started the engine. 'I know, I know, before you say it.'

'Well, we are on a murder inquiry. A bunch of old men aren't going to be hiding dark secrets among their tools, are they?' Dave rolled his eyes up and choked a forced laugh, tipping back to exaggerate the effect.

Barbara put the car into gear. She took one last look at the shed and the large padlock on its door. She would still like to poke around inside it, despite her partner's impatience. Obviously she didn't have any evidence to justify a search warrant, but she wondered if there was some way of her engineering a quick look round. She imagined trying to explain to the Chief Inspector about an old shed on an allotment. No chance.

Richard Owen-Davies had parked a little further down the road, watching in his rear-view mirror. Eventually he saw the Ford Focus leave the allotment and waited a few more moments before restarting the Renault and turning back. Richard didn't have a torch with him and he knew he had to be quick, since the light was fading fast now. Pulling in by the shed as close as he could, Richard unlocked the padlock and hurriedly peered round, checking as thoroughly as the light would allow. *No jars left here. Nothing to worry about.* Feeling some sense of relief, he left the shed, snapping the padlock back in place and giving it a final tug to make sure. Then he drove back home.

DS Wallis had argued that they go back to the station to assimilate what little they had gleaned from their day's inquiries. 'Not a lot,' he concluded, 'but it has to be done.'

As they climbed the stairs to their office, he called over his shoulder, 'I must admit, Babs, I still think you're imagining things. I fail to see how that shed, and that car returning to the allotment, can have any bearing on what we're dealing with.'

'My instinct was right, though, Sarge,' Barbara replied as she followed him up the stairs.

The two police officers had driven round the block quickly after they left the Elms allotments, and they had seen the Renault pull in again.

DS Wallis tutted loudly, shaking his head disapprovingly. 'Dave, not Sarge.'

'Yes, Dave, I know.'

They had not taken the number of Richard's car, but Barbara wanted a look inside that shed more than ever now. She had made a mental note to find time in the near future and regretted not having taken the Renault's registration number.

When Richard reached home he rang Ernie and then Brian to suggest that they call off their usual visit to the allotments the next day. He thought they should not make any more plans for the immediate future; no pest control for a while. Ernie and Brian both agreed but expressed concern over whether Bill would agree. Richard told them he would ring Bill and tell him about today's events.

Richard tried again, but Bill was either out or not answering his phone. He tried several times during the evening, without success.

'You seem to be making rather a lot of telephone calls, Richard,' Daphne observed.

'I'm trying to get through to a friend. He's not responding, that's all.'

Daphne peered into Richard's study. 'I had lunch as usual with Rose today. Have you eaten anything, Richard?' She glanced around disdainfully, he considered.

'I'll have some boiled eggs later. I'm not hungry.'

'Has something exciting been happening down on your silly allotment lately?' Richard straightened at his desk. 'Why do you ask?'

'No reason, really. It's just that you seem … well … different lately.' Daphne was not sure what she meant herself.

'Not unless you call the strange death of a friend and his wife – both poisoned – an everyday event,' Richard snapped sarcastically. 'A friend with whom I shared the silly allotment.'

His wife shrugged, and left for their comfortable lounge without giving their conversation another thought.

Ernie watched the early evening news on his television. He had prepared himself some bacon and eggs. Never having improved his cooking skills since Grace had died, Ernie still missed his wife's cooking on a daily basis. When on occasion he had bought a pie for his dinner, that was when he really yearned for her food. Grace had been famous among their family and friends for her pastry. For weeks before Christmas she would be cooking mince pies by the hundred. Everybody they knew would ask her to make some. The neighbours (when they had friendly neighbours) and their daughter (when she was at home) always took a batch to work. Grace had spent her early years in service and she had learned well in that large kitchen. Grace's steak and kidney pie had been Ernie's favourite meal.

Tonight Ernie could not settle. He could not relax, however hard he tried. After mopping the juices from his plate with a slice of bread, he took the plate to the kitchen, then put on his coat, found his car keys, turned off the television and headed towards Bill's house. Ernie Evans was not an educated man nor a person to question things usually. Though he felt tired and miserable as he parked his VW Golf outside Bill's house, Ernie felt he ought to be doing something.

Music throbbed from the unlit house. Ernie received no response from his repeated ringing on the doorbell, nor a reaction from his hammering on the door. The music sounded even louder as he opened the letterbox to peer through and call out to his old friend. The side gate was locked, preventing him from getting around to the back of the house. Ernie tried banging on the door a few more times but was unheeded still. *He's in there. He wouldn't go out and leave his music on.* 'Come on, Bill, I know you're in there,' he muttered to himself. Ernie was puzzled but had no idea what to do next. Frustrated, he decided to give up; it was cold and he didn't have a clear idea of what he would have said to Bill. He sniffed miserably and as he climbed back in his car it began to rain. Flicking on his headlights and wipers, he set off for Richard's house.

Ernie had never been to see Richard in his home, regarding him as an allotment friend only. He was feeling self-conscious as he rang the bell of the large detached house, admiring the polished hardwood front door while he waited. Ernie pondered his feelings of failure in his own life. These unwelcome thoughts seemed to creep into his mind so easily, they just arrived unwanted. Suddenly the door opened, the black lantern light came on over his head, and Ernie glanced upwards to the source of light, blinking.

Richard stood in front of him with a puzzled look on his face.

'Hello, Ernie. What are you doing here?'

He shifted uneasily on his aching legs. 'I've just come from Bill's. I'm worried.'

'Come in a minute. I'll make you a cup of coffee and you can tell me.' Richard put his hand on Ernie's elbow gently. 'Come in,' he repeated.

Ernie wiped his feet thoroughly on the coconut mat on the other side of the threshold. Richard pointed towards the doorway of his study off the hallway where they were standing. Ernie looked around the hallway, then walked through to the study, admiring all the books, the old photos on the wall and not least the desk.

'Take a seat, my friend. I'll just go and switch on the kettle.'

'Don't bother for me, thank you.' Ernie fingered the bunch of keys in his hand.

'Sit down, Ernie, sit down. Tell me what's wrong with Bill.'

Richard sat down behind his desk. He was aware of the psychological barrier this might present to the man opposite but had no option. Ernie took a seat on the plain wooden captain's chair on his side of the desk. He studied the book spines behind Richard. The thought crossed Ernie's mind that he hadn't read that many books in his whole life. He perched on the edge of his chair and continued to fumble with his keys.

'I'm worried about Bill,' he began cautiously.

He described his sense of uneasiness, and how he couldn't settle at home earlier. He told Richard how he had called at Bill's house and heard loud military music coming from inside, how he had tried the bell, banged hard on the door and could see nothing through the letterbox.

Richard listened intently from his side of the desk. He waited a few moments after his friend had finished talking. He noticed the man's shoulders sag into his overcoat like an upright tortoise, Richard thought. He saw the anxiety in the tired thin face, the watery old eyes fixed on him.

'It does sound very odd, I agree, but I'm sure there's a very simple explanation. Perhaps he always plays his records as loud as that. Maybe he simply couldn't hear the doorbell. Probably nothing to concern us.'

Ernie was a little reassured by Richard's suggestions. 'I'm beginning to wonder why I've come here. But Bill was so agitated when he left us this morning. I've been thinking about him since then. Then there was Brian's visit from the coppers.'

Richard polished his gold-rimmed glasses with a small cloth and put them back on after inspecting them. 'I went to our shed this afternoon, just to make sure we had nothing there to cause a problem.' He decided not to mention the two people he had seen there.

Ernie stood up and studied the bunch of keys in his hands. 'You're right. I'm wasting your time. I'll get off home.' He felt more relaxed, still tired, but slightly less anxious.

Outside the front door, Ernie Evans stood in the pool of light from the overhead lantern in the porch, the rain glistening in the brightness.

'Well, goodnight, Richard. I'm sorry I bothered you. I'll see you next Monday morning at the allotment. We'll give it a miss, all of us, for the rest of the week, like we agreed on the phone earlier.'

'Goodnight, old friend. Now don't you worry. I'll see you on Monday. And it was not a bother. I trust I've reassured you.'

Richard paused for a moment before he closed the front door against the rain and switched the porch light off. Then he shrugged and decided to go through to the kitchen to boil two eggs for his supper. He checked the bread bin, took the butter from the fridge and reached for the salt cellar from the cupboard by the sink. He watched the saucepan of water, waiting for it to boil.

'Who was that?' called Daphne.

'Oh, only Ernie,' Richard called back from the kitchen.

Daphne did not enquire further.

When he arrived back at his flat, Ernie sat down heavily in his worn armchair with a resigned sigh and was asleep before he knew it.

Brian meanwhile was telling Debbie about his visit from the police. 'One bloke and a young policewoman asking about what happened in the pub the other night.'

Debbie ruffled what was left of his hair. 'You're too old for all this excitement, Bri. Do you want a cup of tea?'

Bill heard thumps on the wall from the adjoining semi-detached house. They made him snarl and mutter but he did turn the record player's volume down. Then, snatching the stylus arm from the disc, he threw the LP across the room, aiming it at the wall. Bill paced up and down slowly now, not marching. A wave of exhaustion overtook him. He had been marching for hours after he had finished the pickled onions and cheese. The glass jar on the mantelpiece contained only cloudy vinegar now. Bill wiped his shirt sleeve across his mouth and nose, slumped into his chair, rubbed his itching eyes and drifted into a deep but fitful sleep.

In his dream, Bill met his father, and his sweet old mother soothed him. Then he found himself sitting at his desk in the biscuit factory office, watching the new girl Brenda as she walked past the half-glazed panels that separated his office from the corridor. Brenda glanced into his office as she went by and smiled at him shyly.

Bill shifted in his chair, his long legs aching, his eyes stinging as he stirred. He shivered involuntarily. Slowly he became aware of his trousers, cold-wet in his lap still from the vinegar. Bill sniffed as he recognised the smell. The wooden-cased clock on the mantelpiece ticked loudly. He peered through the dark room at it: quarter to three, he could just make out. His head was full of a drowsy dull pain, and his legs would not move at first when he tried. Shifting his weight up the chair, he shuddered with cold. The wind was driving rain against the windows noisily. He went back to sleep. Snoring and snuffling noises filled the sparse room, competing only with the clock's *tick tock, tick tock, tick tock*.

The next time Bill woke he was shivering violently. His stomach cramped in pain. Letting out a moan, he gazed around his dark room. Four thirty now, the clock said. He staggered uncomfortably to his feet, slapped the kitchen light on and reached in the cupboard for a bottle of milk of magnesia. Dropping the cap on the quarry-tiled floor, he gulped the white chalky liquid noisily and drained the bottle. Then he ran some water from the tap into the bottle and with his large thumb over the neck shook the bottle and drank the diluted result. Rubbing his stomach, he filled his kettle and lit the gas ring. Aware again of his wet trousers, he climbed upstairs, removed his trousers and threw them across the balustrade on the landing, then searched his wardrobe for more. His blue-serge suit trousers would do. Shiny from wear at the office, this had been this favourite work suit. It hung more loosely on him now. Bill had worn it recently to Pete's funeral. He kicked his slippers out of the way and dragged a large pair of black Oxford shoes from the bottom of the wardrobe. The leather on the shoes was cracked with age but the soles were sound from their recent trip to the shoe mender's. Having tightened the leather belt around his waist, he straightened carefully after doing up the shoelaces. Bill caught sight of himself in the wardrobe mirror set on its single door. The mirror's silvering had perished in the corners; there were small rings and blotches from cold nights when a dew even formed on his bedcovers. No central heating in this house. The grey and torn sheets on his unmade bed were crumpled just as he had left it. A single 60 watt bulb in its dust-laden fringed lampshade shed a gloomy light over the double bed. He studied the face in the mirror, and Bill saw his father.

'William, my boy, do not disgrace me. You know what to do.'

'Yes, Father, I do.'

Back down in the kitchen he made some tea, stirring the pot slowly. His reflection in the kitchen window was now mirrored by the night-blackened glass. Rain was still beating hard on the outside. The milk of magnesia announced its arrival in his stomach, and he felt slightly nauseous as he sipped the sweet tea. His innards cramped again as the hot liquid coursed through his body, and he winced. Aware now that it was another day, William Arthur Choules listened to his father. Bill thought he could see his mother's back at the sink, her red hands busy, the small frail body, her straight white hair cut short. Then he blinked and she was gone.

He ground his jaw as he studied his steaming cup. 'I know what to do, Father,' he told it.

CHAPTER 22

It was Monday morning, and Brian, Ernie and Richard sat in their communal shed drinking tea. They had not mentioned pest control at all. The talk was of the coming spring, and Ernie spoke about last season's runner beans. The weather had been discussed at length. They had at least agreed that they had neither heard from nor seen Bill. Concluding that he was best left alone, they still hoped he was not ill.

An aircraft overhead had brought the Twin Towers in New York into the conversation. They shared opinions on terrorism and the Irish troubles but didn't refer to their own evil deeds. It was unsaid, but each understood that their own activities would be shelved for now. Brian asked the other two if they thought Pearl Harbor or September 11, New York, had been the biggest disaster that had occurred during their long lives. The others had disagreed; they had lived through the Second World War. The war news had been present in their lives but not so vividly portrayed in an era long before everyone had a television. 'Everyone except Bill, that is,' Brian had added.

Richard supposed that their own parents had known even worse times. He asked if the others knew of 1 July 1916. How many Germans had died he didn't know, but on that day, the first day of the Battle of the Somme, there had been 60,000 casualties, 20,000 killed. The families of those 60,000 young men would never have been the same again.

'If each family only consisted of four, that would directly involve 240,000 people.' Richard speculated with the statistics. He supposed most families were much bigger then. 'Young men with their lives before them ... The knowledge of this period of history is lost to all but a few of the 58 million or so people in this country today.'

'How could people ever forget?' Richard sighed and shook his head.

Ernie pictured the fading photograph in his bedroom that included his brothers before the Second World War. Richard noticed the faraway look in Ernie's crumpled features; so did Brian.

'Not to mention the horrors of the Second World War that we all went through.' Brian touched Ernie's sleeve gently in acknowledgement.

Brian found himself justifying their own dark deeds as somehow excused by the tragedies of the past. Richard preparing the poison for all five men to perpetrate their newsworthy events of only a few weeks ago seemed insignificant by comparison.

The conversation continued in its self-conscious way. Each man was silently aware of their stilted awkwardness with each other this morning. Each vainly attempted to recreate the comfortable bonhomie of their shared hut's more comfortable past.

Brian attempted to lighten the mood by introducing fresh subjects. He tried football but with no takers. Gamely he tried house prices, regretting it immediately when Ernie began expressing his personal regrets.

Brian, Ernie and Richard continued self-consciously trying to avoid the subject that bound the gardening club together – together, that is, with Bill and Pete. Although they talked the whole morning away, the atmosphere remained strained. It was a relief to all to lock the shed and set off to their respective homes after subdued goodbyes.

None of them noticed the young woman in the Ford Focus. Not one of them spotted the binoculars hanging round her neck.

DC Barbara Booth had watched the shed for several days now in her own off-duty time. DS Dave Wallis would not listen to her intuition that the shed on the allotments was in some way significant to their solving the mystery of the poisonings. It was the first time during her visits that she had seen anybody there, and that Monday the only people to appear were three elderly men. She had written down the registration numbers of each of the vehicles – the Renault, the VW Golf and the battered Ford Escort van, which the newly promoted detective already knew belonged to Brian Young.

At first she had laughed at her own silliness when she saw how old her 'suspects' were. Barbara knew she would be severely embarrassed if Dave found out that she had privately been making an observation of these three vehicles and their owners. She would be equally embarrassed if he had seen her drive by each address that the vehicle registration check had provided. Except Brian Young's address, maybe.

When Detective Chief Inspector Harris had discussed the toxicology report with DS Wallis and herself, Barbara's suspicions were fuelled by the report's conclusion that the main poison used was atropine, derived from the plant known as deadly nightshade. Colchicine was the other poison found by the toxicologists, again derived from botanical origins. She had researched both of them on the internet, discovering the painful results of ingesting either of these.

Plants ... gardeners. The thought reverberated back and forth in her mind. Gardening, plants and gardeners continued to direct her thoughts towards the allotments. One moment it seemed ridiculous to suspect the three old men she had seen entering and leaving the allotment shed of somehow being involved, but she was unable to dismiss her recollection of Brian Young's uneasy manner when she mentioned the poisonings to him.

Barbara weighed the possible connections as she tidied her flat. Round and round the facts revolved in her brain. The prison. The Wicket Keeper pub. Mr Kool's Bar in town. The moneylender. The family from 37 Wycliff Road. Each fact led her to deny her suspicions, until again she remembered that the married couple, the Wilsons, were friends of Brian Young.

According to the autopsies and toxicology reports, both poisons seemed to have been used at the prison, where there were dozens of seriously ill young men ... and several deaths. What link could there be between convicted criminals in the prison and a group of elderly gardeners? The pub and the bar were both frequented by drug dealers – more criminals – and some members of the family at 37 Wycliff Road were also known offenders. Why would these villains be targeted by a bunch of old men who met in an allotment shed? There was no sense to it.

Barbara gazed out of her kitchen window lost in thought as she filled her kettle to overflowing. She poured some water away and clicked on the switch.

DCI Bob Harris had elaborated at length a tedious theory of terrorist activity, a small cell of terrorists in Willbury whose intention was to disrupt the town's police, hospital and other services. Barbara was not convinced, even when he announced that the Chief Superintendent had put forward the same theory as the DCI.

'The Home Office has of course been notified, and no doubt MI5 or MI6 or SO15 will soon be in our vicinity,' he had informed them at the briefing.

It seemed absurd to Barbara when he had added pompously, 'Do not exclude from your thoughts the fact that we have a large community of Muslims in Willbury these days.' He had raised his eyebrows ostentatiously as he said this.

Barbara Booth had sniggered to herself at this statement but she hadn't noticed any amusement among any of her fellow officers present at that meeting.

'One of those old men from the allotment brought Peter Wilson to the hospital when he was dying from the poison,' she had mentioned to DS Wallis, who showed no interest in her observation. 'It was Brian Young, the old bloke we went to interview.'

A specialist unit of the national Counter-Terrorism Command, SO15, had indeed been brought into Willbury to follow up this 'terrorist group' theory, and they were already busying themselves among local groups in the area. However, both the Bob Harris and Dave Wallis agreed they would continue to investigate locally as well.

'Willbury Valley Police CID's pride is at stake,' the DCI told his DS with a knowing nod. 'Nothing should be overlooked, but everything will have to be reported back to the SO15 unit's Command.'

DC Booth had received some serious mickey taking towards the end of the meeting. Even the DCI had ridiculed her theories when he asked for opinions. Dave Wallis had just managed to sway DCI Harris to allow them some more time on their own inquiries.

'I hope your intuition has some foundation, my girl,' he grumbled on the way to the canteen. 'It's my credibility on the line as well as yours.'

'Thanks for backing me, Sarge. I'll buy the teas.' She smiled at her partner.

Richard Owen-Davis planned to visit his daughter for lunch at her dance studio. He hadn't seen her for months. He had rung her over the weekend to invite himself, so Bobbie was expecting him.

Brian returned to his house after a visit to the bookie's to place a few pounds on a horse running at York, in a race that Channel 4 was showing that afternoon. His date was with a cup of tea and his sofa. *It's nice to do something normal*, he thought as he switched the television on.

Ernie spent the whole afternoon washing out his ancient greenhouse with disinfectant. The old wooden greenhouse tucked in the corner of his small garden needed a dose of Jeyes Fluid, he had decided some time ago. Job done, he fell asleep in his armchair after a meal of baked beans on toast. He missed the early evening news, sleeping well into the evening.

Roberta and Richard Owen-Davies had a pleasant hour with the fresh bread rolls he had promised to bring and her microwave soup in the back office of her dance studio. Bobbie had even kissed her father when he arrived.

'Nice to see you, Daddy. How is your allotment growing?' She knew of her mother's distaste of his hobby, and it was her regular tease when they got round to seeing each other.

They skimmed the surface of a few subjects, and both expressed their pleasure with themselves that they had bothered to arrange the lunch.

'When are you ever not going to be too busy to cross this town to visit your mother and me at home?' Richard asked his only daughter before he left. He knew she wouldn't, however.

Bobbie hugged her father but avoided his question. 'Bye, Daddy. See you soon.' She squeezed his hand, lifted it to her mouth and kissed it. 'Say hello to Mother for me.' She watched him climb into his car and waved from the stone-arched doorway.

Sally, Pete's elder daughter, had accepted the offer made through the estate agents Owen-Davies and Blagrave. She phoned her sister Vanessa to tell her.

'I've accepted an offer ... Yes, a widow's buying it. I've also agreed that the agents will arrange for Mum and Dad's stuff to be cleared out ... Yes. When I take the keys into their office I have to sign that we don't wish to remove anything else once we've taken what we want for ourselves ... Yes, come and get the key ... Yes, you can take whatever you like. Anything ... Yes. I don't want anything else. I've got all their papers still but there's nothing else there that I want for myself ... Yes, it was a very quick offer ... No, I don't know how many the agents showed around ... No ... No ... I'll be glad too when it's been sold ... Yes, the money will be handy. Don't cry. No. Please don't cry ... Yes, I'll come to see you. Take care. Bye for now.' Sally dabbed a tissue at her own eyes and put the phone down.

Back on duty with her sergeant, Barbara Booth admitted that perhaps he was right.

'We need to be looking at new areas, to find who was responsible for the poison job. There were so many affected and apart from the prison they were all pretty much from the same parts of town. The answer must be somewhere within that small area.'

They then admitted to not knowing where to look next.

'Let's have another look at the arson case at the cycle shop. See if we can't do better at clearing that up. Or maybe there is a connection there to the other events, the poisonings.'

DC Booth glanced at her partner to discover whether this was a sarcastic comment or whether he was being serious. She couldn't tell. He was slumped in the passenger seat of the Ford Focus, intently unwrapping a Mars bar.

'You've read the fire report, I take it?' He took a large bite of his chocolate bar and chewed appreciatively.

Barbara acknowledged that she had.

'The Bastin brothers who owned the shop are a couple of villains, you know,' Dave informed her through a mouthful.

'I didn't know that,' Barbara confessed.

'Oh yes,' said Dave. 'I know those two very well. David and Graham Bastin. Our paths have crossed before. They are a choice pair. Both have form.'

'Perhaps I should meet them as well.' Barbara raised her eyebrows playfully. 'Where will we find them?'

'You drive, I'll take you there.'

He guided his partner across the town to a row of shops.

'That's it there. The Bastin brothers will be in their shop most probably, unless they're up to no good somewhere else. It's Second Hand World.'

'SINGLE ITEMS OR WHOLE HOUSE CONTENTS, FAIR PRICES FOR CASH,' the fluorescent posters in the grimy windows announced.

'Our boys prefer old to new. They've got two shops then?' Barbara speculated.

'Bent goods of any sort,' Dave added. 'Yeah, this shop and the bike shop.'

A scruffy, unshaven man in his thirties was sitting in an ancient upholstered armchair at the back of the cluttered shop.

'Hello, Mr Bastin.' DS Wallis showed his warrant card.

'No need for that card, Wallis. I know who you are.' Graham Bastin glanced at DC Booth. 'I don't know who this bit of stuff is, though.'

He looked Barbara up and down slyly but obviously. Barbara showed her warrant card. His leer vanished.

'Too good to be true, might have known you couldn't pull a bird like that, Wallis.'

DC Booth wandered about the shop, ignoring the following eyes. Office desks, sofas, bookshelves, old pine chests of drawers. The smell of dust. Wicker chairs, a stuffed owl in a glass case, a dark-stained Welsh dresser with chipped china plates displayed on the shelves. A portable television on a small table. The shop was crammed. Barbara ran a finger through the dust on a table top as she edged through the shop.

'Found the bastard who burnt our bike shop down yet?' The shopkeeper hoisted himself straighter in the armchair.

'DS Wallis to you, my friend,' Dave snapped.

'I'm no fucking friend of yours, Wallis,' Graham Bastin retorted, laughing. He stood up and lit a cigarette with a snap of his Zippo lighter. 'Coppers getting younger, eh, Wallis?' He nodded in the direction of DC Booth. 'Or am I getting old?'

'My partner DC Booth would like to know if you have any idea who may have set your bike shop on fire. I, on the other hand, would be more interested in where you bought your stock for it. How you can have an endless supply of second-hand bikes?'

'I think I would sooner answer DC Booth's question.' Bastin wandered over to Barbara Booth. 'The sergeant says you'd like to know if I've got any idea who torched our bike shop.' He grinned obsequiously, showing nicotine-stained teeth.

Barbara swung round to face the man. 'He's right. I would like to know. It would be my guess it was either a dissatisfied customer or another bicycle shop owner. I would imagine you have plenty of dissatisfied customers, Mr Bastin.' Barbara smiled sweetly at him. 'Or someone getting their own back on you maybe?' She continued to smile at him.

Bastin's smirk vanished. 'Smartarse, your bird, Wallis, just like you. I thought the police were supposed to be polite these days, you being public servants and me being a taxpayer paying your wages.' His sly grin returned.

'We're polite to polite members of the public,' Barbara said, equalling her previous sweet smile.

'Who steals the bikes for you? You and your brother are too lazy to do it yourselves.' DS Wallis moved over to Barbara's side.

'Perhaps you don't pay them enough,' DC Booth suggested.

'Disgruntled supplier maybe?' Dave Wallis added, to make it clearer what his partner was saying.

'You're wasting my time, you two. Bugger off and find who torched our shop. Or better still find who's poisoning all the people in Willbury.' He lit another cigarette and blew smoke rings with the first drag.

'Know something about that, do you?' This was Barbara's subject now.

'What I read in the papers and see on the telly.' He hitched his tracksuit bottoms up with one hand.

DC Booth studied him for a few seconds. 'Come on, Sarge. I think we're wasting out precious time here. Just one last thing, though, Mr Bastin –'

'No more, DC Booth. We've wasted enough time on him. By the way, where is that brother of yours?'

Bastin blanked the question.

DC Booth persisted. A shot in the dark sometimes hit. 'Just one last question for you. Do you know any of the people who were poisoned? You know, from the newspaper or television reports?'

She watched Graham Bastin's face. She knew the answer before he gave it. She had read the slight twitch, the merest sideways movement of his pupils.

'Yeah, as a matter of fact I know the family who had two kids killed by it.'

DS Wallis could see his partner's back straighten at hearing the answer. He let her go on.

'The Johnsons? You mean the whole family or part of it? Who exactly do you know?'

'I've had a beer or a cup of tea with his mum or dad occasionally, but I know the eldest son – actually the wife's son by her first marriage.'

'Jason Kelly? And how do you know him? He's a bit young to be a friend of yours, isn't he?' Barbara's concentration was visible.

'I don't know what you're getting at. He's a mate of my brother's son.' He hesitated.

DC Booth continued to study his face closely this time.

'They play football together.'

Barbara considered the answer. Perfectly plausible, she concluded to herself. Probably true, but there was a hint of uneasiness in his manner. She went on to probe this discomfort a little more.

'You go and watch them play football then, do you? Is that how you know him?'

'Yeah, he plays football with my teenage nephews. Nothing wrong with that.'

His tone was just a tiny bit too enthusiastic, she reckoned. DC Booth was confident there was more to the acquaintance, that the link was stronger.

'Perhaps you like watching boys,' DS Wallis threw in.

Graham Bastin stood up. He reacted angrily to this jibe. 'Why don't you fuck off and find who murdered Jason's little sister and brother, who tried to kill the whole family? Instead of pestering me. I've got work to do even if you haven't.'

He lit yet another cigarette and went through to the rear of the shop, ignoring his visitors.

'Goodbye then, Mr Bastin, if don't want to co-operate in helping us find the arsonist. We may be back,' DS Wallis called through to the back of the shop.

The two detectives left the shop and returned to their car, where they sat for a while. DC Booth placed both hands on the steering wheel and stared through the windscreen, not looking out at anything.

'There is a link there, Dave, I know it. Jason Kelly is probably one of his bike suppliers. The teenager nicks bikes. They buy from him. That would be my theory.'

'I've no doubt your assumption is correct. Well done for pushing that point.' Dave Wallis sat sideways in his seat, studying his partner's face. 'We'll bear him in mind. Keep an eye on him. But I'm not sure what it's telling us overall.'

Barbara confessed that she was not sure either but she was beginning to think it was a part in the jigsaw. Then she banged both hands on the steering wheel. 'Let's go.' She started the car. 'I think I'll check some stolen bicycle records later. There just might be a connection somewhere in that list.'

'Good idea, Babs. You do that.'

She glanced sideways at her superior officer, again to see if he was being serious or sarcastic. She concluded the latter.

CHAPTER 23

Bill Choules was hungry again, hungrier than yesterday. He propped his bike against the wall beside the door of the Parade café, knowing it opened early, although he had never been in before. He had ridden by the café many times on his way to the allotment. The windows streamed with condensation. The smell of fried food would still be in the walls when they knocked the building down some time in the future. In this street the shops changed hands often. The owners of the Parade café had seen many hopefuls come and go in the adjacent shops.

Darkie Green and his wife Pam had lived above their café for the whole eighteen years they had owned it. 'Pam's dream': Darkie had been reluctant originally to buy a café but Pam's heart had been set on it. He was called Darkie because he used to have a shock of jet black hair along with heavy black eyebrows. That was over eighteen years ago, however. Now his hair was pure white, with not a trace of colour in his still thick hair. Darkie served and Pam cooked but retirement loomed. They would sell the café soon while the trade held up. Darkie said this more often lately. Pam was coming round to his way of thinking. The husband-and-wife team were both in their sixties now and they had put a bit of money away in better times. They would get a reasonable figure for the business, they supposed, while it was a going concern. The business transfer agent was coming round next week. They already had their accounts of recent years out to show him.

'What a pity,' Darkie had said to Pam only the previous night as they watched television, 'that the accounts don't really show how profitable it is.'

'Can't have it both ways with the tax man,' Pam had observed. 'Nice little bungalow in the Bournemouth area. See our days out.'

They had made their minds up that the time had finally come to retire.

Bill stood at the counter and pointed to the chalk board.

'Big Boys' Breakfast, guv? Here's your tea. Sit down. I'll bring your breakfast over in a minute or two. Find a table. Knives and forks there.' Darkie pointed to a cutlery tray at the end of the counter. 'Help yourself.'

Bill paid for his breakfast, picked up a knife and fork and found a table by the front door. The gloss-painted wall ran with little rivulets of condensation nearly as much as the front windows. Bill watched one of these run down to meet another.

Darkie put a large plate down in front of Bill. 'One Big Boys' Breakfast.'

'Could I have some toast?' Bill asked him.

'Yes, 'course you can. It's included with your Big Boy, mate. The tea and toast are included in the price. Coming up in a mo',' Darkie said with a well-practised friendliness.

It wasn't long before he returned with two slices of buttered toast. 'Real butter as well, mate,' Darkie informed Bill as he put the plate of toast on the Formica-topped table. 'Not margarine.'

Bill produced a ragged blue handkerchief and wiped a drop from his nose. His mouth watered as he rubbed his unshaven chin. He shook some salt and pepper over the plate, which was piled with sausages, eggs, beans, a few black mushrooms, tinned tomatoes and a slice of fried bread hiding two slices of bacon. Bill ate hungrily and quickly, egg in the corner of his mouth, bean juice on his rough chin among the short white bristles.

Two builders entered noisily.

'All right, Darkie, where's that sexy Pam?' one of them greeted the café owner.

The younger of the two leaned over the counter and made as if he were going to climb over it. 'Pammie, Pammie, where are you? I'm coming to get you! Where are you?' The young man put a knee up on the counter.

Pam popped her silver head out of the hatch behind the counter. 'If you're man enough, Gary, come and see me at three o'clock this afternoon when I finish here.' She cackled and her head disappeared into the grimy kitchen.

Darkie laughed. 'You can have her, Gary. No charge. Usual, boys? Two Big Boys' Breakfasts for two small boys. Extra beans on one of them, Pam.' He called across his shoulder to the hatch.

The two men sat down with their mugs of tea; they knew the form. They glanced across at Bill. He noticed them looking. The two builders came in most mornings on their way to work. There may have been some fat on the plates but there was none on the men's hard bodies. One lit a cigarette, the other studied the back page of his newspaper, while they sat in silence.

A postman shuffled in and stood at the counter drinking a coffee that Darkie poured as he saw the postman arrive.

'Anything from Ernie today?' asked Darkie, a question he'd asked many times before. 'About time my Premium Bonds came up with a big 'un. Only ever seem to get fifty quid – 'bout time I had a big prize.'

The postman shrugged.

Bill wiped the remaining juices from the plate with his second slice of toast. The best he had felt for days, he thought. As he stood to go, his stomach cramped. He screwed up his face and winced out loud.

'You all right, mate?' The smoking builder looked over to Bill. He shrugged and winked at his mate, who had looked up from his paper.

Bill left with no answer.

The cold air hit Bill Choules. He took a huge gulp. He leaned one arm on the wall by his bicycle. His eyes streamed. Groping in his coat pocket, he produced the blue handkerchief and mopped them, blew his nose into it and mounted his old black bike uneasily. His Timex watch told him it was still only 7.30. He had treated himself to this watch on his thick wrist many years ago but it still kept good time. He had in fact bought the watch from Wise the Jeweller's from this same parade of shops long before it had closed down. The traffic was building up already on the road outside the Parade café. Bill rode out around the small pickup truck parked outside. A horn sounded, and he involuntarily waved a fist in anger at the car's rear. The start it had given him cleared his head to the job in hand. Bill peddled purposefully, his big legs pumping hard at the pedals. The ancient dynamo was still working well on his front and rear cycle lamps.

The arsenic had been in his garden shed for years. Bill had cleared the mass of cobwebs from the box when he had found it. He didn't know whether it had lost its effectiveness to kill rats over time. How could he? He wasn't a chemist. He was a gardener. 'That's a start,' he told himself and his father as he mixed a solution. 'Rats are pests.' He would continue the good work on his own.

So many in Willbury had heeded the warnings and ceased having a milk delivery – indeed, as most had anyway in recent years.

Bill hummed a deep rumble quietly to himself as he injected the solution of arsenic into the milk bottles by the back door of the Green Man public house. He had decided they were all scum at these premises. *Stupid people with milk bottles – don't they learn?* Nobody noticed the old man mount his bicycle and ride away, the cars and their occupants were going by much too quickly. He didn't think one dose would kill anybody. *More's the pity.* But they could suffer like him.

The traffic was really building up in Willbury town centre as Bill made his way back to his house. He rode past the Wicket Keeper pub. *No milk bottles there any more. I must find a way to get in.* The arsenic Bill had discovered in the dusty corner of his shed had been left there by his father. He didn't know whether over the years it lost his effectiveness to kill rats. He had made a solution anyway, and it was there in his pocket. *The others aren't going to continue to get rid of pests*, Bill sneered to himself. For all their talk of leatherjackets, aphids, slugs and snails and weevils, it was up to him now. He had had enough of life now. What had it been anyway, he had asked himself many times recently. What was the point any more? Even if he was ill, so long as he could keep going with his own pest control at least he could help clean up a few corners of Willbury. The anger consumed him once more. *William will find a way to get rid of all the scum.*

He passed the small red-brick chapel. 'A dance studio. Huh!' he exclaimed out loud. The service for Brenda had been at this chapel all those years ago. He caught a sob in his throat, which seemed to come from deep inside. His eyes burned with involuntary tears, welling up so unwanted that they made him angry. Grinding his teeth, he wiped first one then the other eye with the back of his hands. Bill's whole body shuddered. A high-pitched moan escaped from his mouth. He pulled on to the pavement, straddling the cycle crossbar to gather himself. The pain in his stomach distracted his thoughts as he stood astride his bike. It made him wince, and he gulped the cold morning air while the pain eased slowly away. As he looked both ways back and forth along the road, its slow stop–start of endless cars and trucks filled his nostrils with their filthy acrid exhausts. Then he saw a young woman squeeze her car into a space in front of the chapel. He watched. *Not Brenda.*

He had no idea it was Richard Owen-Davies's daughter, even though Richard had probably mentioned in conversation in their hut at the allotment that his daughter was a dance teacher. His thoughts were elsewhere, certainly not making any connection to the woman unlocking the front door of the chapel.

Bill got off his bike and began walking back along the pavement, pushing his bike towards the chapel. The young woman had gone inside, leaving the passenger door open and revealing an assortment of items on the seat. Bill noticed a carton of orange juice among them. Quickly he fumbled in his pocket, drew some fluid from the bottle into the syringe and stabbed it into the carton.

His hands shook as he emptied the syringe contents. Nobody took any notice of the old man leaning against the car door.

Getting on his bike as fast as he could, he pushed himself off. The young woman watched him go as she returned to her car to collect her possessions from the seat. Bobbie Owen-Davies locked the car door and watched the old man ride off. She checked to make sure that all her things were still there. He had seemed to be near her car but apparently he hadn't stolen anything, as she had first feared. Her suspicions evaporated and she thought no more of it, except to remind herself to lock the car in future.

A large white box van narrowly missed Bill; the driver hooted his horn and shouted something Bill didn't hear. The horn's noise brought him to his senses. CRISPS AND SNACKS TO THE LICENSED TRADE in bright red lettering on the side of the van registered with Bill.

'Maybe, maybe, William,' Bill muttered to himself.

It was easy to keep the van in sight, since his bike allowed him to keep moving inside the traffic queue. Bill Choules wondered how he might inject some of his hideous fluid into some deliveries. He watched the van pull into a pub forecourt. The driver went inside with a clipboard and after a few minutes returned to the van, climbing up a couple of steps into the back. The rounds-man carried several cartons of crisps and a few boxes of peanuts and other snacks into the pub. Bill watched. The driver returned, got into the cab and reversed further into the pub's car park, where he waited to cross the traffic and turn back the way he'd come. A builder's pickup let him out into the traffic. *Could he be delivering to the Wicket Keeper?* Bill wondered. He mounted his bike across the road and made his way back towards the Wicket Keeper, concentrating as he rode, and all of a sudden his mood lifted.

Bill stopped along the road from the pub. He had arrived there before the van, which was now in view, indicating to turn in there. Bill smiled to himself and began humming.

The driver hopped out and strolled round to the kitchen door at the back corner of the pub, carrying his clipboard as before.

Bill caught the eye of a passenger in a car in the traffic queue as he tried the van's back door. The car moved a few metres forward and the woman driving the car took no more notice. He tried the back door handle. Open. The inside of the van had racks either side of a narrow aisle piled high with crisp cartons and cards of snacks in boxes. Bill drew some fluid from the bottle and stabbed the needle into individual bags of peanuts and through the sides of crisp cartons. Frantically he stabbed, then refilled the syringe and continued stabbing wildly. He nearly fell down the steps at the rear of the van and hurriedly grabbed his bike from where he had propped it against the pub wall. He heard a voice call out, 'Won't be a minute, I'll just get your stuff!' The driver appeared round the back of the van. He saw the old man mounting his bike, and it occurred to him that it might be the same big bloke on a bike he had yelled at, but he thought no more of it. Not with twenty or more calls yet to make.

Bill gasped to a stop in the municipal gardens in the centre of Willbury. He propped his cycle against a bench. There was no one in sight at this time of morning. No townsfolk were enjoying the gardens on this cold grey day. He fished in his pocket. The bottle containing the solution he had made had emptied its contents into the pocket of his blue-serge suit jacket. It had soaked into his overcoat and through to his shirt. Bill groaned his disappointment. He realised he hadn't tightened the lid, and the bottle was empty. Angrily Bill threw it into some laurel bushes nearby.

After pushing his bicycle to the gate of the gardens, he set off once more towards home, muttering to himself as he went. He was unaware of two schoolboys laughing at him. They mimicked the old man talking to himself.

No more left. Wasted, William. Naughty boy, William. You're a clumsy boy.

'I didn't mean it, Father. I have done some.'

You're useless, William. You'll come to nothing.

'But I have done some, Father,' he argued with himself as he walked along.

He threw the bike down on his own front path, opened the door and went straight upstairs. Bill lay on the bed and studied the cracks in his ceiling. Nine o'clock, the yellowing white plastic alarm beside the bed pointed out. His stomach growled as he drifted off to sleep.

The sky was darkening, and the clock showed ten past four when he awoke in his shadowy bedroom

'Can I come down now, Mother? Has Father gone out?' he whispered.

Rubbing a fist in his eyes, Bill looked around the room warily. He heaved himself up on his elbow. *No father. No mother to be seen or heard.* He had been dreaming. He was cold, even though he still had his coat on over his suit. He swung his legs over the side of the bed and rubbed the stubble on his chin.

Down in his kitchen he put the kettle on and made tea. His mouth was dry and caked from sleep and fried food. He took his tea through to the back room, blew the steam away and sipped earnestly and noisily. Peter Schmalfuss caressed the piano to Chopin's direction on his music system. Nocturne in E flat major flowed from his hi-fi as night fell, surrounding Bill Choules and his semi-detached house. Opus 9 number 2 filled his head. Sitting in the gloom, he allowed the music to fill his being. So beautiful. The tea warmed him through. He felt safe. The needle scratched the centre of the disc for a moment and the arm returned automatically to its rest, interrupting Bill's reverie and breaking the spell of the music. Bill switched the light on and returned to the kitchen for more tea. He wished once more his clumsy fingers could have mastered the piano. Six lessons in, his father had told him he would pay for no more lessons. He would never be able to play and it hurt his ears, his father had said impatiently.

Bill shuffled through his records. Tommaso Albinoni's Adagio for Organ and Strings in G minor was a piece he enjoyed, though the organ phrases reminded him of his father. His phone rang. He ignored it. It insisted for some minutes. It competed with Liszt now. *No competition*, Bill thought, irritated at the intrusion. The music flowed through him as the tea did. *If only I could play like that.* He closed his gritty eyes but not to sleep this time; rather, to soak up the Liebestraum No. 3 in A flat major, Dieter Goldman showing Bill what could have been. His mind drifted, luxuriating in the music. The phone shrilled out again, but he tried to ignore it once more.

Bill snatched the needle arm from the record deck.

'Leave me alone, leave me alone, all of you!' he shouted at the telephone.

He buttoned up the overcoat he still had on, looked around the room and snapped the light off. With his hand in the damp coat pocket, he fleetingly recalled the reasons. *This morning in the town gardens.* His head throbbed at the temple. He rubbed his large pink forehead with the back of his hand. *I'll get them anyway.* Again a wave of pain seared through his stomach. He closed his eyes in the cold air of his front garden and halted, to allow the pain to subside. When it eased, he picked up his bicycle and set off once more.

Bill pushed on, breathing heavily at the exertion of his peddling. He hummed a tuneless noise, the music jumbled in his head. No melody was recalled correctly, though he knew so many so well. He took one hand from the handlebars and checked his pocket once more for the matches he'd taken from his kitchen. He always kept them for his old gas cooker or the little stove in the shed. Tonight, though, he had another gardening aid – his Weed Wand. This was a very handy tool with push-button automatic ignition. The spare gas bottles bulged in his overcoat pockets as he leaned his bike against a wall. The bottles of methylated spirits chinked in a coat pocket. He'd bought these a few days ago when this idea had come to him. In his saddlebag there was also a two-litre plastic tub of white spirit from his shed. That might be useful too. Bill was well prepared. He had also stuffed his pockets full of rags. *Smoke out a few pests*, he thought.

'Yes, Father,' he agreed, 'the town hall offices do hold too many cheats and liars. Councillors out to line their pockets, giving contracts to their friends. Pests.

Purporting to serve the community but in reality working for their own advantage. It has gone on for years. For ever.' He had not discussed these pests with the gardening club but now they were high on his list. 'What would those fools call these types of pest. Slugs?' He didn't care what the others might call them. Their agreed code had come to nothing anyway.

The glass doors of the Civic Centre offices reflected Bill Choules. He frantically looked around. Brick and glass would not burn. *Must be something somewhere.* He went down the side. 'Ha!' he exclaimed out loud. He heard himself and checked over his shoulder anxiously.

'Keep quiet, William. Shush, boy.'

The discarded Christmas tree, the tall spruce, lay between several wheeled bins in a service area. Still not cleared, it had lain there for over a month now, drying, ever since it had been removed from the reception area behind the glass doors. Those automatic doors that invited people into the sumptuous reception to report their petty problems. Two discarded wooden pallets leaned on the wall beside the bins. Bill poured some white spirit over the tree and paper and splashed some over the pallets. He pulled the tree nearer to the wooden side access service door, the needles forming a trail, and doused more of the spirit over the door itself, not knowing what lay behind it. Bill quickly struck a match and lit the vapours from the spirit, the blue flame almost invisible initially. Searching frantically in a bin, Bill pulled out paper, lots of paper. He stuffed bundles of paper around the needles into branches of the prone tree. The big man propped the wooden pallets across the tree, stood back for a few seconds to assimilate the whole effect. *That will do*, he concluded.

His eyes shone in contemplation of the fire before he rode away on his bike, puffing, puffing and cackling, steam pluming from his mouth as he exhaled with exertion. He stopped not too far away in a shop doorway. A group of young women, out for an early-evening drink, went by arm in arm, giggling at the sight of the old man. Ignoring them, he gazed in the direction he had come from. The whole area was illuminated by streetlights and low path-lights set in the terrazzo pavement. *Was that a flame? A glow certainly.* An orange glow flickered beside the building, lighting the red bricks. Would it catch properly? He could not tell, but this was promising.

'Got a fag, mate?' Bill was suddenly aware of a scruffy man beside him. 'Got a spare fag, old man?' the stranger said through his matted beard.

Bill walked away, pushing his bike. 'I don't smoke,' he replied gruffly over his shoulder

The man shrugged and shuffled off, looking down at the ground and the lights set in the pavement, mumbling and cursing to himself as he went.

Bill mounted his bicycle and set off once more, irritated that he could not watch. Continuing down a side street of smaller shops, Bill could see rubbish was piled outside each door waiting for collection in the early hours, black bags and cardboard boxes flattened and tied into bundles.

Bill lit or tried to light each pile. He could not wait to watch these, he realised only too well. 'Good job the street was quiet, though, William,' a voice told him as his mounted his bike once more.

The next object to attract Bill's interest was a doorway, in which there was a varnished door leading to offices above a shop. The ornate brick Victorian architecture was discernible above the modern shop fronts. He fished some rags out of his pockets and pushed them through the large letterbox, then poured more methylated spirit through it, inserted his Weed Wand and sparked its ignition. He knew it had taken on something in there, plenty of old wood to burn.

Two doors down he tried to pour more liquid under the plate-glass doors of a shop. Again he ignited the gas in his Weed Wand and the clothing just inside the doorway quickly caught fire from the rivulet of burning methylated spirit. This long-handled tool was perfect for this job, as well as burning weeds from a pathway. Buoyed by this success, he tried an optician's shop. The spirit caught fire, then fizzled out as he watched. The methylated spirit glowed blue for only a few seconds, blackening the doormat and no more. Bill decided to leave it.

He checked his pockets, and found two more gas canisters for his Weed Wand. He mounted his bike and rode around the corner towards other shops. A Debenhams department store caught his eye. Some people were walking along the pavement towards him, but they passed by, talking loudly and seeming to take no notice of the old man holding a bicycle. More plate glass doors. He poured yet more methylated spirit from the bottle, sweeping it under the door with side of his hand. His hands were cold from splashes on his hands as it evaporated. Some liquid had seeped beneath the door. Placing the Weed Wand on the ground, he set off a jet of flame which blackened the brass strip at the bottom of the door and then rushed on inside. *Success!* Bill tried to splash the second bottle of spirit between the doors. He checked behind himself and up and down the road. More people were coming. He must go. Again he mounted his bike and rode off, glancing back but seeing nothing. *Would it or wouldn't it catch fire?*

Bill cycled slowly now, away from the town centre. His body was aching and his head whirled. Just then he noticed a decorators' merchants down a side street where a small industrial estate began. The whole area here was quiet and deserted. Ignoring the cold creeping to his core, he gulped in a few deep breaths. 'Come on, William, come on, keep going, keep going,' the voice urged him. Pain washed through his gut as he rubbed his hands together, rubbing life into his cold stiffening fingers.

The building in front of him was in complete darkness. He stuffed rags soaked in methylated spirit through a letterbox in the panel beside the glazed doors, pushed his Weed Wand through and ignited it. The jet of flame lit the inside of the building with a blue glow and he could see shadowy displays of stacked paint and decorating sundries. Racks of brushes and rollers hung there. A wooden rack of Anaglypta textured wallpapers was just to one side. Turning the Wand and its flame towards the wooden shelving, Bill manoeuvred the tool so that it reached near to the rolls of wallpaper. It didn't take much lighting. Bill smiled with satisfaction and looked over his shoulder. *Still quiet.* General Decorating Supplies was alight. This one would go well, thought Bill. The fire was already raging through the building interior long before he heaved himself back on his bike. An overwhelming exhaustion came over him, making it difficult to pedal. He urged himself on. *I must get home, I must* … Small explosions from paint cans filled the air as he cycled away.

With stiff and aching hips he climbed awkwardly back on to the bike and headed for home. Each push of his legs became and more difficult. He felt almost faint, and had to stop a few times because he was giddy with exhaustion. However, whenever he noticed a possibility for his magic wand, he couldn't resist an urge to use it again. He started several more fires before he eventually travelled the last few hundred metres up his own suburban road and to his own dark front door.

The old man slumped painfully into his armchair, soaked with sweat, every muscle in his body hot with pain. His ears stung as he slid lower into the chair. He sat for some minutes and rested, his shins now agonising. He rose unsteadily to ease them and as he chose some more Chopin he could hear sirens whooping in the distance.

He was fast asleep in his armchair before the first side of the recording was through, oblivious to the crisis he had caused.

CHAPTER 24

A taxi driver had called 999, the first of many to see the fire at the council offices. Calls came into the emergency services switchboard thick and fast. The whole town was on fire, it seemed to the operators. If Bill had gone to his front gate right now to investigate the cacophony of siren sounds, if he had looked back towards the town centre, he would have seen the orange, yellow and blue glow across the silhouettes of rooftops. He would have been happy with his handiwork. However, he bathed in the sounds of Chopin in the back room of his house as sleep overtook him.

Richard and Daphne, united in his Renault, were on their way home from the hospital. Roberta had called herself from her cell phone. Earlier, she had felt so ill that she had locked up her studio and driven to the hospital Accident and Emergency department. She had telephoned them from there, breathlessly telling them that she was being kept in overnight for observation, some sort of poisoning. Arsenic, they had said. Richard's scalp had prickled all over at her words, but he reassured her that he and her mother would be down shortly. They would check at reception to discover which ward she was in and he told her not to worry herself. But he was worried.

They had heard the sirens. They could clearly see the glow coming from the direction of Willbury town centre on their way home.

Fire appliances had been called out from many surrounding towns. This was a major incident class A, and substations were all rapidly recruited.

Richard switched the television on to a 24-hour news channel when they were back indoors and he and Daphne sat down together, expecting a report on what was happening. Neither spoke as they kept watch on the screen in the corner of their comfortable sitting room.

Ernie already knew about the major fire in Willbury. He had been listening to a phone-in on BBC Willbury Valley local radio. It had been interrupted for a special announcement. It did not occur to him that his friend Bill Choules could have any knowledge of how it all started. He wished he could share a chat with Grace about what was happening, and exchange views about which shops might be on fire in their town.

Throughout Willbury, news of the fires was emptying the bars and restaurants. The town centre was full of people rushing in all directions. Club owners would count the cost later, glad only that it was a quiet February weekday. Sirens screamed everywhere, flashing blue lights were reflected in shop windows, and police cars, ambulances and yet more fire appliances gathered in groups.

Richard and Daphne watched as the television report of the fires in Willbury came around every fifteen minutes on the news channel. They knew the presenter's views by heart as they waited for another update from the outside broadcaster. The reporter was cued on her earpiece each time. Over her shoulder the sky glowed, and the camera managed to capture it each time she gave her latest report.

Richard stirred and turned off the television.

'Time for bed, old girl. What a catastrophe. I can't watch it any more.'

Daphne agreed and they went upstairs to their bedrooms.

When Bill woke at 6.15 the next morning he remained unaware of the smouldering black hole in the cluster of buildings that formed Willbury town centre.

In a house not far away, Debbie shook Brian's shoulder. 'Cup of tea, love.'

Brian blinked. Debbie told him about the fires in Willbury, having seen the news on television as she had her breakfast of cereal and toast.

'I told you it must be something big, the number of sirens we heard last night,' she added. 'I'm off to work now, love. I'll see you later.' She kissed him on the cheek. 'Drink your tea before it's cold. See you later.'

'Bye, love.' Brian did not dress; he went to the toilet, rushed down the stairs and switched the television on. A police spokesman was talking.

'We believe the spate of poisonings, another fire we had a few weeks ago and now this catastrophe are connected.'

Brian felt for his tobacco on the coffee table in front of him, unable to take his eyes from the screen.

The television reporter pushed for more. 'How do you think they are connected? Do you think you could expand your theory a little more?' He probed earnestly.

The Chief Inspector checked some notes in his hand. 'We have been making inquiries about the last series of poisonings. Obviously the poisonings attracted your interest. The fires last night we already know from early investigations were caused by arson attacks. There have also been more people admitted to the hospital with suspected poisoning. Some of these were victims on the previous occasion – a local publican, his wife and staff, and some of their customers this time. It seems that Willbury is under some sort of attack. However, the situation is now under control, and investigations are well under way.'

Brian listened aghast. He blew air and lit his first roll-up of the day.

'Back to the studio.'

The camera now showed the reporter huddled in her fashionable fake-fur-trimmed coat.

Brian blew smoke at the screen. 'Oh no, Bill! What have you done now?' he said out loud. Somehow he knew Bill was involved.

He telephoned Ernie but there was no answer. Then he rang Richard, who answered straight away.

'Yes, I know,' said Richard. 'Yes, I've had the same thought ... Yes, probably Bill, I fear... No... I've tried to ring Ernie too ... No, I haven't seen him ... Well, yes, we did agree to leave him alone. Must go, Brian. I'll see you at the shed ... Yes, about eleven ... Yes, that's fine ... No, nothing we can do. Bye – must go.'

Brian replaced the handset, staring at it for a few seconds.

Richard had sensed Daphne was listening.

'Who was that?' she asked her husband.

'Only Brian from the allotment.' Richard was afraid his uneasiness showed.

'What did he want? You don't ring each other normally, your allotment friends. What's going on, Richard?'

'Oh, he only wanted to know if I was going down the allotment or not.'

Richard looked at his wife. He was still attracted to her, standing there in the silk dressing gown that he had bought for her himself. Well, Roberta had chosen it but he had paid. A sadness came over him. The crass stupidity of what the so-called gardening club had started had culminated in this ... and Bobbie being poisoned!

Richard lied that it was a few days since they had seen each other at the shed. 'We haven't been every day lately, that's all.'

Daphne seemed satisfied with this explanation; at least she didn't pursue him any more. When they discussed the fires over coffee at the kitchen table, Richard did wonder if she suspected he had been lying. They did not know yet but the fire had consumed Bobbie's studio. Not only that, but Terry's car showroom had been badly damaged.

The town was in chaos. The police traffic department had sealed the town centre itself as a crime scene. Their diversions had worked to some degree. They had shut off major routes into the town centre, trying to get traffic on to the ring road. The ring road traffic was now stationary. Every department had been called in. Forensic teams were working alongside the fire service. Home Office forensic experts were also on their way down the motorway.

The town's traffic was at a standstill from every direction. Willbury Valley police force's Chief Superintendent was furious about how many people had ignored their radio and television appeals to stay at home today if they were heading into Willbury town centre. It was grid-locked. Nothing moved. Tempers were short. Drivers trying to do U-turns added to the problems. Numerous cars were trying to get out of the town as well as in. Several fights had been reported. Police cars were unable to get to these incidents to calm things down.

'An early-morning delivery van left the road. He had braked too late, not expecting stationary traffic round the corner. The van driver lost control and drove straight through a shop front on a parade. It was a café, a greasy spoon.' The police sergeant was explaining to the cadet driving him. 'Over on Griffin Street, two people were hurt,' he continued. 'The ambulance is trying to get through just as we are.'

Two of his own officers had already got there when they finally reached Griffin Street. The radio alerts were directing whoever was available to go to an incident.

The constable already at the scene opened the car door for the sergeant. 'The elderly café owners are in shock. But two men are still in their own pickup. It's been pushed through the window by the bread truck,' he quickly informed his senior officer. 'We're waiting for the fire service now. They'll have to be cut out from the pickup's cab. It's a bloody mess in there, Sarge,' the officer said, pointing to the rear end of the builder's vehicle, which was almost level with the shop front.

'Can we get to the men?'

'You had better see for yourself, Sarge.'

'An elderly lady in a car on Church Road, suspected heart attack ... the car blocking the side street completely,' the sergeant's driver now informed him. 'Just come over the radio now, Sarge.'

'Bloody hell. You try to get over on your own and I'll stay here.' The senior officer quickly made the decision. 'Go on now. I'll stay here.'

On the slope of the motorway exit slip road to the south of Willbury, a BMW had sounded its horn just once too often. The driver of a van in front got out and walked back to the car behind him. The BMW's window slid down. The van driver punched the face hard. The BMW driver's nose burst in a bloody mess.

'You don't own the road, mate,' the van driver said. 'We all have to wait, not just you.' He returned to his stationary van and turned the engine off.

The BMW driver cursed and put a clean handkerchief to his nose, which was now pouring blood and probably broken, he suspected.

Bill Choules lit the gas stove in his kitchen, and put two spoons of tea leaves into the teapot. He hummed to himself as he stirred the pot.

A helicopter roared low across his rooftop, carrying out general surveillance and reporting back on the traffic situation. Bill saw it from his kitchen window. He scraped a small amount of mould from a slice of bread and popped it under the grill on the gas stove.

Schoolchildren were forming in bigger groups than usual in different parts of town. They told each other lurid stories containing barely half-truths about the town centre fires. No buses could get out of the bus garage down town, so they would have a long wait to get to school today. Gangs of schoolchildren began roaming the streets, some even intent on trying to get to their schools. Some would get there only to find them locked. Their schools would be still in darkness. Boys pushed each other playfully. Some were dodging in and out of the slow cars. The groups seemed to snowball as they gathered up stragglers. The grammar school boys were normally earlier than the comprehensive school pupils. They didn't often meet but as they could not get into their school this morning they gathered at the locked gates of Willbury Academy, the grammar school. A huge semicircle of the more academic youth discussed the night's events; they too were restless. Unable to get into the school, some of the younger ones had set off back home. These were the first to see the swarm of massed youth heading towards them – boys, girls, black, white and brown, short-skirted girls, their exotic hairstyles now visible. The mayhem that ensued would set a rivalry between these two schools to a pitch it had not reached in previous years. It would last for many years to come, long after the town returned to normal. The girls from the comprehensive were equal to their male classmates in sorting out the grammar school 'shits'. Scores would have to be settled for weeks to come. Adults from the houses opposite the grammar school gradually came out of their homes – those that were not already in traffic queues elsewhere. Some shouted, some pleaded, for order. Aroused and enjoying it, some of the boys turned on these good citizens. When finally one single police car sounded its advance up the road, the area cleared almost magically. Children scurried in all directions, apart from those too injured to move. There were many unfortunate enough not to be able to run. Books, clothing, pens, papers and mobile phones were strewn across the road outside the school.

Boys nursed bruises and cuts, dizzy and disorientated children comforted each other. The hospital A & E would be even busier.

Central government had of course been informed. This was unprecedented, the civil servants agreed. The television stations' crews that weren't stuck in traffic were everywhere. Every part of the town held a story. Was it terrorists?

Bill ate his toast and sipped his tea in his kitchen, wondering how he might spend his day. He cut another thick slice from the loaf and put it under the grill. Having spread hard butter on to the toast, he watched it slowly melt into the toasted bread and then scraped just enough marmalade from the sides of the jar.

Brian rolled his sixth cigarette of the morning, hardly able to take his eyes from the television screen long enough to lick the gummed paper.

Debbie came in through the front door. 'There's no way I can get to work today.' She nodded towards the set. 'Not with that lot going on. The traffic isn't moving at all.'

She sat down to watch what was happening in Willbury. The reports were changing by the minute. The studio presenters introduced reporters from different locations all over the town. A reporter described a fight he had witnessed. Car horns and sirens could be heard in the background as he gave his report. The screen switched to show a smouldering building. A young reporter 'on her first assignment' described the events she had seen inside the hospital. A camera then followed the progress of a helicopter across the grey sky, the *clack-clack* of its blades clearly heard. Then another police spokesman was interviewed.

Brian and Debbie exchanged looks throughout as they watched the screen change from the studio to locations they recognised so well.

Willbury town centre had all major and some minor routes sealed. The hospital was coping as best it could with yet more poisoning cases. Willbury mortuary was busy with autopsies. All police leave had been cancelled, and off-duty personnel had been called in. Gradually police efforts were succeeding in gaining control of the traffic. The Chief Constable was determined to keep control locally. He was sure they could cope.

Darkie sat in the kitchen at the rear of the café comforting Pam. He looked through the hatch at the pickup truck still there in their café.

'Those lovely boys,' Pam sobbed. 'Never mind our smelly old café, never mind our Bournemouth plans. Those lovely boys are dead.'

Oliver had rung his mother to report his problem. His town centre office had been gutted by fire. It was insured, of course, but what could this do to his business? Daphne in turn told him his sister was seriously ill in the general hospital with suspected arsenic poisoning.

'Who would do these things, Oliver?' she asked.

Oliver was sure he had no idea, he told his mother, who put the phone back in its cradle and slowly sat back down, totally bewildered. Richard stayed silent as he watched his wife return the telephone to its stand.

The police helicopter had been joined by another, both trying to report back to traffic control from overhead. The motorway in the region was slow but moving now.

Brian held Debbie's hand as they watched the reports flooding in.

Richard glanced at his wife as she sat there, still in her dressing gown.

Anil Athwal had never completely sold out of morning papers ever before. Even the *Independent* and the *Guardian* had gone from the shelves. His wife was on the mend and he was happy with the morning takings, even though he surmised that he could not get to the cash-and-carry today.

CHAPTER 25

Brian Young set off to walk to the allotments. He was glad to be out in the fresh air and to be on his own. The traffic around was still heavier than usual but it was beginning to move. Stopping at the gateway to roll a cigarette, he licked the paper and cupped his hands to light it. As he reached The Elms and gazed across to the hut, the allotments seemed more desolate this morning. He trudged across towards their shed. Nothing moved anywhere.

The February morning sky was slate-grey, the day was dull but dry, the air cold but not freezing. An eerie stillness exuded from the shed as Brian unlocked the padlock. An involuntary shudder ran down his spine. He looked around the hut's gloomy interior as if expecting to see something ... or somebody. The old brickie filled the kettle and lit the gas ring. Then he sat watching the blue, yellow and orange flames licking around its blackened base.

It had been difficult explaining to Debbie why he had to meet Richard at the allotment today of all days. She could not understand why he was so anxious to see him there and had argued with him not to go.

Brian had not bothered to light the wood-burning stove and he was beginning to wish he had. He pulled his coat tighter round his chest. The kettle began to boil and he made himself a cup of tea. The silence of the shed engulfed him. No Pete, no Ernie, no Bill. He waited for Richard. What a stupid thing they had started. How on earth had it come to this, he asked himself as he warmed his hands on his steaming mug of tea.

Richard Owen-Davies swivelled in the chair at his study desk, fidgeting with a ballpoint pen, trying to rationalise the gardening club's recent activities. Today, though, he was fully aware of what was happening out there in Willbury. Periodically he got up and paced backwards and forwards a few times, then he would sit down again, remove his gold-rimmed glasses and rub his eyes. Finally, after staring into space for several minutes, he fetched his coat, deciding in the end that he would walk to the allotments to meet Brian as agreed. Daphne did not hear him leave.

When at last he reached the entrance he surveyed the quiet allotments. At first Richard thought he was on his own. There were no signs of life, not even Brian's van, as he had expected. Now wishing he hadn't bothered, he wondered again why he had agreed to come. Then as he approached the shed he could see that the padlock was loose and he began to feel apprehensive. Cautiously he pushed the door open and stepped inside. It was with some relief that he saw Brian's familiar face looking up from where he sat clutching a steaming mug cupped in his hands. Brian had brought some milk, he noticed, almost with amusement. *To think of that practicality at a time like this.*

Brian stood and grunted something that Richard didn't quite catch. Richard watched Brian put the kettle back on to the lit gas ring, then sat down gratefully and rubbed his aching shins. He took the cup of tea Brian handed to him with a mere nod of his head. Then Brian returned to his seat and busied himself with Old Holborn and Rizla green paper. They sat in silence, neither man knowing what to say or perhaps where to start. After some minutes while each man remained lost in his own thoughts, it was Brian who finally broke the spell.

'What have we done? What have we bloody done, mate?' Brian eyes sparkled and he automatically wiped a freckled fist into each in turn.

Tobacco smoke curled above the small gas flames. Richard shook his head, his eyebrows moving to his thoughts, not to the words. Brian stopped fingering his cigarette and pinched a strand of loose tobacco from his lip, glanced idly at it, then wiped it on a trouser leg and took a deep drag. He coughed before continuing.

'How did it come to this, Richard? Pete's dead, the town was on fire last night, the hospital's full, and Willbury's in bloody chaos.'

Brian sighed noisily and leaned forward with his hands on his knees, studying the dusty shed floor for his answer, not waiting for Richard's.

Richard sucked hard, filling his lungs with air in a huge gulp, and his back straightened in his chair. 'This is better than we could have hoped for. This is beyond what we set out to do … to make our point.'

Brian stared at the retired civil servant, taken aback by Richard's answer. He had expected to hear some remorse, just as he felt. Now, though, he was confused by the response he had received. Their eyes met, they examined each other, but neither spoke. The shed glowed from the gas ring and Brian now watched its reflection in Richard's glasses.

'This is way beyond what I thought we were supposed to be doing, Richard.' Brian drew on his roll-up, smoke pouring from his nose. 'I thought we were supposed to be targeting pests, not the whole flipping town – not the whole bloody area. Not indiscriminately either. We are just five' – the word 'five' caught in his throat – '*four* silly old buggers who somehow got carried away with doing instead of talking.' He emphasised the word doing. 'Everybody moans like we do to each other, it does no harm. But we should have kept it to talk only. This is fucking crazy, Richard.'

Richard put his hand on Brian's arm to interrupt him. Brian glanced down at the small well-manicured hand.

'Brian, that was what we set out to do.' Richard self-consciously removed his hand. 'Bill has now taken things this far on his own, and I must admit I fear for his sanity, but this will make a huge statement to the whole country, not just our town. Not just in Willbury. The media, when they begin to analyse what's happening here, will draw conclusions. They will realise why this situation came about – I'm convinced of that. I've no doubt the government are fully aware of what's happening in Willbury. Maybe, just maybe, they will do something nationally. I think it's fantastic, the TV and newspaper coverage Willbury is getting. I've heard plenty of discussions on Radio Four bulletins with ministers and the PM. *Respect for others* keeps getting mentioned. *Respect of property* too has been talked of endlessly. That was our intention, wasn't it? To raise awareness of the decline in standards that we all used to discuss. Willbury was even a topic on BBC's *Question Time* the other night on the television.'

'I wish I could believe what we've done would make the government do something to improve things.' Brian shook his head once again. 'And I bloody wish we'd never started, if you want to know the truth as I see it.' He rubbed a meaty hand on his forehead. 'All I know is it's sent Bill nuts. He's the bloody pest now.'

The two men began to discuss individual events they had seen reported on the television or heard on their radios. They related different aspects to each other, as if the other was unaware, as if the other man had not seen it on his own television set or read it in his newspaper or heard it on his radio.

Brian suddenly asked, 'Richard, have you heard anything from Bill or Ernie?'

'No, I haven't.'

'What should we do now, Richard?'

'I really don't know,' Richard sighed. 'I think we should perhaps find Bill and Ernie to see what they make of the situation.'

They agreed that Brian would walk over to Ernie's flat and Richard would go round to Bill's house and they would give each other a ring later. They also, however, agreed it had been pointless to come to the shed. Brian turned the gas ring off. It sputtered and went out, cancelling the shadows in the hut.

'Let's go, shall we.' It was a statement from Brian, not a question.

They locked up the shed and walked stiffly together across the deserted allotment to the gateway. Then they parted company without even a goodbye.

Brian knocked on Ernie's door but received no answer. He peered through the letterbox but could not see any movement. After knocking several more times he gave up and decided to try a neighbour. Brian rang the bell of the ground-floor flat next door and asked the elderly lady who answered the door if she had seen her neighbour, Ernie Evans. She had not, she informed him, and she added that it was unusual for nobody to have seen Ernie. Puzzled, Brian went home.

Richard meanwhile had reached Bill's house. He rattled the letterbox noisily. The house had the look of somewhere unoccupied. It's strange, thought Richard, that one can sense when a house is empty; it has a certain atmosphere that conveys to some forgotten primeval sense that nobody is there. The retired civil servant shrugged, assuming that Bill was temporarily out somewhere, and set off for his own house.

But Richard's primeval sense was incorrect in this instance. Bill had heard the banging on his front door but was not even curious who might be there. He had no trouble ignoring whoever it might be. He put on another CD. Soon he was soothed and lost in the resonance of the strings.

Richard's phone was ringing as he put the key in his front door. The telephone stopped as he reached it. He dialled 1471 to find out the caller's number and rang Brian back immediately. Each related his story. Both Ernie and Bill appeared to be out, they concluded. Brian told Richard he was puzzled when Ernie's next-door neighbour said she hadn't seen him for a while. Richard reassured Brian, suggesting that he relax and wait, and try Ernie again later.

An occasional siren could be heard across the Willbury rooftops, and, although the traffic around the town was beginning to move, there were still some bottlenecks.

Traffic was still congested on the motorway to the south but at least it was moving now. Members of the police traffic department were beginning to find their way back to their canteen and some were even being allowed to sign off duty.

As afternoon darkness began to close in around the town, the police had managed to gain control. There were extra patrols out, but nothing new had been reported to the control desk. The main incident room would now be able to concentrate more fully on what had happened. The causes and the culprits could now be considered.

No shops had opened in the centre of town. The smaller local district shops had therefore profited well from the disaster.

Willbury General Hospital A&E department was beginning to catch up with its backlog. Doctors and nurses were more exhausted than usual, and trolleys had had to be utilised as beds in some corridors. A management meeting was convened for two days' time to go over the day's events and discuss the strengths and weaknesses of the hospital's major emergency contingency arrangements.

The fire service had contacted some outside contracting structural engineers to assist their own experts in assessing which buildings in the town centre would need making safe.

Another side of Willbury had been busy all day. Business owners had been contacting insurance firms, who in turn had been calling in the loss adjusters. The decorators' merchants would not trade for many months to come. The premises of General Decorating Supplies had been gutted before the fire service had even arrived. The vans left overnight in the adjacent yard, which belonged to Willbury Seafood Ltd, would not be delivering to any restaurants. Tyres had burst in the heat. Windscreens and van paintwork were blackened beyond repair. The delivery vans stood forlornly in a row.

When Fred Thompson, managing director of Willbury Seafood Ltd, had finally reached his business premises next to the decorators' merchants about lunchtime, tears had stung his eyes. Years of sacrifice and hard work to build up his company were now in ruins. Fortunately his building had not suffered too much and his stock was still safe in the fridges and freezers, but there were no vans to deliver it. The cash-flow interruption would be difficult to get through until new vans could be obtained, sign-written and commissioned again. All nine vans were useless. Three of his drivers were still hanging around in the yard when Fred arrived. He found it difficult to contain his anger and disappointment when they accosted him about their wages at the end of the week. Perhaps it was not unreasonable, he concluded later, when he'd had time to think. He had resolved to rebuild his business. He had been studying his insurance policies in the office.

Fred had started out with a single second-hand refrigerated van, picking up directly from Grimsby in the small hours and selling all day in the Willbury area, with long exhausting hours daily. This was only another problem to solve, but he did feel the loneliness of running his own small company when, as he came to terms with this latest setback, he wondered what the next few days would mean to him. Looking at the blackened shell of General Decorating Supplies next door as he drove away with a few files, he wondered how or if they could ever recover. Fred knew that they too were just a small independent company – two partners who had changed their occupation from working painters to suppliers of paints and materials to the trade. *It's tough enough at the best of times, running a small business*, Fred thought. But at least it had happened at night and nobody was hurt. As he reached the junction with the main road, he shuddered to imagine what it would have been like if all that paint had caught fire during the daytime.

The *Willbury Reporter* building was further down on the same road, on the trading estate. They had geared up to sell even more copies today. Not all the staff had made it into work, and those who had were exhausted from the extra effort to get the paper out this day, even if it was later than usual. Extra pages were filled with photographs of the town centre, the shell of General Decorating Supplies and the row of blackened Willbury Seafood delivery vans next door. The editor's column reported cautiously that as far as he knew not a single person had perished in any of the fires. 'Few people actually lived in the areas affected, and what a mercy that was.' A small amendment was crammed in at the end of this column but only in the final edition: 'Firemen have found the burnt remains of one body in the vicinity of the Town Hall offices. The pathologist has concluded it was a male, perhaps in his thirties. Further investigation will be carried out.'

Queen Victoria Street, which linked the High Street to Station Road, was the worst-affected area. Many shops and fine Victorian buildings were in ruins. Several solicitors had offices above the shops in this part of the town centre, the paper reported, and speculated that the loss of records in these offices would affect far more people than the staff alone. The *Reporter* observed that they were 'privileged' to have been granted a brief interview with a Scenes of Crime officer and also the Deputy Chief Constable of Willbury Valley police force, both of whom remained guarded but had suggested a terrorist link.

The *Willbury Reporter*'s editorial column caused anger in police headquarters, whose press office immediately contacted the *Willbury Reporter*'s editor to complain about irresponsible speculation about terrorism and the unnecessary fear it might create. In recompense, the editor quickly agreed to use his column the next day to commend all the emergency services, to congratulate the police on the speed with which they had contained the events, and to express his confidence in the Willbury Valley force to find out exactly who had caused the catastrophe.

The Deputy Chief Constable would not be drawn on any more speculation at the official press conference, but in response to a question from a *Daily Mirror* reporter he agreed that the fires and the recent poisonings probably did have a connection.

'This is as far as I can answer. Any more questions, ladies and gentlemen?' Deputy Chief Inspector Roland Iles added: 'You cannot expect me to speculate at this point in time, but rest assured that we will – indeed are already – following up several lines of inquiry.' He stood up, fitted his cap on carefully and declined more questions by raising one hand, palm opened in the direction of the throng of reporters. 'At one p.m. tomorrow lunchtime, ladies and gentlemen, we should have more answers for you then. But I have a lot of work to do right now.' Cameras flashed as he left the podium.

Jane Hopkins, the local Labour MP, had set up office in a pub near the town centre that had not been affected by the fires. There she had met fire officers, councillors, police inspectors, television crews, and radio and newspaper reporters. 'Unprecedented events' had become her catchphrase in almost every interview she had given. Members of the public had shouted at her for answers. Jane now felt browbeaten, and she wondered how she had managed to get to this pub about lunchtime through the traffic, then walking and dodging the crowds on the pavement, comforted only by the recognition she had received. Somehow she had found her way here. Somehow people had found her here. Parliament had been interrupted during the afternoon, she knew, as the Minister related the events to the House. The House of Commons had returned to near normal after the report but without her. Ms Hopkins now wished she could go home. She lived in a pretty village just outside Willbury, and she wanted to be there, although she knew she couldn't. It would doubtless take weeks, if not months, to sort out this mess. She tried to order a sandwich at the bar. 'We don't have any sandwiches,' the barman told her perfunctorily, 'because no bread has been delivered.' Jane Hopkins had settled for a bag of crisps.

The Chief Inspector from Willbury Valley headquarters had arrived to assess the situation. He was proud of his officers, he told those present at 6 o'clock that evening. The Chief Inspector sat down with local councillors and all those called in to discuss the Willbury emergency contingency plan. He opened by asking for a calm assessment of recent events and a pragmatic approach towards a resolution. Several times he reprimanded Julian Harradance, a local Tory councillor, for interrupting. He condemned Harradance's 'out-of-place comments', as he described them, 'comments with racial implications about Muslim terror groups'.

'If indeed Mr Harradance will allow us time to investigate a possible terrorist cell in Willbury, time will give us the answers. And may we please stick to the agenda, Mr Harradance.'

The meeting decided that it was only a local problem but with national implications. When the traffic department officer spoke, he made a point of reiterating his Chief Inspector's confidence in a speedy investigative resolution to both the fires and the poisonings. 'I don't apologise for talking outside my jurisdiction about the investigations.' He then proceeded to draw a few yawns from those present with interminable praise and even self-congratulation of his department's speed and efficiency in bringing the morning's traffic situation under control. He was seen to glance in the Chief Inspector's direction occasionally during this speech. The meeting concluded with a resolution to get back to normal, 'the British spirit' being mentioned more than once.

Brian stood at the reception desk in the police station. He was arguing that he needed a policeman to break the door down at his friend's flat. Finally he convinced them and he left with a young constable. Brian had knocked and knocked so hard on Ernie's door that the woman in the next flat complained of the noise, warning that she would call the police if he didn't stop immediately and stressing that she had told him earlier that nobody was in.

Brian asked the young policeman to slow down as they walked back to Ernie Evans's flat. He was still exhausted from tramping to the police station and the trudge back was hurting. His heart pumped hard in his chest and his legs and hips ached.

'Who lives here?' the constable asked when they finally reached Ernie's door.

'I told you on the way,' Brian snapped impatiently. 'A mate of mine. He's an old bloke, he's not been seen around for a while, and I'm worried about him, with everything that's been happening.'

The policeman peered through the letterbox.

'Can I break the door open or not?' Brian asked, wheezing.

The young constable gathered himself and crashed his shoulder into the door. The doorframe splintered away from the lock. They looked at each other as if to ask 'who first?'

Brian led the way. He shuffled about the shabby flat, followed by the police officer.

'It seems, Mr Young, that your friend is not in.'

Brian looked confused and uncomfortable. 'No ... sorry,' he mumbled. 'I was worried, though. I was sure something bad had happened to him.'

'Well, I'm off back to the station,' said the constable with a sigh. 'I'll leave you to sort out the broken lock and doorframe,' he added with a sly grin as he walked away.

Brian looked at the split in the doorframe where they had shouldered the front door in. 'Where the hell are you, Ernie?' he said out loud to no one. He pulled the door closed as best he could after checking around the flat once more. Ernie wasn't in.

'I felt so stupid,' he told Debbie when he arrived home.

'Where is he then?'

'I don't bloody know, do I?' Brian went to his pocket for his tobacco pouch.

'Don't snap at me, Brian Young. Sit down, I'll make you a cup of tea if you'll stop being so grumpy, you silly old fool.'

Brian winced slightly at the reminder of their age difference as Debbie left the lounge for the kitchen and he heard her filling the kettle.

'Sorry, love!' he called out.

'Yeah, well ...' he heard her say from their kitchen. 'Look, it's not your fault all these things are going on in Willbury. I wish you'd stop acting as though it was.' Debbie returned and placed a mug of tea down beside her husband. 'At least I've had a day off that I didn't expect. I'm happy enough about that. Put the telly on and see if there's any more news. I guess it's all calmed down enough for me to get to work tomorrow.'

Debbie sat down opposite Brian with her own tea. 'Don't you want the news then?'

Brian hadn't moved. 'No, I was just wondering where Ernie can possibly be.'

'Do you think there are foreign terrorists around here?' Debbie asked.

'No,' said Brian abruptly.

'Who then? Somebody's doing it – the poisonings and now the fires. Sharon next door thinks it's terrorists. So does Paul, her new partner. He's a nice-looking bloke.'

'Who's nice-looking?'

'Paul, Sharon's new bloke.'

Brian cursed.

'All right, I won't talk if you don't want to, love.'

'It's not you,' Brian said, trying to smile. 'I burnt my mouth on the tea.'

Debbie laughed, then suddenly turned to Brian. 'Hasn't Ernie got a daughter? Maybe he's gone to see her. Haven't you got a number for her? She lives in one of those horrible blocks of flats over where the gasworks used to be, doesn't she?'

'You're right, he's probably there, or could be, I don't know.' He reached under the coffee table for the telephone directory and flicked through it. 'Here she is. Evans, A. Pass the phone, Deb.'

He rang the number. Debbie watched him draw on his roll-up, thinking how she must try again to get him to give up smoking.

'Hello, Anne. It's Brian, Brian Young, a mate of your dad's ... Ernie, your dad ... Is he there by any chance? ... He is!' Brian glanced at Debbie and grinned with relief. 'Good, can I speak to him please?' He put his hand over the mouthpiece and whispered to his wife, 'She's a horrible woman, that daughter of his. And thick. I don't know how Ernie and Grace had a daughter like that.' Brian turned back to the phone. 'Hello, Ern, how are you, mate? ... Where have you been? ... Staying there? ... Of course you couldn't get back to your flat, mate ... Yeah, I understand ... What? Pardon?'

Ernie's voice sounded very feeble to Brian.

'Can't hear you, mate, say again ... OK, mate, cheerio, see you soon.' He put the phone back down .

'You didn't tell him about his flat door, Brian.' Debbie peered over her cup as she took a sip of tea.

'Oh Christ, no,' said Brian. 'But I'll have it fixed before he gets home. He's ill. His daughter is supposed to be looking after him.'

'Poor old Ernie,' said Debbie. 'What's up with him?'

Brian sat back and drank his tea. He fought a compulsion to tell Debbie about the gardening club. He was confused about all the feelings he was trying so hard to contain. He wished none of it had happened – the bloody gardening club and its pest control.

'What's up, love? Are you worried about Ernie? You look …' She was going to say, *You look older lately*, but stopped herself in time.

'No. Yes, I mean yes, I'm worried about Ernie, and I miss Pete.'

Debbie got up and sat at his feet after kissing his cheek. 'Cheer up, love. It will all sort itself out.'

'I truly hope so,' Brian replied without conviction.

'What's up with Ernie then?' Debbie asked again

'Shingles,' Brian answered curtly.

'Oh dear, he's in trouble then. That's painful, I've heard. And it's generally caused by stress.' Debbie looked up into her husband's weary face. 'What do you think brought that on then?'

CHAPTER 26

DC Barbara Booth and DS Dave Wallis had been working non-stop for days and there seemed no end to their inquiries. That day had thrown up so many more issues to sort out – fights, the fires and yet more cases of poisoning. It still did not make sense to either of the detectives. It was mysterious, they both agreed from time to time, until Detective Sergeant Wallis, spluttering with laughter, said to his partner, 'Please stop saying, "It's mysterious"!' They both laughed together. This was what made the job interesting and worth doing, they also agreed. It made it very tiring as well.

They were feeling extra pressure too because the specialist unit of the national Counter-Terrorism Command, SO15, were still handling the investigation into possible terrorist activity, and Willbury Valley Police CID's reputation depended on Wallis and Booth's ability to come up with ideas based on their local knowledge.

Barbara looked across the desk to her partner, who was sitting opposite. 'Dave, I think we have a gang of anarchists at work here. I also believe that these fires and the new poisonings are all connected to the first poisonings and the early arson case. Worse, I suspect we still haven't seen the end yet. And I'm sorry but I can't help thinking that the anarchists may be old ones.' She raised her eyebrows in a self-deprecating way, waiting for her sergeant's expected dismissal of her oft-expressed theory.

Dave raised a sceptical eyebrow. 'I'm beginning to agree.' He loosened his tie as he spoke. 'I agree there's some connection but I still can't see where to start. We've spoken to a lot of people so far, and I don't think we're any nearer to putting it all together. Yet we've got murder, arson, attempted murder, and anarchy on a grand scale.' Dave rubbed his chin and leaned back in his chair. 'Somebody, whoever they are, is very angry, and if we can figure out why perhaps we'll be a little nearer.'

Detective Constable Booth chewed the end of her ballpoint pen. 'They brought the town to a standstill, put the whole force into a state of panic, they've filled the hospital, half the town centre needs rebuilding, and we are left wondering why.'

DS Wallis looked across the desk at his partner. Something told him she would have an answer before he did. He didn't really like to admit it but that was what he had concluded, sitting here watching Barbara. This was the biggest inquiry he had ever been involved in. He had been a detective for many years longer than she had, and, although he had solved plenty of local crimes, they were simple by comparison to this situation. Some years ago he'd accepted that he wouldn't go any higher than sergeant. Now he was just waiting for retirement, his pension – and that bar in Spain. Barbara, he concluded, would go far.

She broke his train of thought. 'Let's look again at what we have. The local criminals and villains are disrupted as much as regular people, if not more so. Each situation has involved or centred on either villains or their hangouts. That's how it started.'

'The latest fires don't bear that theory out,' Dave argued. 'Innocent businesses were the worst affected this time. A dance school and town centre shops don't have any connection as far as I can see – or a decorators' merchant or a car showroom.'

'Let's go over the facts we know.' Barbara was determined not to be deflected.

'OK,' agreed Dave. 'First, we've seen the forensic report from the toxicology department. Belladonna poisoning, colchinine or whatever it's called poisoning –'

'Both plant extracts,' Barbara interrupted.

'Yeah, right, both derived from plants. You got that information from the internet before we even had it from our own department. Clever girl. But who could have managed to get access to the milk, for example? The lab is very sure that was the source. The forensic guys have crawled all over the Wicket Keeper, the old moneylender's flat, the house in Wycliff Road and the others. How could that poison have been administered? Injected through the cap maybe?' He laughed at his own suggestion.

Barbara punched air with a small fist. 'Why not? Of course! I've never had milk delivered. My mum and dad used to, though even they haven't for years. But we forget that some still do. Bet that's it! How else could the poison traces have been linked to milk bottles in most of the cases.'

'Except the Wilsons,' Dave chipped in. 'And the prison. There was poison present in prisoners' bread. Nothing to do with milk bottles.'

'Yes, but hold on, Sarge … Dave … How the poison got into the milk and the bread is one thing. But we were talking about similarities in the type of poison used. And we'd noticed another thing in common – that villains were victims of some of the poisonings, weren't we? And where is the biggest concentration of villains?'

'The prison.'

'Yes, the prison, Dave.' Barbara sucked the end of her Bic. 'The same poison was used there as in the Wilson case – colchicine, also obtained from a plant, autumn crocus, or *Colchicum autumnale*. Like *Atropa belladonna*, the poison swallowed by the people at the Wicket Keeper.'

'Steady, girl. Latin plant names? Proper little Charlie Dimmock, aren't you?'

The young detective sat forward, ignoring her partner's tease. 'Remember old Mr Young, who'd been involved in a fight at the Wicket Keeper, and who has an allotment? He's the same man who brought Mr Wilson into the hospital and said he'd been poisoned. They were friends. So maybe Wilson had an allotment too.'

'Yes, that's definitely worth finding out,' Dave conceded. 'But how do we connect the fires with the poisonings?'

'You've forgotten the arson at the Bastins' bicycle shop,' Barbara retorted. Don't you remember that Graham Bastin knows Jason Kelly, the teenager who lives in Wycliff Road, the one we thought might have been stealing bikes for the Bastins?'

'Yes, 'course I remember, Babs.'

'Well, I've checked through the records of stolen bicycles, and one name on that list interests me. Owen-Davies.'

'What's so special about Owen-Davies?'

'Remember the car, the Renault, that was hanging around the allotments the day we went there? I checked the registration number with Swansea, and they said the owner was a Richard Dillingham Owen-Davies.'

Dave Wallis stopped doodling on the pad in front of him, and looked up. 'That's interesting, Babs. Owen-Davies isn't a common name round here. You might be on to something, maybe a connection between the arson and the allotments. We'll have to go and have a word with some elderly gardeners again.' He paused, then continued, 'The links are a bit tenuous, but three old men do seem to be connected somehow to the earlier crimes. There's old Brian Young, his deceased friend Peter Wilson, and now your Renault driver, this Owen-Davies character. Do you think they are angry old men? Are there any more of them out there? The bike shop arson is perhaps significant after all. I'm sorry I didn't take you seriously then.'

'That's OK, Sarge ... Dave. Better late than never, eh?' Barbara said nothing about her reconnaissance of the allotments, her checks on Brian Young's van and the VW Golf that turned out to belong to an Ernest Evans. Nor did she reveal that she had driven past the addresses supplied by the Driver and Vehicle Licensing Agency. She was too embarrassed to tell her sergeant, especially since her activities hadn't turned up anything useful to their investigation.

'Could these more serious fires also be connected?' her partner was saying. 'And the new cases of poisoning?' Dave Wallis placed both his palms flat down on the desk. 'Toxicology reports from the hospital show that the poison used this time was arsenic. Who uses arsenic nowadays? I'm not sure whether they still put it in rat poison. Do gardeners use arsenic? We need to find that out before we jump to conclusions.'

'Should we discuss this with the Chief, with Bob Harris?' Barbara was hesitant. 'I think perhaps we should.'

Dave thought for a moment. 'It may be protocol but perhaps we should first see if we can get more information. I really don't think he'll take us seriously. The counter-terrorist boys are following up the terrorist line of inquiry, so whatever theory we put forward has got to be convincing. Let's go see what new connections we can make. It still seems ridiculous that a group of old men might be the perpetrators, so let's not make idiots of ourselves with ol' Harris, eh?'

DC Booth sighed. 'You're right there, but the timing of all the events, the number of coincidences ... there must be a link.'

'I know, Babs, but I can't see any logical explanation, and a gang of geriatric anarchists in dear old Willbury does sound far-fetched.'

'Since when did logic have anything to do with criminals?' DC Booth stood up and tidied her side of the desk. 'These crimes are not for gain, so there must be some other motive. We just need to figure out who and why. What sort of motive.'

'Let's go to the canteen first, though. I'm starving.'

Dave Wallis got up from the desk and rubbed his abdomen in an exaggerated circular motion. Both detectives stretched, stiff from sitting at the desk all morning, and made their way upstairs to the canteen.

At the counter, Dave went for the shepherd's pie, Barbara a chicken salad. Dave chatted to a small group of uniforms when he returned to the counter for more tea. After he returned with fresh cups of tea, Barbara persisted.

'Let's go and put our theories to somebody else, the Chief Inspector perhaps, Bob Harris.'

The detective sergeant leaned forward across the table. 'Barbara, I think we need more evidence before we discuss it with the Chief. For all we know, we might be spending our time looking at a bunch of old geezers whose only crime is to spend their time gardening when they should be sitting by a fire and talking about old times, telling each other how good life was when they were young. As I said, I'll go along with it but we don't want to look foolish in front of the Chief, do we?'

His partner sat back and ran each hand alternately through her hair. She frowned. 'I think we should first go and talk to Brian Young again. I sensed that we made him feel uneasy. Something about him wasn't quite right.'

Dave shook his head. 'DC Booth, you may have a degree in psychology but the motivation is much more likely to be political. Even if these old blokes are involved somehow, there's no way they could have caused such devastation in Willbury on their own. There would have to be some link to a political group of anarchists or terrorists of some sort. The counter-terrorist unit are covering this angle, but we might be able to uncover something local.'

Barbara was not fully convinced but nodded her agreement. They speculated on who could gain from what had happened, some political group based in Willbury. They dismissed Middle Eastern terrorists, al-Qaida, the IRA, the Real IRA, Russians or other Eastern Europeans. As they theorised back and forth, Dave began to focus on student groups. Suddenly he stood up.

'I think we should visit the university,' he announced. 'That's the most likely place to find student agitators.'

'Yes, but you agreed downstairs to follow up my hunch about the old men, and you said yourself that the counter-terrorist unit was dealing with the political aspect.'

'Does modern policing allow for hunches?' Dave laughed and shook his head in an exaggerated way. 'But let's go to the university before we visit the old men.'

Barbara pushed her chair back. *Here we go again.* 'OK,' she said, 'let's at least do something before anything else happens.'

Bill had not left his house for two days after the fire, seemingly oblivious to the situation he had caused. He had popped out to the local shops and bought a few groceries but nobody had talked to him.

A few flakes of snow began to fall. By the time he had put the kettle on in his cold kitchen it was snowing hard outside. He fried some sausages in a pan and hummed to himself.

The two detectives sat in their car in the university car park. The car windows misted from the cold outside.

'Start the engine, Barbara. It's bloody cold in here.'

Barbara started the car and set the blowers going, de-misters on.

'That was a waste of time,' she said with a grin.

'No, it wasn't. We have all but eliminated any likely connection with the students. I didn't like the economics professor we spoke to. He gave me the creeps. I wouldn't trust him with my kids and I wouldn't eliminate him either. He was a smartarse.'

Barbara turned to study her partner's face. 'You're joking, I hope.'

Dave Wallis looked offended. 'No, as a matter of fact I'm not joking, I don't trust anybody with a beard like that.'

She laughed out loud. 'Dave Wallis, that is ridiculous. He may have a bad beard but that doesn't make him a terrorist.'

Dave countered, 'It wasn't just his beard. He didn't answer one straight question with a straight answer.'

'He was merely being evasive because he couldn't understand what you were implying.' She did her best to imitate Dave's voice. '"Tell me, professor, is there any political group in this university with a grievance against society."'

The detective sergeant squirmed in his seat. 'He obviously had sympathy for students leaving college with large debts, he said so, he got all fired up about it. That's political.'

'Of course it's political but not exactly revolutionary. I feel sorry for working-class students starting working life thousands of pounds in debt before they even begin their careers. That is if they can even get a job.'

Dave sneered but did not interrupt. '*You* did,' he said, and regretted it immediately.

Barbara ignored the remark. 'If you train to be a policeman, a firefighter, a nurse or many other jobs, you get paid while you train. The armed forces, fighter pilots ... many, many jobs in the public sector and private industry are all paid while the employees train. Lots of students struggle hard for years to pay their way through their learning. You don't ask doctors to pay for their training.' Barbara could sense she was mounting a personal hobby-horse and stopped herself.

'You sound as bad as him,' Dave remarked straight-faced.

'Yes, but I don't have a beard, so does that exempt me from suspicion?' Barbara was unable to contain her laughter at her superior officer.

'This is a waste of time,' Dave Wallis observed.

Barbara agreed it was a waste of time. 'Where next then? The Irish Club?' She put on Dave's voice again. '"Tell me, Mr Murphy, are there people in this club who would poison our citizens and set fire to our buildings?"' She continued with an Irish accent, '"Oh no, Detective Sergeant Wallis, the Brits have never done anything wrong, never in history, of course not."'

Dave cut her off. 'All right, all right, you've had your fun, but I'm not going to harass the horticultural clubs or the Dahlia Society either. And I've seen what the IRA got up to in the past, and it wasn't funny.'

They sat in silence for a while, the engine still running while the car warmed up. Then Barbara put the car into gear and drove out of the university car park. Students were coming and going, hunched against the cold air, jeans dragging on the wet pavement.

She pulled into the allotment. Dave looked at her and tutted as loud as he could. He smiled and shook his head again.

'You don't give up, do you?'

She turned off the car's engine by the shed on The Elms allotment, which appeared to be deserted apart from two squabbling crows that had flown off at the car's approach. The detective constable got out of the car, leaving her partner still hunched in the passenger seat. Barbara rattled the padlock on the shed door, then went round the side and tried to peer through the dirt and condensation on the small window.

'I want a proper look in here,' she said.

'You're not serious, are you?' Dave said, coming up behind her.

'Yes, Dave, I am.'

'Well, just to satisfy you, let's go and have a word with that bloke Brian Young then. Let's ask him to unlock the shed. And we'll ask him if he knows anybody called Richard Dillingham Owen-Davies.'

The car doors slammed, echoing in the silence of the allotment. Barbara checked her notebook for Brian Young's address and started the engine. A single rook squawked and flew off.

CHAPTER 27

Debbie Young jumped when the doorbell rang. Brian got up to answer the door and both knees cracked audibly. Debbie listened to hear who was at the door as Anne Robinson on television fired questions at the contestants on *The Weakest Link*. Brian came back into the lounge followed by a middle-aged man and a young woman. The young woman said hello to Debbie. Debbie gave her husband a puzzled look.

'This is Detective Sergeant Wallis and this is Detective Constable Booth,' said Brian, introducing the police officers to his wife. 'They just want to chat with me.'

'What about?' Debbie asked her husband directly.

'I don't know, love,' he replied, avoiding her gaze.

Brian waved the detectives towards the sofa as he sat down in an armchair.

'Make some tea, love.' He looked at Debbie now. 'Please.'

She got up without question and went to the kitchen, switched on the kettle and then returned to the lounge. 'Would you like tea or coffee?'

'Tea, please,' Dave and Barbara answered in unison.

Brian turned the television off with the remote control. The room remained silent until Debbie returned with a tray bearing four cups of tea, which she placed carefully on the coffee table.

'Help yourself to sugar.' Debbie waved a hand in the tray's direction and sat down again in her armchair, her confusion obvious to Brian.

'Thank you, Mrs Young.' Barbara smiled across at the other woman, who she noticed looked much younger than her husband.

Dave Wallis grinned sheepishly at the couple. He wished he wasn't here. *This is embarrassing*, he thought.

Barbara stirred her tea, although she hadn't put any sugar in. She directed her gaze at Brian and cleared her throat.

'Mr Young, does the name Owen-Davies mean anything to you?'

'Yeah … it does.' Brian shifted in his chair. 'Richard Owen-Davies has an allotment down at The Elms.'

Barbara leaned forward. 'Do you happen to know if he reported having a bicycle stolen recently?'

'Let me think …' Brian began hesitantly. 'I remember … he did say something about his grandson's bike getting stolen.'

The detective constable caught her partner's eye and he nodded back at her with a faint smile.

'Mr Young,' Barbara said quietly. 'Does Mr Owen-Davies visit your shed?'

Brian glanced uneasily at Debbie, who managed to refrain from asking what was going on.

'I haven't got a shed.'

'I mean the shed at your allotment, the one you share with your friends. Does Mr Owen-Davies share your shed?'

'Yes, he does,' Brian replied, struggling to appear unconcerned.

Barbara tried to sound casual and relaxed but adrenaline was already beginning to kick in. 'Who else do you share the shed with?'

Brian reached for his tobacco and began rolling a cigarette. 'I used to share it with four others, but one has died recently.'

He cleared his throat with small coughs as he spoke, interrupting his own sentence. Staring at the carpet, he lit the cigarette that he was fingering and looked back at the policewoman as he blew out a small cloud of smoke.

'What was his name?' she asked.

'Pete Wilson. He was an old mate of mine. We'd known each other most of our lives. We worked together, drank together, we'd known each other for years ...' His voice tailed off.

'That's very sad,' Barbara commiserated.

'What happened?' asked Dave. 'I mean, how did he die?'

Brian hesitated, his mouth dry, and coughed as he drew on his roll-up. 'He committed suicide.' Smoke was emerging from his mouth and nose as he answered Dave Wallis's question and he absent-mindedly fanned a hand through the small cloud.

'That's awful. Do you know why, Mr Young?' Barbara continued as gently as she could. She could see the old man was growing uncomfortable. 'I mean why he killed himself.'

It was Debbie who spoke next, though. 'Pete's wife had been ill for years, and when she died he just couldn't live without her. He killed himself later the same day.'

Barbara raised her hand slightly in Dave's direction, as if to signal, *I will do the talking.* Dave caught on and sat back with his tea.

'I'm sorry, Mr Young,' Barbara went on. 'I can see this is upsetting you but please, what happened? I mean, how did he kill himself, what method did he use?'

Brian took a deep drag on his roll-up. He looked at Debbie as he spoke, all eyes on him.

'He swallowed some poison. He drank some poison, poor bugger. His wife had taken something earlier that day. She'd had enough, he told us – I mean, she wanted to die.' His voice cracked.

Barbara changed tack at this point, keeping her voice as sympathetic as she could. She asked how they had come to work together. She let Brian tell some stories about building sites they had both worked on, him and Pete. He talked about Liz's illness, their lovely little girls, building their patio. Barbara prompted now and then to keep Brian talking. Debbie occasionally added small anecdotes, explaining how she and Brian had met. When they seemed to be drying up, Barbara asked for more tea.

'Yes, of course,' said Debbie. 'Who would like another cup?'

While Debbie was in the kitchen, Barbara leaned over to Brian, putting her hand gently on his thick forearm.

'Do you know what sort of poison he used or where he may have got it?'

Dave remained quiet, allowing Barbara to continue on her own.

'I don't know,' Brian mumbled.

Barbara squeezed his arm confidentially. 'I think you do, Mr Young ... May I call you Brian?'

Brian looked into the young policewoman's face as Debbie returned with more tea. He glanced at his wife and their eyes met momentarily.

Debbie sensed something was wrong with Brian. 'What is it, love?' She stood by his chair and put her arm across his sagging shoulders.

Brian's head rolled forward and hung down as he stared at the carpet. A huge sigh escaped from his mouth.

Barbara kept her hand on Brian's arm and glanced up at Debbie. 'I think Brian wants to tell us something.'

She exchanged eye contact with her partner and transferred her gaze to the top of Brian's head, then almost whispered, 'Do you know what sort of poison your friend used to kill himself, Brian?'

A silence filled the room.

The old man couldn't think what to say. His mind raced and his thoughts seemed to trip over themselves – swirling thoughts of the gardening club meetings, their plots, the poison, Richard's poison, pests. *Why, oh why? How did I get involved? I never dreamt it could get as bad as it did.* He didn't want to implicate Richard, but he didn't know how to explain the poison Pete had used.

'Brian,' Debbie coaxed, anxious to know herself, 'tell them what happened.'

'Pete used a poison he had made himself.' Brian sat back up straight and looked in turn at the three faces staring at him.

Debbie took her arm away, and sat down abruptly in her chair. Barbara removed her hand. Brian's eyes glistened now, and a single tear rolled down the weather-beaten old face.

'Did he give some to his wife as well?' Barbara probed.

Brian cleared his throat. 'Yes, he gave his wife some of it early that morning and then swallowed the rest himself later that day.' His cheeks filled with air and he blew it out in a slow stream, then continued. 'It was a mercy killing. His wife … Liz. He'd had enough, I guess. The future looked too …'

His voice cracked again. He cleared his throat noisily, making no attempt to hide the tears flowing down his face or to wipe them away. The room was tense as Brian continued.

'Liz had multiple sclerosis. Life was getting too much for both of them. I had no idea at all what he was thinking. I hadn't a clue he might do something like that, until that day.'

'What happened that day?' Barbara Booth's voice was not much more than a mere whisper.

'He gulped it down in front of us all in the shed. Liquid in a coffee jar. Looked like lemonade or something.'

Barbara waited a few moments. 'In the shed at the allotment? Was the poison colchicine, Brian?'

'I don't know what that is,' he said flatly.

'Poison made from autumn crocus bulbs,' Barbara informed him.

'I remember he said something about bulbs, yes.'

'Do you know where your friend obtained these bulbs?'

Brian shook his head. 'I just saw him with some liquid in a coffee jar.'

Barbara continued, 'Is there a plant called deadly nightshade growing on your allotment, Brian? Or on any of your friends' allotments?'

'Not to my knowledge,' said Brian, shaking his head again. 'We don't have poisonous plants anywhere near the plots where we grow vegetables or flowers for our homes.'

'Would you like to tell us what happened when your friend, Mr Wilson, swallowed the liquid in the jar?'

'Not long after he drank it he started getting ill and I took him in my van down to the hospital.'

'What a day that was.' Debbie was regularly mopping her eyes with paper tissues as she said this. She was forming a pile of used wet tissues in her lap.

Brian looked at no one but stared straight ahead. He told the police officers in detail about the time he spent at the hospital when he took Pete there. He told them how bad he had felt at the funeral, how upsetting it was to see their daughters and their grandchildren. 'Two coffins at the front of the church.' Brian fell silent then.

He'd left out everything concerning the gardening club's pest control plans and activities, he was aware he'd made a few bits up, but his long monologue had the other three present open-mouthed and incredulous by the time he finished. His wife was particularly wide-eyed, and she wiped flowing tears from her reddened cheeks without taking her gaze off her husband.

'Brian,' Barbara said softly. 'We'd appreciate it if you would allow us to look round your shed.'

'Oh, Brian, love … oh, Brian.' Debbie continued to cry, her head shaking in disbelief. She put her arm back round his shoulder and sobbed more loudly. 'He murdered her. Pete murdered Liz.'

'I am sorry, Mrs Young, but we'll have to ask Brian to come with us and make a formal statement.' Barbara placed a comforting hand on Debbie Young's shoulder, then turned to Brian. 'And we do need to see your shed.'

Dave Wallis stood up, and he too expressed apologies to Debbie. 'We'll be in touch later to keep you informed, and we'll bring your husband back. But we will have

more questions for your him, as I'm sure you understand.'

Brian took his coat from the hallway and accompa-
nied the police officers out of the house. At the gate, he
turned and looked back up the path at Debbie, who was
standing in the front doorway. She put a hand to her
mouth and a sob caught in her throat at the sight of his
crumpled old face as he climbed into the rear seat of the
unmarked police car. She half raised her hand to wave.
He did the same. The Ford Focus pulled away and she
watched until it was out of sight. Then Debbie closed the
door, returned to the empty lounge and cleared the cups
into the kitchen, still sniffing and sobbing, bewildered
and confused.

'You have the padlock key to the allotment shed?'
Dave enquired over his shoulder to the old man slumped
in the rear seat.

Brian nodded and grunted agreement.

When they drew up beside the hut, Barbara let
Brian out of the back of the car. He pulled himself
slowly upright, fishing in his coat pocket for the padlock key.

The police officers exchanged glances as the old man
fumbled with the padlock and key. Brian pulled the door
open and took a pace sideways. The door creaked open.
The two detectives peered inside. Leaving Brian just
outside the door, Barbara stepped in first, Dave close
behind her. They looked around the dark dusty shed
almost with disbelief at what had brought them here.
Dave could not help shaking his head.

'Good job we have decent torches,' murmured
Barbara as they searched the shed, careful not to touch
anything.

Dave sniffed the teabags. 'We'll have to get the forensics boys to do a thorough search in here, but there doesn't seem to be anything mysterious. No laboratory of poisons, no arsonists' kit if you discount a box of matches.' Dave said this with a grin, pleased at his attempt at a joke as he pointed towards the box of matches beside the little gas ring.

'You're not taking this seriously, Sergeant.' Barbara glared at him in mock annoyance.

'You must admit, Detective Constable, that the idea of five old blokes sitting here plotting to destroy Willbury is hard to grasp.' Dave shook his head again. 'Still, the forensics team will need to search the shed, for traces of atropine, colchicine … and arsenic. Not to mention fire accelerants such as turpentine, petrol, meths or white spirit.'

'What about Brian Young?' Barbara wondered. 'Can we take him back home? At this stage we don't have enough on him to arrest him, do we?'

'Not without forensic evidence, or information from his mates or other witnesses. And we need to call in botanical experts to search the allotments for poisonous plants.'

'It's too dark now for anyone to do a search,' Barbara observed. 'And I reckon the old man is too tired now to face a formal interview.'

'Obviously we need to question him,' Dave added, 'to find out any links he might have to political activists. It's hardly likely that these old blokes are responsible for carrying out the major arson and poison attacks on their own, whatever their involvement.' He gestured round at the humble contents of the shed. 'But it's a bit late now to start interrogating him, and we can't hold him indefinitely. Better if we track down his allotment mates first. Old Brian's not going to do a runner if we take him home, is he?'

Back outside the shed, Dave Wallis snapped the lock back on and popped the key in his pocket. Then they escorted Brian back to the Ford Focus, climbed in and set off to take him home.

They pulled up outside the Youngs' house. Debbie was standing at the front window, behind the net curtains. The sky was dark overhead, pricked with stars.

Dave Wallis leaned across and took a pad from the glovebox. 'Before you go in, Mr Young, we need the names and addresses of anyone who shared your allotment shed with you. We know about Peter Wilson, and Richard Owen-Davies, but not the other two men you've mentioned.'

Brian screwed his eyes shut momentarily. 'There's Ernie Evans.'

He gave them Ernie's address, although Barbara had already discovered this by getting the registration number of his VW Golf checked with the DVLA. Not that Dave knew about this.

'Ernie may not be at home. He's got shingles and he's staying with his daughter Anne at her flat.' Brian gave them Ernie's daughter's address. 'No, same surname as Ernie,' he replied to the detective sergeant's question. 'She's not married.'

'And the fourth man?' Dave asked.

'Bill Choules.' Brian felt apprehensive as he gave them Bill's address.

'Anyone else we should know about?' the sergeant enquired, but the old man shook his head. 'Well, perhaps you might think of something else that might help us.

I don't think you'd like to see any more poisonings happen in Willbury. No more fires. And no more ...'

Dave glanced across at his partner in the driving seat. She had remained still, with both hands on the steering wheel, staring directly ahead through the windscreen.

'And no more deaths,' Dave Wallis finished, after deliberate hesitation, turning back to the old man in the back seat as he added this last warning.

'OK, Mr Young ... Brian. Hold tight and I'll let you out.' Barbara got out and opened the rear door for Brian. 'We'll be back to take you in for a proper statement, or we may ask a PC to pick you up tomorrow morning. So please stay at home until you hear from us again.'

Brian tensed at this news and muttered quietly, 'Yes, of course.'

'We'll have a lot more questions for you in the next few days. You may hear something about the arson in town. Or perhaps you know already?' She couldn't see any facial reaction in the dim light but she saw the old man stiffen slightly.

'Oh.' Brian could think of nothing else to say. He watched the car drive away down his road.

'He reminds me of my dad,' said Dave, blowing air and sliding lower into the passenger seat. 'What a result, though.'

Barbara glanced over at her partner momentarily as she changed up a gear.

Next morning Bill got on his bike and set off to have another breakfast at the café. He was puzzled when he arrived to see a line of Acrow props holding up the front of the Parade café. The café front itself was boarded up. He noticed that the boards seemed new, and wondered briefly what had happened. Undeterred, he set off for Tesco, thinking that their café served cheap good food. That would do. He was hungry. He hummed to himself as he rode, plumes steaming from his mouth.

Richard Owen-Davies sat in his study reading. It was hard to concentrate but it filled the long morning. Daphne was at the hospital or over at Oliver's, he wasn't sure. So much had happened, he didn't know what to do next to fill his time. He felt as though he was waiting for something else to happen. Pete had given him the novel by Robert Tressell, *The Ragged Trousered Philan-thropists*. Richard had found it hard-going and repetitive when he had tried reading it once before. He couldn't really relate to the book, but with Pete on his mind he was trying again. He picked it up from time to time but had never read it fully. When the doorbell rang he was pleased at the distraction.

The man and woman standing on his doorstep identified themselves as police CID officers. Both held up their warrant cards, and the man spoke first.

'Mr Richard Owen-Davies?'

Richard replied, 'Yes, I'm Owen-Davies.'

'I'm Detective Sergeant Wallis and this is Detective Constable Booth. May we have a few words?'

Richard's chest deflated. He wanted a brandy. 'You had better come in.' He took a pace backwards.

Inside his hallway, the detectives explained why they were there. His name had been given to them by a Mr Brian Young, who was helping them with their inquiries into the deaths of Peter and Elizabeth Wilson.

'We understand that you share a shed at an allotment with Mr Young, Mr Evans and Mr Choules. Is that correct?' DS Wallis asked.

Richard murmured agreement.

'And is it true that you reported a stolen bicycle a few weeks ago?'

'Yes, I did,' Richard replied. 'It was a very expensive bicycle that belonged to my grandson, but it was never recovered.'

'I see …' DS Wallis began. 'Now, Mr Owen-Davies. Is there somewhere we can sit down and ask you some questions?'

'Yes, yes, of course,' said Richard. 'Please come into my study. Anything to help.'

'And we'd like to see your garden if we may, sir,' Barbara added.

'Oh … of course. There isn't much to see, I'm afraid, at this time of the year, though.' His voice had dropped to not much more than a whisper.

'We'll be the judge of that.'

DS Wallis studied the man. Balding head, wisps of white hair – what there was of it – neatly trimmed, and unusually coarse-haired eyebrows. He had half-moon spectacles hanging on a cord on his chest as well as the gold-rimmed glasses that he was wearing. The detective noted Owen-Davies's expensive clothing too. Dave could smell the cleanliness of the man and the house.

'This is my study.' Richard pushed the door open and waved a hand towards the open doorway.

Barbara followed the two men in. Wallis began taking in the surroundings casually. He picked up the book on Richard's desk. 'Socialist, are you, sir?'

'No,' said Richard defensively, 'of course not' – as if that explained everything. 'Oh, I see ... that book. How do you know it?'

'My father was a carpenter, sir, in the building trade, you know. He was always waffling on about *The Ragged Trousered Philanthropists*, how everyone should read it.'

'Have you read it, Sarge?' Barbara asked, not grasping the significance. She had never heard of *The Ragged Trousered Philanthropists*, although she was well read, and she was curious about it by now.

'No,' said Dave, 'even though I tried many times. Not your usual sort of reading then, sir?'

'No,' Richard answered. 'A friend gave it to me, a friend from the allotments.'

'Who would that be, sir?'

'Oh,' said Richard, 'a friend who died.'

'You mean Peter Wilson perhaps then, sir?'

'Yes, I do.' He explained briefly how Peter Wilson had come to his house to decorate this very study, how it was Peter Wilson who had invited him down to the allotment in the first place.

'I think he was teasing me by giving me that book. I mean, I think it was his idea of a joke to give a civil servant a book that, as he put it, is "a study of the working lives of poor people and their conditions in the early 1900s". Building trade workers, like Peter. I think he believed it would give me a different understanding of the politics of the last century. He and Brian Young liked to tease me about my ... as they put it ... "soft life" as a career civil servant. Oh, it doesn't matter, does it?' Richard smiled weakly.

'No, sir,' Dave agreed.

Barbara made a mental note to read it some time. She enjoyed social history. A book on the well-filled shelves suddenly caught her eye – *Garden Pests and Nature's Poisons* by G. P. Alexander. She reached for it while Richard watched, his eyebrows becoming active. He'd completely forgotten that the book was sitting there in the bookcase, for all to see. Now he wished he had got rid of the book, wished he'd not invited the police officers into his study. What was he thinking of?

'This is very interesting, Sarge,' said Barbara, flicking through the pages. She turned to the back of the book and searched through the index. '*Atropa belladonna* or deadly nightshade' and '*Colchicum autumnale* or autumn crocus' were both listed. She leaned across from the bookcase and showed her partner. Dave acknowledged it with a startled glance.

'May we have a quick look round your house, sir?' the detective sergeant said quietly.

'Look, what's all this about, officers? I thought you just wanted to ask me some questions.'

'We do, sir, but we need to have a look round first. If you refuse, we can always return with a search warrant, sir, but you might prefer it if we do this informally.' Dave Wallis studied the retired civil servant's face closely.

'Yes, yes, of course, if you must … Come this way.'

Richard tried to disguise the trembling of his hands as he led the police officers across the hallway to the sitting room. His heart was racing and he felt giddy. He propped a hand against the sitting room doorway.

'This is the sitting room.' He stepped back.

'Yes, very nice, sir,' said Dave Wallis, his gaze taking in the expensive furnishings, the neatness, the immaculate appearance, not an object out of place. 'A very nice room indeed. I think we would like a look at your garden now, sir. We would particularly like you to show us where you have some deadly nightshade growing, and maybe some autumn crocus out there.'

Barbara only just contained an involuntary gasp at her partner's adept directness, which caught her by surprise. She noticed immediately the effect it had on the house's owner.

Richard Owen-Davies stumbled. His dizziness increased, as he felt blood drain from his head. His scalp prickled. His eyes began to water. The pale skin on his forehead began to glisten.

'I don't feel too well,' he said. 'May I go to the kitchen for a glass of water?'

'Where is your kitchen, sir?' asked Barbara. 'I'll get you one. Where do you keep your glasses?'

Richard pointed towards an open door at the far end of the hall, and muttered, 'Glasses in the top cupboard.' Then he walked unsteadily back across the hallway to his study and sat down heavily in the captain's chair, putting his head in his hands. DS Wallis stood in the doorway, stepping aside to let his partner through with a glass of water.

'When you have drunk that, sir, we'd still like to look in your garden.'

'No need.' Richard's voice was barely audible. 'Thank you,' he said, half raising the glass towards Barbara.

'No need, sir? You were saying …?' Barbara prompted.

'No need to look in the garden. I have both plants growing here in my garden.' Richard Owen-Davies glanced from one police officer to the other. He did not register the knowing look they exchanged.

'I think you had better get a coat and come with us down to the station, sir. We will have forensics make a closer inspection of your garden tomorrow. Perhaps you may help us later on at the station and sketch a layout of your garden, showing where our specialist team may find these plants.'

'Yes, of course.' Richard's reply gained no volume. 'The autumn crocus is not from the crocus family. At this time of the year the bulbs are still under the soil. They flower in autumn.'

'I thought so,' Dave said, poker-faced.

Barbara had difficulty stifling a laugh at her sergeant's mock solemnity. But she surprised him when she added, 'I had a look out of your kitchen window, Mr Owen-Davies, and I noticed you have a shed in your garden. Have you been using it recently, sir?'

Richard turned pale as he remembered the preparations he had carried out in the shed. He had thoroughly cleaned up afterwards, but now he worried about traces that might remain there. Slowly he murmured, 'Yes … yes … I have.'

'Right, sir. Our forensics people will need to examine your shed. Finish your water if you wish, sir, but I think you'll have a lot more to tell us down at the station.' Dave addressed his partner, 'Bring that book with us now please, DC Booth. Not *The Ragged Trousered Philanthropists*. The other one.'

'I know which one you mean,' said Barbara, feeling a surge of satisfaction as she carried out the copy of *Garden Pests and Nature's Poisons*.

DS Wallis and DC Booth interviewed Richard Owen-Davies for over two hours. During this time he confessed to having prepared the noxious liquids from the plants, and to carrying out the poisonings, including those inside the prison. He explained how he had injected poison into milk bottles on doorsteps and into the bread being delivered to the prison. He even owned up to setting fire to the bicycle shop.

When the detectives asked about Richard's friends at the allotments, he denied that they were in any way involved. He had prepared the poisons in his own garden shed. Yes, they had all talked about pests in the community, and fantasised about some kind of 'pest control', and that had given him the idea of concocting liquid poisons from the plants in his garden. But he was the only one who had taken any action. The other men, he said, were unaware of what he had done.

'Why did you take a jar of colchicine to the allotment shed, and how did Peter Wilson come to be in possession of some of it?' DS Wallis asked.

There was a pause. Then Richard said, 'I did tell them I'd mixed some poison, and suggested we use it against the drug dealers and other criminals in Willbury.'

'What was their reaction?'

'Peter Wilson seemed interested, and he took home a jar. The others thought I was joking.' Richard's eyebrows were moving up and down, and he fiddled with his spectacles. 'I had no idea what Peter had planned ... with his wife. And it never occurred to me that he would take poison himself.'

'What about the latest poisonings? Did you ever use arsenic? Do you know who started the latest fires?'

'No,' said Richard. 'I don't know anything about the recent events ... those fires in the centre of Willbury ...

any of that. My own daughter was poisoned, and her dance studio was burnt to the ground. My son's office was gutted by fire. You can't imagine I had anything to do with those terrible things.'

They discussed the recent catastrophes, but the detectives were satisfied that Richard Owen-Davies had not been involved, although Barbara had a strong suspicion that the man knew more than he was telling them. After exploring all the possibilities, they decided they would get no more information from Richard at this interview. Perhaps new evidence would be uncovered by the forensics people.

'Thank you for your co-operation, Mr Owen-Davies.' DS Wallis concluded the interview by stating the time clearly to the recorder and switching it off.

Richard's solicitor, Philip Smyth, had tried to help him through the interview, but Richard had explained to the lawyer in advance that he would be relieved to get it off his chest. In any case, he was not prepared to tell Philip Smyth what his allotment friends had been doing. In Richard's mind, his friends believed the poisons would not kill anyone, and so he was willing to take full responsibility. When he was charged with murder, attempted murder and arson, he said nothing, but signed the statements that had been prepared for him. As the detectives went to leave, he asked DC Booth whether Brian was all right. She assured Richard that he was, apart from being a bit confused and upset, and commented that his wife would look after him. Richard nodded as the uniformed officer led him away to the cells.

'There is something very, very sad about these old blokes, don't you think, Barbara?' Dave pushed his hands deep into his trouser pockets. 'I know what Owen-Davies is responsible for, but somehow ...'

'Yes, I know what you mean, if you forget what he has done. And if you believe that the other old men did no more than dream up plans they never intended carrying out. I'm not so sure they are as innocent as Owen-Davies made out,' Barbara quietly said. 'And don't forget that we have two more to pick up yet. Ernest Evans may still be with his daughter, but this Bill Choules character isn't answering his phone. We need to get over to his house and find him as soon as we can.'

The uniformed officer who led Richard away had been in the force for more years than he cared to think about but he didn't remember ever taking anyone as old as this one to the cells on a murder charge. He had come to believe that there was some sort of mysterious age limit for murder.

'In there, sir, thank you.' He locked the cell door with a clank.

Richard Owen-Davies lay awake in his cell, his despair complete. He had spoken to Daphne on the phone. For very many minutes she had not understood what he was trying to explain, and he'd had to repeat several times what was happening and why. She had become almost hysterical and then she had banged the phone down, saying she would call Oliver. She had told him that she had collected Roberta from hospital and that she would be spending a few days in her mother's care.

'Without her insane father!' she had screamed.

Those words were the last he had heard from Daphne so far. His wife had expressed no sympathy for him, no understanding of his plight. Sitting in his cell, he felt overwhelmed by self-pity, and the tears flowed freely. The loneliness of his childhood dormitory bed weighed heavily in his thoughts. He recalled that same remembered desperate, chest-heaving despair of homesickness. Alone here in this police cell, now awaiting his appearance in court and God knows what, he no longer felt the defiance he had recently expressed to Brian in their allotment shed.

Chapter 28

Bill Choules tucked into the meal he had collected from the counter, a slightly scorched cottage pie and garden peas that were a little too dry. Earlier in the day he had eaten a late breakfast here, and a few hours later he was hungry again.

The supermarket restaurant was packed. Groups of young mothers were wiping sauce from children's mouths, old men were wiping sauce from plates and chins. A few working men were having a cheap fry-up, pairs of women were taking breaks from shopping. Bill got back in the queue for another cup of tea after he had emptied his plate, but by the time he returned with fresh tea his table had been cleared and wiped clean, and he had lost his seat. Irritated, he sat down at another. He looked at his watch; it would be getting dark soon. He finished his tea and left the warm, brightly lit supermarket where everyone seemed to him so intense and busy.

His bike was gone! It was not where he'd left it outside the shop. He'd had the bicycle for so many years, it was almost a part of him. It had taken him to work, to church sometimes … everywhere. At first he was confused, and paced up and down angrily looking for it. Who would steal his precious bike? He walked back into the supermarket and asked at the customer services counter for someone to call the police.

The woman sympathised with him. 'Was it a new bike?' she asked. 'Nothing is safe these days.'

She clicked her tongue with a *tut-tut* and called over a uniformed shop security man, who said he would check around the car park in case it had merely been moved. When he returned to confirm the bike was still missing, she picked up the phone. Then she found Bill a seat and told him the police were coming.

For nearly an hour Bill sat watching the endless stream of shoppers pass by with their laden trolleys. He was becoming very tired.

'Mr Choules?' A young uniformed policeman stood in front of him, his cap in his hand. 'You have had your bike stolen, I believe, sir? Would you like to describe it to me?'

The officer scrawled a few notes as Bill spoke. He might be new to the job but he knew there was no chance of getting the bicycle back.

'Where do you live?' he asked finally.

Bill told him.

'How will you get home?' the policeman asked. Without waiting for an answer he continued, 'Come on. Hop in my car. I'll drop you off. It won't be far out of my way.'

Bill stood and thanked him, then followed him meekly from the supermarket to the police car.

The PC tried to chat to the old man to pass the time in the late-afternoon traffic. Bill stared ahead in silence.

'Here will do,' Bill said when they reached the corner of his road. He pulled his overcoat tighter as he heaved himself out of the police car.

'Take care, old chap. Sorry you lost your bike. We'll let you know if we find it.'

Bill leaned into the passenger door from the pavement and thanked the young officer before the car pulled away. The police constable rolled his window down and fanned a hand across his face. The old man stank.

The streetlights were on as Bill slowly made his way the short distance home. It was cold and a fine drizzle had started. As he approached his house, Bill could see another car parked outside his gate. Two people had just climbed out and were walking towards his door. He didn't want to talk to anybody, so he walked slowly by as a middle-aged man with a young woman knocked on his door. He continued on further up the road and waited until they returned to their car.

Dave Wallis radioed back to Chief Inspector Harris, asking him to send some other officers to keep a watch on the house. 'We're just leaving for the other address,' he reported.

'Somebody is looking for you, William. Nobody ever visits me,' Bill muttered to himself. The car remained outside his house for several minutes. He was growing impatient for them to go. The rain had increased, and he was getting cold and wet. At last the headlights were switched on and the car pulled away. He tried to see into the car, but he didn't recognise the two people inside.

Bill put the key in the lock and opened his front door. He didn't switch any lights on. *They might come back and realise I'm in.* Continuing through into his back room, he put on a CD compilation, turned the volume down, his anxiety eased by Mozart on the first track. He slumped into his armchair with his damp overcoat still on. His stomach knotted; the pain made him close his eyes tightly, but it passed after a few moments. Rain spattered the windows. Bill was fast asleep long before the music ceased.

He awoke in the middle of the night with sore eyes, and his face and his hands were cold. His back ached when he tried to sit up straight. Struggling stiffly to his feet, Bill went into the kitchen, filled the kettle and lit the gas. He checked his watch in the blue glow of the gas ring: 1.15. He made some tea and put an extra spoonful of sugar in his cup and stirred. As he held the hot cup in both hands, he willed his brain to wake up properly. He thought about his bicycle and the car parked outside his house earlier. The steam from the cup warmed his face as he sipped. He rocked slightly on his feet as he stood alone in his dark kitchen, with no light other than the glow from the hissing blue ring of flame on the gas stove, which was casting wavering, gloomy shadows. It gave him a little heat at least, though.

Bill had lived alone for many years, hardly seeing anybody but the gardening club, but he had never felt lonely. It was his life, that's all, he concluded, on the rare occasions he ever gave it any thought. He continued pondering over the day's events – his meal, the crowds in the supermarket, his stolen bicycle, the policeman giving him a lift, and the man and woman at his door. He wondered who those two strangers were. Nobody ever knocked on his door. Well, maybe a few people trying to sell him double-glazing or conservatories, or very occasionally Jehovah's Witnesses. Nobody ever came into his house, apart from his friends a few weeks ago, when they had the meeting to decide about pests. That was the only time they had come round. His thoughts returned to his bike. Where was it now? Who had taken it? Pests, he supposed. Pests! He poured another cup of tea and drank it slowly. Suddenly he felt the need to talk to one of his gardening club friends.

Shutting the front door behind himself as he stepped outside a few minutes later, he murmured, 'Goodbye, Mother. Goodbye, Father.'

He didn't notice the unmarked car with steamed-up windows parked across the road. The car's occupants didn't notice him either.

The other houses in Bill's road were in darkness and the rain had ceased. He ignored the cold and strode down the quiet street, having decided to go to see Ernie, who lived nearest to him. When he reached Ernie's flat, he knocked repeatedly, but no one came to Ernie's door. Somebody shouted to him to shut up and go away. Bill felt for the matches in his overcoat pocket. He saw the badly mended split in the door frame but took no notice.

A free newspaper was still sticking from the letterbox. He couldn't see the pile of junk mail on the floor inside the door when he pushed the lighted newspaper through. He couldn't know as he walked away how quickly it would all catch fire. He didn't care. He would try Peter. His house was not far away. A taxi drove by as he strode out towards Pete's semi.

Pete will have a chat with me. He will talk about chrysanthemums, have a natter about this and that.

Pete's house was also in complete darkness, but Bill rang the doorbell and rattled the letterbox. No light came on, no one answered the door. He saw more free newspapers sticking from the letterbox. His anger and disappointment began to mount. After soaking the paper in methylated spirits from the bottle he produced from his pocket, Bill pushed it further through the letterbox slot, lit it with a match and walked away. He wished he had brought his Weed Wand with him.

Bill was surprised to see lights on at Richard's house. As the curtains were not drawn, he could see a young man with a drink in his hand sitting slumped, legs straight out, in an armchair.

Daphne and her daughter were asleep upstairs. The two women and Daphne's son had exhausted themselves with talking, still not fully comprehending why their husband and father was spending the night in a police cell. Bill hesitated, unsure what to do. The man wasn't Richard, obviously. He couldn't have a chat with a stranger, somebody who didn't share his hobby. Three cars were on the driveway – a little sports car, a Range Rover and Richard's Renault. The side gate between the house and the garage was open, and Bill found himself walking through it. He crept round to the rear of Richard's house, lifted the lid of a wheelie bin, peered into its dark interior and let the lid back down quietly. Then he tried the door to the wooden shed behind the garage, and found it unlocked. He struck a match and went in. On a cluttered bench in the wooden shed there was a candle stub, which he lit with another match and left standing on the bench among plastic seed trays. Noticing a half-filled creosote can, Bill poured the contents into the wheelie bin. Then he found a full plastic container of white spirit on a shelf, and emptied it out on top of the black rubbish sacks in the bin.

They're not my friends any more ... not my friends any more. They soon forgot about aphids and leather-

jackets and weevils. He smiled when in the flickering light from the nearby open shed he saw two snails halfway up the side of the bin.

Back in the shed he set fire to a rolled-up garden magazine from the candle, then went back out and dropped it into the plastic bin and wheeled it against the back door to the house. As an afterthought he brought an old teak armchair out of the shed, laid it on top of the bin and poured over it the last remaining drops of methylated spirits from the bottle in his pocket. He stood and watched for a moment. Visible from the guttering candle in the open shed, the plastic bin lid began to change shape and a hole in it appeared. Smoke swirled from the widening hole and from the edges of the lid. Soon flames appeared and licked the bottom spars of the wooden chair.

As Bill crept back through the side gate between the house and the garage, he glanced over his shoulder, and when he reached the pavement in front of the house he saw through the window the man still sitting in the armchair.

He walked back home, tired and cold, his head throbbing. He rubbed his forehead, kneading it with his fingertips as if to rub away the ache.

The car's occupants did not notice the big man until they saw him walking up the path to his front door.

'Christ!' one said to the other. 'There he is! What do we do now?'

The other policeman shrugged. 'What's the time?'

'Nearly five o'clock. DS Wallis won't have come on duty yet. Nobody said pick him up. Just keep watching.'

'Yeah, but we should report that he's back in his house, shouldn't we?' the first said.

'No rush, is there? No one's going to come out to visit him at this time.'

'No, I suppose not. But watching a doddery old man's house when so much else is happening round Willbury doesn't make sense to me.' He rubbed his eyes.

'Me neither,' said the other officer.

Much later, they would have to explain to a formal police inquiry why they failed to report Bill's arrival back home as soon as they saw him.

Bill lit the gas oven and opened its door to try to warm the kitchen, then filled the kettle, lit a gas ring and put the kettle to boil. He searched his cupboards for some aspirin or something for his headache. In the distance he heard a siren. He sipped the sweet tea he had made and returned to the back room, feeling slightly warmed by the tea. He sat down awkwardly, and a pain passed through his stomach in a sweeping wave. The tea seemed to soothe it a little. He shivered as he relaxed, his headache began to subside and he dozed off.

When he awoke an hour later, the streetlights shining through the window were casting shadows around the room. He still had his overcoat on and it was still damp from the afternoon drizzle, its sour smell filling his nostrils. Bill rubbed his temple. A dull awareness was beginning to enter his brain, as he seemed to remember saying goodbye to his parents some hours ago. He rubbed his sore eyes with his knuckles. Had he dreamt that he'd been out for a walk and had gone to see his friends but they wouldn't let him in? Were they real memories or a dream recalled? Bill was cold and hungry, he knew that. His whole body ached. Thin wispy hair had dried flat to his head. His teacup was beside him, still full. Picking it up, he tasted it, but it was cold. Bill cursed, 'Damn and blast!'

Seven thirty, his watch told him. Bill supposed Tesco would be open and he could get a breakfast there. It was a long walk, and with anger he remembered his bike was gone. He shut the front door and shuffled off. There was no rain but it was cold, a damp bone-aching cold. The thought of the warm supermarket restaurant and hot food kept him going.

CHAPTER 29

'It can only be the fifth one,' Detective Sergeant Dave Wallis said as climbed into the Ford Focus. 'Let's get round to his house quickly. Three more fires, four more people dead. Owen-Davies's house ... two females upstairs, one male downstairs – his family, I assume.' Dave slapped the dashboard. 'One empty house was torched, but at least the next-door neighbours were saved by the firefighters. It was Peter Wilson's old semi in Glendevon Road. The other property was a ground-floor flat that was unoccupied, but an elderly woman was overcome with smoke in the flat above. All three addresses are on our list of five – three of our gardeners' homes. Richard Owen-Davies, Peter Wilson, Ernest Evans. That leaves Brian Young and Bill Choules.'

'Of course you're right, Dave. It must be Bill Choules who started the fires. We should have waited there yesterday,' Detective Constable Booth proffered, aware of her senior officer's anger.

'Christ Almighty, Barbara, his house was bloody staked out all night. According to the officers in the car outside, he didn't turn up until five in the morning, long after the houses had been torched. But they've only just reported his appearance, and now they've gone off duty! What the fuck did those idiots think they were doing?' He had become red in the face now.

'We didn't know then for sure that Bill Choules was connected to the major Willbury fires. We only wanted to interview him when he got back home. There were no grounds for arresting him.' Barbara added, trying to console her partner. 'The idea that he might be dangerous seemed surreal all along, even to me. You know we never seriously suspected our gardeners of burning down the town centre. Old men don't do those things, do they?'

'This bloody lot do!' Dave clicked his seatbelt in. 'Let's go, and quick.'

'What a start to the day, Sarge.' Barbara quickly put the car into gear. 'That was Richard Owen-Davies's family. His wife, his son and his daughter. And him locked up. Not him then?'

'Great detective work, DC Booth,' snapped DS Wallis.

'I was joking, Sarge.'

'I was being ironic, Constable. And now who is being inappropriately glib?'

'Sorry, Dave. I can't believe nobody went round to Ernie Evans's daughter's house yesterday evening.' Barbara accelerated towards Bill Choules's house.

'They did. I can't believe you didn't know that. He was lying on his daughter's sofa. He's got shingles, just as Brian Young said. His daughter had been looking after him for days.' Dave steadied himself with one hand on the glovebox.

'So when do we get to speak to Evans?' Barbara asked.

'As soon as we find Choules and get back to the station. Some uniforms are picking up Young and Evans and bringing them in this morning.' DS Wallis glanced at his partner with a frown. 'Did you actually attend the briefing last night, DC Booth?'

'No need to be sarcastic, Sarge.' Barbara frowned back at him. 'Brian Young was brought into the station to make a statement yesterday morning, but that only covers Peter Wilson's suicide and the murder of his wife. We still haven't questioned either Young or Evans about the arsenic poisonings and the town centre fires. We can't just assume that Choules is responsible for all that.'

'I'm not assuming anything. Just making sure that we locate Choules, because right now he's the only one who hasn't accounted for his presence last night.'

'But the others may have dreamed up some of the plans,' Barbara countered. 'We still need more evidence, more information. Even if Bill Choules has been on the rampage.'

'Is the back-up team behind us?' Dave asked, then answered his own question. 'Yeah, they're just behind.'

Bill had to pass Pete's house on his way to the Tesco supermarket. An observer would not have seen any hint of acknowledgement of his involvement as he walked by. He registered a burnt-out house. He may even have registered Pete's burnt-out house. But it did not appear so. No sign of guilt crossed his face.

The far side of the semi-detached house was charred black with smoke. Some window-panes were broken but most were intact. The fire brigade had saved half of it when a neighbour across the street had called 999 in the early hours, but they were only just in time. Three house fires at once set a new record.

'Quite a night, so soon after the town centre fires,' a group of firefighters on the next shift were agreeing at the Willbury fire station on this side of town.

'Whatever next?' one man had wondered to his mates. The police had instructed the fire chief to be on extra alert.

Dave and Barbara jumped out of the car together. A couple of schoolboys watched as they marched to the front door of Bill's house.

'Bet they are cops,' said one boy to the other.

They stood and watched the two detectives banging on the door. An armoured Transit with its crew had parked up behind the Ford Focus. Dave hurried round the side of the house and Barbara stayed at the front door, peering through the letterbox.

'Clear off, you two!' DC Booth turned to the boys.

The boys leered at each other but began slowly to move away. They called for their mate Ben, who lived next door, and glanced over the fence at Barbara as they dawdled down the pathway. When Ben emerged, the three boys stood and watched as Dave tried to see through the kitchen window. The detective continued on to the back room windows, with his face cupped in his hands against the glass, misting the window with his breath. 'Nobody,' he muttered to himself, and cursed. The boys watched Barbara banging on Bill's front door.

As Dave walked back round the front, he saw the boys. 'Clear off, you lot!' The boys ignored him.

Barbara moved to the low fence between the houses. 'Have you seen anybody in this house in the last few days?'

The boys sniggered. 'Who wants to know?'

'We are police officers and I won't ask again.'

Ben approached the fence. 'There's an old man who lives there on his own. Haven't seen him lately … don't see him much anyway.'

'You haven't seen him in the last few days?'

'You said you wouldn't ask again,' sneered one of the other boys from the pathway. The second giggled.

'No, I live here, but I haven't seen him for ages.' Ben looked at his watch. 'Got to get to school. Come on, you two.'

The three boys wandered off up the road, each making up his own story as to what the police were doing, what the old man had been up to. Even their imaginative fantasies were not as lurid as the truth. When the full story became known in the neighbourhood, Ben would claim he had told the coppers that the old bloke was responsible for everything.

'Well, Dave, do we break in or not?' Barbara peered in once more through the letterbox. 'The house is empty, no one's in, that's obvious. It's funny how you can tell by looking through the letterbox.'

'I think we have to break in,' replied Dave. 'We can't be sure the old bloke isn't hiding in there somewhere. Whatever, the back door will be easier than the front.'

'The back door down the side,' Barbara said with a wink.

'You know what I mean.'

Dave had little problem shoulder-charging the back door. The old rim lock split away from the frame and they were in. They quickly searched the house, commenting on the ancient furnishing and equipment, but finding no sign of Bill Choules. Some of the rooms had obviously not been used for years and were so full of junk that they could barely open the doors, let alone conduct an exhaustive search.

'It's like a museum of a 1950s house,' Dave remarked quietly. 'It certainly seems empty, but we'll need to have it thoroughly searched, with a warrant too. We'd do better to start looking for our Mr Choules somewhere else.'

'Can we leave the house like this, with all the damage?' Barbara looked dubious.

'I'll call the station, tell them about the back door and let them know that nobody is in. I'll get a maintenance team to fix the doorframe and put a new lock on the back door.'

'What if he comes back and can't get in the house? Won't he get suspicious and do a runner?'

'No, I'll instruct the maintenance people to take one key back to the station but leave the other inside, still in the lock. And leave the door unlocked.' Dave reached for his mobile phone. 'It's time to involve the media, put out a description. I didn't see a photo of the old man anywhere in the house. If the station can't get hold of one, I'll ask them to get Brian Young to help them mock-up an e-fit of Bill Choules. Have them issue it to the media, say we're wanting to question this man in connection with last night's fires.'

Stepping outside the house, Barbara spotted the garden shed and gestured to Dave to have a look inside. The door creaked when he opened it, and both officers peered inside. There was no old man hiding there, but Barbara let out a cry.

'Now what do we have here, Sarge?' She pointed to an old container of rat poison on the workbench.

'Don't touch it, Babs,' Dave warned. 'Forensics will need to examine it for prints.' He squinted at the dirty label. 'Well, it definitely contains arsenic. Looks like we've found our poisoner.'

As they returned to the car, Barbara asked across the roof, 'What now then, Sarge? Where to?'

Dave blew air and shook his head as he clicked his seat belt in. His partner started the engine but they couldn't decide where to go first, and they sat in the car for a while with the engine running.

'One old man can't be hard to find. But where to start? The allotment shed maybe?' Barbara suggested.

The detective sergeant got out of the car again and had a brief chat with the Transit's driver. It left at the same time.

As the two vehicles pulled away, a squad car took up position opposite the house, to begin a round-the-clock surveillance.

Bill's stomach growled. Inside the supermarket restaurant, he checked what cash he had in his pockets and studied a handful of coins and a crumpled five-pound note. A fry-up would taste good this morning, he thought.

He chose his breakfast: sausage, egg, bacon, baked beans and two slices of toast. His mouth watered as he sat down with the tray of food. Slowly he sipped his tea and buttered the toast, doing so deliberately to savour what he was about to enjoy.

News of the fires in Willbury the previous night had filled the local radio airwaves and television news. The reported speculation that the police were hunting for a suspected arsonist was the topic of conversation of many this morning. National television crews had been dispatched to Willbury yet again. When the police spokesman had linked them to the recent 'terrible events' of the poisonings, the town centre fires and the deaths that had taken place during those unforgettable days, all stations had been alerted, and reporters and television crews with their vans and cameras were appearing all over town again. To find an outside broadcast crew in a Tesco restaurant was not a surprise. 'Always get a good cheap breakfast at a big supermarket restaurant,' most of the crews knew that. 'Cleaner than a greasy spoon café on the road. Cleaner and cheaper than a motorway café.'

The crew behind Bill were loudly discussing their plans. Bill had noticed that they spoke in raucous voices. He simply did not know why they had 'Sky' printed on their clothing and equipment. But he had overheard enough to understand who or what they might be.

When the young policewoman gently broke the news to Richard Owen-Davies of the fire at his house, and told him that the bodies of three people had been found there, he let out a strangled noise that sounded like 'Bill'. After the duty sergeant had joined the policewoman, they gradually calmed him down and made sure that this was precisely what he had yelled out. 'Bill.' Just 'Bill', they agreed the prisoner had repeated. Not 'Old Bill', as they had at first wondered.

Within half an hour, Bill Choules and his description were common knowledge throughout the station building. The incident room buzzed with activity. Word quickly spread that the counter-terrorism unit were about to leave Willbury Valley police headquarters. There was widespread relief that local CID detectives were solving Willbury's wave of crimes.

Ernie propped himself up on one elbow as he lay on his daughter's sofa fully dressed but covered with an old

Superman duvet she had unearthed from a cupboard somewhere. He felt himself shrink. As he stared at the television screen, the e-fit likeness of Bill was easily recognisable. His heart gave a lurch. This was the first news he had seen for days.

His daughter Anne had told him with a mean resentment that he would have to stay with her. She had told him curtly that his flat had been burnt out. Despair and confusion seeped through the pain in his body. He scratched absentmindedly at the rash. He knew he should ring the police to tell them he knew the man in the e-fit but felt unable to get up to the phone. In any case he was expecting an officer to pick him up from the flat and take him into the police station. He lay back staring at the ceiling and listened to the television in the corner of the room. The police would be here any minute now, he concluded. He closed his eyes and tried to sleep off his exhaustion.

Anne showed the uniformed police officers into her lounge. 'There he is,' she simply said, pointing to the sofa.

Brian, like Ernie, had been collected by uniformed officers and brought into Willbury Valley police headquarters. They now sat in their respective interview rooms.

Brian already knew about last night's fires, but when he arrived he was told about the deaths, and was asked to help them compile an e-fit of Bill Choules. When he asked why, he was informed merely that they wanted to question him. Brian thought they shared his own suspicions about who was responsible for setting fire to three of the gardening club members' homes, although he had no idea why Bill should have done this. He presumed that Bill didn't know Richard and Ernie were not at home, but why would he want to harm them or destroy their homes?

He sipped a mug of tea and begged a cigarette, but he could not stop shaking. Debbie was safe for the moment, he knew, but that seemed more by luck after what he'd just been told. What if his house would be the next to be set on fire? He knew only too well that it was Bill's sole responsibility, and the shock still stunned him as he tried to focus on his own immediate future.

Bill mopped the plate with his last half-slice of toast. He felt warm and comfortable. One more cup of tea, he told himself. He went back up to the counter to get in the queue. One of the men with 'Sky' on his chest seemed to be looking at him. Staring, in fact, he considered with irritation. It annoyed him; he did not like people staring at him at any time. He was unaware of what an unkempt and sorry sight he portrayed. His presence was noticeable by smell; he was unaware of that too. This large dishevelled man, unshaven, wearing a huge overcoat, attracted plenty of sideways glances. He averted his eyes from the staring man and shuffled forward in the queue. Sitting back down, he drank his tea, growing ever more uneasy now with the man still looking at him.

Unsettled completely, he rose from his seat to go and a fury began to well up inside him now. As he marched along the pavement, his mind was full of overwhelming bitterness and the disappointment his life seemed to him. He muttered and ground his jaw. The continual anger was becoming exhausting.

It seemed a very long walk home and Bill Choules thought he would never get there. He was having terrible stomach pains now and at times almost doubled up with agony. He would stop walking for a few moments and breathe cold air deeply until it passed. Then on he trudged.

As he turned into his street, Bill saw a car parked directly opposite his house, and he stopped in his tracks. A man in overalls was walking round the side of the house to the back. *No going back home then.* Bill retraced his steps as far as the next street, where he knew there was an empty house with a 'For sale' sign outside. There were high hedges round the front garden, and inside the garden was a summer-house. Bill opened the gate and tramped across the overgrown lawn to the small wooden structure, which consisted of a roofed-over bench facing where the sun would be if it wasn't clouded over. Almost collapsing on to the bench, Bill wrapped his big overcoat tightly around his body, stretched out, cold but exhausted, and slept the sleep of the innocent for the rest of the day.

The incident room had just been informed of what had happened in a downstairs cell. It was announced at the one o'clock press conference that a Mr Richard Dillingham Owen-Davies, most certainly one of the perpetrators of the heinous multiple crimes in Willbury and probably a leader of a criminal group, had been apprehended but had been found hanged in his cell during the morning.

The press officer enjoyed telling the *Sun*'s questioner that the police had never given too much credence to any sort of terrorist conspiracy. He wondered if he would be out of order if he passed judgement on the sensationalist headlines the paper had been printing.

'Irresponsible alarmist headlines have caused unnecessary public anxiety,' he said. 'We have contained what was merely a local problem,' he understated, to the *Sun* newspaper reporter's dismay.

'How was it possible for Mr Owen-Davies to hang himself while in police custody?' a reporter from the *Guardian* butted in.

'We do not have the details at this moment in time,' the press officer replied, keeping his face expressionless. 'But I can assure you there will be a full investigation of the matter.'

'Is it all over now then?' the *Sun* reporter came back.

'Good day, ladies and gentlemen. That is all I am going to say today. The briefing is over. No more questions, thank you.' He glanced at the last questioner coldly and left.

As the day progressed, television crews were once more appearing throughout the town centre. Reporters from television news channels conducted interviews with the public and officials at every opportunity to the point of irrelevance. A first-year constable in uniform was described as a police spokesman; a firefighter returning from sick leave was asked for his opinion. The views of the local MP, Jane Hopkins, were sought at Westminster, but not before her career had been discussed at length. Journalists at the local radio station were barely able to contain their excitement that Willbury was the focus of national news coverage again. One crew had somehow managed to unearth Ben and the other two boys who had witnessed the scene at Bill Choules's house that morning. The boys described with an unnerving glee how they had seen the man and woman break down the old man's back door. A report of the Owen-Davies family tragedy, 'while the father was in custody', was carried out in the street with Richard's gutted house in the background. Police forensics team members could be seen in their white Tyvek overalls.

DC Booth and DS Wallis had wasted much of the morning trying to find Bill Choules, having visited The Elms allotments fruitlessly.

'You'd think he might return to the allotment shed, if he's avoiding his house,' Dave had reasoned with exasperation. 'He can't just vanish.'

Later that morning the two detectives had returned to the station to start questioning Ernie Evans and Brian Young, who they hoped might know where Bill Choules might be hiding. Maybe there would be some forensic evidence to shed light on the complexities of the case. There would be lengthy interrogations throughout the day, as CID officers tried to establish which of the old men had committed the crimes, who was involved in the planning, and what charges might be brought against the two suspects who had been brought into the station.

Police headquarters had dispatched more cars to cruise round Willbury, stopping at libraries or parks to search for the man they only knew to be a big man in his seventies. All officers had been furnished with copies of the e-fit, which was also being broadcast on the television news bulletins. Television crews continued their coverage from various corners of Willbury, each crew afraid not to be first to the scene, to see this old man that everyone was looking for, the man who had caused so much grief and havoc in this provincial town.

Early in the evening, Debbie picked up Brian and Ernie from outside the police station. After several hours of questioning, they had been released without charge. As Richard had taken full responsibility for the poisonings with deadly nightshade and autumn crocus, as well as confessing to arson at the bicycle shop, there was no evidence against Brian or Ernie. They had admitted to having discussed the idea of 'pest control' but only as a joke, and they had not put their fanciful ideas into practice.

It was clear that Bill had started the recent fires in Willbury, and the empty container of rat poison in his garden shed was evidence that he had possessed arsenic. The detective sergeant still suspected them of conspiracy, or even complicity, but there was no case against them. Both Brian and Ernie knew that the two detectives' reports had exonerated them from the arson or any of the deaths. They would be allowed to go home and be available to give evidence in the future. Both men realised they were lucky to be getting into Debbie's car and going home.

Dave and Barbara looked seriously tired as she dropped her partner off outside his house.

'Do you think it's over now?' she asked.

'How would I know? Probably not until we have Bill Choules in custody. Probably not. I do know one thing, though – you will have to get some rest.' He said it in a fatherly sort of way, his hand on her arm across the gear lever in her car.

'Both of us,' she sighed.

Brian and Debbie were discussing how terrible Ernie looked. 'Poor Ernie,' Debbie kept repeating after they had dropped him off near his daughter's flat.

'Anne wanted him to go back to his own flat. Not much chance of that, ever. Bill torched that as well. He had to go back with her. She didn't want that – it was obvious. Poor old bugger. Let's hope the council will fix him up with another flat.'

When they were finally sitting together in the lounge, Brian lit another roll-up and studied its shape. 'Perhaps he could come round here for a bit, eh, love? We've got two empty bedrooms.'

'I'm not sure about that, love.' Debbie frowned.

'Think about it in the morning then?'

'OK, love.'

They stayed up into the night drinking tea, with Brian smoking endless cigarettes as he related the whole story to his wife. Debbie's feelings were mixed. She was horrified at what the men had done but still sorry for her husband. Brian had allowed her to believe that, although he was aware of what was happening, he hadn't been directly involved. When he talked about the gardening club 'pest control' activities, he referred to 'the chaos they had brought about' and 'the deaths they had caused', as if he'd not played any active part in the plot.

Debbie easily persuaded herself that Brian had been led into the conspiracy, that he would certainly not have considered such a plot on his own. He was such a kind, gentle, simple man – a bricklayer, not a terrorist. Brian was certainly not a killer, a poisoner or an arsonist. She believed that Richard and Bill had the most to answer for. As he fell asleep in his armchair, she tucked a blanket round him and went up to bed herself, exhausted. She would ring in sick to work in the morning, she had decided. They could talk it all through again tomorrow. She would stand by her husband if the police decided to arrest him and charge him with any crimes. Debbie could hear his snores coming from downstairs as she drifted into a shallow, fitful sleep.

When the doorbell rang, Brian woke with a start. He gazed around the familiar surroundings of his own lounge. He looked at the clock on the mantelpiece: 11.30 a.m. Where had the night gone? Where had the morning gone? Where was Debbie? The curtains were still drawn from last night. He scratched his head and rubbed his eyes, shifting in the armchair, trying hard to gather his senses.

The bell rang again, it seemed more insistently to Brian as he tried to dispel the cobwebs from his brain. He coughed, straightened himself and glanced around the darkened room. Finally he pushed the blanket back, his body aching as he stiffly got to his feet and stretched. He rubbed his neck, digging his thumbs in hard, massaging. Then he trudged across to draw back the curtains. He jumped when he saw the face at the window. *Bill! Christ! What is Bill doing here?* Brian remembered his friends' houses being burnt down and felt a twinge of alarm. The doorbell insisted again, then there were more thumps and knocking at the front door. Hesitating for few seconds, he drew breath and opened the door with some trepidation. Bill stood there, clothes smelly and dishevelled, pink forehead dirty, eyes wide.

'Can I come in?'

Brian stepped back a pace and waved Bill in. The events of the past two days raced through Brian's mind, and his head suddenly cleared. He forced a friendly smile and tried not to show his fear of the big man.

'Come in, Bill. I'll get us a cup of tea.'

CHAPTER 30

Two uniformed policemen had been dispatched to Bill Choules's house. They had been instructed to take the back-door key and search the house thoroughly for the old man. His description had been given to them and a copy of an e-fit likeness. One officer was to wait outside in the car. The other was to search the house, but they had been ordered not to try to apprehend the suspect, just to report back to the station. DS Wallis was to be informed immediately if he was there. Their duty officer had also emphasised that back-up was to be requested if the old man was found at the property.

PC Rick Jones had knocked on the front door, rattled the letterbox and peered through it into the hallway. The house appeared very quiet, he told his partner in the car, whispering into his radio.

'I don't think anybody is in. I'm going in the back.'

Rick unlocked the back door. The police constable shook his head in disbelief at the messy, old-fashioned kitchen as he went through. Slowly he opened the door to the back room, calling out, 'Anybody there?' He saw great piles of old vinyl LPs lying around and small piles of CDs on a table. Continuing through to the front room, he could see his fellow officer, PC Gary Clark – an off-duty friend as well as a colleague – sitting looking towards the house. It gave him a little reassurance, although he realised he could not be seen through the filthy net curtains at the window. Still nobody had appeared, though. Rick moved back into the small hallway to the foot of the stairs, listened carefully, and held his breath as he slowly began to climb the stairs. 'Anybody at home?' he called again. He winced as a step creaked part way up. He murmured into his radio to the waiting officer outside, 'No one downstairs, on my way upstairs.'

He reached the top of the stairs. Four doors, he registered. Three bedrooms and a bathroom, he surmised, a typical old semi-detached house layout. The dirty worn carpet silenced his steps. Gingerly the young policeman pushed a door open. Bathroom, no body in the bath. Then the next: back bedroom. Rick peered in, again holding his breath, ready to act. A roomful of dark furniture glowered at him. Ragged curtains at the window, half drawn, added to dinginess of the room. Thick dust covered every visible surface. Cobwebs filled each corner and drooped in swags from a picture rail. A black-and-white wedding photograph that stood on a narrow mantelpiece above a small tiled fire surround was fluffed with dust and cobweb.

What a bloody mess. Rick screwed up his face at the sight.

He could hardly get the door open to the smaller front bedroom, so much junk was in there, but no old man.

'Just going into the last room, Gazza,' he radioed in a more confident whisper to his mate Gary.

Slowly he pushed the door back. He listened intently for the tiniest sound that might signify a person in the final room in his search. Finally he stepped in. A large bed dominated the room, a double bed with an old dark-stained headboard, the varnish lined with horizontal raised cracks in the veneer. It had been slept in recently, he guessed. Sheets and blankets on the unmade bed were crumpled. The sheets, once white, were now grey with age. A double wardrobe with the same dark stain stood against the wall. Rick knocked on the wardrobe door and called, 'Anybody in?', then sniggered inaudibly through his nose at his own humour. An old-fashioned dressing table with a few bits and pieces on it – a comb, a hairbrush, a pot of Brylcreem, like the one his grand-dad always kept on his bedroom dressing table. Rick smiled briefly at the recollection. He noted that he had begun breathing properly again and chuckled at himself.

'Not a soul in sight,' he confidently reported to PC Clark. 'Nothing but a load of old junk. The bed looks like it has been slept in recently. Yuk. You wouldn't want to bring your girl back to this house to impress her. I'm coming out. Report to HQ. No suspect at home. See you in a minute. I'm on my way out now.'

He clumped noisily back down the stairs, relocked the back door and returned to the waiting police car.

'Bloody hell, what a museum in there!' he exclaimed as he climbed into the passenger seat. 'How do people live like it? Have you reported back?'

Gary Clark put on his seatbelt again, ready to start the car. 'Yep. They said we could go back to the station. Another couple of other stiffs are on their way to keep the house under observation. Looks like they're here already. Let's go.'

Brian carefully placed two mugs of tea on the side-table near to Bill.

'Sit down, Bill. Sit down, mate,' he urged.

Bill obliged. He sat down and stared straight ahead. Without acknowledging Brian in any way, he picked up one of the mugs and began sipping the tea.

'Enough sugar in there for you, Bill?' Brian's mouth became dry. 'I'll just take a cup of tea upstairs to Debbie,' he croaked breathlessly.

Brian crept out of the room as though he were trying not to wake someone. He almost trotted up the stairs to their bedroom.

'Debs, Debbie.' He shook her shoulder. 'Wake up, Debs. We've got a visitor.'

Debbie rolled over on to her back and pulled the duvet up under her chin. Brian shook her again.

'Debs, wake up. I've got Bill downstairs. He is sort of weird. He hasn't said a word yet. Debbie, wake up.'

His wife moaned slightly as her eyes popped open. 'What is it?'

'We've got Bill downstairs. The whole bloody town is looking for him and he is here, downstairs, drinking tea.'

She sat up rubbing her eyes but was wide awake now. 'Christ, Brian,' she whispered. 'What are we going to do?'

'Get yourself dressed quickly. There's a cup of tea for you on the bedside table. I'll go back downstairs and try to keep him talking. You must phone the police, tell them he's here.'

Debbie was out of the bed, snatched up her tea and gulped a mouthful as she threw on some jeans and a jumper.

'Use the phone up here, but be quiet. I'm going downstairs to keep him talking, or at least keep him here. Oh, and by the way he smells awful and his clothes are all filthy. Try not to look too shocked.'

Brian hurried back downstairs to the lounge. 'Want another cup of tea, Bill?'

'Brian?' Bill sounded surprised to see the retired bricklayer, his friend from the allotment.

Brian shifted uneasily. He took Bill's mug from his hand. 'I'll get us another cup of tea, mate ... two sugars, isn't it?'

Debbie whispered into the phone. She had dialled 999, not the number for the police station.

'No, not an ambulance, not a fire engine ... The police, yes, yes, quickly please.' She whispered her address and rapidly explained as best she could that she had Bill Choules in her house and the police were looking for him. The operator there had been notified to put a call through immediately to the police incident room should any calls come through to the police regarding the search.

Debbie Young put the phone back quietly and went down the stairs slowly, not sure what to expect.

'Hello, Bill.' She tried to sound as cheery as she normally was. 'Brian making you another cup of tea?' she asked. 'I'll have one as well,' she called in the direction of the kitchen.

The three sat silently for a while drinking fresh tea, Brian and Debbie all the while exchanging glances over the top of their mugs. Debbie had managed to convey to Brian that she had called the police.

'Would you like a sandwich, Bill?' Debbie broke the silence.

'Yes please, Mother.'

Debbie jolted at the reply, then caught her husband's eye across the room. Brian shrugged and raised his eyebrows. He rolled a cigarette and lit it. Debbie stood up and went through to the kitchen, glancing at the clock there. 'Come on, come on,' she mouthed to herself and the police. Returning to the room, she handed Brian and Bill a sandwich each.

'How are your chrysanth cuttings this year, Bill?' offered Brian, trying desperately to think of something to say, something that might start a harmless conversation.

Bill's face lit up, as he hungrily ate the sandwich, and he replied with his mouth full. 'Plenty ready for this year, plenty ready. It will be a good year.'

Debbie tapped her watch for Brian to see. Brian looked out of the front window as discreetly as he could.

'Been down the allotment lately, Bill?'

Bill looked confused, his eyes vacant once more. He took a huge gulp of tea, crammed the last of the sandwich into his mouth and stood up.

'Must go to the allotment.' Then he simply walked out of the room to the front door, leaving Brian and Debbie dumbstruck.

Brian jumped to his feet and followed him quickly. 'No need to go, Bill. Come and have a chat … more tea, another sandwich.'

'No thank you. I must go. I have a lot of jobs to do.'

Brian held his arm. Bill stared at Brian, then gently but firmly removed Brian's fingers and set off down the short pathway.

'Aw, bloody hell! Come on, coppers,' Brian said as he returned to the lounge. 'I couldn't hold him here by force, could I?' He felt the need to explain to Debbie. 'What could we do? He's weird, he's very strange. Did you ring the police?'

'Yes, of course I did!' snapped Debbie. 'A whole bunch of them looking for him … so slow … Oh, Brian, what a bloody mess. Bill seems not to know what's going on. He's obviously completely unaware of what he's done.'

The Ford Focus screeched to a halt outside Brian and Debbie's house. Both doors burst open. Dave Wallis and Barbara Booth jumped from the car and ran towards the house. Brian and Debbie recognised the detectives, and Brian was standing at the open front door when a marked police car pulled up behind the Ford. Two uniformed policemen leapt out, pulling on their caps. A white Transit van parked up behind them.

'He's gone! He was here but he's gone.' Brian breathlessly explained to the detectives how strangely Bill had behaved. 'Quiet, yes. Not agitated or aggressive, but weird.' Quickly he told them that Bill had said he was going to the allotment. Then he described what Bill was wearing, as if a big old man like Bill couldn't be easily recognised. 'He's about ten minutes or so ahead of you,' he called to the police officers as they got back to their car.

The detectives and the uniformed officers started their cars simultaneously and sped off, followed by the Transit.

Brian returned to the lounge and sat down next to Debbie on the sofa. He put his arm round her shoulders.

'I'm so sorry to put you through all that, Debs. Bill going crazy...' His eyes began to water and a fit of coughing left him breathless. 'All this chaos ... the fires, the deaths ... Looks like I got out of my depth.'

During the weeks ahead, the couple would spend many hours talking through the gardening club plot, but Brian never told his wife some of the things he and Ernie had done. He could hardly believe it himself, and it began to seem like a bad dream.

As Barbara climbed out of the car at the allotment, it was obvious that no one was in the shed. The padlock was still on the door. The marked car pulled in beside them and the uniformed officers jumped out. Then the Transit van drew up, with six men in full black body armour waiting inside.

'Not here then?' PC Rick Jones, one of the uniformed officers from the marked car, appeared behind the two detectives.

They turned to him and both gave him a look as if it was his fault that the suspect wasn't there.

'You could make a detective,' Dave replied with heavy sarcasm.

'So this is where the old bastards did their scheming, is it?' Rick rattled the padlock and walked right round the shed.

Barbara nodded in the direction of the shed's locked door and shrugged her shoulders with an exaggerated gesture to signal to the Transit driver that there seemed to be no need for the armed officers after all.

Rick came back round to the front of the hut and addressed Barbara. 'It's hard to believe that five old men sat in this rickety old shed and held so much anger between them that they planned to do so much harm to local villains. I wonder if they wanted so many to end up dead ... to cause so much damage, running into millions.'

She shook her head. 'It's difficult to realise that five ordinary old blokes could plan so much destruction and mayhem. The two who we know for sure actually killed people are now dead themselves. But so many lives have been changed for ever, because of five apparently ordinary blokes. Probably none of them ever broke the law before. It just doesn't make any sense.'

'Got rid of some villains off our patch, though.' Rick grinned from ear to ear. 'Put our little town on the map, haven't they?' he added.

Rick's partner Gary, having wandered over to the group, now gazed at the sky. Barbara glared at him. Dave glared at him. Rick grinned and held his arms out, both palms up.

'What? What have I said?'

'It looks like it did start that way,' Dave observed. 'It has ended up a major catastrophe, though, hasn't it? Five old blokes wanted to change the world. Why didn't they stick to talking about it, like the rest of us?' Dave Wallis shoved his hands into his trouser pockets and kicked a stone at his feet towards the shed.

Barbara shook her head again. 'We still have one to pick up before he does anything else. Gentlemen, let's go and find him.'

'Yes.' Dave nodded his agreement. 'It may not be over yet.'

'Do you still need us?' asked Rick.

No one answered. The detective sergeant sidled away a few paces, staring into the distance across at rooftops beyond the allotment, in the direction of the town centre, trying to focus on the possibilities of where Bill Choules might be found.

Rick had already told his partner that if he ever got the opportunity he was going to try to chat up DC Booth, and he was now attempting to indicate to Gary to give him the chance to be alone with her. Gary got the eye-contact message and followed Dave Wallis.

Gary repeated Rick's question, 'Do you still need us, Sarge … er, DS Wallis?' 'Yes, stay with us and help look for him, but, if you see him first, radio us immediately.

He won't be far. After all, he was supposed to be heading here. We'll just have to drive round the locality until we find him. He can't be far away. He's on foot, and he's old.' Dave then added to the constable, 'Go and tell the "riot squad". Tell them what we're doing.'

Gary strode over to the Transit, tapped on the van's window and explained the detective sergeant's decision. All the officers returned to their cars and drove away from the allotments in what looked like a solemn procession.

Bill had seen the two cars and the van and several people standing near the shed. He may have been in a state of confusion, but he knew to stay where he was. He wasn't going to talk to anybody. Those people over by the shed weren't his friends.

Chapter 31

Bill sat at the back of the church. He imagined his father playing the organ. The organist had come in to practise, having only recently taken over in this parish. He wanted to get used to the unfamiliar organ. It was a good time to practise on weekday afternoons when there was usually no one else around, except sometimes a funeral. He was enjoying himself.

'Onward Christian Soldiers.' Bill's favourite tune boomed from the pipes. He mouthed the words to the ancient hymn. '*Onward, Christian soldiers, marching as to war, with the cross of Jesus going on before.*'

The organist was engrossed in his music, unaware of the old man at the back.

When the hymn finished abruptly, Bill sat upright in his pew. When the organ struck up once more, Bill was startled by the next piece of music. The organist would be playing at his first funeral service this Friday. It was part of his plan this afternoon to practise the funeral march from Chopin's Sonata in B flat minor.

Bill turned the big iron key to lock the heavy wooden double doors to the church, then swivelled back to gaze up at the vaulted timber ceiling.

He walked slowly and quietly down the aisle. His head was bowed down towards the chequer of worn red, black and off-white quarry tiles that formed the floor.

His mind was lost in the slow march soaring from the organ. Tears sprang to fill his eyes. Their salt stung his eyes but he made no attempt to stem them or wipe them away.

Gradually, step by step, he continued towards the altar. His eyes were fixed on a brass cross there. Noiselessly he shuffled up the aisle. A pain in his stomach rippled through him. One foot forward and then the other, he advanced in a slow march, his legs moving stiffly. Bill raised then bowed his head in the direction of the altar and large teardrops fell and glistened on a black tile. He turned left beneath the pulpit. The organist was absorbed in Chopin's poignant music.

Bill stepped quietly into the vestry in the front corner of the church, and gently closed the door. Inside, the music was slightly deadened by the stone walls, but Bill was still lost in Chopin's funeral march. It filled his mind and his heart.

The oak-panelled walls of the vestry were covered with vestments hanging from brass hooks. White cassocks and choristers' cottas drooped limply, along with an embroidered chasuble greyed by shadows. Richly coloured preaching scarves were folded neatly on a rough oak table top.

Bill felt devoid of all senses. His mind was focused on the muffled organ music. A shelf of large candles caught his eye. He took down one at a time, lighting each from the first that he had lit carefully with a match. His hand was perfectly steady. He lit one after the other, setting each down wherever he could. He placed them carefully, the guttering flames lightening the oak panels. 'One more for Brenda.' He dripped melting wax on to the clean white vestments, held the candles near, and gradually they smouldered, then flared. Smoke began to sting his eyes, but onward, onward he methodically lit candles. A choirboy's cotta slid from its hook, blackened by fire, still burning. It fell on to the polished wooden bench beneath it.

A throaty cough escaped from the old man. Candle flames dazzled his eyes. Smoke stung them, red-rimmed now. Tears ran down his face.

Bill Choules was slowly losing consciousness. Smoke invaded his lungs. An altar set smouldered without flame beside him. He lay on the stone floor and went to sleep.

The organist marched to a halt.

Was that smoke he could smell, he wondered.